Welcome back home

....

Nina McKenzie

Contents

Chapter 1

----

6 years earlier

"Aves, I'm running out to grab dinner. Sawyer is on his way, he'll probably get here before I get back." My brother, Callum, said as he grabbed his keys off of the island.

"Okay." I said in response, not looking up from the book I was reading.

I heard the front door open and close, signaling that Callum had left to go pick up food for the three of us. It was a normal occurrence at this point, our dad was often gone and Sawyer was always at our house.

Sawyer Evans was Callum's best friend of many, many years. They were the typical football player popular boys and I was the typical little sister, crushing on her older brothers best friend.

I was 17, Sawyer and Callum were both 20. I was getting ready to go into my senior year of high school, they were going into their junior year of college. They were both still popular and making themselves known in university. I was stuck in the same small town, keeping myself in the background away from the crowd.

The front door opened again less than 10 minutes later. I knew it was Sawyer. He never knocked anymore; he didn't need to. This was basically his house too.

"Ave?" His deep, rich voice called out. "Cal said you were home." He called out again.

I shoved a bookmark in my book and stood up from the island. I ran my fingers through my hair, trying to smooth it out a little bit as I walked into the living area to greet him.

"Hey, welcome home." I smiled my stupid, brace covered smile. I couldn't wait to get these things off.

"Good to see you, it's been a couple months!" He kicked his shoes off and walked up to me, wrapping me in a hug without hesitation.

I couldn't help but notice that his arms were a bit more muscular. I also couldn't help but notice that he smelt just as amazing as he always did, he always smelt of vanilla with a hint of something that I could never quite put my finger on.

"Good to see you too." I said softly. He released me from his arms moments later and took a seat on the grey sectional. I took a seat as well, keeping some distance between the two of us. "How's college treating you?" I asked.

"It's great. Football team is treating me well. It still sucks not playing with Cal, but it's always cool when we get to play each other." He grinned.

I listened to him go on about how college was going. He seemed to be doing well, just as I expected him to be doing. He didn't play very often, but he was happy with what he did get to play. He told me that he thought he'd be able to play more this year, which was exciting.

"Senior year, how exciting. Little Avery is about to be an adult." He chuckled. I blushed, grabbing a pillow from behind me and throwing it at him. "Hey! What was that for?" he laughed as he caught the pillow.

I pulled my knees up to my chest and hugged them as I looked in his direction. "What if I don't get into a good school? What if I can't figure out what I want to do? What if I can't figure out how to adult?" I asked, feeling stupid for talking to him about everything but they were genuine questions and fears I had. I had a routine, I knew how to be a high schooler. I didn't know how to do anything else.

Sawyer reached over, putting his hand on my knee. "Ave, calm down. You don't need to have everything figured out right now. You still have the entire senior year, the only thing you need to worry about is who you're going to prom with." He chuckled.

Maybe that's the only thing he needed to worry about, but that was literally the least of my worries.

"Sawyer, I'm probably not even going to prom. That's not on my list of worries." I said and glanced at his hand that was still on my knee.

"Why wouldn't you go to prom? It's senior year, that's like... the second most important thing." He looked at me like I was crazy for even thinking that I wouldn't go.

I couldn't help but laugh at his comment. Our priorities were definitely different. "Because it's just a dance? I probably won't have anyone to go with and I'm not going by myself. Sawyer, if prom was the second most important thing for you when you were a senior, how on earth did you make it into such a good school?"

He gave my knee a quick squeeze before moving his hand and leaning back on the couch again. I didn't miss the squeeze though; it sent chills up and down my leg.

"Shit, Jones. If you don't have anyone to take you to prom, I'll come back up and go with you."

My eyes widened. "You don't mean that." There's no way he meant that and I wasn't about to get my hopes up thinking that he would actually do that. If anything, he definitely wasn't doing it because he wanted to go to prom with me. He was doing it because he felt guilty that his best friends little sister was talking about not going to prom because she didn't have a date.

Why were we even talking about this? The year hadn't even begun and it wasn't even close to prom season.

"Why would I say that if I didn't mean it? You need to go to your senior prom and I will happily go with you if it means you'll go." He folded his arms over his chest and looked at me with a smile that simply melted my little heart.

"I'll think about it," was all I said back.

"Oh, you'll think about going to prom with me?" He asked with a chuckle.

I could sense the mood was lightening back up, which made me feel relieved. "Yes. I will think about it. Maybe if you come home early with some flowers and a sign or something I'll think about it a little harder." I smiled back at him. "Oh no, better yet. Get the football team to help you ask me like you did with Madison Yanky your senior year." I grinned, teasing him about how he'd asked out his prom date.

This made him laugh. God he had the most beautiful laugh. He'd always had it, it was something that never changed. Well, it got deeper... but that only made it that much more beautiful.

"I'll see what I can do for you, Jones." He chuckled.

I liked when he called me Jones. When he wasn't calling Callum 'Cal', he called him Jones. It was a football thing, I think. So it always made me feel cool when he would call me Jones as well.

"Anyway, do you have any ideas what you want to do after graduation?" He asked, changing the subject again.

I shrugged. "I've always thought I wanted to be a writer, but I'm not sure if I have what it takes."

"Avery Jones, don't ever doubt yourself. If you want to be a writer, then be a writer. Who gives a shit what other people think? If it's something that you like, then do it and fuck the rest of the world." He said immediately, his tone quickly becoming serious.

Whoa.

I didn't even know how to respond.

"And if you feel like you can't be a writer here, then pack it up and go be a writer somewhere else. Go to New York or California or something." He added on as I was still trying to think of a response to the first part of his statement.

I laughed a breathy laugh. "California? New York? Sawyer, do you know nothing about me?"

"What? You don't think you'd ever move out of the state?" He asked.

I shrugged. I'd never thought about it before. "I've never considered it. This is home. Dads here, Callum is here, you're here. Can you see me living in a place like California?"

"You never know. You're full of surprises, you know?" His voice had changed just slightly and I had absolutely no idea what he meant by that.

I was about to ask when the front door opened, letting both of us know that Callum was back. Sawyer hopped off the couch to greet my brother.

"Evans! Welcome home." My brother said with a smile.

"Good to see you, Jones." He gave my brother a quick hug before the two of them walked into the kitchen, immediately picking up like they'd never left each other.

I sat on the couch for another couple of minutes, trying to figure out what Sawyer meant when he said I was full of surprises.

He could picture me moving to somewhere like California?

Me? Of all people?

Sawyer, get real.

Chapter 2

"What am I supposed to do without you for the entire summer?" Larissa, my best friend and roommate, asked me as she laid sprawled across my bed alongside my suitcase that I was trying zip shut.

"It's just a couple months, I think you'll be okay." I laughed. "Now sit on this damn suitcase and help me zip it all the way."

Larissa huffed but crawled onto the top of my suitcase in an attempt to add extra weight so I could shut up properly. "Are you sure there's not room in there for me?"

I breathed a sigh of relief when I finally got the suitcase completely shut. "I told you a million times you could come with me. You're the one that couldn't take off work."

"Yeah yeah... and you're 100 percent positive your brother is going to marry this girl?" She threw herself back on my bed, giving me the world's biggest pouty face. It was far too early in the morning for me to be wanting to deal with any of this. I didn't even know how Larissa was so awake right now.

I rolled my eyes at her obnoxious comment. "Sorry to break it to you, they've been together for like.. 5 years now. Pretty sure he's going to go through with it." I laughed.

"Worth a shot I guess. At least you get to spend the entire summer with Sawyer. Oh my god, he's going to lose his shit when he sees what a babe you've become over the last couple of years."

"Thanks Larissa." I rolled my eyes again.

"Shut up, you know what I mean! He hasn't seen you in what? 3 years?"

I sat down on my bed and shrugged. "Since before I left, yeah."

I hadn't been home in about 3 years. I had no reason to, other than seeing my brother. After my dad passed away, I needed to get out of town and be on my own. I couldn't stand our small town anymore, I felt trapped. So I moved to Santa Monica when I was 20, I found Larissa online. She was looking for a roommate and I was practically desperate. I consider myself lucky that she turned out to be pretty damn cool and now she's my best friend.

But I'd be lying if I said I wasn't nervous to go back home. My brother was getting married and he begged me to stay the summer with them, said that it had been too long and that coming home for a week wasn't going to cut it. So, I worked double the last couple of months so that I didn't have to worry about it while I was home. Told all of my clients I'd be back by the end of summer and here we are, hours away from catching a flight back to my small little hometown.

Back to spend the entire summer with my brother.

Back to seeing the boy I had a crush on for 10 plus years.

Back to the place I never wanted to go back.

"He's going to be all over you." She smirked, breaking me from my thoughts about going back home.

I shrugged. "I doubt it. He's probably got a girlfriend. We haven't talked since I moved and he's not on social media, so I literally have no idea what's going on in his life other than the random bits I hear from Callum."

"Babe, if he's got a girlfriend? She better be scared." She said like I was about to be competition for someone.

I threw a pillow at her as I got off of my bed. "You're absolutely ridiculous, you know that? Come on, let's get to the airport. I don't wanna be late and even at this god awful hour, I know we're going to get stuck in traffic."

I practically dragged Larissa out of my bed and shoved her to the front door of our apartment. She helped me carry all of my things down to the car and soon enough, we were off to the airport.

"Text me as soon as you land, okay?" She said as she closed the trunk of her car.

"You got it. I'll see you in three months!" I hugged her for what felt like the thousandth time. She was definitely obnoxious, but she was my best friend and I was going to miss her like crazy while we were apart.

"Send me all the pictures and call me all the time! I'll send you pictures of the west coast beach that you'll be missing out on." She laughed as she pulled away from me. "Love you, babes."

"Love you!" I grabbed my things when I finally let go of my best friend and headed into the airport with another promise that I'd let her know when I landed.

The nerves that filled my stomach had nearly tripled since landing in Maine. I watched the mechanical belt as suitcases that didn't belong to me passed, waiting for mine to come out. I nervously played with the rings on my fingers, trying to suck back any and all nerves. I just had this feeling in the pit of my stomach that things were going to be weird this summer. They were definitely going to be different and I almost wanted to go to the desk and ask the lady at the counter for a ticket back to California. When I finally spotted my purple suitcase, I stepped forward so I could grab it and pull it off. Once it was in my possession, I grabbed my other bags and made my way to the exit.

I sent my brother a quick text, letting him know where I was before sending Larissa a text to let her know I'd landed and was waiting on Callum to pull up.

She sent me back a picture of her sitting outside one of our favorite cafes. I laughed at her picture, letting her know that I was jealous before shoving my phone in my back pocket. I waited for a couple minutes before my brother pulled up in front of me in a black SUV.

As soon as the car was in park, he was exiting the vehicle and running around to me. "Aves!" He threw his arms around me and practically squeezed me to death. "Oh my god, I've missed you."

I hugged him back and fake coughed. "You're not gonna be able to spend the whole summer with me if you suffocate me in the first 10 seconds." I laughed and tried to push him off of me.

He didn't listen, hugging me for another couple of seconds before finally letting me go. "I can't help it, it's been too long." He said as he helped me load all of my things into the trunk of his car. We loaded ourselves in once we were finished and he took off towards the exit of the airport.

"It's so good to see you, sis." He glanced over at me and smiled. "How were your flights?"

I shrugged and looked out the window, watching the scenery quickly become familiar. "They were both fine, incredibly long. Nothing exciting happened on either one, unless you count that a dog was sitting behind me on my first flight." I said with a laugh.

Callum chuckled and nodded. "Glad that everything went smoothly. Dani is really excited that you'll be here for the entire summer."

I looked over at my older brother, giving him a gentle smile. I always liked Dani, she never treated me like I was a baby unlike my brother and most of his ex girlfriends. Even though I was only three years younger than him, everyone always thought I was some little kid that was far too young to spend time with them. "I look forward to getting to spend some time with my almost sister in law. If you guys need any wedding help, let me know. I'm happy to help with anything."

Callum chuckled. "I'm sure she would love that. I know she's getting a bit stressed." Who wouldn't be this close to the wedding? I know if I were in his shoes, my head would be going crazy trying to make sure everything was going according to plan.

I glanced out the window as Callum took a left turn down a road that I knew wasn't his. "Where are we going? I thought we were going straight to your apartment?"

Callum cleared his throat which made me look over at him. "Dani and I are actually staying with Sawyer right now. We're finalizing some paperwork on a house and our lease was up, so we're just staying with him until we've finished that up. We shouldn't be there much longer." He glanced over at me, gauging my reaction.

My eyes widened a bit, mostly out of irritation that he hadn't told me. But I was sure it was because he assumed I wouldn't care.

Sawyer was his best friend and it's not like we didn't know each other.

Only at this point in life, we didn't.

"Oh uh, yeah cool." I replied simply.

Callum looked back at the road before saying, "he's not home tonight. But I told him I was picking you up today, so he knows that you'll be there tomorrow when he gets back."

"What's he doing tonight?" I asked, mostly out of curiosity.

Was he out with a girlfriend explaining to her why there was going to be another girl staying in his house?

Not that it mattered, it'd be an easy explanation.

"It doesn't mean anything, it's just my best friend's little sister. There's nothing to worry about."

He shrugged. "I don't really know. He'll either be back super late or tomorrow morning. But I figured you'd want to just shower and rest tonight anyway so I didn't think it would matter really." He said as he pulled into the driveway of a house that I immediately recognized as Sawyer's childhood home.

Did he still live with his parents?

"Yeah, that's fine." I said as I unbuckled. We got out of the car and Callum helped me bring all of my things inside.

"Dani and I are in the basement. You're in the guest room." He said. I followed him up a quick flight of steps and into a bedroom. I'd never been upstairs in this house, but I had a feeling this was Sawyer's old room. It made me wonder why lived in his parents house if they didn't live here anymore. It definitely felt weird being in here, almost like I wasn't supposed to be. Callum set my suitcase down as I set my other bags down on the bed.

"Ahh, the memories of this room." He chuckled, confirming that this was indeed Sawyer's old bedroom.

"I don't want to know any of the things you two did in here if I'm going to be sleeping in here." I groaned.

Callum laughed and pulled me into another brotherly hug. "Welcome home, sis."

After a couple minutes of chatting to my brother, he let me know which door was the bathroom and then told me that he'd be downstairs with Dani. It was almost 10 and I was pretty tired from traveling literally all day. I grabbed my toiletries and walked into the bathroom, setting out everything I needed for a quick shower.

Once I was out of the shower, I wrapped myself in a towel and headed back to the guest bedroom, shutting the door behind me. I didn't hear anything coming from downstairs so I figured that Callum and Dani were in the basement. I was thankful that we could play catch up in the morning, I just wanted to take everything in for a little bit and I knew I'd be overwhelmed if I was trying to fill everyone in on my life the second I got home.

I threw on a pair of underwear and a tee shirt that belonged to my ex boyfriend. I'd thrown everything at him when we broke up, literally at him. But the one thing I refused to give back was the tee shirt I was wearing. I did it mostly out of spite, because I knew it was a favorite of his. But it was also comfortable.

I brushed through my hair and pulled it into a loose braid, not wanting to deal with drying it fully. I took the chance to really look around the room. I assumed Sawyer didn't have many guests in here, because it still felt like his room. There were some football trophies on the dresser and there were a couple posters on the wall. I wondered why things didn't get taken down or put away. I wondered if he just didn't care to take them down or if he liked that this room still felt like his.

I moved my stuff off the bed and laid down, wondering how many other girls had been in this bed. He was popular after all, there was no way that girls I know from school hadn't been in this bed. "Gross." I mumbled to myself before pulling out my phone and FaceTiming Larissa.

She answered almost immediately. "Hi babe!"

"You'll never guess whose bed I'm sleeping in." I smirked.

"You're joking! I told you it was game over when he saw you!!" She squealed. I'm glad that it was just me upstairs, because anyone around me definitely would have heard her immediately freaking out on the other end of the line.

I laughed and rolled over so I was laying on my stomach. "He's not even here."

"So you just banged him the second you got home and then he left?" She gasped.

"Larissa oh my god." I laughed. "No! I haven't even seen him yet. But Callum and Dani are buying a house and so they're staying with him. I guess he lives in his parents old house? I don't know. So Dani and Callum are in the basement and I'm in the guest room, aka his childhood bedroom." I explained the situation to her, letting her know why I was laying in Sawyer's old bed.

Larissa's eyes went wild. "Oh my god you're in the same bedroom he probably banged all the cheerleaders and smoked pot and — Oh. My. God." She interrupted herself, her eyes widening.

"Please don't say what I think you're going to say." I mumbled.

"Avery Alexandra Jones. You are in the very bed that he absolutely without a doubt jerked off in his entire teenage life." She gasped.

I immediately jumped out of the bed, that thought even more horrifying than him having sex. "You're going to make me sleep on the couch. You have to stop." I fake gagged before I started laughing.

"I don't even know this man, but you're in for it babes. You had a crush on him for how long? And now you're staying in his room? And there's no way he hasn't had at least one thought about you in his life.. and if he hasn't, he will as soon as he sees you."

I rolled my eyes. "And on that note, I'm going to go."

"Happy Summer, Ms. Jones. Let me know how the reunion goes tomorrow." She giggled.

"Goodnight, Larissa."

"Night, babes!"

We hung up and I glanced at the bed, wondering if it really would be better off to just sleep on the couch. "Oh Jesus, Avery. Grow up." I mumbled to myself as I climbed back into the bed.

I let out a huff as I picked up my phone to see what time it was and groaned when I realized it was nearly 1am. I was absolutely exhausted, but I was still on California time so it was only 10pm. Which definitely wasn't early, but I was used to late nights with Larissa so it felt early.

"Fuck me." I mumbled. I climbed out of bed and slowly opened the bedroom door. I peaked out, not hearing anything or seeing any lights. I was sure Dani and Callum were long asleep and he said Sawyer probably wouldn't be back until morning.

I quickly walked out of the bedroom and made my way downstairs, using my phone's flashlight to help guide me. Once I reached the bottom of the stairs, I made my way to the kitchen. The house wasn't huge and the main level was super easy to navigate. I set my phone on the counter face down so I could still use the flashlight and opened up the fridge, trying to see what they had to drink. I found a couple bottles of water and reached in to grab one.

Once I grabbed the bottle, I shut the fridge and spun around so I was facing the light of my phone. I took a drink from the water bottle and looked around the kitchen. I didn't remember much of this house considering I'd only been in it a handful of times, but from what I do remember it was practically the same. It felt almost comfortable knowing that Sawyer hadn't changed anything about it.

I closed the lid of the water bottle and picked up my phone, using the light to guide me back to the stairs so I could go back into the guest room. I made my way up the steps and started for the door to the guest room when the door to the bathroom opened.

My stomach started doing flips as my eyes immediately found a silhouette of what I knew was Sawyer Evans.

The light to the bathroom wasn't on, the only light in the small hallway was that of my phone. I was practically frozen in my spot, unsure if he was going to stop and say anything to me or if he was going to turn and go into his room.

"Avery?" was all he said. His voice came out in almost a whisper.

I cleared my throat. "Yeah." I responded simply, my voice the same level as his.

At that moment, I became hyper aware of the fact that I only had a tee shirt on. It was dark, but my phone was probably providing enough light for him to notice.

"It's late." He said.

"I uh, was just grabbing some water.." It's not like I needed to explain myself to him. I didn't even think he would be back until the morning. I was not expecting to see him, especially when I was wearing nothing but a tee shirt.

"Get some rest. I'll see you in the morning." He moved from the bathroom to the other bedroom door. "Goodnight."

"Goodnight." I quickly responded and walked into the bedroom, shutting the door behind me.

Jesus Christ, his voice had gotten really sexy.

Has his voice always been that sexy?

There's no way.

Did he know I didn't have pants on?

Did he care?

Did he think my voice was sexy?

"Go to sleep." I mumbled to myself as I forced my eyes to close.

Chapter 3

I had to practically force myself out of bed around 11am. I was already over the time difference and wanted to adjust. 3 hours didn't seem like a lot, but it was totally killing me. I changed into a pair of black leggings and a tank top before walking out of the room and into the bathroom. I quickly used the bathroom and brushed my teeth. I pulled the hair tie out of my hair and combed my fingers through the waves caused by the braids. Once satisfied, I walked out of the bathroom and made my way downstairs. I was hoping to see my brother or Dani, but when I walked through the living room and into the kitchen I was met with neither of them. Instead, I was met with a shirtless Sawyer.

"Good morning." I said quietly.

His shoulders tensed just slightly before he turned to face me. I took the opportunity to take him in, looking at the boy... man I hadn't seen in 3 years. He looked the same, but older, more mature. The last time I'd seen him he was my age. But 3 years can do a lot to a person when it comes to maturing, I would know.

I think he was doing the same, taking me in and seeing all of the things that had changed in the last 3 years. "Morning, Ave."

I couldn't help but smile when he called me by my nickname. I have no idea what last night was all about, but it was nice to hear the voice that I'd recognized. "Where's Callum?" I asked.

Sawyer leaned against the counter and folded his arms over his chest. I couldn't help but notice the muscles flex as he moved, my eyes wandering over the tattoos that painted his olive skin. I recognized a couple of them, but some of them were new.

"He went into town to grab lunch with Dani. They will probably be back soon." He responded.

I nodded, tearing my eyes away from his arms and back to his face. "Cool."

I watched Sawyer's eyes as they looked me over again, taking in his best friend's little sister. I wondered what was going through his mind.

Did he think I looked older?

Did he think I looked prettier?

Did he even care what I looked like?

So many questions were running through my mind, none of which I would be able to ask him. He probably wasn't even thinking about anything that I was thinking about, so in reality it really didn't matter that much.

"How's it feel to be back?" He finally asked, which gave me no indication of what he was thinking about the way that I looked.

I leaned my hip against another counter, still facing him. "It's weird. It feels like it's been longer than 3 years. It feels weird being here but not being at my dads house." I answered honestly. It was weird, being here but not being in my home. It was weird that I didn't have the ability to go to my dads house and be in the room I grew up in. Instead, I'm staying in Sawyer's old room. "It's kind of strange being in your house. Feels like I'm not supposed to be here." I added with a laugh.

Sawyer let out a soft chuckle that went straight to my belly, making it erupt in another wave of nerves. "It's a bit weird having my best friend's little sister sleeping in my room-- my old room." He correct-ed.

My best friend's little sister.

There it is.

"Trust me, it feels weird sleeping in the same bed that my broth-er's best friend used to sleep in." I retorted, making it a point to call him my brother's best friend. I know that it didn't affect him the same way that it affected me, but I needed to say it anyway. "I can only imagine the things that used to go down in that room. Why are you living in your parents house anyway?" I asked, curious as to why he lived here and his parents didn't anymore.

"Mom needed a place that didn't have stairs. She didn't want to sell the house though, and couldn't bear to have someone else living here. They found a small house a couple streets over and basically asked me if I wanted the place. I didn't want to upset my mom, so here we are." He shrugged.

I wondered what was going on with his mom, if everything was okay or not. But I didn't want to pressure him for answers, especially if the topic was a sensitive one. He unfolded his arms, each of his hands grabbing the counter behind him. My eyes immediately trailed over his exposed chest again, watching each muscle flex as he moved.

Jesus, Avery. You need to stop.

I was practically drooling over him.

"Right, that was nice of you." I finally said, forcing myself to break away from the thoughts I was having about him.

Sawyer caught onto my staring, a smirk forming on his perfectly plump lips.

"You act like you've never seen me without a shirt on." He chuckled, like it wasn't a big deal. It wasn't, but it was. I'd seen him without a shirt a number of times and I'd always found him attractive, but I'd never looked at him the way I was looking at him right now, which made it a big deal.

My eyes widened the second he made the comment, confirming that he knew I was checking him out. My face heated up immediately. "Still so full of yourself, I see." I shot at him, wanting to redirect the attention off of myself.

Sawyer pushed himself off of the counter and took a step closer to me. "Ave, I've known you for years and it's not the first time I've seen you check me out." He confessed.

I could feel even more heat creeping up from my neck and onto my cheeks. I wanted to play dumb, tell him I had no idea what he was talking about but when my lips parted to respond to him, nothing came out.

"No need to get all shy on me. We know each other better than that." He was standing in front of me now. The look in his eyes was a mix of seriousness and humor, the tone in his voice was something I couldn't quite decipher.

I couldn't breathe.

Did we know each other better than that? At this very moment, I felt like I didn't know anything about him. This wasn't my brother's best friend, this was a stranger who I had no idea how to talk to. This wasn't the boy I had a little school girl crush on for years, this was a man whose voice was shooting straight down to the pit of my belly.

"By the way, you look really good in just a tee shirt." His voice was low, it sounded like something I'd never heard from him before.

The front door opened, causing Sawyer to give me one more look before exiting the kitchen and walking into the living room to greet my brother. I finally let out a shaky breath, frozen in my spot against the counter.

You look really good in just a tee shirt.

He noticed.

He liked it.

The three of them walked into the kitchen moments later, Dani taking me by surprise by throwing her arms around me and pulling me into a hug. I was forced out of my thoughts, forced to shove Sawyer's comment to the back of my brain and focus on Dani as she squeezed the life out of me.

"Avery! It's been so long!" She squeezed me almost as tight as Callum, forcing out a breathy laugh from me as I hugged her back.

"Hey Dani." I smiled at her as she pulled away from me. I'd seen my brother and Dani in the last couple of years, they'd flown out to California a couple of times. It was definitely still hard being away from both of them. Dani and I got on really easily and for that, I was very grateful for.

"How were your flights? Are you excited to be back? How's Larissa!" She threw a bunch of questions at me, just like I knew she would. This was the exact reason why I was glad I didn't have to do any of these greetings last night.

Callum was setting food down on the island when he looked over at Dani and laughed. "Jeez, babe. One question at a time. You act like you never talk to her."

I laughed at my brother's comment. He was right, it's not like I didn't talk to Dani. We did text, but it was nice to know she was excited to have me home. "My flights were fine, long. It's a little weird being back, but I can't complain too much. And Larissa is good, she's sad she's not here. I told her to come with me, but she couldn't get the time off work." My eyes shifted to the island that Callum had placed the food on, my eyes widening when I realized what he'd gone out to grab.

"You're favorite." He grinned, watching my reaction.

"Oh my god, you're the best!" I smiled, immediately reaching over to grab a cheese covered fry. I didn't even care that they weren't as hot as they'd be if I'd gone with him. I practically moaned taking a bite of it. "Best. Fries. Ever."

Callum handed Dani a wrapped sandwich then slid one over to me. "I know I'm the best brother ever. Thanks for reminding me." He chuckled before passing one over to Sawyer, who was standing next to me.

"Let's eat on the deck. It feels wonderful outside." Dani said as she was sliding open the door to the back deck. Callum picked up his own sandwich as well as the fries and nodded towards the back door.

"Let me just grab a drink really quick." I said and turned to grab something out of the fridge. I stopped, seeing Sawyer standing directly in my way with his stupidly hot muscles still out on display. "Are you going to put a shirt on today?" I asked.

Sawyer chuckled and shrugged his shoulders. "Figured you were enjoying the view. Didn't want to deprive you of it. Although, you do have all summer to look." He smirked.

"Jesus, Sawyer. Is that how you got all the girls in high school?" I asked, trying to ignore the fact that I was one in fact of the girls that wanted to make out with him.

"Wouldn't you like to know." He said as he stepped around me to walk outside.

"Gross, I don't want to hear about anyone that you had sex with. Especially not in the bed I'm sleeping in." I opened the fridge and looked inside, grabbing another bottle of water. "You need more drink options." I said as I turned around. My face heated just slightly when I realized that he was no longer in the kitchen but outside. "Cool, just kidding." I mumbled to myself before walking outside to join everyone on the back deck. I took a seat in between Callum and Sawyer at the small table in the middle of the back deck.

I unwrapped my sandwich and immediately took a bite, groaning in appreciation. Callum laughed and gave me a small shove.

"Do you need a room alone with that sandwich?" He laughed.

I looked at him, mouth full of bread and said, "shut up, Callum." I finished chewing and pointed at him. "You can eat these delicacies whenever you want. I however, cannot. So let me enjoy it while I can." I took another bite of the sandwich and turned away from him.

I felt Sawyer's eyes on me, discreetly watching from beside me. I sat up a little straighter and turned my attention to Dani, so I could focus on her instead of Sawyer. "I don't know if there's anything that I can help with, but with the wedding being a couple weeks away please let me know if there's anything that I can do to help. I told Callum that last night, but I wanted to make sure the message actually got passed along."

Dani smiled at me, one of those big appreciative smiles that reached her eyes. "You have no idea how relieving that is to hear. My sister is driving me a bit crazy so it would be nice to talk to someone else that isn't her." She laughed.

"Ahh sisters, aren't they fun?" Callum joked.

This time, I shoved him. "I am fun. That's why I told all of my clients to screw off this summer and I'm here with you instead."

Callum put his hands up in surrender and laughed. "Relax, sis. We appreciate you being here. I'm sure you could find a couple people to work on while you're here if you needed to." He shrugged.

I laughed. "Who the heck in this small town would need me to do their makeup for anything? And if not someone from here, what vacationer do you think would really need that done last minute?"

Callum shrugged, "You never know. Events pop up, proposals, parties. Anything's possible."

"I thought you were moving to become a writer?" Sawyer asked, shifting my focus to him. I once again couldn't quite read his tone. I couldn't tell if there was judgement in it or if it was simply curiosity.

"I think I moved to the wrong city for that. Makeup started off as a hobby and small side thing. Couldn't get into writing like I wanted to and it eventually became a full time thing." I shrugged, answering his question honestly.

"You have clients for makeup?" He asked.

I furrowed my eyebrows, sensing a bit of judgement now. "I mean makeup and skincare... Uhh, yeah. Larissa had a couple connections that helped me get into everything pretty quickly." I answered. It almost made me feel bad, like I was doing the wrong thing. I felt especially bad after admitting that my roommate helped me move forward with things quickly. I moved to California as a way to get out of our little town, but I also told myself I was moving so I could become a writer. And the third strike to feeling bad right now was admitting that it hadn't gone according to plan.

Dani cleared her throat, sensing my obvious discomfort with the turn that the conversation took. "Do you know what you're wearing to the wedding?" She asked, changing the subject to something more light hearted.

I silently thanked her for changing the subject and shook my head. "I brought home a couple of options, but I might go into town and buy something."

"Oh can I help you decide?" She asked with a soft smile.

I couldn't help but laugh. This was her wedding and she wanted to help me pick out a dress. I wasn't even in the bridal party, but she still wanted to help me. "Yeah, I can show you the options that I brought with me and if you don't like them, we can go into town together?" I offered.

"That sounds perfect!" She smiled.

"You guys could go this weekend?" Callum suggested. "I don't think we have much planned. That way you can get it done with so it's one less thing to worry about."

I nodded as I picked up my water bottle. I took a sip from it and put it back down. "Yeah that sounds great." I leaned back in the chair I was sitting in, closing my eyes and just taking everything in.

I forgot how much I loved Maine summers. The weather wasn't crazy different from California right now, but the air was different. As much as I was nervous to come back and even though there was already a part of me ready to go back to Larissa, Maine was home in my heart. Breathing in the air from home was filling me with something I couldn't quite put my finger on.

I think this is going to be good for me.

Chapter 4

"I've just got to go into work for like an hour. Are you sure you're going to be fine?" Callum asked for the millionth time as we walked towards a cafe that was nearby.

"Callum, I said I'm fine. I know my way around everything, I think I'll be okay. Just text me when you're done and I'll let you know if I went anywhere else. Relax, I'll be fine." I laughed. It was sweet that he was worried about what I would do while he was working, but I really didn't care. I wanted to come into town with him this morning so that I wasn't stuck in the house while everyone else was gone.

"I'll text you as soon as I'm done. Or if I'm going to be there any longer." He gave me a quick hug before I practically shoved him off so that he could go to work. If he needed to work longer, I really didn't care. It's not like I had anything else to do so it was the least of my worries.

I walked into the small cafe, immediately inhaling the fresh scent of coffee. I smiled and walked up to the counter, waiting behind an older lady who was asking a bunch of questions about coffee and their food. I pulled out my phone while I waited, seeing a text from Larissa.

Larissa- Hey babes. How are things going?Me- Things are fine. Getting coffee while Callum runs to the office. Larissa- How's the boy situation? Me- Weird. Larissa- Define? Me- Call you in a min.

I shoved my phone into my pocket when the lady finally finished her order and took a step forward so I could order a coffee.

"Hi! Welcome to Sunrise Cafe, how can I help you?" I looked up at the woman behind the counter, immediately recognizing her as someone that went to high school with the boys and I. I prayed that she didn't notice who I was. She was a couple years older than me, so I was hopeful that she wouldn't. I wasn't in the mood for any more chats about how my life was going.

"Can I just get an iced coffee with half and half?" I asked as I pulled my wallet out of my purse.

"Of course! Can I get a name for the order?" She said as she put the order into the system.

"Avery." I said as I took my card out.

"Avery Jones!" She practically squealed. "I thought that was you! You look great girl, oh my gosh. It's been years!"

My shoulders visibly sank when she realized who I was. "Yeah it's been a while." I said quietly.

"You moved to California right? What a dream! What's it like?" She asked, her voice overly cheerful.

I handed her my card, hoping that it would speed up the process. "Yeah I did a couple years ago. It's great."

She swiped my card and handed it back to me. "Your brother's getting married soon, right? Did you and Sawyer ever end up to-gether? I always thought the two of you would make the cutest couple. Whenever the three of you were together, it was so sweet." She smiled at me as she continued to ask questions about my life.

I put my card back in my wallet and looked up at her, confusion written all over my face. She thought it was cute that I hung out with my brother and his best friend? I wouldn't call that cute or sweet. "Uhh, no. We're just... friends." I said, unsure if we were even friends at this point in life.

"Well, who knows what will happen now that you're back home! Never say never." She grinned.

"Have a nice day." I said and walked to the other end of the counter so I could escape the conversation. I quickly pulled my phone out again and dialed Larissa's number. "Please come save me." I said the second she answered the phone.

"Oh god, what did he do?" She laughed, assuming I was talking about Sawyer.

"It's only been like 3 days and I feel like I have so much to tell you." I laughed. I started to tell her about the small interactions I've had with Sawyer since being back. I decided I'd wait until I was out of the coffee shop before telling her about the interaction I had with Madison, the girl from the behind the counter.

"Avery fucking Jones, he thinks your hot." She squealed. I had to pull my phone away from my ear, she was literally screaming in my ear.

"He does not!" I whispered yelled, wanting to yell at her but not wanting to gather the attention of the entire cafe.

"Order for Avery!" A man behind the counter yelled, holding out my coffee. I quickly grabbed it from him, thanking him before walking out the front door so I could talk to Larissa without bothering anyone inside. I sat down at a table outside and put my coffee down.

"You're absolutely delusional, my California best friend. Maine guys are not the same as California guys. They are like 10 times more complicated." I explained before taking a drink of my coffee.

Larissa scoffed. "You dated Jamie, a freaking British footballer for what, like 8 months? And you can't handle a guy that you've known for like... over 10 years?"

I rolled my eyes, sitting back in my chair. "So totally not the same thing at all? Jamie was an idiot first of all. And not even from California, might I add? Sawyer is different and the fact that I've known him my entire life makes everything that much more complicated."

It was true. Things were super weird with Sawyer and part of it was because of how long we'd known each other. With guys from California or even Jamie, it was easier. I didn't have history with them so I was able to start fresh. I was able to give the details I wanted to give them. Sawyer knew everything about me, except for the last couple of years.

"So you admit that you still have a crush on him?" I could feel her grinning through the phone.

I huffed. "I never said that."

"You didn't have to." She argued.

"I don't know! He's like.. not the same person he was the last time I saw him. He is, but he isn't. He's always been hot... but like Jesus, Larissa. He's like... full on sexy now. And I can't get over the fact that I'm sleeping in his fucking bed." I groaned.

Larissa giggled. "And guess what? You're full on sexy too. And he knows it. He saw you for the first time in three years in nothing but a tee shirt. And he knows that you're sleeping in the same bed that used to be his. He probably wants to join you in that bed."

I rolled my eyes at my best friend's ridiculous comments, even though she couldn't see me.

"Babes, the summer is just getting started. He told you he liked you in just a tee shirt. You're definitely going to bang him before you come back to me. And I cannot wait to hear all of the details."

"Don't you have to go to work?" I laughed.

"You called me, remember? But you're right, I do need to go to work." She laughed. "Text me later?"

"Promise." I said before hanging up the phone. I put my phone down on the table and took a sip of my coffee, looking around the area. I wondered how long it would take for things to not feel weird. I wondered if I'd fall back into my normal Maine Routine or if I'd fall back into my California Routine. Or neither. I hated that I just felt out of place.

I wanted to go to my dads old house. I wondered if anyone still lived there. I wondered if it still looked the same. I missed my dad a lot and being back home amplified that feeling a lot. That's one of the things I was scared of. I moved almost right after he died, so I'm not sure I handled it the best. I was afraid that being back home would force me to finally grieve for him in a way that I hadn't yet done. I had all summer to drive by the house and see if it was occupied, I made a mental note that I wanted to do that before the summer was up.

I took in the surrounding area for a couple more minutes, watching people walk past me. It's one thing I did miss while I was in California. I missed the small town feel. It was something I wanted to escape, yet some days I missed being somewhere where I knew everyone and all the shops.

My phone buzzed on the table, breaking me from my thoughts and causing me to pick it up.

Sawyer- What kind of drinks do you like?

I read it over again, confused.

He must have heard me when I said he needed more options.

Me- Anything but Coke. Sawyer- Are you still in town with Callum?

He responded almost immediately.

Me- He's at the office, but I'm here.

I watched the three little dots appear and disappear a couple of times before a text finally came through.

Sawyer- Are you walking distance from the grocery store? Me- I am. Sawyer- Meet me there in 15? You can pick out what you want.

Now it was my turn to make those dots appear and disappear.

Sawyer- Leaving work now.

I didn't have a chance to respond before he sent that, so I responded simply.

Me- Okay.

I picked up my coffee from the table as well as my purse and headed in the direction of the grocery store. I sent Callum a text, letting him know that I was going to the store and he responded saying that he would probably be done soon and that he'd meet me there.

It was a super short walk to the store so I ended up waiting outside for Sawyer to get there. I sipped on my coffee, looking around as people entered and exited the grocery store before he arrived.

"You didn't have to wait outside for me." Was the first thing he said when he walked up to me.

I looked up at him, he was dressed in a pair of slacks and a soccer jersey. I tilted my head, confused by the outfit. "What the heck do you do for work?" Was the first thing I asked him, ignoring his comment about me waiting outside for him.

Damn, I thought he was being judgmental about what I do and here I am, doing the same thing.

"I coach soccer." He said simply.

"Soccer?" I questioned.

I'd never known him to be into soccer, so I was confused on where this came from. Sawyer was always into football. It's what he played growing up and in college. He never showed any interest in the soccer team, so the idea of him coaching soccer was really throwing me off.

"That's what I said, yes." He walked inside the building and I quickly followed him as he grabbed a cart and started walking around the store.

"Since when have you been into soccer?" I asked, still not over the fact that he was coaching soccer. I figured if anything, he'd coach football. I couldn't help but question him, I wanted to know more about why he decided to choose that path.

"Since when are you?" He returned the question.

I looked up at him, immediately confused by his comment. "What?"

He stopped walking and turned to face me. "I thought you were into American football. Not European."

My eyes widened. "How the hell do you even know about that?" His comment threw me off, his tone was a bit harsh and I didn't even know he knew about Jamie and I.

Sawyer laughed and started walking again. "I don't live under a rock, Avery. Callum also came back from California raving about how he met a European Footballer."

I quickly started to follow him again, watching him put things into the cart. "What are you jealous or something?" I asked without thinking.

Sawyer laughed again, but this time it wasn't as light as the first laugh. "What do I have to be jealous about?" And just like that, I was back to being Callum's little sister. Not the girl he thought looked good in a tee shirt, but his best friend's little sister. Of course he had nothing to be jealous of, it's not like he'd ever thought about what it would be like to be with me.

"Right." I practically whispered, irritated by the turn that the conversation had taken. We'd basically just gotten to the grocery store and things were back to being awkward. It was like he was pulling me back and forth and I couldn't quite keep up with everything.

The tension was back between us, the air was thick again and I felt like I was choking. We walked through the grocery store in silence, both of us putting things in the cart. Callum ended up meeting us at the store, he also began putting things in the cart.

"How was practice today man?" He asked Sawyer, seemingly not noticing the tension between us before he arrived.

"Same old same old." Sawyer responded simply to him.

"When's the game?" He asked.

"Saturday afternoon."

"Wanna go?" Callum turned his attention to me. "We don't have anything planned for the afternoon. Other than you and Dani shopping I think. But if you guys go in the morning, you should be able to make it. Right?"

I didn't want to say no and look rude, so I forced a smile and nodded. "Yeah sure. We might not even need to go shopping, but if we do we'll go in the morning."

"Sweet. We can talk to her about it when we get back, but I'm sure she'll be excited about it." He smiled.

We finished shopping and went to the check out. Sawyer paid for his things and Callum paid for his stuff and mine, even though I told him he didn't need to.

"You came all the way out here, the least I can do is buy you a couple drinks. Relax, it's not that serious." He laughed.

"Keep that attitude up all summer please." I grinned, obviously joking.

"Baby siblings always mooching off the older siblings." Callum joked with a laugh.

"Guess some things never change." Sawyer added, causing my eyes to lift to his. I couldn't tell if he was joking or not, but there it was. Another mental punch to the gut.

I wanted to ask him what the hell his problem was. He'd never been this mean to me before. When we were in school and even when they first started college, we had a good relationship. He was super nice to me and never cared that I hung out with them. Something changed after I graduated, it was almost like he'd pushed himself away from me. We didn't joke around as much as we used to and eventually I put what felt like a million miles between us, so now his jokes felt like actual punches to the gut. They weren't light hearted anymore, it felt like he meant everything he said and I hated that.

I looked away from him, deciding it was best not to say anything.

"Sawyer, we'll meet you back home." Callum said as we walked out of the grocery store.

"Sounds good." He said before walking away.

Callum and I walked to his car and loaded the groceries into the trunk before getting in ourselves. On the drive back, I turned to face Callum. "Why does Sawyer have a stick up his ass?" I spit out before I could stop it or lessen the blow.

Callum looked at me with wide eyes. "What the hell are you talking about?"

I huffed and folded my arms. "Did I do something to him? Does he want me to find somewhere else to stay? He's acting like he hates me."

Callum made a right turn before stopping at a red light. "He doesn't hate you, Aves. He's known you for how long? Of course he doesn't hate you. His mom isn't doing great and I know he's stressed about it. Plus he's been talking about finding a new job and I think we're just messing with his routine by being there." He sighed, obviously sticking up for his best friend.

I relaxed my shoulders a bit when he mentioned Sawyer's mom. "Is she okay? His mom I mean." He'd mentioned her needing to move out of their house because she was having a hard time with the stairs, but he didn't really go into more detail than that. I'd hate for Sawyer to feel the things that Callum and I felt when it comes to parent loss. I know that everyone will feel that eventually but it's something I wouldn't wish upon anyone.

"She's okay, just not great. He doesn't like to talk about it a lot, so don't ask him about it. Just cut him some slack, okay?" He asked. I knew that Callum just wanted what was best for everyone and I'm sure to him, everything was normal. Nothing out of the ordinary was going on between Sawyer and I and I was going to have to try and keep it that way.

I nodded and turned to look out the window. "Alright." I said quietly as I watched the outside world pass by me.

I hoped that everything was okay with his mom, but I was sure that if he wanted me to know what was going on he would talk to me eventually. For now, I needed to listen to Callum and cut him some slack. It was the beginning of the summer after all, I'm sure we would find our rhythm eventually.

Chapter 5

S awyer

   "Coach! Think we're gonna win on Saturday?" One of the kids on the team, Matthew, asked me as he was zipping up his bag.

   "Do you think we're going to win on Saturday?" I asked him in return.

   "Definitely!" He grinned up at me.

   I chuckled and nodded. "Then we're going to win. Good job today."

   "Thanks coach! See you on Saturday!" He picked up his bag and ran off to his mom.

   I waited until everyone was picked up before I headed to my car. I threw my own bag in the back and climbed into the drivers side. I started the car and pulled my phone out of my pocket, seeing a text from my dad.

   Dad- I know you've got a lot going on. Can you make time for dinner sometime soon? Me- Yeah, sure. Let me figure out a day and I'll call you later. Dad- Mom misses the house.

   I ran a hand through my hair, sighing.

Me- We can have dinner at the house then. Dad- Call me later with the day.

I tossed my phone into the passenger seat before backing out of the spot I was in. My head was all over the place and I'd never felt the way that I was feeling right now.

My mom wasn't doing well at all, every time my dad unexpectedly asked to set up dinner it meant something happened or something changed, but never in a good way. I almost wanted to tell them that I couldn't have dinner with them because I didn't want to see what she looked like or how much worse she'd gotten.

I love Callum, but I wished that I had the place to myself. I didn't want to ruin his wedding planning or his good moods by talking about depressing shit. I was constantly surrounded by the happiness of two people about to get married and all I wanted to do was sit at home by myself to just give myself a chance to feel sad or frustrated by my own situation.

And to make matters worse, Avery's got my mind even more fucked up than it already was before she got here. I don't see her in 3 years and the first time I lay eyes on her, she's wearing a fucking tee shirt. She walked into my old bedroom in nothing but a tee shirt that barely covered her ass.

I don't know how to be normal around her. How am I supposed to treat her like my best friend's little sister when I can't stop thinking about taking her up to my old bedroom and fucking her brains out? So now I'm just being a dick, I know I am and I feel bad. I don't know how to joke around with her anymore, I don't even know who she is. So everything I mean to come out as a joke has not come out that way and I can see the immediate hurt on her face at each stupid thing I've said to her so far, but I can't stop saying stupid things.

I fucking told her I liked her in the tee shirt the day after she got to my house. I was so caught up in seeing what she looked like after 3 years that I almost forgot who she was. When I realized what I was doing, it's all been downhill since and it's been less than a week of her being back. I needed to really get my shit together if I was supposed to spend the entire summer with her. Especially if she was going to be staying in my house for three months.

I finally pulled into my driveway, thankful I was able to give myself a break from my own head. I didn't see Callum or Dani's car, but that didn't mean Avery wasn't home. I had no idea if she'd gone out with anyone or not. I shut the door to my Jeep after I got out and made my way to the front door. It was unlocked, letting me know that Avery was in fact home.

I kicked off my shoes by the door and immediately went to the stairs so I could go change. I reached the top of the steps just in time for the bathroom door to swing open, revealing Avery with a blue towel wrapped around her body and steam coming from the bathroom behind her.

"Fuck me," She gasped when she saw me standing at the top of the steps.

Fuck me is right.

"You shouldn't shower with the front door unlocked. You never know who might want to come into your house." I stated, my eyes never leaving her.

I watched as she tightened the towel around her just slightly. "It's a pretty safe neighborhood if I recall correctly.. didn't think I had anything to worry about.." Her voice was quiet, like she wasn't sure how to respond. It was probably due to the fact that she didn't know how I would respond.

"Fair point. I do have to ask though, do you always walk around other peoples houses in little to no clothes?" I asked, reminding her that this wasn't actually her house and this was now the second time she's left very little to my imagination.

She shifted on her feet, uncomfortable at my question so I added in, "I'm definitely not mad about it, simply curious. Trying to figure out if this will be a normal occurrence all summer."

I watched as the redness spread across her cheeks as she listened to what I had to say.

I could make her other cheeks just as red if she wanted me too.

Jesus, so not the time.

"I didn't know when you'd be home. Both times, actually." She answered honestly.

I nodded. "Do me a favor? Don't start keeping track of my schedule. I like these little run ins." I grinned before walking into my bedroom, not giving her a chance to respond.

I heard her practically running to the other bedroom and shutting the door behind her. I sat down on my bed and let out a small groan. It was things like that that made me question literally everything.

I was giving myself whip lash with these interactions. One minute, I was accidentally hurting her feelings by telling her I had no reason to be jealous of her ex boyfriend. The next minute, I was flirting with her and basically telling her to continue walking around myself with little to no clothes on.

It was already frustrating.

Avery had become seriously hot since the last time I saw her. Honestly, it started after she graduated. It was little things that she did that made me start noticing her a little more. She lost her braces, her clothing changed a little bit, her confidence increased a bit with college.

But whatever California did to her? It was like meeting her for the very first time. She was no longer someone's little sister. She was a woman and a woman that I wanted nothing more than to bury my cock inside of for days on end.

This was going to be the longest most confusing summer of my entire life. I needed to get it together if I was going to survive the next three months with her in my house. She was Callum's little sister and I needed to keep reminding myself of that.

No matter how hot she'd become, she was my best friend's little sister and I needed to keep that line drawn as best as I could.

Fuck me is definitely right, Ave.

Chapter 6

I pulled back the curtain, stepping out to reveal the dress that I had on. I was truly exhausted, I'd been trying on dresses all morning and I was ready to be done. Dani and I had agreed that we didn't like anything that I brought home with me so we decided to do some shopping before going to Sawyer's soccer game. We were running out of time and I was praying we would agree on a dress soon.

"Oh my god, Avery! This is the one!" Dani squealed. "It's so pretty!" She pushed herself off of the chair and over to me, spinning me around so that I was facing the mirror.

"Jesus, am I getting married or are you?" I laughed. Her reaction was funny, she was really acting like we were wedding dress shopping for me when in reality, I was just trying to find a last minute dress for their wedding.

"Oh shut up and tell me you love this dress." She giggled.

I looked myself over, looking at the dress that I had on. It was a cream colored, satin dress that was covered in flowers or leaves or something in different shades of pink. It went down to my mid calf, with a slit on one side that went up to my thigh. It had a cowl neckline and a strappy back, which was probably my favorite part of the dress. It was really pretty.

"I do love it. But are you sure about the color? Aren't you not supposed to wear anything that is even remotely white to weddings?" I asked, looking back at her through the mirror.

Dani quickly shook her head. "There's enough pink in it that you really don't even notice the cream. I would consider this dress pink, please buy it. Plus it will look cute with the wedding colors!"

I turned to face her, confused as to why that mattered. "I'm not in the wedding party, why does It matter that it goes with the wedding colors?" I asked with a laugh.

Dani shook her head again, but this time in a way that told me she was hiding something from me. "It doesn't matter, it will just look cute."

"Dani, why are you being weird?" I asked.

She just shrugged.

"If you don't tell me, I'm not buying this dress." I folded my arms, giving her a look. Of course I didn't mean that, I was going to buy the dress regardless of whatever she was being weird about. But, I didn't know if she knew that.

"You're buying that dress. Now go take it off so we can pay for it. We've got a soccer game to go to." She shoved me back towards the dressing room, not giving into me. I rolled my eyes and walked into the dressing room, changing out of the dress and back into the outfit I had on earlier which consisted of a black jean skirt and an orange tee shirt tucked into it. I slipped my sandals back on and walked out of the dressing room again so that we could go check out.

I bought the dress and Dani and I headed off to where Sawyer said the game was.

"How does it feel to know that you're getting married in like... less than 3 weeks?" I asked, looking over at her.

Dani giggled. "It's pretty weird! But I'm so ready for it to finally be here. I feel like we've been planning everything for ages and I'm excited to see all the work pay off and to finally marry Callum. He's literally so sweet and just everything I could have ever asked for."

"Gross, that's my brother we're talking about." I joked. I honestly loved that Callum was marrying Dani. She was the sweetest person I'd ever met and I loved knowing that Callum was happy with her.

"Oh you think that's gross? Wait until you hear about what he did to me on---"

"Stop! Stop stop stop stop. I do not need to hear about my brother's sex life!" I interrupted, wanting to put a stop to the conversation before it actually got gross.

Dani couldn't stop laughing as she stopped at a red light and looked over at me. "You are too funny, Avery. But seriously, I'm excited for the day to finally be here and I'm so happy that you're home getting to spend the summer with us. I'm excited that you'll be here even after the wedding."

I smiled at her and nodded. When Callum had originally asked me to come home, I'd told him I would come home for a month and leave after the wedding. But after him telling me that I didn't get to spend enough time with him because I lived so far away, I'd agreed to spend the entire summer.

"Yeah, I came home for your wedding and then you guys are just going to ditch me after so you can go celebrate your love or whatever." I teased.

Dani gave my arm a shove before she started driving again. "It's called a honeymoon. Hopefully by then we'll be in our own house and you can stay there instead." She smiled.

"I'm sure Sawyer would love that. I really don't think he likes that I'm staying there." I started. "He's being all... weird." I sighed. I had no idea if I could talk to Dani about it, but I couldn't talk to Callum about it and she actually knew him. I could talk to Larissa every day about him, but she didn't actually know him so it was harder to get an idea of if I was actually reading too much into things.

"What do you mean by weird?" She asked me.

I shrugged and turned to face her. "Can I be honest with you without you going off and telling Callum everything I said?" I asked. I trusted her, but there was always that part of me that was unsure how much she'd go off and tell my brother when I wasn't around.

"You mean about the fact that you've been in love with Sawyer since I met you and probably before that?" She glanced in my direction just as my eyes went wide.

"I am not in love with him, oh my god." I argued.

Dani laughed. "Yeah sure."

I folded my arms. "I'm not in love with him! I had a crush on him when we were growing up, but who didn't? It's your typical stupid love story, girl likes her older brother's best friend and the best friend sees her as nothing but a little sister. Typical and out done." I huffed. "That doesn't even matter, that's not what I was going to say!"

"Okay then, what were you going to say?" She asked.

"He's just being weird! When we were growing up, things were never weird between us. Whenever he was hanging out with Callum, he would always make it a point to talk to me or to tell me I was allowed to hang out with them. Things were easy. Even after he went to college, whenever he'd come home it wasn't weird. He'd ask me how school was going, we'd talk about life and we'd hang out with Callum like all three of us were friends." I started, thinking back to when we were younger and things were simple. Of course I had a crush on him back then, he was cute and he was nice to me. What more could a young girl want?

"I graduated high school and things got a little weird. He got a little distant, but I didn't think much of it. We were both getting older and had different things to talk about. He was planning what he was going to do after college graduation and I was planning on what to do in college." I sighed. "Then my dad died and I couldn't take it anymore. So I moved and this is literally the first time I've seen him in three years and things couldn't be more different.."

Dani listened to everything I had to say, following it up with, "define different?"

I groaned, throwing my head back on the headrest. "Strange! So fucking strange and different. I don't know! He was all weird the night I got home, then he was all... flirty? the morning after. Then things got weird again when we went grocery shopping and he was making it a point to remind me that he would never be jealous of anyone I dated and that I was just Callum's little sister.... Then yesterday while you guys were at work, he got home when I was walking out of the shower and got all... flirty again." I spilled everything, just needing advice more than anything.

Dani pulled into a parking spot right as I finished rambling. She put the car in park and turned to face me. "Want to know what I think?"

I rolled my eyes. "Duh, that's why I asked you."

"He's confused. You're all hot and stuff now. You get back from California after three years and you're a totally different person. He probably doesn't know what to do with these thoughts because he's probably trying to decide if Callum would be happy or if he'd punch him in the nuts if you two ever hooked up." She said.

I shook my head. "Absolutely not, there's no way that Sawyer likes me." I argued.

Do me a favor? Don't start keeping track of my schedule. I like these little run-ins.

His sentence from last night popped into my head.

By the way, you look really good in just a tee shirt.

Then the sentence from the morning after I landed.

Oh my god, does Sawyer like me?

"He's definitely thinking about hooking up with you." She giggled. "Now come on, we've got to watch some little kids play soccer." She said as she opened the door.

"Little kids?" I asked. I don't know why I assumed that Sawyer coached teenagers. I still couldn't get over the fact that he coached soccer, knowing that it was little kids somehow made it ten times better.

"Yes! It's so stinking cute, let's go!"

I followed Dani out of the car and to the field where two teams of little kids were running around a soccer field. Dani spotted Callum and walked up to him, taking a seat next to him.

"Hey babe! Hey sis. Did you guys find a dress?" He asked just as I took a seat next to Dani.

"Hi babe." She gave him a kiss and then looked over at me. "We found the most perfect dress!"

Callum started laughing. "Who's the one getting married?"

I gasped, "That's exactly what I said!"

Now all three of us were laughing. "You two really are siblings." Dani giggled.

The soccer game was pretty fun to watch. It's always more fun to watch kids play sports, because when something goes wrong people aren't screaming at them to fix their mistakes. We can all sit there and either laugh or continue to cheer them on. Honestly, it's pretty wholesome to watch.

The three of us were standing, waiting for Sawyer to finish up so that we could talk to him when a little kid walked up to him. "Coach! Did you see me make that goal?!" He was so excited and so happy.

I watched Sawyer as he bent down so he could be more on the kids level. He gave him a high five and smiled. "And did we win today just like you said we would?"

The kid gave him a high give back and practically jumped in the air. "Yes! Just like we said we would!"

"That's what I like to hear. You did great out there. You better go celebrate tonight." He chuckled.

"Duh, mom says we can go get ice cream. Wanna come?" The kid asked as he grabbed his bag.

"Not this time, maybe next game." He laughed.

"One of these days you're going to come get ice cream with us, coach."

"Michael, your sister's in the car! Let's go sweetie!" I looked over at an older woman motioning for the kid talking to Sawyer to hurry up.

"Gotta go, bye coach!" Michael, the kid, waved to Sawyer and ran off to his mom.

My heart warmed at the interaction. I'd never actually seen Sawyer talk to little kids, other than when he would talk to me when we were younger but I feel like that didn't count because he's only three years older than me. It was really sweet watching him interact.

"Shit, Dani the realtor is asking to meet us at her office in 20 minutes." I glanced over at Callum as he looked up from his phone. "Needs us to look over some paperwork."

Dani groaned. She looked over at Sawyer and then looked back at me. "You can take my car if you want?" She started to get her keys out of her bag when Callum stopped her.

"I actually rode here with Sawyer. Sis, do you care to catch a ride home with him?" He asked.

Of course this would be happening.

"Uhh, no it's fine. You guys go ahead."

Callum ran over to Sawyer, I assumed he was telling him the situation and that I needed a ride back. Sawyer and I made eye contact and I couldn't quite read the look on his face so I quickly looked away and looked at Dani.

"You'll be fine! If you start losing confidence, just remember.. he already wants to sleep with you." She whispered.

"Dani!" I whisper-yelled.

She giggled and gave me a quick hug. "What? It's true so just keep that in mind. See you tonight!"

Callum and Dani walked away, leaving me standing there waiting for Sawyer to finish up whatever he needed to finish doing. I adjusted the skirt that I wore before I walked over to where he was standing so I could see if he needed any help.

"Congrats on the win." I smiled up at him. It was the first time I'd said that to him in a while. I used to tell him all the time when they would win games, but it had been a while since I'd been able to do that.

"Thanks. It's pretty fun watching them play."

"The little kid that was talking to you, he seems really sweet." I said.

Sawyer nodded and chuckled as he threw a bag over his shoulder. "That's Michael. Always asking me to get ice cream with him after the games, always one of the last ones to leave the games or practice. Always telling everyone to keep their heads up when we lose."

I watched him gather a couple more things, his hands looked pretty full. "Can I help you carry anything?" I asked. "Michael sounds a lot like someone I know." I added on. Sawyer was the same way growing up. He was never your typical asshole football player. He's always been pretty down to earth and actually cared about other people. I think that's part of the reason everything he's doing has been so confusing.

Sawyer motioned to a binder and a bottle of water. "Can you just grab those? I got everything else."

I did what he asked, grabbing the water bottle and the binder. He started walking towards his car, so I quickly followed him.

"And yeah... he reminds me a lot of myself, I think that's why he's got a special place in my heart." He added on.

I smiled, but didn't respond to his comment. I just thought it was sweet, but I didn't want to ruin the moment by saying anything that would make him take it back. When we reached his car, he opened the trunk and threw a couple of things back there. "You can put the binder in the back seat." He said as he closed the trunk when he was finished.

Once again, I did as he asked. I put my binder and my purse in the backseat of his Jeep before climbing into the front seat. I set the water bottle down and glanced over at him. He didn't say anything as he started the car and backed out of his spot. I didn't have much else to say so I turned and looked out the window.

I could feel the tension creeping back up between the two of us and I wanted to yell at him about it, but I decided that I didn't want to ruin the good mood that the game had put me in.

Sawyer wants to sleep with you.

The little voice in my head spoke before I could shut it down. My breathing quickened at my own thought, my legs squeezing together just slightly.

You want to sleep with Sawyer.

The little voice spoke up again. I wanted to yell at it to shut up, but I knew I was fighting a battle that I couldn't win. I couldn't get the image of him standing in his kitchen shirtless out of my head.

We're going to sleep with Sawyer Evans.

Oh my god. Shut up, shut up, shut up.

Chapter 7

I took a step back as I finished Dani's makeup. I grinned, proud of myself. Not that she needed a lot of makeup, but I was proud of what I had done to her. "Dani, you look so hot." I laughed.

I watched her spin around so she could face the mirror in the bathroom we were standing in, her eyes going wide. "Avery! Oh my god, I forgot how much I loved when you do my makeup." She looked at herself over again and smiled.

"My brother is going to drop to his knees when he sees you, especially in the dress! You have to go put it on!" I pushed her out of the bathroom, pointing to the pink sequin dress I pulled out of my luggage. It was a one shoulder dress with a long poofy sleeve, the side that had the sleeve also had a cut out in the mid section. I closed the bathroom door so that she could get dressed and finished touching up my own makeup. I was excited to go out tonight with everyone.

Everyone had been so busy this week, working and doing things to prepare for the wedding that I found myself feeling a bit lonely and bored. I tried to stay out of the way so that I didn't interfere with what everyone was doing. Dani had been asking for my opinion on certain things, but other than that I had been basically on my own for the week. Sawyer and I had a couple chats, but it felt like he'd been keeping his distance since the soccer game the week before.

"I'm done!" I heard her yell from the other side of the door, so I swung it open and gasped when I saw her.

"Oh yeah... on the floor, all night. Do I need to find another house to sleep in tonight? Like a million miles away from the two of you?" I asked with a smile.

Dani walked into the bathroom, giving the dress a small tug as she did. "Am I going to have to tug on this all night? I'm not used to wearing short dresses." She laughed.

I leaned against the door frame, watching her as she messed with her hair. "You'll get used to it. Trust me, it's worth it. Do you have a pair of tan heels to wear with it? They'd be perfect."

"Yeah, somewhere. I'll find them in a second."

I pushed myself off the door frame and smiled. "I'm going to go get changed, I'll be back in a couple minutes. If you can't find the shoes, let me know I think I brought home a pair." I said before making my way out of the basement and upstairs to the guest bedroom. I shut the door behind me when I walked in and stripped out of the clothes I was wearing. I picked up the dress I'd planned on wearing tonight and stepped into it. It was a light blue dress with long, mesh poofy sleeves to match the one Dani was wearing. Both the sleeves had little ties near the wrists to match the tie in the back. I shimmied into it and reached back in an attempt to not only tie the back but zip it up.

"Fuck," I mumbled to myself when I couldn't successfully do either one of those things. I slipped into a pair of silver heels and walked out of the bedroom so that I could have Dani help me.

Like clockwork, as I walked out of the bedroom, Sawyer was walking out of his dressed in a simple pair of khakis and a button down. He made even the simplest of outfits look so good. I quickly moved one of my hands to my back, holding the dress together from the back.

"Need some help?" He asked, noticing how quickly I'd moved to hold my dress together.

"Oh, I was actually going to ask Dani for help. You don't have to." I said, not wanting to make him help me.

Sawyer shook his head, taking a step closer to me. Instantly, I was able to smell that same cologne that he always wore. The one with Vanilla and something else, something woodsy. It still smelt just as heavenly as it did before. "It's fine, I can help. Turn around." His voice was soft, different.

I slowly turned around so that my back was to him. I let go of the dress and instead grabbed my hair, pulling it over my shoulder so that it wasn't in the way. The second I felt Sawyer's hands grip the zipper, I sucked in a breath. I hoped that it wasn't noticeable, but I'm sure that he noticed. He slowly pulled the zipper up until it reached its destination. His hands grazed the exposed part of my back as he moved them up to the strings that needed to be tied. He was silent the entire time, the only thing that could be heard was my shaky breathing. I felt goosebumps arise on my skin each place his hands touched, even if they barely grazed the spot. When he finished tying the strings together, he gently grabbed my hair and pulled it to the back where it had been placed before. I let out another breath before turning around to face him.

I couldn't read his expression, but his eyes were darker than normal. The usual bright shade of green was much darker, something that I don't think I'd seen before. "Thank you." I said, my voice barely above a whisper.

Sawyer's eyes traveled across my body, taking everything in. He wasn't shy about it either. I was watching him check me out.

Sawyer Evans just checked me out.

"You look really good, Jones." Was all he said.

Oh my god, and he thinks I look good.

I felt the blush creep up my neck and spread onto my cheeks. I watched his eyes linger for a moment, I knew they could see my chest rising and falling at a rate that I was too embarrassed to care about. "Thank you, you look good too." I complimented him back.

I wondered what his next move would be, if there was even a next move.

I felt one of his hands grip my waist, pulling me slightly closer to him. I stumbled a bit, not expecting him to do it. My breathing was definitely rapid, my lips parted in anticipation for whatever he wanted to do next. He was in control of this situation, we both knew that.

I swear I saw him glance at my lips.

He's going to kiss me.

"Sawyer! Aves! Are you guys almost ready?!" My brother's voice yelled just as the basement door opened.

Just as quickly as he'd pulled me into him, he was taking a step back and clearing his throat. "Yeah, one sec!" He turned to yell down the steps, letting my brother know that he was coming downstairs.

Sawyer turned to look at me again, I was frozen in my spot. "We'd better get going." He said and motioned towards the steps.

"Right, yeah." I nodded. I quickly walked past him to go to the stairs. Sawyer grabbed my hand to stop me from actually walking. I turned to look at him, wondering why he was stopping me.

"Seriously, Jones. You look... good." He practically whispered before he let go of my hand.

I sucked in a breath and started down the steps, practically in a daze from just his words alone. He almost kissed me. Oh my god.

Dani was walking through the basement door as I reached the bottom of the steps. "You look so hot! We look so hot!" She squealed. My eyes lifted to meet hers and almost immediately, she knew something had changed. "Babe, can you drive us there? I'll drive back obviously." She called out to Callum, her eyes never leaving mine.

"No worries, you guys ready to go?" He asked, glancing at Dani then at me. I tensed, feeling Sawyer's body behind me at the bottom of the steps.

"Yep! Let's go! Sawyer, you can sit up front on the way there. Girls will sit in the back." Dani said as she made her way to the front door, following behind Callum. I was thankful she was sitting in the back with me, even though I knew it meant she was going to ask me what happened upstairs.

I felt Sawyer's hand rest on my lower back, causing me to stand just a little straighter. I quickly glanced back at him and he nodded towards the door, not questioning anything that he was doing. I walked to the door, following behind the other two. Sawyer's hand never left my back as we walked out the front door. He locked the door on the way out and even opened the back door of the car for me. I looked up at him again, confused as to what was going on. I climbed into the back of the door and he just nodded at me before closing the door and getting into the passenger seat.

Callum started the long drive to the club that we were going to to celebrate the two of them. There were no fun clubs in town, so we were going a bit out of our way but none of us really minded the drive.

Dani leaned closer to me, her cell phone in hand and motioned for me to look down at it.

What the heck happened upstairs with you two?

I almost laughed, seeing as she was using the notes feature on her phone to write that so that the boys didn't hear us. I took her phone from her so that I could type a response.

Sawyer likes my outfit.

I handed her the phone back and grinned as her eyes widened, then narrowed at my simple response. She quickly started typing again.

That's it? That's all I get?

She shoved the phone back into my hand.

I think he was going to kiss me.

I handed her back the phone.

She gasped, looking up at me with wide eyes.

"You okay?" Callum's voice came from the front seat. He glanced back at us through the rearview mirror as he asked.

Dani quickly nodded. "Yeah, we're good!" She said, probably a little too quickly. She quickly shoved her phone back into my lap, not even typing anything back. She was asking me for details without actually asking.

He helped me zip my dress up, then he told me I looked good. He pulled me closer to him and it looked like he was going to kiss me when Callum asked us if we were almost ready to leave. He pulled away from me and so I started to walk down the steps but he grabbed my hand and said, and I quote, "Seriously, Jones. You look... good." Then we came downstairs and he put his hand on my back and we walked outside and now here we are.

I typed the long paragraph of details and handed her back the phone so she could read it. Dani read the message and reached over, grabbing my hand and squeezing it, her way of screaming without disturbing the boys.

"Oh my god oh my god." She mouthed.

I started laughing, unable to help myself. I couldn't believe it either, but her reaction was making everything better.

So you guys are going to sleep together tonight, right?

She handed me back her phone and my eyes widened at her message.

"Dani!" I said without thinking about it.

Both of the boys glanced back at us, confused looks on each of their faces.

"Girl talk." She quickly said, giving them both a wave as a way to say it's none of your business. "What? I'm just asking a simple question?" She whispered, turning back to me.

I shoved her phone back on her lap and laughed. "I could ask you the same question." I said, even though I already knew the answer and I didn't want to hear it said out loud.

"A million times yes. I look hot tonight, are you kidding me?" She said out loud, not caring about who heard.

"Damn straight you do!" Callum said from the front seat, causing Dani to giggle.

"Gross." I laughed.

"I think we both look hot tonight, wouldn't you agree boys?" Dani smirked. I narrowed my eyes at her, wanting to tell her to shut up.

Callum glanced back at us again, chuckling. "I'm not about to say that my sister looks hot. But, you do look pretty Aves."

I glanced at my brother and smiled. "Thank you, that's very nice of you to say."

"What about you, Sawyer? Don't you think we look hot?" She grinned.

"Uhh, is that a trick question?" He asked.

"What the hell does that even mean?" Dani questioned.

Sawyer turned so he could see us, then glanced at Callum in the driver's seat. "You're asking me if I think my best friend's almost wife and little sister look hot. If I say yes, he's going to punch me. If I say no, all three of you are going to punch me."

I couldn't help but laugh at his response, although I was sure to hear the part where he once again referred to me as the little sister. I was never going to escape that term and I absolutely hated it.

"You might as well just take one punch instead of three and admit that we look hot." Dani said confidently, not backing down from him. I knew what she was doing and a part of me hated it, but another part of me wanted to see what he would do.

Sawyer shook his head and turned around so he was facing the front again. "Yes, you both look hot." He finally admitted.

"Dude! That's my fiancee and my sister you're talking about!" Callum gave him a shove, but I could hear the humor in his voice so I knew he wasn't serious.

Dani and I were cracking up in the backseat. I liked this. This felt normal, this felt like the way things had always been. I glanced forward, catching Sawyer's eyes in the side mirror. He had a small smirk on his face that I could just barely see. Right before he looked away, he gave me a quick wink. I quickly looked away from the mirror and back to Dani, smiling at her as she leaned forward to say something to Callum.

The rest of the car ride was light hearted, we were joking around with each other and the tension that had been between Sawyer and I was not present. I was sure it would come back at some point, but I was thankful that for the time being, it was gone.

"Have you ever drank?" I asked Dani over the loud music. We'd been at the club for a couple hours and I noticed that she wasn't drinking. I remembered her mentioning that she would drive us home, but I felt bad that we were celebrating them and she wasn't even drinking.

"I mean I've had a drink before, but it's not really my thing." She responded with a smile.

I nodded. "Totally valid. Hangovers suck." I laughed, taking a sip of the vodka cranberry I was holding.

Callum slung his arm around Dani, looking down at me with a drunken grin. "You know, it's really weird drinking with you." He laughed.

I raised my eyebrows at him. "Why is it weird?"

"Because! You left before you were even old enough to drink legally and you never partied with me in high school. So we've never actually gone out together before and it's just weird watching my baby sister get drunk."

I laughed at his words because he was acting like I'd never been drunk before. "First of all, you never let me go to parties with you. Second of all, you act like I've never gone out and gotten drunk." I finished off my drink and set it down on the bar behind Dani.

Callum leaned over to Sawyer, whispering something to him before turning back to me. "First of all," he started in a mocking tone. "That's because everyone we went to high school with were shit heads and I wasn't about to let you get drunk with any of them. Second, I knoooow that you get drunk because now you're a cool California girl, going out and partying with British Footballers!"

He was definitely drunk.

I felt Sawyer's eyes on me the second Callum mentioned my ex. I glanced over at him, his eyes were slightly narrowed like he didn't like the fact that he'd been brought up.

I thought you didn't have anything to be jealous of, Sawyer?

"Well I appreciate the concern, but it was really annoying when we were younger." I tried to ignore the second part of his statement, not wanting to deal with talking about Jamie.

"How'd you even meet that guy anyway?" Dani asked innocently.

"I'm also curious about that." Sawyer finally spoke up.

I looked at him again, but his tone wasn't as innocent as Dani's. "Uhh, I met him on a night out with Larissa. He was friends with a couple of her friends. Why does it even matter, we broke up." I shrugged, wanting to change the subject.

"Here you are, man." The bartender interrupted just in time, passing 3 shots and 3 drinks to Sawyer.

Callum took his arm back from Dani and handed me a shot just as Sawyer picked one up. "To me! I'm getting married!" He said as he raised his plastic cup. Sawyer and I followed suit, tapping the cups together and taking the shot.

I made a face as the liquor burned the back of my throat. "Fuck," I mumbled to myself. Sawyer handed me another cup, this time it was a drink. I quickly thanked him and took a sip of it. "Jesus Christ." I was really about to get fucked up with my brother. Whoever was pouring these drinks tonight was pouring them strong.

"Baby, dance with me!" Dani said, pulling on Callum's arm. Callum took her hand and started walking to the dance floor. "You two, dance with us!" Dani looked back, pointing at the two of us.

I glanced at Sawyer and back at Dani, shaking my head. There was no way he was going to dance with me, especially not in front of Callum. It's not that I didn't want to dance with him, but I think we were both in agreement that we couldn't dance in front of my brother, not the way that people dance at clubs.

We stood awkwardly next to each other for a couple minutes. Sawyer ordered two more shots and handed me one of them when it reached him. We tapped cups and downed the shot before he picked up his drink and put his hand on my lower back again. "Come on, we're not just going to stand here all night."

Sawyer led me to another area of the dance floor. We were standing in a spot that we could just barely see Dani and Callum, but they weren't facing us so the chances of them seeing us were pretty slim. Sawyer stood behind me, the hand that was on my lower back moved to grab my waist. I was tense, not sure how to handle myself in this situation. I'd danced with other people before, but I never imagined dancing with Sawyer Evans like this. He gave my hip a light squeeze and leaned down so he was closer to my ear. "Relax,"

I sucked in a breath, his voice sending a chill down my spine. I tried to loosen up as he started to move my hips for me to the beat of the song that was playing. It took a little bit of time, but I finally loosened up. I think it was mostly due to the alcohol choosing this very moment to finally hit me. Sawyer and I danced together for a while, neither one of us saying much. His free hand held my hip, my hips having a mind of their own and grinding against the front of him. I finished my drink eventually and tilted my head back against his chest so that I could look up at him through my hazy eyes.

He was so handsome it almost wasn't fair. It was like God had taken a little extra time to sculpt every single inch of his body. Sawyer looked down at me, a questioning look on his face.

"What?" He asked, although his voice was soft.

I think it was the alcohol talking for both of us when I asked, "Were you going to kiss me earlier?"

Sawyer chuckled, tilting his head back so it was facing the ceiling. When he looked back down at me, he turned me so I was facing him completely. "Did you want me to kiss you earlier?"

I liked it better when he was calling the shots. It felt too vulnerable for me to admit that I did indeed want him to kiss me. "I asked you first.."

His hand moved from my hip, back to my lower back where he pulled me closer to him again. "Would you have kissed me back if I had?" He questioned. He still didn't answer my question, but this time I answered his.

All I did was nod, I couldn't find the words to say that I would have kissed him back because I did want him to kiss me, that I've wanted to know what it felt like to be kissed by him since I was 13 years old and everyone around me was starting to kiss other people.

"What about now?" He asked.

I was about to respond with a yes, please for the love of everything that is good in this world, just kiss me when I heard Dani's voice asking us if we were okay with leaving. I quickly pulled away from Sawyer and looked at Dani, who was eyeing me down like she'd caught us with our clothes off.

"Callum's pretty wasted and it's a long drive back." She grinned.

"Yeah, let's go before Sawyer has to carry him out." I smiled, trying to ignore the heat that I felt throughout my whole body.

The four of us walked back to Callum's car, his arm wrapped around Dani in an attempt to keep himself up. "Shotgun!" He yelled as we reached the car.

Dani helped him into the front seat and turned to look at me, "He'll throw up if he sits in the back." She said as a way of apologizing.

I shook my head and laughed, "It's fine. Don't want to deal with throw up tonight." I said as I climbed into the backseat next to Sawyer. Once everyone was in the car, Dani took off back to Sawyer's house. I was looking out the window, everything was dark and blurry and it was making my head spin a bit. I closed my eyes, trying to ignore the feeling in my head that was telling me I might get sick tonight instead. I felt warmth on my exposed though, causing me to open my eyes and look down at it. Immediately, I saw Sawyer's hand covering my thigh.

My eyes shot up to look at him, but his head was facing the window. I looked back down at his hand, watching his thumb gently move back and forth on the exposed skin creating goosebumps under it and sending a volt of electricity straight up the remainder of my leg and to my core.

Sawyer's hand didn't move the rest of the car ride, and it was a long car ride. He also didn't say anything, he just looked out the window and held my thigh. When we got back to his place, he helped Dani get an almost passed out Callum into the basement. I heard him tell her goodnight and to come get him if she needed any help with him before he shut the basement door. I was standing by the steps, holding the heels that I'd just taken off. I wasn't sure what the next move was. Was he going to try and kiss me? Was he going to brush everything off and tell me he was going to bed?

God I hope not.

Sawyer nodded towards the top of the stairs, silently telling me he was going upstairs. I nodded, walking upstairs, knowing that the night was about to come to an end and that he was about to pretend nothing happened. I stood in front of the guest bedroom, shoes in hand looking over at him.

Please don't say goodnight.

"Tonight was fun." He said, keeping a slight distance from me.

I nodded in agreement. "Yeah, it was." I glanced down at his hand, the one that had been on my thigh the entire car ride home. The one that I wanted to feel against me again.

"We should probably get some sleep. We're both probably going to be hungover tomorrow." He lifted his hand and scratched the back of his neck.

Fuck.

"Right, uhh. Goodnight then." I said quietly before quickly turning and walking into the guest bedroom. I shut the door and leaned against it, letting out a sigh. A part of me was mad, I wanted to run into his room and tell him to just shut up and kiss me. I wanted to tell him to pick a side, either kiss me and act like you want me or stop doing all those little things that make me think you do.

It was definitely the alcohol talking as I swung the door open again, prepared to storm into his room and tell him the exact thoughts that were going through my head. Only, I didn't need to go anywhere because he was standing at the door.

He looked at me for less than 10 seconds before muttering a quiet, "fuck it" and grabbing my face in his hands. I dropped the heels that I hadn't even realized I was still holding, grabbing a hold of his arms just as he connected his lips with mine.

Almost immediately, I melted into the kiss. The kiss that I'd been waiting 10 years for, I was finally getting it and let me just say, it was not disappointing. Sawyer kicked the door shut with his foot and spun us around, pressing my back into the door. One of his legs came between mine, his thigh pressing into me with the slightest amount of pressure. I gasped, giving him the opportunity to sneak his tongue in to invade my mouth. My hands found their way to the back of his neck, his hands still cupping my face. Both of us doing what we could to keep the other in place while our mouths worked together like we'd done this a hundred times.

Sawyer's thigh pressed into me again, an unintentional moan slipping past my parted lips. As soon as the sound came out, he pulled away from me. Neither one of us said anything, we just looked at each other for a minute. Sawyer finally stepped away from me, leaving me feeling cold and slightly unsure of what he was going to say next.

"We should go to bed.." He said, although this time I could hear it in his voice that he didn't want to.

"Was it that bad?" I blurted out.

Sawyer quickly moved closer to me, cupping my face in his hands again as a light chuckle slipped past his lips. "Jesus, no. Avery, it was the exact opposite of bad. But we've both been drinking and I don't want you to wake up in the morning regretting something."

I looked up at him, my mind not processing his words properly. I just nodded, trying to make sense of everything that had just happened. "Right, yeah. We should go to bed." I agreed.

Sawyer pulled me closer to him, kissing me again but this time it was a lot gentler. He snuck his hands around my back, quickly untying the knot that he'd tied earlier and unzipping the dress. When he pulled away from me, my hands immediately found the back of the now unzipped dress, holding it together.

"Goodnight, Ave." He almost whispered.

I moved out of his way as he opened the door. "Goodnight, Sawyer." I whispered when he looked back at me from the open doorway. He nodded and walked out of the room, closing the door behind him.

I didn't even change out of the dress, I just laid down on the bed, staring up at the ceiling.

Oh my god. I just kissed Sawyer Evans.

Sawyer Evans told me I was a good kisser.

I touched my lips, a smile forming on them the second I did.

I kissed Sawyer.

Chapter 8

A knock at my door, followed by my brother's voice forced me to sit up in bed. I felt like I'd been hit by a truck, literally every part of my body hurt.

"Come in," I groaned in hopes that he'd hear me. Callum walked into the room seconds later, looking just as bad as I felt. "What on earth do you want?" I didn't even know what time it was, but I wanted to be left alone.

Callum took in my appearance and nodded. "Me too, sis. Me too." He leaned against the door frame, not walking fully into the room. "Dani and I, unfortunately, need to run out for a couple of hours. I was going to ask if you wanted to come into town, but I'm going to assume the answer is no. So instead I'll say there's a pot of coffee, I just made it."

As much as I appreciated him asking me if I wanted to go with him, he was right in assuming I absolutely did not want to go anywhere. "Thanks, but I'm not leaving this house today." I brought my hands to my head, letting out a soft groan. "I will take some coffee though, I'll grab some in a couple minutes."

Callum nodded. "Cool, text me if you need anything while we're out."

"Will do." I said before he walked out of the room. I stretched my legs out as I tossed the covers off my them and stood up. I was currently wearing a pair of sweatpants and a tank top, I thought about changing out of it but quickly decided against it. I grabbed my purse that was sitting on a desk in the bedroom and pulled out my glasses, pushing them onto my face. I didn't wear them often, but my eyes were feeling extra blurry this morning. I grabbed my phone off the charger, shoving it into my pocket before I made my way to the bathroom.

I did a quick check to see if Sawyer was in the bathroom and when I realized he wasn't, I slipped in so I could use it and brush my teeth. Once I was finished, I ran a brush through my hair and pulled it into a quick side braid. "Good enough." I mumbled as I walked out of the bathroom.

I heard the front door close right as I was making my way downstairs, letting me know that Callum and Dani had gone. I made my way into the kitchen, inhaling the scent of the freshly brewed coffee that my brother promised. I saw an empty mug next to the coffee pot, it made me smile because I couldn't remember which cabinet held the mugs. I opened the fridge and pulled out the coffee creamer, pouring some into my cup as well as the coffee. Once I was finished, I shuffled over to the back door so I could sit outside.

Immediately after opening the door, I was hit with a bit of a breeze. It wasn't cold by any means, but the breeze sent chills up my exposed arms. I sat down at one of the chairs, bringing my feet up into the chair as well and holding my coffee close to me.

The fresh air was what I needed. Breathing it in immediately made me feel less sick than I did curled up in bed. I closed my eyes and rested my head against the chair, my mind thinking back to the previous night's events.

Taking shot after shot with the boys.

Sawyer telling me to dance with him.

The car ride home, Sawyer's hand on my thigh.

Sawyer kissing me.

I sucked in a breath, remembering the feel of his lips against mine. The way he mumbled fuck it right before he grabbed me. The way he told me that it was a good kiss but he didn't want me to have regrets in the morning.

I didn't have regrets, Sawyer. I want to do it again.

I remembered the way his leg pressed against me, the way that one simple action sent a million tiny volts of electricity right through me. I wanted to feel it again from him, but I wanted more than that.

I could feel my body getting hot and I knew I needed to think about something else. I set my coffee down on the table and pulled my phone out of my pocket. My eyes widened when I saw the time, it was already almost 1pm. I also saw that I had a bunch of missed texts from Larissa. I opened the text thread to read the messages, only I found a couple from myself last night that I didn't remember sending to me.

Me- We da mced Me- I live uuuuuuuuuu – Larissa- Morning Sunshine, have a good night? Larissa- Okaaaay wake up pls. Larissa- I need to know what drunk Avery did!

I quickly typed her a message back, letting her know that I was alive. She texted me back almost immediately.

Larissa- What. Happened.

I didn't even know where to start.

Me- We went out. We drank. We danced. We kissed.

I watched the three dots appear and disappear for a couple minutes and I couldn't help but wonder what she was thinking or doing.

Larissa- You kissed!?

Was all she responded back with.

Me- Sure did. Me- And then we stopped because he didn't want me to regret anything. Larissa- You HAVE to call me later. I'm on my way to a shoot right now, but I need all the details later today!!

I laughed as I set my phone down after telling her to have a good shoot. The sliding glass door opened, causing me to look back and see Sawyer walking outside with a cup of coffee in his hand. He had on a pair of sweatpants, much like the morning after I got here, he wasn't wearing a shirt. His hair was messed up and I wondered if he also felt like he'd been hit by a train. I wondered if he was going to mention anything about last night or if he was going to sweep it under the rug like it didn't happen.

"What's so funny?" He asked as he walked up to the table. He took a seat and leaned back in the chair, bringing the coffee mug to his lips.

I watched him as he took a sip of his coffee, his eyes meeting mine over the mug. The chill I had felt when I first walked outside had amplified, but I knew it wasn't due to the weather outside. "I was just talking to Larissa." I leaned forward and picked up my coffee cup, copying his actions and taking a sip.

"So why California?" He asked as he brought the mug back down. He crossed one of his ankles over the opposite knee and after turning a bit so he was facing me more.

I shifted at his question, wondering if I wanted to be honest with him about the answer. There were definitely many reasons why I moved away from home, but the specific picking of California, I wasn't sure if I actually wanted to tell him that. "Do you want the basic answer that I give everyone or do you want the real answer?" I asked.

His eyebrows furrowed in confusion, obviously not knowing what I meant by that. "Both?" He chuckled.

I nodded. "The basic answer is that I'd never been to California before, it was literally on the opposite side of the country from home, and it sounded fun." I took another sip of my coffee, waiting for him to say something.

"Fair enough. What's the real answer?" He asked.

I leaned my head back against the chair again, closing my eyes so that I didn't have to look at him when I admitted the reason I'd chosen to move to California. "You."

I heard him shift in his chair, but I didn't open my eyes to see his expression. I didn't give him much to work with other than saying that one simple word, so I'm sure he was trying to figure out the meaning behind it.

"Me?" He asked, just like I knew he would. He wanted more of an explanation.

"Yes, you." I started. "When I was 17, you came home from college and we were talking while we waited on Callum to come home with food. We were talking about school, prom, college. You asked me what I wanted to do and I told you I wanted to be a writer, but that I was scared." I sighed.

"I told you to go to New York or California." He finished for me. I opened my eyes and looked over at him. I couldn't read the expression on his face, but I nodded to let him know that he did in fact say that and that the reasoning behind me moving across the country was him.

"Yep, you did. I told you that everyone was here, this was home. I asked you if you could see me living in a place like California and you told me I was full of surprises. I had no idea what you meant by that, but after my dad died... you and Callum were both doing different things. You'd both graduated college and you were both busy. I didn't feel like I had anything keeping me here, so I moved. I looked up places in both New York and California, but California was further away from the pain I was feeling and I think I just, for once, wanted to surprise everyone by doing something I know no one expected." I admitted, for the first time. Not even Larissa knew the entire reasoning behind my moving.

Sawyer looked at me for a minute, just taking everything I'd just said to him in. "It definitely surprised us all." He looked like he wanted to say more than that, but after a couple of minutes of nothing else, I finally spoke up again.

"Yeah but then things didn't go quite according to plan. Becoming a writer is not as easy as you'd think. I had more than one thought about coming back home, but I didn't think I could. I couldn't come home knowing things didn't work out." It was part of the reason I hadn't come home in a couple of years, I didn't want to explain to anyone that things weren't as glorious as they seemed. "For fucks sake, I come back home and I feel like I don't know anyone anymore. I come home and one comment gets mentioned about me not writing and doing makeup instead and you of all people act like that's a crime." I sat up, turning so I could face him completely so he'd know that I didn't appreciate the way we'd talked about my job before.

Sawyer sighed. "I wasn't trying to make you feel bad, I was just... surprised I guess. It didn't seem like something you'd want to do and I don't know, just didn't know what to say I guess. I'm sorry, Ave. Really."

I couldn't help but laugh. "Makeup isn't something you could see me doing, but you believed I could be an author?"

He put his foot back on the ground and leaned forward a bit, leaning on his elbows on his knees. "I don't know how to say this without sounding like a dick." He chuckled.

I copied his actions again, putting my feet on the ground and leaning on my knees. "What? That you were used to seeing me with my nose shoved in a book and not used to seeing me do any sort of makeup?" I answered for him.

"Well yeah... that's pretty much it exactly." He started. He leaned forward and grabbed one of the legs of the chair I was sitting on, pulling it towards him. My legs rested in between his legs, my heart immediately beating faster at the sudden change in proximity.

"So is it a bad thing that I do that instead of writing?" I asked quietly.

Sawyer shook his head, one of his knees lightly knocking into mine. "I didn't say it was a bad thing, I just said I was surprised. You did yours and Dani's makeup last night, right?" He asked.

I nodded. "I did, yes."

"You're really good at it then. I don't really know much about it, I mean I don't know much about writing either and I'm sure you are good at that. But if you do what you did last night on people all the time, the people that get to look at them are very lucky." His tone changed again.

"Thank you, Sawyer." I wasn't sure how to respond, so I just thanked him.

"Speaking of last night.." He started.

And the whiplash is about to come again. He's about to tell me that we both had too much to drink and that we should forget it ever happened.

"Is this the part where you tell me how much you regret kissing me?" I asked, wanting to just get the conversation over with. I started to back my chair away from him, but he put his hand on my leg, immediately stopping me from going anywhere.

"I don't regret it." He said, this time surprising me.

"You don't?" My voice was quiet, barely above a whisper.

Sawyer shook his head. "I don't. But I don't know if we should do it again."

Oh no, there is it.

I looked down at the hand that was on my leg, wanting to push him off of me. "Oh." Was all I was able to say in response.

"I just, things are weird. I've got a lot going on and I don't want to drag you into any of it. Plus, you're going to move back to California in a couple of months and I don't want to start something that's just going to end in two months. And... There's always Callum. You're his--"

"Please don't fucking say that I am his little sister." I cut him off, not wanting to hear him say it.

"Ave, it's true... how's he going to feel knowing his best friend kissed his little sister?" He said with a sigh.

Nope... nope there it is.

"Have you ever considered the fact that I am more than Callum's little sister? That I am in fact my own person and can make my own choices?" I was focused on any of the other excuses, I was only focused on the biggest one that involved my brother. I was so sick of people using that as an excuse, I was so sick of being tied to my brother in everything I do.

I pushed his hand off my leg and backed up so I could stand up. I grabbed my coffee and turned to walk inside the house, not wanting to be a part of the conversation anymore.

"Ave, stop." He said as I reached the door.

I ignored him, walking inside the house and aggressively sliding the door shut behind me. I walked to the sink to put my mug in it, not even caring that I didn't finish the coffee. My head was still pounding and the conversation just made it pound a little harder.

I heard the back door slide open and shut as I was turning off the water in the sink. I felt like I wanted to cry and the last thing I wanted to do was cry in front of him over something like this.

I spun around so that I could walk upstairs, but Sawyer was standing directly in front of me now. I gasped, my back hitting the counter behind me when I jumped, not expecting him to be so close to me. "Sawyer, what the hell are you doing?"

Sawyer placed his hands on either side of the counter behind me, trapping me against the counter and his bare chest. "Don't walk away from me."

I lifted my gaze to meet his eyes, forcing myself not to look at his chest. "I don't need anymore of this conversation, Sawyer. I've spent my entire life being Callum's little sister, not being old enough to do things or not being cool enough to do things. You've always been the one person who didn't say shit like that to me! You've always been the person who included me in everything and then you finally kiss me and then tell me you don't regret it, but that you can't kiss me again because I'm Callum's little sister." I sucked in a breath once I was finished.

Sawyer looked at me for a minute, taking in everything that I'd said to him. I could see thoughts crossing his mind, I could see him contemplating on his next move. I could sense it was another fuck it moment, he just didn't say it out loud this time. His hands moved from the counter and face again, cupping my cheeks in his hand like he did last night. He pulled me into him and pressed his lips to mine, taking my breath away for a second time.

Whip. Lash.

I hesitated just slightly before my hands found their way around his neck, pulling him closer to me. Our lips worked together in sync, our tongues exploring one another. Sawyer shifted our bodies until my back was against the island instead of the sync. He moved his hands down to my hips, lifting me up and placing me on the island. My legs instinctually wrapped around his waist, pulling him closer to me.

I could feel him press against me, causing me to gasp. Sawyer finally pulled away from my lips, only to kiss down my jaw and to my neck. I tilted my head back, a small whimper slipping out. God everything about this felt so good that it was almost overwhelming.

Sawyer's squeezed my thigh with one of his hands, his other hand moving up my side and closer to my boob. He gently bit a small on my neck that made me gasp. "Sawyer.." I whimpered.

"Fuck, Ave." He groaned into my neck, his voice sending chills down my spine.

I want to hear that voice again.

I was about to pull him closer when the front door opened. I gasped, shoving Sawyer away from me and hopping off of the counter. I heard footsteps making their way into the kitchen as Sawyer was opening the fridge and I was trying to regulate my breathing.

"Sawyer, can you toss me a water bottle." I heard Callum's voice enter the kitchen. I turned to face him, hoping that he didn't catch onto anything that had just taken place.

"Didn't you like, just leave." I said, leaning against the island and facing him.

"Yeah... we rescheduled a couple things, I feel like ass." He laughed. I heard Sawyer close the fridge. He leaned against the island next to me, passing a water bottle over to Callum. "Thanks man."

"Guess we're ordering in for dinner later?" Sawyer asked, not giving any indication that the two of us were just making out or that he was hiding a hard on from my brother.

Callum fake gagged. "The thought of food sounds terrible... but yeah, we can order in. I'm going to go take a nap." He grabbed the water bottle and turned to walk out of the kitchen. Sawyer and I waited until the basement door shut before he turned to face me.

Sawyer scratched the back of his neck before speaking up, "I'm uhh, gonna go take a shower. If you want to pick dinner tonight, we can either order or we can go pick it up later."

I nodded, not missing that fact that he said we could go pick it up later. "Yeah sure, I'll think about it."

Sawyer nodded and walked upstairs to go take a shower. I walked into the living room, sitting down on the couch. I grabbed a blanket and pulled it over my body, leaning my head back. I turned the tv on, but I wasn't focused on it at all. All I could think about was how good Sawyer's lips felt against mine and how I wanted nothing more than to feel him pressed against me again.

I don't think I could take much more of this back and forth.

Chapter 9

5 years earlier

What a disaster of a night.

My arms were folded as I looked out the window of Jake Kellers Audi. I didn't even want to go to the dance. It's not that I thought that Sawyer would come to the prom with me, but the way that I felt when he told me he wasn't going to be able to come home was surprising. I was disappointed and I absolutely hated that I felt that way. There was no reason for me to feel disappointed, it's not like we were dating. I was pretty sure I heard from Callum that he'd been seeing someone anyway, so he had literally zero obligations to me. Jake asked me to go with him a couple weeks ago and instead of being an ass and saying no, I decided that I'd suck it up and go with him.

I should have been an ass and said no.

I spent the entire morning trying to get myself ready, doing my own hair and makeup. I was pretty impressed with myself by the time I was finished. I wasn't one for doing makeup, but everything turned out really nice. My dad had taken me shopping to pick out a dress. I picked out a beautiful purple dress that had a deep v cut and a little poof at the bottom, with a slit up one of my legs. I'd never felt so beautiful in my entire life when I'd finished getting ready.

Jake was late picking me up, which should have been the first red flag of the evening. I decided that it was fine and I'd cut him some slack, thinking he got busy with getting ready or something. The second red flag should have been dinner, he practically ignored me the entire time. I had no idea why he'd even asked me to come with him. I spent the entire dinner wondering if he'd done it out of pity or if he'd done it as a joke. He talked to his friends the entire time, I only engaged in conversation a couple of times the entire dinner.

The third red flag was at the actual dance. He'd brought a flask with him and practically made me take a drink out of it before forcing me onto the dance floor with him. I tried to tell him that I didn't feel like dancing, but he told me to loosen up and have fun. He held my hips and was practically moving them against the front of him for me the entire time. Each time a slow song would come on, he'd tell me that he had to go to the bathroom or that he wanted to take a break. By the end of the dance, we'd finished the flask. I was more than sure I'd drank more than he did and for someone who didn't drink, I was feeling the effects of it.

The fourth and final red flag was in the car after the dance. He'd mentioned wanting to go to an after party, but I didn't want to go. He told me it would be fun, I told him I wanted to go home. He asked me if he could at least kiss me before he took me home. He told me it was all he'd been thinking about all night. I agreed, figuring it was one kiss and it was Jake Keller, I'd heard he was a good kisser. When he leaned over the middle of the car to kiss me, it started off gentle but quickly turned into more than what I wanted. His hand was on my boob, squeezing it before I could push him away.

"Jake, stop." I mumbled against his lips that refused to part with mine. I shoved him a bit, trying to push him back into the drivers seat of his car. He moved my hands out of the way with his free hand, giving my boob another squeeze before it shoved it's way under my dress.

"Jake, I said stop!" I cried when he moved his lips away from mine, pressing them against my neck instead. "I said no!" I was starting to panic, my chest rising and falling at a rapid pace. He let his hand slip, releasing my two hands from his grip. I used all the strength I had to push his chest so he'd fall back into the other side of the car. "I said no." I whispered, tears pricking my eyes.

Jake looked at me and I hated the look on his face. "Guess it's still true, it's still impossible to get with Little Avery Jones." He muttered.

I folded my arms over my chest, wanting to cover myself up. "What the hell are you talking about?" I practically spit at him.

Jake laughed as he started the car. "You're fucking impossible. Your stupid brother kept everyone from getting with you when he was still in school. Thought after he'd graduated you'd be a little easier to get with." He said as he backed the car out of the parking spot.

"Take me home, now." Was all I said back to him before I turned to look out the window.

We didn't speak to each other the rest of the car ride. As soon as he'd pulled up to my house, I got out of the car and slammed the door behind me. I didn't care if he wanted to yell at me about it, I wanted to get away from him as quickly as possible. What I hadn't noticed when I was walking to the front door of the house, were the two cars parked on the street that didn't belong to my dad or I. By the time I'd pulled my keys out of my purse and unlocked the front door, Jake was long gone. When I walked into the house, I was met with four people, none of whom I was expecting to see. My eyes widened at the sight of my brother, Sawyer, and two girls that I didn't recognize.

"Surprise!" Callum said the second he saw me. He pushed himself off the couch and practically ran over to me. I didn't even have time to shut the front door when he wrapped his arms around me and pulled me into a hug. I wasn't expecting anyone to be home, my dad had left after I did for a work conference and the fact that they were here was almost overwhelming.

The fact that Sawyer was here made me angry.

He said he couldn't come home.

He was home.

I probably wouldn't have cried if I hadn't been crying in Jake's car, but the overwhelming feeling took over and I immediately started to cry into my brothers chest. I wasn't even hugging him back, I was just standing there crying.

"Ave, what happened? What's wrong?" Callum pulled back slightly, his hands rested on my shoulders as he looked down at me.

I didn't want to tell him what happened, I didn't want him to freak out and go attack Jake or something. "I just... wasn't expecting you to be home." I lied.

Callum pulled me into another tight hug. "You don't have to cry about it, oh my gosh sis." He pulled back again and looked down at me. I forced a laugh so he'd believe what I'd said. "Have you been drinking?" He asked, narrowing his eyes at me.

I just looked at him, not saying anything in response.

"I can smell it on your breath. Jesus, is that why you're crying? Are you a drunk cryer?" He chuckled. He wrapped his arm around my shoulder and pulled me into the living room, kicking the front door shut as we walked away from it.

"Dani, this is my little sister. Ave, this is Dani, my girlfriend." He pointed to one of the girls on the couch who immediately smiled at me, one that was mixed with pity and genuine happiness.

"It's nice to meet you." I said quietly to Dani.

"Callum has told me a lot about you, it's nice to meet you. Your dress is gorgeous by the way!" Her voice was nice, she was nice. She was also absolutely stunning.

He motioned over to Sawyer, obviously not needing to introduce him. "And that's Britt. Sawyer's girlfriend."

My breath caught in my throat at the mention of Sawyer having a girlfriend. So it was true, that's why he couldn't come with me tonight. The way that she was looking at me wasn't as kind as Dani, she was looking at me like she was annoyed that I'd interrupted whatever they'd been doing.

"Nice dress," was all she said to me.

"Thanks.." I said quietly. I looked at Sawyer, waiting on him to say hi or hug me like he always would when we hadn't seen each other in a while, but he just nodded and turned back to the tv. My heart sank even further down into my stomach.

"So how was it? Did you have fun? Who'd you go with?" Callum sat back down on the couch next to Dani. I stood by a chair, not wanting to sit because I didn't want to stay in here for long. I wanted to rip this stupid dress off and burn it. I hated that I was still feeling Jake's hands on me.

"Uh, it was okay. I went with Jake Keller and--" I started, but was interrupted by Sawyer.

"You went with Jake Keller?" He asked, turning to look in my direction.

"How'd you end up going to prom with that dickhead?" Callum asked me.

I shrugged, twisting a couple rings that I had on my fingers. "He asked me a couple weeks ago. I thought I was going with someone else, but I got bailed on and I don't know, thought it would be fun. Turns out, I was definitely wrong." I glanced over at Sawyer when I mentioned getting bailed on, his shoulders tensed just slightly before he turned his attention away from me. His girlfriend shot me a look and it made me wonder if they'd talked about it.

"Shouldn't you be at an after party or something?" She asked, her voice filled with annoyance.

This time, my shoulders tensed. It was obvious she didn't want me hanging out with them and even though this was my house, I figured it was best to give her what she wanted. "I'll just uh, leave you guys alone. I'm going to change and lay down." I quickly turned away before anyone could argue and ran upstairs. I walked into my bedroom and practically slammed the door shut. I threw myself on my bed and covered my face with my hands, fresh tears spilling out before I could stop them.

I hated everything about what the night had become. I sat on my bed for what felt like ages, crying until I didn't have anymore tears left. I eventually forced myself off of my bed so I could change. I reached around to the back of the dress, reaching for the zipper. I stretched my arms as far as I could, but I couldn't reach the zipper. "For fucks sake, could this night get any worse." I mumbled to myself. I did not want to go back downstairs and ask for help. I contemplated on what I was going to do for a couple minutes, before a knock at the door caused me to stop.

I walked over to the door, ready to tell Callum to help me with my dress and leave me alone. But when I opened the door, it wasn't Callum standing on the other side, it was Sawyer. "What do you want?" I didn't want to talk to him, he was actually one of the last people that I wanted to talk to.

"Have you been crying?" His facial expression immediately changed to concern.

I folded my arms and shrugged, even though it was more than obvious that I had been. I hadn't taken my makeup off yet so I was sure my face was a mess. "It's just been a long night."

Sawyer shifted on his feet. He glanced at the staircase before looking back at me. "Can I come in?" He asked hesitantly.

I wasn't sure I wanted to invite him in, but I was curious to hear what he had to say so I stepped out of the way. He walked into my room and I shut the door behind him. "I'll only hear what you have to say if you unzip my dress for me." I said and turned around so my back was facing him.

Sawyer moved closer to me with little to no hesitation. I felt his fingers grasp the zipper, causing me to tense. He unzipped it and stepped away from me. I immediately grabbed the back of the dress, holding it together before I walked over to my closet. "Turn around or something, I'll tell you when I'm done." I wasn't facing him, but I also didn't want him facing me.

"I'm looking at the wall." He said. I peaked around my shoulder to check, not that I didn't believe him but I wanted to be safe. I quickly slipped out of the dress and pulled a sweatshirt that had

Callum's college name on it over my head before slipping into a pair of comfortable shorts. I walked over to my bed and sat down before grabbing his attention again. Sawyer turned around when I said his name and slowly walked over to my bed, hesitantly taking a seat. "Are you crying because of me?"

I almost laughed, surprised that he even cared. "Why would I cry over you? You didn't do anything wrong." I said honestly. I was upset with him, but he technically hadn't done anything wrong.

"I told you I'd take you to prom, then I told you that I couldn't come home, and then I came home with a girl." He said, summing up exactly why I was upset with him.

I shrugged. "You didn't have any obligations to take me other than the conversation we had over the summer, but it wasn't that serious. You didn't have to lie to me though, you could have just told me you got a girlfriend and couldn't come with me. I'm upset that you told me you couldn't come home and then you still came home." I admitted to him.

Sawyer sighed and ran a hand through his hair. I wasn't sure why he was getting worked up, but it made me feel bad. "But I still said I would take you. Britt just kind of showed up and I made the mistake of mentioning it to her and she freaked out. I didn't know how to tell you, so I just said I couldn't make it. Then Callum wanted to be a good brother and surprise you. I told Britt I was coming home and she insisted on coming with me." He admitted.

"Your girlfriend doesn't like me." I said with a small grin.

"I wouldn't go as far as calling her my girlfriend and she just... I don't know, I don't even really have an excuse for her." He chuckled. "But seriously, are you okay? You never cry like that when Callum comes home, did something happen tonight?" He asked, his mode quickly changing back to a serious one.

I let out a small groan. "Jake was just... being an ass all night. Seriously, it's fine. I'll get over it." I shrugged.

Sawyer narrowed his eyes at me. "Did he do anything to you?" Now he was definitely serious.

I hesitated on answering because I didn't know how. He didn't really do anything but he also didn't not do anything. "I mean, like.. he didn't--" I started.

"What the fuck did he do to you?" Sawyer interrupted, catching onto the fact that I was trying to slide it under the rug. "Don't lie to me."

I turned away from him so that I didn't have to look at him. "He just... he tried to touch me! Okay? I told him I didn't want to go to the after party with him and he asked me if he could at least kiss me before he took me home. So I said that he could and then he basically got on top of me and was kissing me and trying to like, you know... touch me.."

Sawyer practically jumped off my bed. I lifted my gaze to look at him again, his face full of rage. "Callum and I will go kick his ass right now. Where's the party he's at?"

I shot up, grabbing his arms. "Please don't. Don't tell Callum, please. I was able to push him off of me before he could really do anything. I'll get over it, seriously just don't tell Callum. You aren't here to kick someone's ass for me, you're both trying to spend time with your girlfriends. Please let it go and in the morning, if I changed my mind then you can both go after him. But tonight, please. I don't want to deal with anything else tonight..." I begged him. I knew the second he told my brother, there would be no stopping it and I just didn't want that to happen tonight.

"Are you sure?" He asked me. Quite the loaded question too. Am I sure I don't want him to tell my brother that my prom date wanted to force himself on me? Am I sure I didn't want the two of them to go beat him up. Am I sure that I'll get over it? I wasn't sure of anything right now.

"Yes, I'm sure." I let go of his arms and took a step back. "I just want to go to bed.."

Sawyer looked at me, trying to make sure I was serious. He sighed and nodded. "Please text me if you need anything, okay? We'll be downstairs. And I'm asking you first thing in the morning if you're still sure and if you even so much as hesitate, I'm kicking his ass." He pulled me into a tight hug before letting me go and walking to the door. "Get some sleep, Ave."

"Thanks, Sawyer." I said before he walked out the door. I laid down on my bed after he closed the door and closed my eyes. I wanted nothing more than to forget this night happened. Maybe forget everything but the way Sawyer's hug felt. I'd hugged him plenty of times before, but this one felt more protective and I didn't want to forget that feeling.

Chapter 10

"**A**re you sure you don't want to stay any longer?" Dani asked her sister as she was grabbing her bag and standing up to head out for the night.

"I need to get Joseph from Dan, you know I'd stay if I could." Dani's sister, Rebecca, said with a sad smile. She gave her sister a hug and waved goodbye to me. "It was nice meeting you, Avery!" She hugged Dani again before walking out of the bar that we were currently at.

I looked at Dani, unable to hold back my laughter. "Your sister was married to a guy named Dan?"

Dani started laughing immediately. "You know, I said the same thing when she brought him home for the first time! He turned out to be a real dick though, I'm glad they aren't together anymore." She smiled.

"Are you mad she had to leave?" I asked. I felt bad that this was basically Dani's bachelorette party and her own sister was leaving early.

"Some Maid of Honor she is, right?" She joked. "No but I don't mind. I get it, but at least I still have you for the rest of the night!" She grinned.

I lifted my plastic cup up and tapped hers, the only difference was that mine had alcohol and hers didn't. "Cheers to that!"

I looked at Dani for a minute, smiling because I really did like her a lot. She was so good for my brother and I was so happy that they'd ended up together. "Dani, I'm really excited that I officially get to call you my sister in law soon. I knew I liked you from the very moment I met you."

Dani reached across the table, giving my hand a squeeze before saying, "I'm really happy to hear you say that because I'm really excited to call you my sister too. God, do you remember the first time we met?"

I nodded, remembering it like it was yesterday. There were parts of the night that I'd tried to block out, but as hard as I tried it never worked. I remember walking into my house, fully prepared to sit alone and cry for the rest of the night. But my brother wanted to surprise me and with him was Dani.

"I was coming home from prom, my idiot of a date dropped me off and you guys were in the living room." I smiled lightly.

"Were you as drunk as I remember crying over Callum surprising you??" She asked with a light laugh.

I sat back in the booth, taking a sip of my drink. "I had been drinking and I did cry, but it wasn't because of Callum. My date was a dick and.. it wasn't who I was supposed to go to prom with." I admitted.

Dani gave me a confused look, not quite understanding what I meant. "What do you mean?" She asked.

"I'd rather not go into details about my actual date. But Sawyer and I had talked about going together." I shrugged it off like it wasn't a big deal, even though back then it was the biggest deal in the world.

"What!" She gasped. "But he'd already graduated? What do you mean?" She leaned forward so she could hear me better, but also because she was clearly interested in the details.

I laughed as I set my cup back down. "The summer before senior year, Sawyer had just come home from school. We ended up talking about prom and I said I didn't want to go. He made a huge deal out of it and told me that he would come home to take me if it meant I would go. Told me he'd find a way to ask and everything." I smiled thinking about the conversation. It was one of those conversations before things got weird between us.

"Okay and!? Why'd he not go with you? He brought a girl to your house that night, what the hell was that girl's name?" She said.

I couldn't help but laugh at her comment. "Britt." I said her name before I could explain what happened.

"That's it! She was so rude. I was so happy when he called that off." She shook her head. "Anyway, why didn't he go?"

"He told me he couldn't come home for it. So I was pretty angry when I walked into my house and saw him sitting there with Britt, who I immediately knew didn't like me." I thought back to the way Sawyer had looked at me, or avoided looking at me when I'd first got home. It was the first time he didn't hug me to greet me. The first of many more to come, I might add.

"What a dick!" She shook her head again.

"Well yeah, sort of. When I walked upstairs, I was so overwhelmed with everything that I just cried. Then I couldn't get my dress unzipped and I was about to go ask for help when he knocked on the door. I let him in so we could talk. He helped me with the dress and then told me that the reason he didn't come was because Britt didn't want him too, but he didn't know how to tell me that.. so he just lied. And then he felt bad annnnd yeah." I shrugged, not going into details about the second part of the conversation we had that night.

"Wait, he helped you out of the dress? Oh my god, it's like history is repeating itself!" She squealed.

"What the hell are you talking about?" I asked.

Dani looked at me like I was crazy. "The last time we went out! When he helped you zip up your dress! That's not the first time he's done that for you!!" She was saying it like it was a big deal. I didn't quite understand what she was getting at, so I just nodded.

"Avery, it's the little things like that that you need to pay attention too. Duh." She said it like it was obvious.

"Uhhh, yeah okay." I said and picked my cup up to finish it off.

"Wait a minute, that doesn't explain what happened the morning after? I saw you talking to Sawyer the next morning and then all the sudden, he and Callum were running out of the house like they were going to murder someone." She asked.

I set the empty cup down and laughed. "I told you, my date was a dick." I didn't need to say more than that. Sawyer had followed his promise the next day, asking me if I was okay and sure he didn't need me to do anything. I hesitated on my answer and without question, he grabbed Callum and the two of them left the house for a couple hours. Jake missed a couple days of school and when he came back, he had a black eye. It didn't take a genius to know what had happened.

"Why are we even talking about me? Shouldn't we be celebrating you and your love for my brother?" I asked her, hoping to get the subject off of me.

Dani waved her hand in front of me, brushing me off. "We talked about Callum and I the entire time my sister was here. Same old love stuff. Yours is way more exciting!" She laughed.

"Dani, you're getting married and you think my confusing... whateveritscalledship with Sawyer is more exciting?" I said with a laugh.

She nodded immediately. "Absolutely. You need another drink because I'm not done talking about your whateveritscalledship with Sawyer."

I shook my head but stood up so I could talk to the bar. "Need another?" I pointed to hers.

"Please!" She smiled.

I made my way to the bar, pushing my way to the front so that I could order two more drinks. I waited until the bartender walked up to me before asking for a sprite and a vodka cranberry and asked them to put it on my tab. I pulled out my phone while I waited for the drinks.

I went on Snapchat and started looking through stories. I clicked on Callum's, smiling at a picture of him and Sawyer out at the one of the only other bars in town. Sawyer also had a picture of the two of them. I swiped to the other screen, seeing I had a message. My eyes immediately rolled when I saw it was from my ex.

When the bartender came back, I put my phone in my pocket and grabbed the drinks, quickly thanking him and walking back to the table where Dani was sitting. "Sprite for you! Vodka cran for me." I smiled as I passed her the drink.

When I sat down, I passed her my phone. "Wanna open that?" I nodded to the open Snapchat app with a message from Jamie.

Dani gasped and grabbed my phone, "the footballer!?" She squealed. "Wait, I better not open a dick pic." She paused, looking over at me with narrowed eyes.

I started laughing and motioned to my phone. "I cannot guarantee that it isn't, but it's probably not. He's probably going to make a comment about the picture I posted of us. Just open it."

Dani hesitated but clicked on it. She gasped, which immediately made me reach over for my phone thinking that it really was a picture of my ex-boyfriend's dick. Dani started laughing as she turned my phone so I could see the screen. "Just kidding!"

I rolled my eyes and leaned forward so I could read the text. It was just a picture of him asking me where I was. "You can respond to him if you want, I don't care." Jamie and I had ended on not so great terms, especially after I threw all of his stuff at him. But we'd talked a couple times since and I'd pretty much gotten over everything.

Dani grinned, clicking out of the picture so she could respond. "Lean forward a little more, your boobs look great, let's make him mad." She said as she turned the camera on front mode.

"Dani!" I laughed. She told me to shut up and do it, so I leaned forward a little bit more. Dani was surprising me a lot the more I hung out with her, she reminded me of a slightly more toned down Larissa and I think that's why it was so easy for me to get along with her.

She snapped a quick picture of the two of us before asking, "what do I say?"

"Tell him I'm at a bar in Maine." I had no idea if he'd run into Larissa since I left, so I wasn't sure if he knew I was home.

Dani did what I said and sent the picture. It only took a couple of minutes for him to respond. When she opened the snap, this time she gasped for real. When she turned the phone to me, Jamie was now shirtless in the picture and I couldn't help but burst out into laughter. "That's because of the boobs." She laughed.

He'd asked why I was in Maine and asked who I was with. Dani took another picture of us, typing out that I was home for my brother's wedding and that she was the bride.

When he responded again, Dani handed me my phone back with a laugh. "I'll leave that to you, hottie." I looked down at my phone, looking at the picture of Jamie that said I looked hot.

"Jesus." I just responded with a quick thanks in the chat, checked the time and put my phone back in my purse. "Holy shit, it's almost 1am"

Dani pulled her phone out of her pocket and set it on the table. "I didn't even realize it was that late! Should probably watch that for when Callum calls."

Callum and Sawyer both wanted to drink so Dani told them that she would pick them up whenever they were ready to go home. I had no idea if she planned on staying out as late as they were going to, but I was really open for anything that she wanted to do so it didn't matter to me. The night had been a lot of fun and I'm glad that we had ended up just hanging out because my feet were killing me from the heels I was wearing. We'd gone to dinner and then walked around the town for a little bit, stopping in at a couple different places that Dani wanted to go to. We went down to the water for a little bit too, which was extremely nice. The water on this side of the country was different, but with everything else in this state, it would always be home and it would always hold a sense of peace for me. Callum had told Dani which bar he and Sawyer were at and she didn't want to ruin their guy time or our girl time, so she decided on one of the only other nicer bars in our town to spend the remainder of the night.

Dani and I spent another 20 or so minutes talking about the wedding and Sawyer before her phone rang. She picked it up and pressed it against her ear, covering her other one so that she could hear better.

"Be there in 5 minutes!" She said before she hung up the phone. "Oh my god, he's so drunk." She laughed.

"Let me go close the tab. Meet you outside?" I asked. I picked up my cup, downing the remainder of my drink before setting it back down. Dani and I stood up from the table and she headed outside while I walked to the bar again. I grabbed the bartender's attention and told him my name so that I could close out the tab. I got everything sorted and tucked my card into my purse before heading outside. I walked up to Dani when I saw her. "All good to go! Think he's going to make it on the walk to the car?" I asked because she said Callum was pretty drunk.

Dani laughed as the two of us started walking in the direction of the other bar that the guys were at. "Sawyer might have to carry him this time." She laughed. "Oh god, what if he's just as drunk!?"

I stuck my arm through Dani's so that I could hold her arm as we walked. "They can just drunkenly hold each other up." I giggled. I was definitely feeling all of the alcohol that I had throughout the night, but I was more than sure I could help her get the boys to the car if they couldn't get themselves to the car.

Dani held my arm as we walked. "Jeez, are you as drunk as them?" She giggled.

I shook my head and pointed to my feet. "No! My damn feet hurt from these stupid shoes. Terrible idea, I didn't think about all of the concrete we were going to be walking on all night."

Dani smirked. "Maybe you can ask Sawyer for a piggy back ride. You're wearing pants, so you have no excuse!" She squealed.

I gave her the tiniest of shoves, obviously taking myself with her when I did. "How about my excuse is that he's probably super drunk and I don't wanna crash into a tree tonight!"

"Yeah yeah, whatever I guess that's a valid excuse." She giggled. We arrived at the bar a couple minutes later, even though Dani had said we'd be there in 5 minutes, we were definitely not there in 5 minutes. The boys weren't even outside though, so it didn't matter. "Ugh, I should have peed before we left the other bar. Can you go find the boys and I'll meet you outside again?"

I took my arm back from her and nodded, "On it!" We walked inside the bar and Dani headed straight to the bathroom. I looked around for the two drunken idiots, spotting them pretty quickly by the bar. I walked over to them and smiled, but Callum shouted before I had the chance to say anything.

"Sister! Hello!" He threw an arm around me and pulled me into him, making me stumble into his side. "Where's my fiancee?"

I wrapped an arm around his side and laughed. "Hi brother. She's in the bathroom, told me to find you two and wait outside. Soooo let's go, I bet you could use some fresh air!"

Sawyer and Callum both finished their drinks and followed me outside so that we could wait for Dani like she had asked me too. "You know, I am so happy that you're home? I've missed hanging out with you so much and I'm just really glad that you're here." Callum said after we got outside.

I watched him for a minute, his body was swaying a bit and I could tell he was the drunkest one out of the three of us. "Have you always been like this when you get drunk?"

"Yes." Sawyer said before he could answer himself.

"Hey! I just have a lot of love to give around. That's my baby sister, I'm allowed to be happy that she's home." Callum defended.

I started laughing, finding this whole thing ridiculous. "I'm happy to be home and spending time with you."

"Aren't you happy she's home, Sawyer? It's just like old times, the three of us hanging out and doing stupid shit." He turned his attention to his best friend at the same time I did. I wondered what he'd say. Was he going to brush it off and say nothing? Would he admit that he was happy I was home? Considering how the last few weeks had gone, I really had no idea which direction he was going to pull me in tonight.

Sawyer's eyes locked with mine before he said, "Yeah. I'm happy that she's home too." He was talking to Callum, but his eyes never left mine. I saw his lips turn just slightly into a grin, if you weren't paying attention to it then you would have missed it. It was only for me.

I blushed immediately but before I could respond, Dani had walked outside. Callum immediately threw his arms around her, giving her the sloppiest of kisses and telling her how happy he was to see her. "Seriously, he's always been like this?" I asked Sawyer.

Sawyer chuckled and nodded. "I wish I was kidding, but yeah.. he's always been like this."

"Ready to go?!" Dani asked us all.

The four of us started walking back to her car. Callum still had his arms around Dani, holding onto her as they walked so the two of them were not walking very fast and it looked extremely awkward. I couldn't help but laugh at the sight. I pulled my phone out of my purse so I could snap a quick picture of them, posting it onto my snapchat story to go along with the others. I thought for a minute before looking up at Sawyer. "Take a picture with me."

"What?" He asked, glancing down at me.

"You heard me, take a picture with me to remember this wonderfully drunk night." I flipped back to my front camera and stopped walking. "I'm not going anywhere until you take one picture with me." I argued.

Sawyer started laughing, "Fine." He took a couple steps back until he was next to me again and lowered just slightly so he was closer to my height. "What do you want me to do?"

I held my arms out so that I could get us both in the picture. "I don't care, smile, stick your tongue out, flip the camera off. I really don't care." I leaned into him just slightly and smiled. Sawyer tilted his head towards me and smiled before I snapped the picture. I quickly saved it and posted it onto my story before we started walking again. Dani and Callum were a ways ahead of us now as they hadn't noticed we'd stopped walking.

We walked down the street, my heels clicking along the pavement. I felt Sawyer's hand slid into my back pocket which immediately made me look up at him. He continued to walk like it wasn't a big deal before he leaned down to me and said, "You look really good tonight."

I grinned and looked forward again so I wasn't looking at him when I said, "You do too."

We walked to the car, his hand in my back pocket the entire time. I wasn't really sure how that was comfortable for him to walk like that, but I liked the small gesture so I didn't question it and I let it happen. It felt like something out of a movie, which made it feel that much better. When we reached Dani's car, her and Callum got into the front seat and Sawyer and I climbed into the back.

"Let's get you drunkies home so you can sleep this off." She laughed before she started on the drive home.

Sawyer placed his hand on my thigh, much like he did the other day. When I glanced at him, he was looking out the window again. It was exactly the same as the first time we'd gone out. I looked out my own window and bit down on my lip, trying to hide the smile that was quickly starting to show.

Chapter 11

Sawyer

After all of the things that felt like they were going wrong in life or just going a little bit off the direct path, going out with my best friend was exactly what I needed. I felt like I didn't have direction right now and it was starting to drive me a little insane. My mother's health was questionable, I had absolutely no idea what to do with the thoughts I was having about Avery, and Callum was extremely busy getting last minute things done for the wedding. Of course, I'd never blame him for that, especially considering his wedding was only a couple days away, but it was nice to just be able to go out with just the two of us for a couple of hours.

Callum didn't care what we did for his makeshift bachelor party, he just wanted to get drunk. Seeing as I was his only groomsman, it was pretty easy to 'plan' the night for the two of us. We'd basically been at the bar the entire time and I was buying him drink after drink. Dani was probably going to be mad at me about it later, but it was his party and he could throw up later if he wanted to. I wasn't going to stop him.

"How weird is it that you're about to be married?" I asked him right as the bartender handed us both another drink. I'd honestly lost count of how many both of us had combined.

Callum took a sip of his drink before laughing at my comment. "Pretty wild, right? But damn, she's so great man. She's literally the nicest person I've ever met but she keeps me in my place. And she gets along with everyone we are around and she's so damn hot." He rambled on about Dani for a couple of minutes, going on about all of the things he loved about her.

I was happy for him. It was nice to see him find someone that made him that happy, Dani was good for him. She'd really calmed him down without changing who he was as a person. If I was being honest, I was a bit jealous of their relationship. Of course, there was no one to blame for my lack of relationships but myself. I'd never been a huge relationship person anyway, but in recent years it was pretty non-existent. I was just busy and didn't feel like I had time for one. Now with Avery showing back up, my thoughts were all sorts of confused.

"What's on your mind?" Callum asked.

I hadn't even realized I had zoned out a bit and I really must have if he'd actually noticed.

"Oh nothing, I'm good." I lied before taking a sip from my plastic cup.

Callum shoved my shoulder with a laugh. "Come on man, I know you better than that. What's up?"

It's not like I could tell him that the main thing going on in my head right now was that I made out with his sister and I wanted to do a lot more than that. He'd punch me right in the jaw. "Ehh, my minds all fucked up right now. I'll be fine." I said with a chuckle.

"Cut the shit, dude. What's going on? Are you good? Seriously?" I knew he wasn't going to take my bullshit; he never did. That's the one thing that Callum did that never changed, no matter what kind of stupid arguments we would get into, he was always without a doubt a good friend. He was almost too caring.

"Why do you have to be so fucking nice, dude?" I joked.

"It's just everything with my mom, stressing me out I guess. I'm all in my head about something and I'm just trying to navigate it without fucking everything up." I tried to be honest, without letting him in completely. I was never one for talking about my feelings anyway, so it's not like he wasn't used to these bland answers.

"Because you're my friend, that's why." He answered the first part of my question before continuing. "I know that everything with your mom has been hard and I do hope that everything is okay. But whatever else you've got going on up there, stop telling yourself that you're going to fuck something up. Get out of your own head and just let whatever is supposed to happen, happen."

Fuck me, he really was too fucking nice.

Especially on a night like tonight, that was supposed to be focused on him and the fact that he was getting married in a couple of days. But here we were, talking about me and my fucked up, confusing mess of a brain.

What is even supposed to happen? Am I supposed to be making out with Avery? Am I supposed to want her as bad as I do?

"Shit, dude it's after 1. I'm gonna call Dani. I should probably call it." He picked up his phone to call Dani and let her know we were ready to go.

I took in everything that he said. I did need to get out of my head, but that was so hard when I didn't know how to handle the situation.

Avery was always cute, she was never bad looking. When we were growing up, she was like a little sister to me though. We were always hanging out, she was always tagging along with us when she could. I never minded, Callum liked hanging out with her and she never bothered me. Even after I went to college, whenever I'd come home I started getting a little more excited to see her each time. I figured it was just because I'd been away and it was nice coming home to someone who felt like family. Something shifted after she graduated though. She was still the same Avery that she'd always been, but something in her shifted and it was like overnight she was different. I hated the fact that I was starting to look at her differently so I started to pull away from her. I'd forced myself to stop getting excited when I'd go home knowing I would see her. I'd force myself to look away from her when we'd go down to the beach over the summer. Then tragedy struck the Jones family and before I knew it, she was gone.

Three years had gone by without seeing her, which helped get over the thoughts I'd been having about her. I'd see pictures that she'd post on her snapchat or from Callum, but that was about it. From the pictures I'd seen, she had definitely matured since moving away but nothing could have prepared me for seeing her for the first time in three years in nothing but a fucking tee shirt.

"They're on their way!" Callum shoved his phone back in his pocket a couple minutes later and looked over at me again. "Thanks for everything tonight man. I feel like we haven't gotten the chance to go out with just the two of us in a while and it's been super nice."

I couldn't help but chuckle, he was definitely drunk. Callum was always one of those super sappy guys when he was really drunk. Sometimes it was annoying, but for the most part I thought it was funny. It just showed what kind of heart he had.

"I'm glad that you had a good time, man." I turned towards the bar so that I could grab the bartender's attention and close the tab that I'd started. It took a couple of minutes for him to get back to me, but I put my card in my wallet and signed the check when he did. Callum and I talked for a couple more minutes before his attention shifted from me to Avery when she'd walked up to us.

"Sister! Hello!" Callum tossed his arm around Avery's shoulders and pulled her directly into his side, causing her to stumble a little bit. "Where's my fiancee?" He'd asked her, making me realize that Dani hadn't walked in with Avery.

Avery wrapped one of her arms around Callum, it looked like a really awkward hug but it made her laugh. Her laugh was so pretty, it was like music to my ears. "Hi brother. She's in the bathroom, told me to find you two and wait outside. Soooo let's go, I bet you could use some fresh air!" She'd said before looking up at her brother. She looked so good tonight, her outfit was so simple but she pulled it off so well. She pulled everything off well.

Callum and I finished up our drinks at the same time before we followed Avery out of the bar. Callum was stumbling behind her and it was making me want to laugh. I hadn't realized how drunk he was until we'd started to walk away from the bar. I was definitely not sober, but Callum was clearly much drunker than I was. "You know, I am so happy that you're home? I've missed hanging out with you so much and I'm just really glad that you're here." There it was, the lovey dovey Callum.

"Have you always been like this when you get drunk?" Avery asked her brother with a laugh.

"Yes." I said, cutting him off before he could answer. I didn't want him to try and deny it because he most certainly always, always like this when he'd been drinking.

Callum immediately got defensive. "Hey! I just have a lot of love to give around. That's my baby sister, I'm allowed to be happy that she's home."

Avery started laughing, that pretty laugh once again as she told Callum that she was also happy to be home. I wasn't sure if she was really happy to be here with him or if she just didn't want to hurt his feelings. I chose to believe that she was being genuine and that she was happy to be back with all of us, even if I was making things complicated.

"Aren't you happy she's home, Sawyer? It's just like old times, the three of us hanging out and doing stupid shit." Callum and Avery both turned to look at me. I felt like I was immediately put on the spot and I wasn't sure how to answer the question at first.

I looked at Avery and the second I did I said, "Yeah. I'm happy that she's home too." I was responding to Callum's question, but my eyes remained locked on hers. It was true, I was happy that she was home because at this point, I never wanted to stop staring at her. Dani walked out seconds later and Callum's arms were immediately around her, smothering her in drunk kisses.

Avery leaned over to me and quietly asked, "Seriously, he's always been like this?"

I laughed at her question but nodded, "I wish I was kidding, but yeah... he's always been like this."

Dani had asked us if we were ready to leave, so the four of us started walking back to her car. I couldn't help but laugh at the way that Callum and Dani were walking. He was holding onto her for dear life and she was doing her best to keep him up and walking straight. They were cute, sweet even. It was kind of gross, but again I was happy that my best friend had someone in his life like Dani.

"Take a picture with me." Avery said to me with her phone already in her hand.

"What?" I asked, not having a clue why she wanted to take a picture with me.

"You heard me, take a picture with me to remember this wonderfully drunk night." She sounded serious. I wanted to laugh and tell her that I didn't want to take a picture but before I could she literally stopped walking and said, "I'm not going anywhere until you take one picture with me."

This time I did laugh.

Get out of your own head and just let whatever is supposed to happen, happen.

I don't really think that's quite what Callum meant, but it helped to go along with it so I said fine and took a couple steps back until I was standing next to her. She was a little shorter than me so I leaned closer to her so it was easier to take the picture. "What do you want me to do?" I asked. It almost felt awkward, like I'd never taken a picture with her before.

"I don't care, smile, stick your tongue out, flip the camera off. I really don't care." She said as she held out her arm to take the picture. She leaned into me, it wasn't a lot but I could feel it, before she smiled. I decided to do the same, tilting my head down towards her a bit and smiling towards her phone. She snapped the picture and the two of us started to walk again.

I listened to the heels of her shoes click against the pavement, trying to focus on the sound instead of the thousands of thoughts crossing my mind. I heard Callum's words in my head again before I slid my hand into the back pocket of Avery's jeans. We walked for a couple of seconds, she didn't say anything to me so I leaned closer to her and told her that she looked good.

I watched the grin spread across her face before she looked forward and told me that I looked good too. The rest of the walk was pretty quiet, I kept my hand in her pocket the entire time. I don't know why I did it, I don't know why I didn't put it on her lower back but as soon as I did, I couldn't take it back and it felt comfortable there. When we got into the car and Dani started driving back to my house, I immediately rested my hand on her thigh and looked out the window. I felt her tense for just a few seconds before her leg relaxed under my hand. I liked the way it felt, I liked the way she tensed and immediately relaxed seconds later. It let me know that she wasn't expecting me to do it but that she was okay with my hand being there.

My thumb just barely moved back and forth on her thigh the entire car ride home. I liked it better the last time, when my hand was touching her bare thigh. I liked the goosebumps that I'd created on her leg under my touch, but I was sure they were there under her jeans. I just hated that I couldn't feel them.

When we'd arrived back at my house, we filed into the front door. "You need help downstairs?" I asked Callum after I closed the door.

Callum moved away from Dani and wrapped his arms around me. "I'm good. Thanks again for tonight man, you're the best friend ever. And seriously, stay out of your head. Things are gonna be okay. Okay?"

I patted him on the back before Dani grabbed his shoulders and pulled him away from me. "Let's get you to bed, baby." She laughed. "Thanks for tonight, guys!"

"Let me know if you need anything." I said before the two of them walked downstairs. I turned so I was facing Avery and nodded towards the steps, much like I'd done the first night we'd gone out.

We walked upstairs together, when we got to the top Avery busted out laughing. "I just cannot believe that my brother acts like that when he's drunk. How have you put up with him all of these years?!"

I started to laugh with her. "You get used to it." I shrugged.

She was leaning against the door to my old bedroom, one of her feet was kicked against the door. Jesus Christ she looked so fucking hot and she wasn't even doing anything.

"Sawyer?" Her voice was quiet, almost like she was unsure of her next move.

"Hmm?"

"I want you to kiss me." Now her voice was barely above a whisper, but I heard it and it took me by surprise. I wasn't expecting her to tell me she wanted me to kiss her, but I immediately knew I wasn't going to not give her exactly what she wanted.

I immediately walked closer to her, as I did she opened the bedroom door and stepped back into it. I followed her without hesitation, closing the door behind me. One of my hands found its way to her cheek, I was realizing I really liked putting them there. The other found its way to her hip, pulling her into me before I crashed my lips onto hers.

God I loved the way she tasted. Her lips were absolutely perfect and I wanted to kiss them all the time. I loved that her body immediately reacted to mine, immediately melted into mine. It was like we'd been doing this for years. Without thinking, I walked forward forcing her to walk backwards until she fell backwards onto my old bed breaking the kiss momentarily. I immediately hovered over top of her, joining our lips once again.

If you would have asked me 8 years ago if I'd be making out with Avery Jones in my teenage bedroom, I would have laughed and said fuck no.

But here we are.

I bit down on her lower lip, almost instantly earning a small whimper from her. God I loved that sound, it went straight through my ears and down to my cock. I felt myself growing stiff and I pulled back, not wanting to take it too far with her.

"Ave," I groaned, lowering my head so I could peck her neck.

"I'm not that drunk." She whispered.

I lifted my head and looked down at her. "I'm not that drunk either, but we've still been drinking."

Avery shook her head. "I won't regret anything in the morning if you won't."

I let out another small groan, internally battling what the next move should be. We didn't even have to have sex, I just wanted to feel more of her. "Are you sure? Like, really sure. I really don't want you to regret anything tomorrow." I leaned down, pecking her neck again as I waited for her to answer.

I wasn't trying to do it to help her answer, I literally couldn't get enough of her.

She immediately tilted her head back, giving me more access to kiss her neck. "I won't regret it. I'll tell you if I want to stop, I promise."

"You're going to be the death of me, Jones." I groaned before smashing my lips into hers again.

My hands explored her body as we kissed, earning small whimpers and gasps every few seconds. I used one arm to prop myself up over her while the other slid down her side and to the jeans that she was wearing. My fingers started to play with the button, popping it open and slowly lowering the zipper.

"This okay?" I asked in between kissing her.

Avery quickly nodded, breathing out a yes. One of her legs was bent, her knee brushing against me as she lifted her lips ever so slightly almost as if to tell me to hurry up. I let out a breathy laugh as my hand slid into the front of her jeans. I wasted no time, my thumb meeting her core almost immediately, earning an immediate moan from her.

My lips met her neck again, nipping at it in between kisses. Two of my fingers sank into her with ease causing Avery to let out a moan a little louder than the rest of them. I immediately moved back to kiss her on the lips, muffling the sound of her.

"I know they're in the basement, but better safe than sorry." I mumbled before kissing her again. I quickened the pace, her body reacting to each pump of my fingers. One of her hands was gripping the comforter we were laying on while the other was gripping my arm, her long nails digging into my skin.

"Sawyer," she breathed out against my mouth. Her breathing had changed and I knew she was close. I kept up the pace, wanting her to ride it out. She let out a gasp, her back arched off the bed as she tensed up.

God she looked fucking stunning.

Once she relaxed, I slipped my hand out of her jeans and kissed her lips again. I rolled over so I wasn't laying on top of her anymore and was instead laying on my side. She turned her head and looked over at me, a lazy smile playing on her lips. I couldn't help but chuckle, if she acted like that with just my hand I couldn't imagine what she'd be like after more than that.

I'm pretty sure I could watch her do that every single day for the rest of my life and not get tired of it.

What a beautiful sight.

Chapter 12

I watched as Sawyer pulled the bag that held his suit out of the closet, laying it across the bed. My legs sat crossed, my elbows resting on my legs as I leaned forward to watch him.

"Is this fun for you to watch?" He asked with a laugh.

I nodded and shot him a smile. "Yes, very much so. I've always been very interested in how men get their shit together for important events." I giggled.

Sawyer laughed and sat down on the bed in front of me, his legs hanging off the side so his feet were still on the ground. "Shouldn't you be getting your shit together?" He asked pointedly.

I shook my head. "My shit has been together for days now. I am a girl, that's what I do." I laughed. "My dress is already downstairs and my bag is packed by the steps. The only thing I need to do today is put some shorts on."

Sawyer grinned as he wrapped his arms around me and pulled me into his lap. I quickly adjusted my legs so they were straddling him instead of crossed. "You don't have to put on pants." He held my hips, bunching the shirt I had on under his grasp. "Kind of like it when you aren't wearing any."

"Sawyer Evans. Did you just hit on me?" I joked.

He chuckled and leaned forward, pressing a light kiss to my lips. "Don't act like you don't like it."

I grinned against his lips before I pulled back. "I'll admit to no such thing. But maybe I'll admit it later if you tell me that you also like the dress that I'm wearing."

Sawyer grinned, kissing me again before saying, "I'm sure that you're going to look hot, but I can't wait to finally see the mystery dress that you keep going on about. Hiding it from me like it's a wedding dress and we're the ones getting married."

I groaned, shoving his shoulders. "God, Callum and I also joked about Dani and I acting like it's my wedding dress. Why are we all the same person?"

"Please do not say I am the same person as your brother, things will get weird fast." He laughed.

"Things are already weird, but I see your point. I take it back, I take it back." I was going to lean in and kiss him again when my phone started to ring. "Shit, hang on." I leaned over and grabbed my phone off the bed, Sawyer's hands never leaving my hips so that he could pull me back onto his lap after I grabbed it. I didn't even have a chance to say anything after answering because all I could hear was Dani freaking out and what sounded like crying but I couldn't understand her.

"Whoa, whoa! Dani! What's going on?!" I immediately started assuming the worst. Was she getting cold feet? Did Callum back out? Did someone get hurt? She was crying so hard, I literally couldn't understand anything that she was saying on the other side of the line.

"Dani, I can't understand you. I need you to take a breath and tell me what happened." I said calmly. Sawyer was watching me, both of us wearing concerned looks on her face. He silently asked me what was going on and I shrugged, mouthing to him that she was crying.

"I... she... canceled..." Was all she could get out.

I ran a hand through my hair as I tried to make sense of the little she had given me to work with. "Who canceled?" I was trying to think of all of the people that would have canceled on her. There were so many different people, I couldn't even begin to think of who she was talking about. I heard some scuffling over the other end of the line, it sounded like someone else was trying to calm her down. I sat there, waiting for someone to tell me what was going on when her sister started to talk.

"Hey Avery. Sorry, mom took Dani outside so she could try to get her to calm down but we're all kind of freaking out. The girl that was supposed to do Dani's makeup canceled on her. I told her I'd try to help her but I'm definitely not as skilled as what she wants. She wanted to call you, but she's really stressed out now.." I listened to Rebecca explain what was going on, my eyes immediately widening.

"Tell her Sawyer and I are on our way. We'll get there as fast as we can. If you can, get her to put some cold water on her face to try and help with the puffiness from crying." Rebecca and I spoke for maybe another minute before I hung up the phone and climbed off of Sawyer's lap. "We have to go. I need to grab a couple more things for Dani, can you grab my bag for me and take it downstairs?"

Sawyer was immediately off of the bed, understanding that something was wrong and we needed to leave. "Yep, let me just throw on some shoes. I'll meet you downstairs."

I practically ran out of his room and to the guest bedroom, grabbing another small makeup bag and throwing a couple more things in there for Dani. I grabbed the first pair of jean shorts that I saw and threw them on before booking it downstairs. Sawyer was already by the door with both of our outfits and my bag in his arms. I slipped into a pair of sandals and the two of us were out the front door, in the car, and on our way to the venue.

"So what happened?" Sawyer asked as he sped down the road, knowing that I wanted him to get to the venue as quickly as he could.

"I don't really know what happened, but Dani's makeup artist canceled on her. She's totally freaking out. Her sister asked her to help and I think that made it worse." I said, wanting to laugh but holding it back. "She said she wanted to call me but then couldn't even talk so then I told Rebecca we were on the way and here we are."

Sawyer glanced over at me and grinned. "Well I'll be damned, I guess you really did find a client while you were home."

I actually laughed this time, reaching over and giving him a small shove. "That's sooo not what we were talking about when we were talking about finding someone to work on this summer!"

It had probably been about 30 minutes by the time we had arrived at the venue and I was finding Dani. The second I walked into the room she was in, her eyes started to tear up again. I immediately shook my head and ran over to her. "Hey! No more tears, not until you see Callum standing there waiting for you. Okay? Then you can cry all of your makeup off, but for right now... I can't have you crying while we put it on." I said with a soft smile.

Dani threw her arms around me, giving me a tight squeeze. "Thank you thank you thank you. I know you weren't supposed to be here this early, but seriously thank you." She sniffled and wiped her eyes as she pulled away from me.

"Don't worry about it, anything I can do for you I am happy too. I was going to be here early anyway because of Sawyer and I was just going to see what I could help out with." I patted her leg and walked back over to my bag so that I could open it up and pull out a bunch of different things. "Can you show me what you were going for today so I have any idea?" I glanced over at her as I started to make a mess on one of the tables that was in the room, spreading out different things so I could see what I had.

Dani asked Rebecca to hand her her cell phone, when she did she pulled up a picture and handed it to me. "This is what I wanted, but honestly if there's something you think would look better or anything it's okay."

I took in the picture for a couple minutes, glancing between Dani and her phone. "Can you send this to me so that I can keep it up for reference. This is absolutely stunning, let's do it." I handed her the phone back and waited for her to text me the picture so that I could look at it on my phone versus having to ask her to pull it up for me a bunch of times. "Rebecca, do you need me to do yours too?" I asked, genuinely unsure.

Rebecca glanced from Dani, to the table of makeup, to me, back to Dani seemingly unsure of what to say.

"Totally up to you, Rebecca. I know you don't really love makeup so if you still want to stick with light it's fine with me." Dani said with a gentle tone. I smiled at her, she was so sweet. This was her wedding day and she was basically saying sis, wear whatever you want.

"I'm happy to help if you want me too. Even if you just want me to do a little bit, totally up to you just let me know. I can do it when I'm finished with Dani." I offered. I didn't want her to feel like she had to let me help her, but I was more than happy to do so if she wanted me too. "If you need to borrow anything too, just let me know!" I smiled. I just wanted to ease both of their nerves a little bit more because I was sure that Rebecca was just trying to stay calm for Dani.

I moved Dani so she was facing in a different direction and got to work. I'd done her makeup for both of the nights that we went out, but this was totally different. It's not that I didn't take my time before, but this was for her wedding, of course it was going to take more time because I wanted to make sure every little detail was perfect for her. I kept glancing down at the picture and back to her, using the picture as a reference but working it with the colors that I had and Dani's face shapes.

"Are you nervous?" I asked as I worked on her eyeshadow. She was fidgeting every now and then and I thought that talking to her might help to calm her nerves a bit.

"I mean not in a having second thoughts kind of way.... but more so... like..." She trailed off, trying to put her thoughts into words but struggling.

"But in a holy fucking shit I'm getting married today kind of way?" I asked with a smile.

Dani giggled and nodded when I took a break to pick up more color on my brush. "Exactly like that actually. I just can't believe the day is finally here. All of the ideas we've had, all of the time and effort and money we've put into this day and we're finally about to see it pay off. I think I cried most of my tears out.... but I'm just ready to walk outside and see him standing there." She smiled, her voice full of love for my brother.

"Dani, everything is going to be perfect. But even if it's not, the only thing that matters today is you and Callum. As soon as you see him, nothing else is going to matter. You're not going to think about all of those little things, you're just going to think about your love and that's amazing." I smiled.

"He's really lucky to have you." She said.

I pulled back, giving her a confused expression. "Who?" I wasn't sure if she was talking about my brother or if she was talking about Sawyer. I was confused about what she meant either way.

"Well, both of the boys actually. Callum is lucky to have a sister like you. You're so kind and all you want is for him to be happy and I'm grateful that you know I can do that for him, because he makes me really happy. But Sawyer is also lucky to have you. I haven't known him as long as you have, but he's been in a real shit mood for the last couple of months, maybe even years. I can see that slowly changing with you being back here."

I was taken back by her words, mostly the ones about Sawyer. It's not like he had me officially, we hadn't actually defined what the heck we were so it was hard to tell. "Well, I am also lucky to have Callum. He's a great big brother and there's no one else I'd rather have marry him." I smiled at her. "But Sawyer, that's just.... Sawyer. I don't know, it's just confusing but that's so not what we're here to focus on today." I quickly tried to change the subject, not trying to make her wedding day about me and my whateveritscalledship.

"It's confusing because you two are making it confusing, it doesn't have to be. You clearly are still crushing on him and it's pretty obvious he's crushing on you. I'll bet you any amount of money that by the end of the night, y'all are doing more than kissing." She giggled.

"Dani! Oh my god, stop." I laughed.

"I'm just saying." She grinned.

When I was finished with Dani's makeup, Rebecca had me do a little bit to her as well. It wasn't anything crazy, she just wanted a little help with her eyeshadow and I touched up her base. By the time I was done, the woman doing Dani's hair was ready to continue working on it. I gathered up all of my things so I could get out of the way and gave Dani a quick hug.

"I don't want to take up too much space, but I'll still be here if you need anything at all. I'm going to go see if the boys need any help with anything or if your parents need help setting anything up. I can't wait to see you when you walk out there. Remember, the only thing that matters are you and Callum. You got this babes." I smiled, mentally laughing at myself for using Larissa's favorite word 'babes'.

"Thank you again, seriously Avery. You're an absolute life saver." She said to me with a smile.

I walked out of the room that they were in so I could leave them to it. I walked to the other side of the building we were in where Sawyer told me they were and knocked on the door. I heard one of them say come in and pushed the door open to greet the boys. "Just came to see if you guys needed help with anything."

Sawyer and Callum were both seated in a set of chairs. Sawyer had one of his ankles rested on top of the other while Callum was more leaned back, both of his legs stretched in front of him. Both of them turned their heads when I walked in and I couldn't help but notice that not only did Callum smile when he saw me, but Sawyer did too.

Callum immediately pushed himself off of the chair and walked over to me, pulling me into a hug.

"Sawyer told me there was a little mishap, thank you so much for taking care of it." He said before pulling away from me.

I smiled up at my big brother. "Happy to help in any way that I can. Do either of you need anything?"

Sawyer shook his head, letting me know that he was good. Callum shook his head as well. "No, I think we're good. You're welcome to hang out in here if you want to, plenty of space."

This time, I shook my head. "Heck no. It's your wedding day and you need to have some guy time before, I'm not getting in the way of that. I think there's a bathroom right next to your room, I'm going to get ready in there. I might just throw my stuff back in here when I'm done but I'm not going to interrupt you guys!" I laughed. It was true though, this was the part in the day where the groomsmen and the bridesmaids hung out and got ready. I did my part for Dani and I just wanted to check on the boys, I didn't want to get in the way of the boys and whatever they needed to do to get ready.

Callum laughed as he walked back to the chair he was seated on before, taking a seat in it. "You're not a bother, but thanks sis."

"Let me know if either of you need anything, yeah?"

When they both agreed, I walked back out of the room to leave them alone. I found Dani's parents and asked them if they needed any help and when they said they didn't, I made my way to the bathroom next to the boys room. I locked myself in the bathroom and turned to face the mirror so I could get myself ready. I made a mess of the bathroom as I did my makeup, happy that it was just me in there so that no one had to deal with it being in their way. Once I was finished with that, I fixed my hair. I'd woken up far too early to curl my hair before any of the craziness started so that it would fall nicely. I ended up not having to do much to it, just pinning a couple pieces back so that they weren't in the way all night. Once I was finished, I slipped into the dress and a pair of heels. I gathered up all of my things and walked back to the boys room.

I was about to knock when the door opened and Sawyer walked out in his suit. My eyes immediately landed on the blue tie that he was wearing that had little specks of pink in it. I couldn't help but laugh when I remembered that Dani had gotten mysterious about my dress matching her wedding colors, but not telling me why.

"What's so funny? Do I really look that bad?" Sawyer asked with a grin.

I smiled and shook my head. "Oh nothing. Just laughing at something Dani told me a while ago. You look really nice." I said.

Sawyer's eyes scanned over me, I watched as they softened while simultaneously grew darker taking in my appearance. "You look stunning." He almost whispered.

I felt the blush immediately creep up my neck, "Thank you." was all I was able to say back. I quickly cleared my throat, "Uh, is Callum still in there?" I nodded towards the door, needing to change the subject before I pulled him into the bathroom and kissed him.

"He is. We're getting ready to walk out."

"Got it, I just need him for like 2 minutes. He'll be right out!" I smiled and squeezed past Sawyer and into the room where my brother was standing, finishing tying his tie. I set my bag down and grabbed something out of it before walking up to him. "Hi brother."

Callum finished with his tie and looked at me with a smile. "Hi again, sis." His voice was a little shaky, like he was nervous. "I'm about to be married."

I laughed and nodded, "You are."

"Holy shit."

He was definitely nervous.

"I just wanted to come say that you got this. I told the same thing to Dani, nothing is going to matter but you and her. You guys got this." I said in an attempt to calm his nerves. "I also wanted to give you something." I motioned for him to give me his hand. He stuck his hand out to me, palm up so I could place something in it. I placed the little keychain in his hand before putting my arms back down to my sides.

I watched him as he looked down at it, his eyes widening. It was a picture of our parents on their wedding day and on the back it read you are my sunshine. I don't really remember our mom, she died when I was really young but Callum and my dad would tell me stories about her all the time. They would tell me that was my moms favorite song and that she would always sing it to Callum and I. My dad would also always refer to her as his sunshine.

"Aves, thank you so much." He closed his palm around the keychain and pulled me into a hug.

I hugged him back, trying to hold back the tears that were threatening to spill. "I know it sucks that they aren't here, but I wanted to make sure you had a little piece of them with you on your big day."

Callum gave me another squeeze before he pulled back and put the keychain in his pocket. "Thank you."

I smiled and nodded towards the door, "Let's get out of here before we start crying. You have to go get married!" I grinned.

Callum and I walked out of the room and I followed him to where Sawyer was standing as well as the officiant. "You got this!" I whispered to him one more time. I smiled at Sawyer before I made my way outside so that I could take a seat.

Callum and the officiant walked out minutes later, followed by Sawyer and Rebecca. When the music started for Dani to walk out, I gave my brother a quick thumbs up before standing up and turning so I could watch Dani. My eyes immediately started to water when she started to walk. She looked absolutely beautiful. By the time she'd walked to Callum, both of them had tears in their eyes as well. I loved the way that my brother looked at Dani as she walked down the aisle and up to him. His eyes were so full of love and it made me so incredibly happy to see. The way he was looking at her, it was like there was nobody else in the room and it was just the two of them.

The actual ceremony didn't last long, but I had to keep dabbing tears out of my eyes the entire time. I had one tissue that I'd grabbed on my way out and by the time the ceremony was over, I'd used it as much as I possibly could.

"And now for the first time, I'd like to introduce to you Mr. and Mrs. Jones!" The officiant said as we all stood up to cheer and watch them walk out. I watched my brother and his new wife walk back down the aisle together hand in hand, the biggest and brightest smiles on each of their faces. Rebecca and Sawyer walked out after them, followed by Dani's parents and myself so that we could go celebrate some more, only this time with more dancing and alcohol.

And just like that, my brother was a married man.

Chapter 13

I sat back down at the table after setting my plate of food down. I was happy that I was seated at the table with Sawyer and his parents. I knew exactly why Callum had seated me with him and his family, but I was sure that Callum did not know why that made me as happy as it did. I hadn't seen Sawyer's parents in years, but I obviously had heard that his mom wasn't doing well. She looked a lot skinnier than what she had the last time I'd seen her and she definitely looked tired. But she also looked like she was trying to remain in good spirits. Sawyer's dad had gotten her food for her and she looked at him with so much love when he returned with it, it was honestly adorable.

"Avery, sweetheart I know I've said this already but it's so good to see you again. You look so beautiful." His mom said to me as we were eating dinner.

I smiled over at her. "It's good to see you again too, Mrs. Evans." I definitely didn't know Sawyer's parents like Callum did, Callum referred to them as mom and dad but he was literally always with Sawyer when we were growing up. I saw them at football games or parties, but I obviously wasn't as close with them as he was. They were always extremely nice to me though, so it really was good to see them again. "Pretty weird that Callum is married, right?" I laughed.

Sawyer's dad laughed at my comment. His mom smiled again. "It's nice to see him so happy. Maybe one day I'll get to see this one get married." She pointed at Sawyer who shook his head awkwardly.

"Jesus, mom." He practically scoffed.

"You're acting like I said you're going to go off and get married tomorrow. I'm just saying, it'd be nice to be able to see my baby boy get married."

I nudged Sawyer and whispered, "Be nice to her."

He gave me a look before shaking his head and returning to his food. The four of us carried on talking while we ate, telling stories about Callum and Sawyer when they were younger, each one making me laugh harder than the last. It was fun getting to hear Sawyer's parent's sides to stories. I'd been a part of plenty of their stories growing up, but of course they had their fair share without me. I'd heard them talk about different things and funny memories on lots of occasions, but it was fun getting to certain things from his parents point of view. I could tell that they really did love Callum almost as much as they loved Sawyer and I thought it was incredibly sweet.

Eventually, the DJ got on his microphone again to let everyone know that they'd be doing the first dance followed by the parent dances. I internally cringed when he said dances because I wondered if he'd forgotten that Callum wouldn't actually get to have one.

I turned in my chair so that I could watch as Callum and Dani walked onto the dance floor and started dancing to the song that had started to play. I smiled, watching my big brother dance with my new sister in law. I watched them talk while they danced, I watched them laugh at each other, I loved watching how in love they were. I loved seeing them so happy together.

When the song ended, Callum walked off of the dance floor and Dani's dad took his spot. I sucked in a breath as soon as the song started to play, emotions quickly coming to the surface as I watched her dance with her dad. I knew that this moment would be difficult, but I had underestimated the emotions that were surfacing. Watching her with her dad, I was so incredibly happy for her that she was getting to share this special moment with him. But it hurt to know that I wasn't going to be able to experience this with my dad one day.

I felt a hand under the table touch my thigh and I looked down, seeing Sawyer offering his hand to me. I quickly took it and he interlocked our fingers together, his thumb gently rubbing back and forth on my hand as if to tell me that I was okay. I used my other hand to wipe under my eyes as I watched the two of them dance. It was almost as if Sawyer was listening to my breathing or at least paying attention to it, because every time I'd tense and my breathing would get caught, he'd squeeze my hand as if to tell me to relax or take a breath.

I was thankful for his silent comfort. I liked that he didn't have to say anything to me, but that he knew what I needed.

The second song ended and I watched as Callum walked up to the DJ, I assumed to tell him that he was mistaken and that it was just them dancing. Instead, he was handed the microphone. He cleared his throat and started to speak. "This is the part of the night where I'm supposed to have a dance with my mom." He started.

Sawyer squeezed my hand again when I sucked in another breath.

"But as most of you here know, I lost my mom when I was younger. I always thought that instead of doing a dance, I'd do something cool with my dad at my wedding. But, I lost my dad a couple years back so I'm not really able to do that anymore.." He trailed off.

Another squeeze from Sawyer.

"Now I'm sure you're wondering why I'm talking about my parents who aren't around anymore on my wedding day. Ahh, why's he making the day so sad?" He said in a joking tone, an attempt to lighten up the mood. "Well that's because it's the important backstory that leads me into talking about my sister, Avery. The one who, even though she's the younger sibling, was the one who unintentionally took the role of a mom when we were younger. If you know anything about my sister, it's that she always helped make sure I had my shit taken care of. Oh, excuse the language."

Another squeeze and a bit of a laugh.

"She's the one that was cheering me on at all of my games, cheering extra loud when our dad couldn't make it. She's been one of my biggest supporters, even from a million miles away in California. She was going to come home for the wedding and I somehow convinced her to spend the entire summer with us, because Dani and I missed her too much." He laughed.

Squeeze.

"Before I ramble on too much.. While I'm not able to have the traditional mother son dance, I'd like to do something special and have a quick dance with my little sis." He finally finished his speech. Sawyer gave my hand one more squeeze before letting go and nodding towards Callum.

I quickly got out of the chair and walked over to him. I didn't even know what to say, it was something I wasn't expecting. I wrapped my arms around my older brother as the music started playing and immediately, more tears started to pool.

"It was the song I would have danced with mom too, I hope that's okay." He said as You Are My Sunshine started to play.

"Jesus, we really are the same person aren't we?" I asked with a laugh.

Callum laughed and nodded, the two of us dancing to the song that was playing. "I've been planning this for a while now and when you gave me the keychain earlier, I wanted to say the same thing but I couldn't yet. I think we were supposed to be twins or something." He chuckled.

"But seriously, thank you Callum. This means a lot to me." We danced for a few minutes as the song played, I let the tears fall down my cheeks. I was overwhelmed with emotion, especially with it being so unexpected. Nothing could have prepared me for Callum doing something like this. I figured that he was just going to move on after Dani and her dad's dance. I never in a million years thought that he would pull something like this. I was so incredibly thankful for my older brother and the heart that he had.

When the song ended, I gave him a tight hug before he walked back over to Dani and I returned to the table with Sawyer and his family. "Did you know he was doing that?" I asked Sawyer when I sat back down.

He immediately handed me a tissue so that I could wipe my eyes and nodded. "I did, but he made me promise to keep it a secret."

"Traitor." I joked.

"Can't be a traitor when I was technically his first." He said with a grin.

Callum and Dani cut their cake and then the DJ started playing music that people could dance too. I ended up on the dance floor with Dani very soon after the music started to play. I danced with her and a couple of her friends after being introduced to them. Callum had been walking around talking to people, he ended up at the table talking with Sawyer and his parents. Dani and I gave them a couple songs to talk, but eventually the two of us walked over to them. She grabbed Callum's hand and grabbed Sawyer's, mostly out of copying Dani's actions. We dragged them to the dance floor and practically forced them to dance with us. Callum and Sawyer gave each other a look, but danced with us anyway. I was more than positive Callum wasn't thinking anything about it but more so that we all just wanted to dance together.

We took a break after a while, Sawyer and I going back to the table to grab a drink while Dani and Callum went around to talk to people again. Sawyer started talking to his parents while I sipped on my drink and looked around, taking everything in. Everything turned out so beautiful. There were some guys that we'd all gone to school with here, mostly guys from the football team. It was cool to see where they were at now. I hadn't really talked to any of them, but they were talking to Sawyer and Callum so I was able to hear a little bit about where they were all at in life. I recognized a couple other people from the university Callum went to, but everyone else was on Dani's side and I really didn't know any of them.

I watched as couple started moving onto the dance floor when a slow song came on. I don't think either one of us knew what to do, because neither one of us got up. It was one of those moments where I think we were both questioning what would be the easiest move. Do we get up and dance and risk questions or do we sit and wait it out, both being a little disappointed.

I didn't miss the little shove that Sawyer's mom gave him before she nodded in my direction. I don't think she knew that I could see her from the corner of my eye, but I did and I couldn't help but grin against the rim of my glass. Sawyer stood up seconds later and held out his hand to me. "Wanna dance?"

I quickly set my glass down and took his hand, following him out to the dance floor. He wrapped his arms around my waist as I wrapped mine around his neck. The two of us swayed to the song that was playing. "Think we'll get caught?" I asked, half joking.

Sawyer shrugged, "I don't think he'll think anything of it, but if he does then I'll tell him my mom made me." He joked.

I looked up at him, raising an eyebrow. "You're like 26 and you're going to blame this dance on your mom?"

"Absolutely I will." He chuckled.

"Or you can just tell him that you have owed me a dance for like... 5 years and that you're finally making it up to me." I said pointedly.

Sawyer pulled me in a little closer, moving us around in a circle. "You got me there, this dance is definitely long overdue." He smiled. "I should have danced with you like this at prom."

I looked up at him, searching his green eyes. "You would have slow danced with me at prom?" I asked, even though it felt like a dumb question.

"If I would have taken you, of course I would have. Why wouldn't I?" He asked like the answer was obvious.

"Jake didn't slow dance with me." I shrugged.

Sawyer rolled his eyes at my response. "Jake was a dickhead. He didn't deserve a slow dance with you anyway."

"You're not wrong there..."

"I really want to kiss you." He whispered, changing the subject.

I blushed. "I really want you to kiss me too." I almost wanted him to have another fuck it moment and just kiss me, but I knew this wasn't the place to do that. This wasn't our show and I wasn't about to have anyone get mad at anyone, which meant the kissing could wait until after.

Sawyer leaned down so he was closer to my ear when he whispered, "the good news is that Dani and Callum are staying in a hotel tonight. Which means the second we get inside, I can kiss you wherever I want, for however long I want."

I tensed just slightly, his words lighting a small fire in me. "Is that so?" I whispered back to him.

"Mhmm. Also means that you can be as loud as you want to be."

I sucked in a breath. "I don't think I'm that loud of a kisser." I said, trying to make a joke so I could calm my body down.

Sawyer did the exact opposite though when he whispered, "Oh no no, I plan on doing a lot more than kissing tonight. I'll give you a reason to be loud." He planted the lightest of kisses just under my ear. "That is, if you want me too?" He whispered before lifting his head up so that he could look at me.

My lips were parted as I looked up at him. My body was on fire and I wanted nothing more than to smash my lips against his and let him take me in the bathroom. "Okay," was all I could get out as a response. I wanted that so badly that it hurt.

Sawyer chuckled lightly and gave my hip a small squeeze. "You do look really good in this dress. But I'm excited to take it off of you."

Sawyer grabbed my bag out of the backseat of his car while I was grabbing my heels off of the floorboard. We shut the doors at the same time and headed towards the front door to go inside of his house. The minute we were both inside and the door was shut, Sawyer dropped my bag and pulled me into him, causing me to drop my heels. He connected our lips and I melted into him almost instantaneously. My arms quickly wrapped around his neck as he held my hips. He backed me up until my back was hitting the wall and pressed himself against me, his lips never leaving mine.

He just barely pulled away from my lips and mumbled, "let's go upstairs."

I nodded in agreement and Sawyer took my hand, leading me upstairs. I wondered which room he was going to take me into, his old bedroom or his new one. Not that it really mattered. The only thing I truly cared about was feeling him against me. We could have stayed downstairs on the couch and I would have been on cloud 9. I followed him into his bedroom, his new bedroom, where he immediately led me to the bed.

We stopped at the edge of the bed and I immediately took off the suit jacket that he was still wearing. I undid the tie and unbuttoned the shirt, slowly pulling it off of him. Once he was without a shirt, his hands grabbed the bottom of my dress and lifted it up and off my body. I immediately shivered, wearing nothing but a pair of underwear under the dress.

"You're so beautiful." He whispered before connecting our lips again. Sawyer helped me lay back on his bed and hovered his body over mine. His hands explored my body, leaving a trail of goosebumps everywhere he touched. I whimpered under his touch, wanting more but also enjoying the little bits of teasing he was doing.

He moved from my lips to my neck just as one of his hands reached the hem of my underwear. I gasped when his hand dipped into them, immediately finding the little bundle of nerves that was practically begging for his attention.

His thumb circled me while his mouth trailed down my neck and to my chest, nipping and sucking on my skin. My back arched into him, begging for more. He continued to trail his kisses lower and lower until he was fully in between my legs. He quickly removed my underwear fully, leaving me bare while he still had his dress pants on. I wanted to tell him to let me finish undressing him, but the words got caught the second his tongue connected with my core.

I gasped, tossing my head back. "Yes," I breathed out. My fingers immediately tangled themselves in his hair, pulling on his hair. My body was still on fire from his words earlier so it didn't take long for that feeling in the pit of my stomach to build up.

I cried out his name along with a couple oh gods as that feeling took over my entire body only minutes later. I was trying to catch my breath as Sawyer was kissing his way back up my body, eventually pecking me on the lips again. He had a grin on his face and I knew he was going to say something.

"I don't think you even realize that I could listen to you do that every single day." He complemented.

I smiled at him and grabbed his face, pulling him down so I could kiss him again. We kissed for a couple minutes before I flipped us over so he was laying on his back. I shifted myself so that I could undo his pants and pull them down. Once he was fully undressed I threw a leg around him so I was straddling him before leaning down and pressing my lips against his again.

"Mmm, you look really hot when you're sitting on top of me like that." Another compliment.

I liked that he was being vocal about what he was thinking right now, it was giving me more confidence in everything that I was doing.

"You look really hot too." I complimented, only it sounded slightly more awkward when I said it.

Sawyer chuckled before he reached out to his side table, he opened the drawer and pulled out a condom. "S'cuse me babe," he said and nodded towards where I was sitting on him.

He called me babe.

I lifted myself off of him just enough so he could roll the condom on. When he was finished, he grabbed my hips and looked up at me. "You're sure about this? No regrets tomorrow?" He asked.

I quickly shook my head. "No regrets tomorrow, I'm sure."

Sawyer nodded and guided my hips down onto him, immediately earning a gasp from me. My hands were on his chest, my nails digging in just slightly as my eyes fluttered closed.

He waited a minute, giving me time to get comfortable before he gently guided my hips, helping me find a rhythm that I liked because the second I lowered down onto him, I lost all ability to think for myself.

It's not like I'd never had sex, but this felt so different than any of the other times I'd had sex. This felt right, natural. Our bodies worked together perfectly and it was almost overwhelming.

Once I found a rhythm I liked, Sawyer's grip on my hips loosened. He was still holding them, but giving me more freedom to move on my own. When I looked down at him, he was staring up at me and I loved the look in his eyes. I loved the way he was looking at me like

I was beautiful, like I was sexy, like I was his. My lips parted, moans escaping past them with no remorse.

My eyes fluttered closed again as my head fell forward towards my chest, I was starting to lose the rhythm as the feeling was building back up. Sawyer quickly caught on, his grip on my hips tightening again to help me.

"Yes, yes.." I breathed out, my nails digging into his chest again. I was on edge, just waiting to jump over and into the deep end. Sawyer stopped moving my hips and instead, thrusted his up into mine causing me to cry out.

I couldn't take it anymore, it was beginning too be too much. "Sawyer..." I tossed my head back and cried out, letting the feeling consume me again. He didn't stop moving, prolonging the waves and waves of pleasure rushing through me.

Before I could even understand what was happening, Sawyer had flipped us over so he was once again hovering over me. He grabbed one of my hands in his, interlocking our fingers as he continued his movements. I whimpered at the feeling, my core feeling overwhelmed with sensitivity but wanting him to also feel the way I was feeling.

It didn't take much longer, his thrusts became sloppy and then stopped all together. His forehead rested against mine and I looked up at him through tired eyes.

"I could watch you do that every day too." I whispered.

Sawyer grinned and kissed my lips before pulling out of me and getting off the bed. He threw the condom in the trash before sitting down next to me again.

He asked me if I wanted to take a shower.

That sounds heavenly.

We showered.

Then we had sex in the shower.

Then we showered again, for real this time.

And then I went to bed cuddled again Sawyer Evans.

Chapter 14

----

4 years ago.

I sat on the couch, a blanket covering my legs and a hood covering my head. My notebook sat on my lap, my pen sitting between my teeth as I wracked my brain trying to think of where I wanted to go next with the story I'd been working on. I'd been staring at the piece of paper in front of me for so long that the words didn't even make sense anymore. At this point, I was just frustrated. I knew I needed to walk away from it, but I couldn't seem to put the pen down. I'd written down a bunch of different ideas, but as soon as I wrote them down to get them out of my head, I immediately hated them. My laptop had turned off a while ago, it was sitting next to me on the couch waiting for me to pick it back up and continue where I had left off.

The front door opened, startling me to no end. "Fucks sake." I muttered, turning my attention away from the notebook and to the front door where my brother and Sawyer were walking in, both with bags in their hands.

"I thought you'd be asleep by now." Was the first thing that Callum had said to me.

Sawyer kicked the door shut behind him and immediately walked to the kitchen, not saying anything to me. I watched him as he walked by me. He didn't even say hi. He'd been acting really weird since they'd gotten home from school for Winter break. He was barely talking to me, when I'd seen him for the first time it wasn't like it normally was. He didn't hug me, he barely said hi. We talked about school for maybe 5 minutes before he ended the conversation. I'd been trying to figure out what I had done to upset him, but I couldn't think of anything. I hadn't even seen him since the school year started for all of us, so I really had no idea what I had done wrong.

"What time is it?" I asked.

Callum started laughing as he walked over to the couch. When he saw the notebook in my hand, he immediately knew that I had lost track of time. "It's like 10:30."

I shut the notebook and then my laptop before standing up from the couch. "I'm not an old lady, Callum. I don't go to bed when the sun goes down." I joked. I followed him into the kitchen where he set the grocery bags down. Sawyer had already taken the groceries he'd brought in out of the bag and I immediately noticed snacks and alcohol. "It's a little late for a party, don't you think?"

Callum eyed me and laughed. "Not an old lady, huh?"

I rolled my eyes, even though his joke was totally valid.

"We are having a couple friends over, but nothing crazy. Ran into a couple guys from high school while we were out and I told them to come over. Hope that's okay?" Callum said as he pulled different items out of the bags.

I sat on one of the stools by the island, watching the two of them. "I don't mind, I can go upstairs. Don't wanna interrupt or anything."

Callum shrugged, opening up the fridge and putting some beer in it. "You're not a bother, but it's up to you." He put a couple other things away before he walked over to the oven to preheat it. "I'm going to hop in the shower, can one of you put the pizzas in the oven when it goes off? I'll be back down in like 10." He didn't wait for either of us to answer him, he just ran upstairs to shower before whoever was coming over got here.

Who the hell had friends over this late? Didn't people normally leave to go back home at this time? People really came over to start hanging out at 10:30? Was I really that lame that the thought of this sounded absolutely wild?

Sawyer opened the fridge and pulled a beer out for himself. "Want one?" He asked without turning to look at me.

I almost asked him if he was talking to me before I remembered I was the only one downstairs. I sat up a little straighter, my nerves suddenly all over the place. "Uhh, yeah sure."

I hate beer.

Sawyer grabbed another bottle out of the fridge before closing it and sliding one of them over to me. "When did you start liking beer?" He asked, like he hadn't been the one to just offer one to me.

I suddenly felt the need to look cooler. I almost wanted him to think that I had changed since starting college, I wanted him to think that I went out and partied. I'd never been one to go out and party like they did, so a part of me wanted him to think that had changed since I'd graduated high school and started university. I shrugged, twisting the cap off of the bottle. "Recently." was all I said back.

What a stupid response.

Sawyer did the same, twisting his cap off only he immediately took a drink of his. I watched him bring the bottle to his lips. I watched his lips part so he could take a drink. The same lips that I wanted to kiss for years now. I would do anything to know what those lips tasted like. He leaned against the counter, one of his hands stretched back to lean against the counter while the other held his beer. We didn't speak for another few minutes and I hated that there was some sort of tension between us. The air was thick and I had no idea how to walk through it. Things had never been like this between us, they'd never been weird or uncomfortable and now I couldn't seem to even navigate a conversation with him.

"Did I do something to you?" I finally asked after a couple of minutes. It came out more timid than I meant for it to, but I couldn't help it.

Sawyer looked over at me, his face changed just slightly but it was hard to read. "What do you mean?" He asked.

Before I could answer him, the oven beeped, letting us know that it was ready for the pizzas to go in. Sawyer pushed himself off the counter to once again open the fridge. I felt the need to help him, so I got up so I could get him the pizza pans. I opened up one of the cabinets, grabbing two pans and setting them down on the island just as Sawyer was taking the first pizza out of the box. I helped him with the second one, taking it out of the box and putting it onto the pan. Once both of the pizzas were on the pans, he put them into the oven and started a timer.

Once he was done, he leaned against the counter again. I didn't sit back down, I leaned against the island so I could face him. "You didn't even hug me when you got home." I said, continuing the conversation that I had opened up.

"What?" was all he said back to me.

I let out a small huff. "You didn't hug me when you got home from school. You've barely spoken to me. I thought we were going to catch up on things like we always do when you come home. We always have so much to talk about and now you're just acting like I pissed you off." I admitted.

This was my first year of college and I had so much that I wanted to tell him and so many things that I was excited to talk to him about. I wanted to tell him all about the classes that I was taking for my journalism major, I wanted to talk to him about the classes I was planning on taking in the Spring. I wanted to ask him how his senior year was going and hear all about how the football team was treating him because he told me that he would be getting a lot more time on the field with it being his last year.

How's school going? Oh it's great! I have so much to tell you. How are things with you though? I want to hear all about your senior year! Good. How's the football team? Good. Are you excited to be home for a couple weeks? Yeah, hey I gotta go help Callum with something.

I'd seen him multiple times since that conversation and I still hadn't had the chance to tell him anything that I wanted to tell him because he was acting like he wanted nothing to do with me.

Sawyer just looked at me. He didn't say anything right away, he just kept his eyes on me. I was trying to figure out what was going through his head, but I couldn't read his expression. After a couple minutes of just watching me, he took a step closer to me. He set his beer on the island behind me and the second he was standing in front of me my breath caught in my throat. He quietly raised his hands up and lowered my hood that I'd forgotten was on my head.

"You didn't piss me off." was all he said when he finally spoke.

Then why are you acting so weird?

He looked me over again and I almost wanted to shrink back. I hated that I couldn't understand what he was thinking or that I couldn't understand the look he was giving me. None of this was making sense and I hated every second of it. He was acting like he didn't know who I was, like I was some stranger that he had met for the first time and didn't care to get to know. I'd known him basically my entire life and I'd never felt more uncomfortable in a conversation than I did in this moment. Even after years of crushing on Sawyer, he'd never made me feel as nervous as he was making me feel while he stood so close to me.

"Then what did I do?" I asked. If I didn't piss him off, I had to have done something to make him act like this. But I couldn't wrap my head around what I would have done to him.

Sawyer's eyes were trailing across me again, looking me over and again, I wanted to hide. I wanted to pull my hood over my head and run away. "Ave, you don't even realize it." His voice was just barely above a whisper, I could barely hear him.

I looked up at him, his expression was a mix between soft and hard. His eyes kept changing and it was making the anxiety in my belly bubble up. "Don't realize what? Sawyer, if I did something you have to tell me so I can fix it." I felt bad. I had obviously done something to him. He was telling me I didn't even realize what I had done but he wouldn't tell me what I had actually done to him. I just wanted to fix whatever I had done to him so that we could go back to normal and I could talk to him without feeling like I was talking to someone I'd never met before.

"You don't need to fix anything."

I was about to respond when we both heard footsteps coming down the staircase. Sawyer quickly backed away from me like he'd done something wrong. I gave him a confused look before walking around the island to take a seat on the kitchen stool again. I was even more confused than I was before I had asked him what I did wrong, but I guess now I knew I hadn't done anything to make him mad. But I still didn't understand what I had done to him in the first place.

Callum walked into the kitchen again. The second he glanced at me, he raised an eyebrow. "Since when do you drink beer?"

I rolled my eyes. "Could you two be any more similar? Maybe I started drinking when I went to college. Ever think that I could actually go to a party?"

Callum looked at me, then to Sawyer, then back to me. He started laughing and when I glanced at Sawyer, I could see him chuckling. "Sorry sis, it's just hard to imagine you going to a college party. But hey, live your life and have fun while you're doing it. Just be careful too. I don't wanna have to drive up there and kick someone's ass." He grinned. He walked to the fridge, pulling out a beer for himself before closing it and leaning against the counter, copying Sawyer's actions.

I didn't party, but I was okay with them thinking that I did. My roommate had dragged me out a couple times, but I'd ended up leaving earlier than she did each time. I lifted the bottle up, taking a small sip from it.

Yep, I hate beer.

I tried not to make a face, not wanting to let either of them know that I actually did hate the way that it tasted. I didn't want to give either one of them a reason to make a comment or question what I was doing in school.

The doorbell rang moments later, shifting the attention off of me and drinking and to whoever was on the other side of the door. Callum walked out of the kitchen, beer in hand, and to the front door to let his friends inside. I couldn't see anyone that had walked in, but I could hear a couple of voices. It didn't sound like a lot of people, but I wasn't sure if anyone else was coming. I could hear Callum say that Sawyer was in the kitchen and that he'd grab them a beer before their voices got louder as they actually walked into the kitchen.

Following behind Callum were three guys that I'd recognized from Callum and Sawyer's high school class. When he walked into the kitchen, he opened up the fridge and grabbed three more beers. Sawyer said hello to everyone as Callum handed them each a bottle.

"I don't know if you remember my sister, Avery." He motioned over to me. "Ave, I don't know if you remember any of these dip shits. James, Tyler, and Lukas." He nodded to each of the guys as he said their names, even though I had remembered all of them.

"Good to see you again." I smiled over at them. I hated the fact that all three of them were looking at me, more like staring at me, like they'd never seen me in their lives. I know that I was three years younger than them, but we did go to high school together for a year and I went to literally every single football game, so I was always walking out with Callum at the end of the games.

"Shit, Avery. You like.. grew up." was the first thing out of any of their mouths.

I almost wanted to laugh, but a small part of me was also grossed out. The last time I'd interacted with any of them I was 15 at Callum's graduation party. I was now 19 and the fact that after four years the first thing that is said to me is that I grew up, it gave me weird vibes.

"Dude, that's my sister." Callum groaned.

"Uhh thanks?" I shifted uncomfortably in my stool.

"Ignore him, he's still an idiot." Lukas said, giving me a soft smile after apologizing for his friend.

I shrugged it off and glanced over at Sawyer, who was still leaning against the island. He was glaring at Tyler. I couldn't help but wonder once again what was going through his head, I wanted to know why he was looking at him like that. But the second he noticed me looking at him, the glare was gone and replaced with another look that I couldn't read.

When the pizzas were finished, Sawyer took them out of the oven and placed them on the stove. Each of the boys grabbed a couple pizzas and headed into the living room. I grabbed my beer, knowing that I wasn't going to drink it, and headed for the stairs after grabbing my notebook and laptop.

"You don't have to go upstairs if you don't want to." Callum called out to me.

I glanced over at him and laughed. "I'm okay, you guys have fun." I said before walking upstairs so that I could go to my room. If it would have been just Callum and Sawyer, I may have stayed downstairs but I didn't feel like sitting downstairs with the other three guys who had been looking at me like I was a piece of meat. I figured it was best to just let them play catch up and I would stay upstairs where I could be alone in my thoughts yet again. Maybe even try to figure out what the hell Sawyer was trying to say to me before my brother walked downstairs.

I shut the door behind me and set the beer down on the desk in my room. I laid down on my bed, opening up both my laptop and my notebook to try and see if I could come up with some sort of idea that would get things moving again.

My eyes fluttered open slowly, groaning at the light coming through the window in my room. I slowly lifted my head and looked down at my bed, realizing that I'd fallen asleep on my open notebook. I slowly sat up on my bed, stretching out my neck and letting out a small whine when I realized that I'd slept a bit weird and my neck was sore. I got out of my bed and glanced at the time on my alarm clock, it was still pretty early so I was sure no one else would be awake. I had no idea if any of the other guys stayed the night, but I was quiet as I exited my room just in case. I walked downstairs, the beer bottle that was still full in one of my hands. I glanced into the living room and saw three boys asleep on the sectional.

I quietly walked into the kitchen so that I could dump the beer out and grab some water instead. As I was pouring the beer into the sink, a voice startled me, almost causing me to drop the bottle.

"I knew you didn't like beer." Sawyer's voice was quiet and raspy, like he'd just woken up and like he didn't want to wake anyone else up. I figured he'd been asleep in Callum's room, but I hadn't even heard him walk downstairs.

"Jesus, you scared me." I whispered back to him. I glanced down at the bottle and shrugged. "You're right, I actually think it's disgusting."

Sawyer folded his arms, leaning against the wall as he watched me. "Why'd you take one yesterday then?"

I finished emptying the bottle and quietly threw it away. "You offered me one. I don't know, just seemed like the thing to do." I didn't want to tell him it's because I wanted him to think I was cool, but I was sure he was going to catch onto it.

"Hey," He said, grabbing my attention and making me look over at him. "I'm sorry for being a dick. I wasn't trying to make you think that you made me angry. You didn't do anything that made me angry or anything like that." He sounded sincere, even through his quiet voice.

"You never told me what I did though or... what I don't need to fix? I don't know, I'm confused by what you meant." I admitted.

Sawyer shook his head. "Don't worry about it. But just know that you didn't do anything wrong and I apologize if I made you feel like you did." He gave me a soft smile. "Want to tell me how your classes are going? I think it's going to be a while before anyone else wakes up."

I couldn't help but smile at his words. I absolutely wanted to tell him about how my first semester of college had been going. I wanted to tell him every little detail and I wanted to hear every detail about how his last fall semester of school was going.

"I have a lot to tell you.." I grinned.

Chapter 15

<hr>

I couldn't get the images of last night out of my head as I stood in front of the coffee pot, the pot of water in my hand waiting to be poured into the machine. I couldn't stop thinking about the way Sawyer's body felt against mine, the way he looked, the way he sounded. It was all so much to take in and I couldn't stop thinking about it.

"Morning," Sawyer's voice came from behind me, startling me. I gasped, not realizing that I'd been that deep in my own thoughts. He wrapped his arms around my waist, pressing his front to my back. "Didn't mean to scare you." He chuckled.

I shook my head, pouring the water into the coffee pot before I started to add the coffee grounds. "Good morning." I said back to him. Once I was finished, I turned on the coffee pot before turning around so that I could face him.

Sawyer grinned and leaned down to press his lips against mine. He tasted minty, like he'd just brushed his teeth.

God I could get used to this.

When he pulled away from me he said, "Does it feel weird, you being here with me without Callum?"

I shrugged, leaning against the counter. "I mean we've hung out before, so no. Not really. It feels weird kissing you behind his back." I admitted.

Sawyer and I had hung out plenty of times, most of the time it was only for short periods while Callum was doing something. But since being home on this trip, I'd spent a decent amount of time with just Sawyer so it felt less strange now. But it did still feel odd making out with him, amongst other things.

Sawyer chuckled but nodded. "Fair enough, it is a little weird kissing my best friend's little sister."

I rolled my eyes, "Yeah yeah, I know. Are we going to tell him about this or?" I trailed off, not even really sure what this was. I thought I was over the crush that I had on him, but it was more than obvious that I was definitely not over it. The problem was that I didn't actually know how Sawyer felt, I didn't know if he liked me or if he just liked the physical stuff.

I watched him as he shrugged, seemingly unsure. "I don't think there's anything that needs to be said right now. Let's just see where things go and we'll cross that bridge when we get there."

I looked at him for a moment, taking in his words. I couldn't quite decipher them the way I wanted to. There's nothing that needs to be said. Does that mean we're on two completely different pages?

"Right," was all I could say back. I turned around, facing the coffee pot again.

Let's just see where things go.

What did that even mean?

Last night they went pretty far. I immediately felt like I was going into this way over my head. It made me question what he wanted out of this. I didn't want to be used for sex, especially not by someone that I knew I cared deeply about. But I also knew how much I enjoyed everything about last night and there was a part of me that did want to see where things went.

"I think I'm going to run out and grab us some breakfast. Wanna come with me?" He asked.

I shook my head, not turning around to face him. "No, you go ahead. I think I might call Larissa for a little bit. She wanted to hear about the wedding." It's not that I didn't want to go with him, but I also just needed a little bit of time to digest his words.

Sawyer spun me around so I was facing him again before he pulled me into a hug. "Did I upset you?" He asked.

I looked up at him and shook my head. "No." It wasn't a lie. It's not that I was necessarily upset, I was just confused.

"Are you sure?" He asked.

"I'm not upset. Just trying to figure out what this is I guess. But we don't have to talk about it right now, like you said we're seeing where things take us. Right?" I said with a small smile.

Sawyer gave me a look before saying, "Ave, I didn't mean it in a bad way. I just mean, this is a new thing for both of us and I think we're both just trying to navigate it in the best way. I don't want to put pressure on it and freak either one of us out. So let's just take it day by day and see where it leads." He explained.

I listened to him explain his thoughts. It didn't make me feel 100 percent better, but it helped. "You're right, we shouldn't put pressure on it. I guess I just didn't understand what you meant."

Sawyer leaned down, kissing me again before pulling back. "I'll be back in about 30 minutes, yeah?"

I kissed him and nodded. "Okay." When he walked out of the kitchen, I turned back to the coffee pot. I grabbed a mug out of the cabinet and poured myself a cup before walking out to the back porch with my phone. I sat down, setting the cup on the table. I looked at the time, it was pretty early in Santa Monica and I wasn't sure if Larissa would be awake or not. I pressed the call button anyway and put the phone to my ear. It rang a couple of times before I heard shuffling coming from the answered line.

"Hello?" A quiet, raspy sounding Larissa answered the phone.

"Did I wake you?" I asked with a small laugh.

Larissa let out a small groan, I heard a door click shut from the other side before she said, "Yeah but it's fine."

"Where are you?" I asked, it sounded a little echoey and she was talking really quiet.

"This guy I met last night, his apartment. Well, I'm in his bathroom right now." She whispered.

I rolled my eyes at my best friend, "Jesus, Larissa. You could have texted me last night or something so I had the address of where you are."

"You're literally on the other side of the country, what the hell would you have done for me?" She asked.

I sighed, "I would have the address of the last person you were with if you had gone missing."

"You watch too many crime shows. How was the wedding?"

I picked up my coffee mug with my other hand, taking a sip of it. "It was really beautiful. The woman that was supposed to do Dani's makeup literally canceled on her at the last second so I got to do her makeup which was cool. Callum loved the keychain that I bought him and he even surprised me with a sibling dance. We danced to You Are My Sunshine, it was kind of funny that we both had similar ideas. Overall, it was a lot of fun." I said with a smile.

"And did Sawyer think you looked hot?" She said, practically ignoring every other detail about the actual wedding and just wanting to know what Sawyer thought about the way I looked.

I grinned, even though she couldn't see me. "I guess you could say that."

"What the hell does that mean?" She asked, her voice slightly louder. When I didn't answer her right away, she gasped. "Oh my god. You totally banged him last night!"

I started laughing, which immediately confirmed for her that she was right.

"Ahh! You did!" She whisper-yelled. "How was it!?"

"We did it more than once." I said first. "Once in bed and once in the shower. It was great, he was great. I felt great." I laughed.

"Oh my god, I'm so dead right now! I knew it, I knew it. I called it. Didn't I call that? I did!" She was quietly squealing, which made it even funnier.

"But I have no idea what that means for us now, that's the problem. He said he didn't want to put pressure on anything and that we should just see where it goes." I said to her. I wanted her opinion, I needed to know if I was reading too much into things.

Larissa let out a small groan. "Guys are such idiots. That's code for I just want sex."

My face fell just slightly at the confirmation that I didn't want to hear. "That's what I was afraid of." She was saying exactly what I was thinking and it was what I was hoping she wouldn't say. I was afraid that Sawyer was going to want just the physical side of things when I knew that I was far too deep in the emotional side of things to be able to maintain just the physical stuff. I'd been emotionally attached to him for years now and even though I thought I was over it, I definitely wasn't.

"But you never know babes, it's different with you guys. You've known each other for so long that he really might just be confused with his own feelings and trying not to freak himself out, you know?" She said, obviously trying to make me feel better. Larissa knew me and she knew I was going to let my thoughts spiral on this before I even had a chance to calm them down.

I leaned my head back in the chair, nodding. "That's what I'm going to keep telling myself at least, it will make me feel better about it."

I heard a knock on the door on the other end of the line. "Shit, babes let me call you back in a little bit."

"Don't get murdered!" I laughed before hanging up the phone. I set my phone down on the table and took another sip of my coffee. I tried to get out of my head, but it was hard when I felt like I had absolutely no idea what I was doing. I also felt like I was making this a much bigger deal than it needed to be, which was equally as frustrating.

I sat on the back deck, my eyes closed and my head rested against the chair as I let my thoughts wander for a little bit. I wondered what it would be like if Sawyer really did like me, in an emotional way. I wondered what it would be like to be in an actual relationship with him. It's definitely not the first time I'd wondered about this, I used to think about it all the time when I was younger. However, this was one of the first times I saw it as a real possibility.

I couldn't help but wonder how Callum would feel about it. Would he be excited that his best friend was dating his little sister? It's not like we didn't already hang out together. Would he be absolutely furious about it? He'd always made it a point to tell his other friends that I was off limits, but I'd never actually heard him say it to Sawyer. It made me wonder if he'd ever actually said that to him or if it was just a silent assumption on his part.

My thoughts trailed back to Sawyer as I once again thought about the way that he looked at me last night. He looked at me in a way that I don't recall ever seeing him look at me and I wanted to relive it over and over again. I thought about his eyes and how they were the most perfect shade of green. They reminded me of the greenery in a forest. They were absolutely mesmerizing.

Sawyer kind of reminded me of the forest in general. His eyes were the color of the leaves on the trees, his hair matched the color of the tree trunks. His personality was even that of a forest, a bit quiet and maybe even a bit scary if you'd never been let in, yet warm and welcoming to those that really got to explore it.

Shades of greens and browns danced around my closed eyes. It was the first time in a while that the little creative wheels in my mind were starting to turn. I hadn't felt inspired to write in ages, nothing brand new had come to mind in what felt like years. Every time I tried to sit down and think, it was like someone had put a wall in front of me that was impossible to climb over. For the first time in a while, that wall was slowly coming down and I was able to step through it.

I almost wanted to get up and go grab a pen or my laptop, but I was afraid that as soon as I did, all of the thoughts that were swarming my brain would disappear. I was afraid that as soon as I actually tried to do something, the wheels would stop turning and I'd be right back where I was before. I was almost afraid to even open my eyes. The colors kept dancing around, different small ideas coming to life. I couldn't help the smile that crept on my face, feeling almost a sense of relief. I thought that I'd lost this form of creativity. Turns out, I'd just lost my inspiration for a while.

-

I couldn't believe that June was already over, I'd been home for about a month now and the time was going by quickly. It's funny how I was so nervous to come home, I didn't even want to come for the summer and now there was a part of me that didn't want the summer to end. This trip had been going a lot better than I expected it to and I was almost afraid for it to come to an end. By the time Dani and Callum got back from their honeymoon, it would be the middle of the month and then I'd only have a month and a half left here. I knew it was silly to think that far in advance but I had so many thoughts floating around in my mind that it was hard not to think about it.

"What are you thinking about?" Sawyer's voice interrupted my thoughts, although I was happy he did. It was easy for them to spiral a little out of control so I was happy to be pulled out of them before I fell too deep into things.

I looked up at him, meeting his eyes. My head was in his lap while I laid down on the couch, he'd turned on a movie but I had no idea what it was even about at this point. I'd stopped paying attention a while ago.

"Time is going by pretty quickly." I said honestly. It's not like I had to hide the fact that I was thinking about how quick the summer was going.

"What do you mean?" He asked.

"I mean, tomorrow is the first day of July. The month went by quickly and I feel like the rest of the summer is going to go just as quickly. I'm just surprised at how quickly things are going by. I think I came into this trip thinking the time would go by slowly, I wasn't really excited to be coming home and I just didn't really know what to expect. But now that I'm actually here, I wish things would slow down a little bit." I spoke, telling him exactly what was going on in my head.

Sawyer ran his fingers through my hair as he looked down at me. "I know what you mean." He started. "Wait, no that's so not what I meant. I wasn't not excited about you coming home, I just also didn't know what to expect." He said, which almost confused me even more.

"What do you mean?" This time I asked for clarification.

Sawyer shrugged. I couldn't tell if he didn't know how to explain what he was thinking or if he didn't want to explain. "You first, why weren't you excited about coming home? Why is it different from what you expected or.. didn't expect?" He asked.

"I haven't been home in three years," I started with the obvious part of my answer. "A lot can change in three years. This is the first time I've been home since my dad passed. I was coming home to attend Callum's wedding, I knew I was going to see you for the first time in years. It was just a lot and I didn't know what I was walking into. Then Callum picks me up from the airport and says surprise, we're actually staying with Sawyer and then I really didn't know what to expect." I didn't want to tell him that I didn't know what to expect from him because things had been super weird the last time I'd seen him. Actually, that things had been weird the last handful of times that I'd seen him.

"I'm sure that was a lot to take in after a couple of years. But what do you mean by you didn't know what you were walking into?" He asked.

I let out a small huff, I had no idea how to explain my thoughts to him without saying because I've had a crush on you for 10 years and the last couple of years before moving you treated me differently and I was half expecting you to tell me to stay out of your way when I got here.

"It's hard to explain.." I started.

"I just... ugh. We used to be close, closer? I don't know. Of course you were always Callum's friend and not technically mine, but I considered us friends. But before I left for California, things got weird between us. I remember you telling me that I hadn't done anything to piss you off, but even after that I felt like I'd done something wrong or that I was doing something wrong. You stopped hugging me when you'd come into town from school. You stopped asking me about how things were going. When you'd come over, you'd talk to me for maybe 5 minutes and that was it. When my dad died, it was the first time in ages that you did anything that made me feel like you cared about me. I decided I was leaving for California and you gave me a gift out of nowhere like things hadn't changed between us.."

"Annnnd then I moved and we didn't speak at all. So of course I had no idea what I was walking into. Was I walking back to the old Sawyer who wanted to know what was going on in my life or was I walking into the recent Sawyer who gave me the cold shoulder almost all the time." I admitted all at once.

Sawyer just looked down at me, taking in everything that I'd said to him. "I didn't know what to expect either," he started.

Immediately, I figured he wasn't going to respond to anything I said. I tried not to let the hurt feelings cross my face but I was sure that it was showing.

"I didn't know what to expect because before you left, I stopped knowing how to be around you. Avery, you went to college and came back as someone I didn't recognize." My expression quickly changed from hurt to confused at his words.

"You were always the girl with her nose stuck in a book, and I don't mean that in a bad way at all. When we were younger, you were like a little sister to me. But the older we got, the more I started looking at you differently. I stopped looking at you as a little sister and I didn't know how to handle it. It felt wrong, so I did the only thing I could think to do in order to stop the thoughts I was having about you. I pushed you away." He said.

My breath quickened just slightly, I wondered if he was trying to tell me that he also developed feelings for me.

"It went from looking at you as my little sister to looking at you and thinking about how much I wanted to kiss you and how much I wanted to go into your room when Callum wasn't home and screw you like there was no tomorrow. I had no idea how to handle anything and it was just easier for me to do that. But then you left and we stopped talking altogether. It helped, but then you came back and I saw you in a tee shirt and immediately, all I wanted to do was push you in the bedroom and take that stupid tee shirt off to see what it looked like underneath." He finished.

Now it was my turn to just look at him for a minute. I was taking in all of his words and trying to make sense of them. A part of me was frustrated by them, because it only made it that much harder for me to tell if he had emotional feelings for me or if everything was just physical for him. But it was also something I wasn't expecting him to say and it, in a way, excited me. It was strange hearing him say that he'd started looking at me differently even before I left for California, but it also stirred up a wave of excitement in my belly.

I sat up and switched positions so that I was sitting on his lap, my legs on either side of him. I rested my hands on his shoulders, still trying to process everything he said and think of what I wanted to say to him next.

"Can you say something? Literally anything?" He said with a light laugh. He seemed nervous, which was a new one for me. Sawyer didn't get nervous around me and it was kind of cute.

I leaned forward, pressing a light kiss to his lips before I pulled away. "So you thought I was hot before I left for California?" I said with a grin, trying to ease his nerves a little bit with a joke.

Sawyer laughed and I think in that moment, we were both breathing a sigh of relief. "That's what you got out of everything I just said?" He joked.

I shrugged my shoulders and giggled, "Yeah I went from being your nerdy little sister to someone that you wanted to have sex with. Go me." I started to laugh but quickly stopped when I'd realized what I had just said. "Ew okay no, don't put it that way that sounds super gross."

Sawyer laughed, a deep laugh that filled my entire body up with joy. "Yeah let's not word it like that ever again, that makes it sound absolutely disgusting and wrong."

My face was red with embarrassment, but I laughed it off. "Okay, let's try again. I went from being your best friends little nerdy sister to... well still your best friends little sister but a less nerdy version and hotter? I don't really know how to make that sound better when I sum it up... let's just stick to what you said."

Sawyer grinned and wrapped his arms around my waist, holding me close to him. "My best friends hot sister that I did have sex with, twice." He summed everything up with a smirk. "And maybe a third time?"

I couldn't help but smile when he used the word hot instead of little. I liked that a lot better. "Maybe, we'll see where the rest of the day goes." I grinned, repeating his words from this morning about whatever the heck this was.

Our whateveritscalledship. I guess that's still the name of it.

Sawyer caught on immediately and rolled his eyes before saying, "Are you mocking me?"

I gasped, "Me? Absolutely not. I'd never do such a thing."

Sawyer stood up from the couch, holding me to his waist as he did. My legs wrapped fully around him, my arms wrapping around his neck to hold myself up and steady. "We're going to go see where the day takes us." He smirked and started walking upstairs.

"Seems like you're putting a lot of pressure on the situation, I thought we weren't doing that?" I joked, taking a small dig at his immediate need to go upstairs and have sex.

Sawyer smirked, taking me into his room. "Oh you want to talk about putting a lot of pressure on something? Let's just see about that. I can put pressure on something for you." He said as he tossed me back onto his bed. His hand immediately made its way between my legs, pressing against my direct center over the leggings I had on.

"Fuck," I whined.

Sawyer wasn't lying. I was quick to find out just how much pressure he wanted to put on me and just where the day was going to take us.

Chapter 16

It had been a couple of days of staying with Sawyer without Callum and Dani around. Things had been going well, but they were still puzzling because I had no idea what we were. We'd been sleeping in his room together and we'd seen each other naked a ridiculous amount of times over the span of a few days. We made out a lot, in his room, in the kitchen, on the couch, literally every part of his house which made me feel that our relationship was more of a friends with benefits kind of thing.

But on the other side of things, he'd brought me coffee on his way home from work one day, I'd made him dinner one night, and we cuddled or held hands on the couch or in the car when we'd go somewhere. All of this was just making the emotional side of things that much more confusing.

I wanted to bring it up again, but it had only been a couple of days and I wasn't trying to freak him out about anything so I kept reminding myself that we were going with the flow and seeing what happened. We still had about a week and a half before Dani and Callum got home anyway. I think I wanted to fully soak up the time that I had with just the two of us a little longer because I had a feeling that things were going to change when the two of them came back home.

I wondered if everything would stop when they got back, if we'd have to be secretive about it, or if he'd tell Callum. I can just imagine the conversation...

"Hey! Welcome back from your honeymoon. How was it? Good? That's great, oh while you were gone I hooked up with your sister. Hope that's okay?"

I know that I made a big deal about being my own person and being more than Callum's little sister, but I did understand why it was a big deal to Sawyer. The thought of telling my brother about whatever this was was kind of horrifying. I had absolutely no idea if he'd be angry or if he'd be happy about it. Callum was a really nice guy, so a part of me thought that if he was upset, he wouldn't be upset for very long because he would just want the two of us to be happy, even if that meant it was uncomfortable for him.

I think it was just confusing for me after the conversation I had with Sawyer about him looking at me differently before I moved away. It did help me to make sense of the way he acted towards me though, he had no idea what to do with his feelings and so he thought it was best to push me away. I think that's why he'd been so back and forth after I got back home too. It was just a lot to take in and a lot to handle. We went from good friends, to distant friends, to gifting me something before I moved, to me putting that special gift in a box somewhere, to no contact, to coming home and being flirty, to rude jokes, to making out, to our confusing whateveritscalledship.

It was definitely a lot to take in and a lot to handle.

"You're thinking about something." Sawyer's voice broke me from my thoughts. I glanced over at him through the sunglasses that I was wearing. We were sitting on the beach, Sawyer was sporting a blue pair of swim trunks and a pair of sunglasses that covered his green eyes. I was sitting next to him in a red bikini. It wasn't crazy hot outside, it was actually the most comfortable sort of warm. The sun was out and it was honestly perfect Fourth of July weather.

"How'd you know?" I asked with a light laugh.

Sawyer chuckled. "You normally answer me when I ask you a question."

I stretched my arms over my head before I rolled over on the towel I was sitting on so that I was laying on my stomach. I crossed my arms and rested my cheek on them so that I was still looking at him. "Oh shoot, sorry. What was your question?"

"I was asking if you wanted to come to my game on Friday." He repeated himself.

Jesus, I totally zoned out on him. I'd forgotten we were even talking about his job.

God, I'm the worst.

It was things like that, him asking me to go watch one of his games, that made me question things even more. I feel like if he didn't like me then why would he ask me to come to his games? It made more sense that he would just tell me when it was going to end and when he would be home. But instead, he wanted me to come with him and it pulled at my heartstrings. Maybe I was reading into it too much and I was just making it a bigger deal than it actually was.

"Yeah! I would love that." I smiled in his direction. "How long have you been coaching them?" I asked him, curious about how he got into everything. I'd been wondering about this since we went to the grocery store and he told me that he was a soccer coach.

Sawyer watched me through his sunglasses. "This is my second season with them. I had been coaching a team with football; soccer was not the start of everything. I guess something happened with their old coach and they were kind of desperate for someone to step in. I had some extra time and thought it might be fun to try something new out, so here we are. I wasn't going to come back for the second season but the kids practically begged me to." He explained before I had the chance to ask him how he'd gotten started with it.

I listened to him explain everything. In a way, I kind of liked that he'd had a similar story with his job. It was definitely different circumstances, but in a way it was the same. "They must really like you if they were begging you to stay." I said with a giggle.

Sawyer laughed. "I guess so. It's definitely been an adventure."

"It's kind of fun watching you interact with them, at least from the last game that I went to. You're really good with kids. It's actually kind of cute." I complimented.

"Oh yeah? You think it's cute?" He grinned, his voice holding an ounce of humor.

I rolled my eyes. "Don't make me take it back." I joked. "It's just different, but it's fun to watch. So yes, I will definitely come to your game on Friday. Plus, you look really good in the soccer jersey. I think I might even like it better than your football jersey." I smirked.

Sawyer shook his head, turning his head back so it was facing forward. "I knew it. I knew that you had a thing for European football over American football."

"I knew it! I knew you were jealous!" I exclaimed. The last time we'd had this discussion was at the grocery store a couple days after

I got home. He'd claimed that he wasn't jealous of Jamie, but I had a feeling that he had been lying about it.

"Me? I don't get jealous." He said pointedly.

"Oh yeah? You're not jealous that I dated a footballer that wasn't you?" I joked, wanting to get a rise out of him.

"American football is better anyway." He shrugged.

I sat up, sitting up on my knees so I could look down at him. I raised my sunglasses over my head and said, "That tee shirt that you keep complimenting me in? Would it make you jealous if I told you it was Jamie's?" I was more than sure I was messing with fire, but I wanted to see how far I could take this before he actually showed me that he was jealous.

Sawyer's body visibly tensed, giving me all the confirmation that I needed. This time he sat up, turning to face me fully. He raised his sunglasses on his head to match mine and looked at me, his eyes growing a couple shades darker. "I wasn't kidding when I said I wanted to rip that tee shirt off of you. Wear it again and I'll do it for a couple different reasons." His voice sent chills down my spine.

He was jealous.

"I won't wear it again if you give me one of yours instead.." I bargained. There was a part of me that almost wanted to wear it again. I wanted to see what he would actually do if I did. But I was also a little nervous to do it. It was obvious that I wasn't as good at playing with fire as I thought I was.

"Maybe I'll let you take one tonight. But you might not even need one." The humor in his voice was gone and it was replaced with pure seduction.

I gasped, my face heating up from his words. All I could do was nod, not really sure what to say back to him.

I'd never in my life given Sawyer a reason to be jealous about anything in my life, it was always the other way around. Me being jealous of all the girls that actually grabbed his attention, me being jealous when he'd talk about a girl around Callum. It was a little strange knowing that I'd actually made him jealous. Even though the conversation had taken a turn in a direction that I hadn't necessarily been expecting, I kind of enjoyed that I had that effect on him.

We'd spent basically the entire day at the beach, talking about anything and everything. We'd taken the day to really catch up on how each of our lives were going, it felt like a conversation that we would have before things changed between the two of us and I was enjoying every second of it.

Sawyer had asked me a ton of questions about what it was actually like to live in California and I'd tried to hint at him that he would have to come experience it for himself. I wondered if he'd consider taking a trip out there, if he'd think about visiting me after I went back at the end of the summer. He didn't really give me much to work with when we spoke about it, so I quickly changed the focus back to him before I got too much in my own head about anything.

I'd thought about asking him about his mom, but I didn't want the conversation to take that sort of turn so I decided not to bring it up. I was still under the assumption that he would talk to me about it when he was ready to talk about it. I didn't want him to feel forced to talk to me about something that he didn't want to discuss.

The sun was quickly going down and the fireworks were starting to go off. Sawyer was still seated on his towel next to mine. We were both resting back on our arms, with our feet stretched in front of us. His foot kept knocking against mine, each time the small bit of contact made me smile. I liked this side of him, this playful side that didn't seem like he was worried about what was going on in anyone else's minds.

But that playful side was quick to disappear when someone said his name, grabbing both of our attention. Sawyer sat up, bringing his legs away from mine and looking up at the figure that was now in front of us. I also looked up to see who the voice belonged to.

Tyler McCowen was standing in front of us with a stupid grin on his face. I hadn't seen him in a couple of years. Actually, the last time I even remember talking to him was when he'd come over to my house with a couple other boys and made a comment about how I'd grown up.

"Good to see you again, Sawyer." He started before he turned his attention to me. "Always a pleasure to see you, Avery." He grinned.

I had no idea if Callum and Tyler were still friends or still kept up with each other, but I knew that they weren't close enough for Tyler to get a wedding invite. I was happy about that because I knew that if he'd been at the wedding that he would have tried to talk to me and that was honestly the last thing I wanted. Even just standing in front of Sawyer and I, I hated the way that he looked at me and I hated the tone of voice that he used when he spoke to me.

"Nice to see you." Was all I said back to him. I didn't care if Sawyer wanted to chat with him, but I definitely didn't feel like partaking in the conversation.

"So you two finally hanging out without the big brother? Did Sawyer finally break down Callum into letting you date one of his friends?" He said with little to no remorse.

My face heated up. I didn't know how to respond to the comment for a multitude of reasons. Sawyer and I weren't technically dating and for some reason, I was bothered by the comment that he'd made about Callum. It's not like I wasn't aware he'd told all of his friends I was off limits, but it was something about the way he'd said it that bothered me.

"I didn't break him down for anything. We aren't dating." Sawyer quickly shut him down. I glanced over at him. It's not that I was surprised that he'd confirmed we weren't together but I was taken back by how quickly it came out of his mouth and how serious he sounded about it.

"You're just watching fireworks together on what looks like a date?" Tyler egged him on, clearly wanting to poke a little further.

"Callum is on his honeymoon. That's why he's not here." I added with half of the confidence that Sawyer had shown. I shouldn't have said anything, I shouldn't have given him the satisfaction of us clearly trying to hide something from him.

"Oh man that makes it even better, sneaking around while the big brother isn't in town. Sawyer, come on man. We all knew you had a thing for her, but you can't date your best friend's little sister, right?" Tyler said.

I tensed at his words, because I knew they were going to have an effect on Sawyer and I was already dreading the aftermath. I knew that Callum was a big thought in Sawyer's mind and it was one of the biggest things that he was trying to navigate. Having an outside person confirm that he shouldn't date me because I was Callum's little sister was just going to make everything that much more confusing.

I couldn't help but notice he said we all knew you had a thing for her. I wanted to ask what that meant but I knew more than anything it was not the time to ask questions or continue the conversation.

"I said we aren't dating. Don't you have something better to do?" Sawyer's voice was sharp, clearly wanting to end the conversation.

I hate how uncomfortable the conversation was making me feel. I knew that I was going to want to bring this up to him later, but I also knew that he was going to want the exact opposite. He wasn't going to want to talk about it, he was going to want to pretend that it hadn't happened.

Tyler just laughed. "Lighten up, dude. I'm just fucking with you. You two have a good rest of your night on your not date." He said before turning around and walking away from us.

Neither Sawyer or I said anything for a few minutes after he walked away, I think we were both trying to figure out what to say to the other person. I was irritated because we'd had such a good day together and that small interaction made the entire night turn on its side. It was almost like we weren't allowed to have fun together, something was always stepping in the way.

"Can we just pretend that he never walked over here?" I finally spoke up. As much as I wanted to talk about it and ask him why he spit out the words we aren't dating so quickly, I knew it was best to just leave it alone right now. I looked over at Sawyer, who was now laying on his back staring up at the sky that was lighting up in different colors.

I watched as his chest rose and fell as he took in a deep breath. He still didn't say anything for another couple of minutes, which only made the anxiety in my body rise. Sawyer finally turned his head and looked over at me. I was ready for him to say yes, but he didn't. Instead he said, "I hope that I didn't hurt your feelings," which took me by surprise.

"What?"

Sawyer pushed himself off the towel so that he was standing on his feet. He held out his hand for me to take, so I did without question. Once I was standing in front of him, he pulled me closer to him, his arms around my waist. I almost wanted to look around to see if anyone was looking at us, but I kept my eyes on him.

"If I hurt your feelings or upset you, I didn't mean to. I know I was quick to shut Tyler down about us dating and I don't want you to get in your head about it or think that I'm completely and utterly against the idea of us being together. It's not totally out of the realm of possibilities, like we said we're just trying to navigate everything together and take things slow." He explained.

My eyes widened at his words. They really took me by surprise. The fact that he was explaining to me that being together was an actual possibility was something that I wasn't expecting. It still wasn't a definitive answer about what this was, but it immediately made me happier.

"It's okay. Like I said, let's just pretend he didn't come over here. I get it, he's annoying and you don't want to give him any sort of ideas that might get back to Callum before we can explain anything himself." I said softly. It was true, even though it had taken me by surprise how quickly he'd answered Tyler about us dating, I did understand. If this was going to evolve into anything then we needed to be the ones to tell Callum about it, not anyone else.

Sawyer glanced around us for a second before leaning down and softly pressing his lips to mine. The kiss didn't last long, but it was enough to make my heart swell. "Thank you for understanding. You're pretty awesome, Jones." He said after pulling away.

I grinned when he called me Jones. "I am pretty awesome, aren't I?" I joked, wanting to lighten the mood back up.

Sawyer immediately laughed, making me giggle. Sawyer turned us so that I was standing in front of him, his arms around my upper half to hold me close to him. I rested my head against his chest, tilting it up slightly so I could look at the sky. There were other people around us, but it was dark at this point and I think both of us just wanted to ignore the others and feel a little normal.

It was nice just standing there watching fireworks with Sawyers arms around me. It felt normal, like we were meant to be here together. I wanted to be able to feel this way with him all of the time. I really enjoyed it and I didn't want it to disappear.

Chapter 17

S awyer

Avery and I were standing off to the side of the counter, waiting on our coffee's to be ready for us to grab. I felt a weird sense of excitement that she was accompanying me to my game today. She'd mentioned to me that she'd liked watching me interact with the kids and I knew it would make her happy to watch it again today. Something about knowing that she was excited to watch the game and that she was happy to tag along, made me happy.

I'd overheard her on the phone last night talking to Larissa while I was upstairs. I didn't hear much of the conversation, but I did hear a small bit of it and I knew they were talking about me. Avery had been trying to keep her voice low and the volume on her phone was turned down, but her friend was loud even through the turned down volume. I heard a lot of I told you so's and I knew it's in a very short amount of time. I'd never met Larissa, but she didn't seem like the type Avery would normally be friends with so it was odd hearing things about her or listening to her talk to Avery. But I guess I didn't know Avery like I thought I did and she really is full of surprises.

I hadn't wanted to eavesdrop for long, so I'd walked down the stairs and into the living room where Avery was lying on the couch. The second she'd seen me walk into the room, she said a quick call you later and hung up the phone. I tried to bug her into telling me why she hung up so fast because I didn't mind that she wanted to talk to her friend, but she insisted that it was fine and that she'd call her later. I knew it was because I'd walked into the room, so I let it go and pretended that I hadn't heard them talking about us.

My phone buzzing in my pocket broke me from my thoughts. I pulled it out of my pocket and looked down at it to see who was calling me. "Your brother is calling, mind if I step outside?" I glanced at her.

She shook her head and gave me one of her perfect, soft smiles. "Go ahead, I'll wait for the coffee. Tell him I said hi!"

I nodded and walked out of the coffee shop. I didn't want to be that annoying person on the phone while people were trying to enjoy their morning coffee. As soon as I walked outside, I answered the phone with a quick hello.

"Hey man!" Callum's voice practically sang from the other end of the line. "How are things going? Just wanted to check in and make sure you and Aves haven't killed each other yet." He laughed.

Oh if only you knew.

I laughed. "We're both doing fine, no we haven't killed each other. We've actually been getting along quite nicely. Maybe you just need to leave us alone together more often." I half joked.

"Damn, I leave for my honeymoon and my best friend has re-placed me with my own sister. Ouch, dude." He joked right back. "But seriously, I'm glad that things are good. Is she doing okay?

Seriously? I figured she'd be trying to find a way to get back to California the second we left."

I ran my free hand through my hair before shaking my head, even though he couldn't see me. "I said I'd take care of her, didn't I? She's doing okay, I promise. She actually hasn't talked about going back early or anything, so don't worry she'll still be here when you get back." I said honestly.

I had promised Callum that I'd look after Avery while they were gone on their honeymoon because he always worries about her. However, I don't think what the two of us are doing together is what he meant by looking after her.

Callum breathed what seemed like a sigh of relief from the other end. "Okay good, you know I just worry about her. Thanks for letting her stay with you even while we're gone. Good news though, we heard back from the relator and we'll be moving into our place basically right after we get back, so you'll have the place back to yourself."

I know that I should be happy about that, but a part of me deflated because I knew it meant Avery would go with Callum and Dani and whatever this was between us would either be out in the open before we figure out what it is, or we'd put an end to it before either of us were ready to do that.

"Oh wow, dude that's awesome. I'm sure you and Dani are happy about that." I said, wanting to keep the focus on the two of them instead of myself and the confusing mess that I had made.

Avery walked out of the coffee shop seconds later with two coffee's in her hand. She handed one to me and motioned to my phone, mouthing a quick everything okay? I nodded in response to her. "Oh, Aves said to tell you hi by the way."

"Hi Ave!!" He practically shouted, causing me to pull the phone away from my ear. Avery started laughing, hearing her brother through the phone that wasn't even on speaker.

"Anyway, I won't keep you guys. I just wanted to check in." He spoke up again in a much more reasonable volume.

"Yeah, we have to get going. Got a soccer game to get too." I chuckled.

"Is she going with you?" Callum asked.

"Yeah." I said simply.

"Thanks for not letting her sit in the house alone. Good luck today! See you guys soon." Callum said before we said our good-byes and hung up. I shoved my phone back into my pocket before glancing at Avery again.

"What'd he want?" She asked before taking a sip of her iced coffee.

"Just checking in. Wanted to make sure we hadn't killed each other yet and that you weren't trying to sneak off to California before he got back." I answered honestly.

Avery rolled her eyes, but nodded. "He really thinks I'm going to leave without saying goodbye to him? That's pretty low."

I shrugged. "You didn't really want to stay here that long and you came home for him. He probably thinks you still don't want to be here and that it would be easier for you to get back if he wasn't right next to you begging him not to go back to California." I explained to her as I was sure that was exactly what was going through his mind.

Callum had told me on multiple occasions that he had been trying to convince Avery to come home for longer than a week when they were planning the wedding. When she'd finally agreed to spend the summer in Maine, it was like he'd won the lottery. He was so excited to spend the summer with his sister.

Avery looked at me for a minute, taking in my words. "You're probably right. But I would never do that to him."

"He's your brother, he just cares about you a lot. You know that."

Avery rolled her eyes again. "Yeah yeah, whatever. Anywaaay, Madison said to tell you that she knew this would happen." She said before she started laughing.

I looked at her, confused as to what the hell she was talking about. Madison who? "What the hell are you talking about? She knew what would happen?"

Avery still had a smile on her face as she motioned to the door of the coffee shop. "Your wonderful prom date. She said that she knew this," She motioned between the two of us, "would happen. She works here, she saw you standing with me and when you walked outside to talk to Callum she told me to tell you that."

Madison Yanky. Jesus, I hadn't thought about her in ages. I honestly forgot that she even worked here. "She said she knew this would happen? What does that even mean?" I asked.

I was still trying to figure out what this was between Avery and I so it felt bizarre for someone else to be commenting on it. First it was Tyler when we were down by the beach watching fireworks and now it was Madison, the girl I took to prom and hadn't thought about in years. I seriously needed to figure out what was going on between us before the entire town was talking about it and spreading rumors. The last thing I needed was for Callum to find out about this through someone that wasn't Avery or I.

Avery shrugged. "She actually asked me about you when I first got home, the first day we went grocery shopping together. She asked me if we ever ended up together and that she thought we'd make a cute couple." She stated as a matter of fact, like it wasn't a big deal. I guess it wasn't, this was just coming from some girl from high school, but it was still weird.

"Weird, my prom date telling another girl that she'd look cute dating me." I said with a chuckle.

"It's not like you guys ever dated, you just went to prom together." She said with a laugh. "You probably hooked up with her though, didn't you?" She asked, but I immediately saw on her face that she didn't want the real answer.

"We didn't date, no." I said, which was an answer without giving her an answer.

"Oh gross, you totally did." Her eyebrows furrowed and she was looking at me like it was gross that I'd slept with Madison. It's not like she didn't know that I had hooked up with a couple girls from school. It's not like I hooked up with everyone I dated, but it also wasn't a huge secret. She'd definitely overheard me talking to Callum about it.

I started laughing this time. "What? It's totally normal to hook up with your date after prom. That's what after parties are for." I said, without even thinking about it. The look on Avery's face immediately made me regret my idiotic choice of words. "Okay, wait I take it back. You know I didn't mean it like that."

Avery shook her head, "No it's okay. You're right, it is a normal thing." I could hear it in her voice that she was trying to really mean it, but I knew that my choice of words reminded her of what happened to her on her prom night.

"It's a normal thing for people that want to hook up. It's not a requirement and if people aren't into that kind of thing, it's fine." I said, trying to make sure she knew that I wasn't trying to say everyone needs to have sex after prom. I didn't want her to feel any sort of guilt for what happened to her because it wasn't at all her fault. She went with one of the biggest dickheads in her class and he definitely got the beating that he deserved after she told me what he'd done to her.

"Anyway. Still gross, I don't like hearing about all the girls you hooked up with." She said, trying to change the subject back to a lighter one.

I placed my hand on the small of her back and started to lead her back to my car so that we could head off to the soccer field. "It's not like this is the first time you're hearing about someone I slept with." I said honestly. Again, she definitely overheard Callum and I talking about girls. I spent a lot of time over at their house and I know for a fact that she heard multiple conversations between the two of us that she probably should not have heard.

"Just because I heard about it in the past, doesn't mean I enjoyed hearing about it. It's not really that fun when the guy you're---" She cut herself off quickly. "Nevermind."

I glanced down at her, my eyebrows raised. "The guy you're what?" I asked, even though I knew what she was going to say.

"No, nevermind. Forget I said anything." She tried to argue.

I shook my head. "No way, you have to tell me now."

Avery let out a loud, defeated groan. "It's not fun when the guy you're crushing on is always going on about the girls he's dating or sleeping with!" She admitted.

I fake gasped. "You had a crush on me?" I joked because it wasn't something that was a secret, even if she thought she hid it well. I'd known for a while that Avery had a crush on me, for a while there I thought it was cute but I also saw her as a little sister, so I never thought about it too hard. She was never creepy about it, so it never bothered me. It was only when I started looking at her differently that I started thinking about things too hard.

Avery shoved me away from me and started walking in front of me. "God, you're the worst. You know that?"

I laughed and quickly caught up to her, pulling her back into me. "Was that supposed to be a secret? Because you weren't very good at hiding it."

Avery huffed, "You were at my house all of the time, it becomes increasingly difficult to hide things from someone that you're constantly around. At least I don't become mean when I like someone!" She said pointedly.

Ouch.

That's what I get for admitting that I started looking at her differently which caused me to push myself away from her.

I deserved that.

"Okay, okay. I think that's enough of that conversation." I shook my head just as we reached my car. I pulled my keys out and unlocked it before opening the passenger door for her. "Truce?" I asked after she was in the car.

"Fine, truce." She huffed. I quickly leaned into the car and pecked her lips before I closed the door and walked around the other side so that I could get in. Once we were both settled, I backed out of the spot I was in and made my way to the soccer field.

The ride to the soccer fields was pretty short, Avery and I didn't hold much of a conversation. Each time I glanced over at her, I could tell she was sorting through her own thoughts. I wanted to ask her about it, but I wasn't sure if she'd want to talk about it. I was almost positive she was thinking about us and whatever we were, but we didn't have much time to dig into it. I told myself that I would talk to her about it after the game so I could see what was on her mind.

We arrived less than 10 minutes later, both of us hopping out of the car once it was parked. Avery grabbed her coffee as well as mine as I opened the trunk to get out a bag of extra soccer balls. I grabbed a couple more things before asking Avery to shut the trunk for me. She balanced the two coffees in one hand as she shut the trunk. I quickly thanked her and started walking to the field where the game would be played.

"You can sit by me if you don't want to sit by yourself." I said as we walked. She sat on the small bleachers the last game with Dani and Callum, but now that it was just her I wanted her to know she didn't have to sit by herself if she didn't want to.

"I don't want to be in the way." She said.

I shook my head. "It's not like this is a professional game, they're kids. Trust me, you won't be in the way. It's totally up to you though, you're welcome to sit over there. But if you get lonely, you are also welcome to move and sit over here with me." I said, wanting her to know that the option was there if she changed her mind later.

When we got to where we needed to be, I set the bag of extra soccer balls down as well as the couple other things that I brought. I was about to say something when I heard a small voice running up to us yelling, "coach!"

Both Avery and I looked over in the direction of the voice, even though I immediately knew who it belonged to. Michael ran over to the two of us, his bag that was far too big for him hanging off his shoulder.

"Hey Michael, you're here early." I said with a laugh. I took the coffee from Avery just as he got up to the two of us.

"Dad had to drop me off today, he can't stay but mom will be here in a little bit." He said slightly out of breath and with a smile. I felt bad, Michael's dad never stayed for his games. I'd never met the guy, he'd normally just drop him off and leave before Michael even got onto the field. "Can you help me warm up since no one else is here yet?"

I glanced at Avery and she nodded, letting me know that she didn't mind that he was taking me away. I smiled at her and set the coffee down after taking a drink. "Grab a ball and come with me." I said before walking over to the net.

"Is that your girlfriend?" Michael asked after he'd made his way over to me.

"What are you talking about?" I laughed.

"The girl with the coffee! She came to one of our other games. Is she your girlfriend? Is that why you can never come get ice cream with us?" He asked in the most innocent way.

I rolled my eyes, my hands on my hips as I stared down at him. "First of all, she's not the reason I can't go get ice cream with you. Second of all, no she's not my girlfriend. Third of all, mind your business kiddo." I was only joking at the last sentence and I knew that he'd know I didn't mean it. Even if you shouldn't have favorites, Michael was definitely a favorite of mine.

"Well, she's really pretty. So if she was your girlfriend, that would be cool. Maybe she can start bringing us snacks to the games. No one has done that in a while." He said before he kicked the ball towards me.

I loved the way his brain worked, he was such a kid. Everything was simple. He literally just said she was pretty so it would be cool if Avery was my girlfriend. No other context needed. She was pretty and she could bring snacks, it was that simple.

I quickly blocked the ball and tossed it back over to him, not wanting to let him have a score that easily.

"She is pretty, you're right, but she doesn't even live here anymore so she can't come to all the games." I said like it mattered to him. I had no idea why I was even feeding into Michael, maybe it was because he was young and didn't actually know our story, so none of his questions were coming from a place of judgment. Again, everything was simple for him.

"Where does she live?" He asked before kicking the ball again.

"California." I answered, catching the ball and tossing it back to him.

"Whoa! That's like... forever away." He said before pausing. "Well, you look less grumpy when she's next to you. So maybe you should ask her to stay." He continued and then kicked the ball. His comment threw me off guard, causing me to miss the ball. I turned and watched as it went in.

"Yes!" Michael exclaimed, proud that he'd kicked the ball into the net.

I grabbed the ball and tossed it back to him. "That's enough of that talk. What do you know? You're like... 7." I joked.

"Hey! I'm almost 11." He shot back.

"Same difference. Come on, keep practicing." I said with a shake of the head.

The game ended up in a loss, but the team wasn't too down about it. They played really well and that was something to celebrate, rather than beat themselves up. That was something I always want-ed to instill in each of them. All of the kids had left and I was just finishing packing up my things. Avery was next to me, helping me clean up a couple of things that the kids left behind.

"You're a good coach." She said, her voice soft.

I glanced over at her with a smile. "Thank you." I responded. "Michael said you were pretty." I said with a laugh, referring back to our conversation while he was warming up.

Avery laughed and shook her head. "He's a kid, what does he know about girls being pretty?"

I stepped closer to her, nudging her arm. "He's pretty smart for his age, he knows a pretty girl when he sees one. I'll have to give him that." I said. Now she was blushing and I was grinning at her red face. We finished packing everything up and she helped me carry everything back to the car. Just as I'd started the car, my phone started to ring through the bluetooth. I was going to ignore it when I saw that it was my dad. "Sorry, let me take this."

Avery nodded, "Go ahead."

I took the phone off bluetooth as I answered it, holding my phone to my ear. I wasn't sure what he was going to say and I didn't want it blasted through the car. "Hey dad."

"Hey son, how was the game?" He asked from the other side of the phone. His voice was quieter than normal, which instantly had me on edge.

"It was alright, we lost. Everything okay?" I asked, wanting to cut straight to the point.

"Everything's fine, but your mother would like to have dinner tomorrow." He said.

Shit.

I'd completely forgotten that I'd been trying to plan dinner with my parents.

"Yeah, that should be fine. Avery is still staying with me, is that okay that she's there?" I asked. I didn't think that they would care, but I had no idea if this was going to be a normal dinner or if this was going to be one of those dinners where they tell me that my mom was feeling worse than the last time I saw her.

I glanced over at Avery and she looked at me the second I said her name. Her eyebrows furrowed in confusion, but I just shook my head to try and let her know that it wasn't anything bad.

"Of course that's fine. How does 5:30 sound? She's got an appointment that afternoon, we should be done by then."

I nodded even though he couldn't see me. "5:30 is fine. I can have dinner ready then." I responded.

"We'll see you tomorrow, son. Love you."

"Love you both, see you tomorrow." I said before hanging up the phone. I looked at Avery again, her face still held confusion. "How do you feel about having dinner with my parents tomorrow?" I asked.

Avery's shoulders relaxed a bit as she nodded. "That sounds like fun. I can help you cook." She offered.

I immediately smiled at her. "Let's run to the grocery store and grab something to make." I reached over, placing my hand on her leg before I used my other hand to shift into reverse and back out of the spot to head to the store.

I was almost uneasy about having dinner with my parents and Avery. It felt like something that couples would do, but we still weren't technically a couple. Even though three different people in the past couple of days had asked us if we were indeed a couple. It somehow made everything in my brain that much more confusing and it was starting to drive me a little crazy.

I knew I needed to figure this out soon or I was going to drive myself mad.

Chapter 18

----

3 .5 years ago

My phone vibrated on my lap for a third time. I looked down at it, noticing it was Callum again. I'd texted him that I was in class, but by the third call my stomach had dropped and I knew something was wrong. I was in the back of the class, so it was easy to sneak out after gathering up my things.

By the time I was out of the classroom, the phone was ringing for a fourth time and then I really knew something was going on.

"Hello?" I said when I finally answered. Callum's breathing was erratic and immediately I sensed he was upset. "What's going on?" I asked.

"It's dad." Was all he said.

My heart dropped. "What's wrong with dad?"

Callum started to cry. He rarely cried. I rushed out of the building so I could make my way to my car.

"He had a heart attack, Ave."

I stopped walking, the world around me suddenly moving in slow motion. "Is he okay?"

What a stupid question.

"You need to come home.."

My eyes shot open, my chest rising and falling at a rapid pace. I must have finally fallen asleep. My room was bright, letting me know that the sun had fully come up. I had no idea what time it was. I'd heard Callum and Dani leave the house around 7 this morning. I was still awake when they left; afraid to close my eyes.

Every time I closed my eyes, I replayed the phone call between Callum and I when he told me about our dad. I could still clearly hear his voice as he spoke to me over the phone, I could perfectly hear the sound of him crying. I could still see the area that I was standing in when he told me dad had a heart attack and I could feel the way my knees buckled when he told me that I needed to come home. If I didn't wake up in time, I pictured myself sitting in the driver's seat of my car wailing and almost screaming in anger.

I couldn't get it out of my head no matter how hard I tried.

My body was exhausted from lack of sleep, I had bags under my eyes that looked like they'd been there for months. My hair was a mess, the funeral was 3 days ago and the only thing I'd done to it since was put it into a bun. I hadn't even brushed it.

I forced myself out of bed. Callum and Dani were gone, which meant I was finally alone and no one would ask me how I was doing. I was so sick of hearing the I'm so sorry's and the how are you holding up's.

I glanced at myself in the mirror, appalled by the reflection that stared back at me. I needed to take a shower today, but right now I didn't care. I had on the same gray hoodie that I'd had on for the past three days paired with some black sweatpants. I grabbed my glasses off the bed and slid them onto my face, my exhausted eyes not functioning properly to see without them.

I walked downstairs and into the kitchen, opening the fridge so I could see what kind of food we had. We had a bunch of leftover meals that people had brought over to us, the second my eyes laid on them I felt sick to my stomach and closed the fridge. I didn't want to eat anyone's sympathy meals.

"You're awake," A voice behind me caused me to practically jump out of my own skin.

When I turned around, I saw Sawyer standing there, a concerned look on his face. I had no idea he was even here.

"What are you doing here?" I asked, my voice slightly colder than I meant for it to be.

"Callum wanted to get out of the house, but he didn't want to leave you here alone. Asked me if I minded hanging out until he got back." He said honestly.

I wanted to roll my eyes, but I wasn't surprised that Callum didn't want me by myself. He was probably concerned with my behavior and just wanted to make sure someone was here if I needed any-thing.

"I'm fine, but thank you." I said, not wanting to force him to spend the day here if he didn't want to. I wasn't a little kid and I would be fine until my brother came back home.

"Callum probably won't be back until later and I know he doesn't want me to leave. We don't have to talk if you don't want to, I won't even ask you how you're doing. But I'm here if you want to talk." His voice was soft, like he was afraid of saying the wrong thing.

Sawyer hadn't said much to me the past couple of days. But it was different than how he'd been treating me for the last year or so. He didn't feel as cold as he had been feeling, he wasn't quite as distant even though he hadn't said much. The warmth was back but this time it was paired with pity that I didn't want from him.

I lifted my gaze to meet his and the second I did, I wanted to cry. I sucked in a breath and quickly looked away, not wanting my emotions to get the better of me right now. "Can we order some food or something? I don't want to eat anything here." I asked, even though this was my house and I could do whatever I wanted to.

"Yeah sure. I can order something, anything sound good?" He asked.

I shrugged. "Pizza?" It was easy and quick, it seemed like the best thing. I knew I probably wouldn't eat that much anyway. I just needed something in my stomach that was currently screaming at me to eat.

Sawyer pulled his phone out of his pocket and I glanced over at the stove, realizing I still had no idea what time it was. It was just after noon, so it seemed fine to order a pizza.

"I'm actually going to grab a quick shower." I announced.

He nodded, "Alright. I'll order this in a couple minutes. I'll wait downstairs if you need anything just let me know."

I quietly thanked him before shuffling back upstairs and into the bathroom. I shut the door behind me and turned on the shower, turning the water up to a decently hot temperature. I waited for the water to heat up before striping out of the 3 day old clothes I had on. Stepping into the shower, I winced slightly at the temperature but stood underneath it until my body adjusted.

The first couple showers I took after I found out about my dad, I would sit and try to scrub away the pain that I was feeling. It never worked, it just ended up with me on the shower floor in tears. Since the funeral, I couldn't even bring myself to care about showering.

I washed my hair before scrubbing my body down. I stood there for an extra couple minutes, trying to wrap my brain around everything that had happened the last week or so. I felt a little numb and I was almost afraid to tell anyone that. Callum was walking on egg shells around me and I hated it. I hated the uncertainty of everything. What was going to happen to this house? Where would I go when I wasn't in school? Did I even want to come back?

A part of me wanted to leave and never come back. I didn't want to be in this town anymore. I didn't want to come back and live in a house that didn't feel like mine. If Callum ever moved away, I'd have no one left and that idea was terrifying. I needed to leave before everyone else left me. Maybe I could look into schools out of state.

"And if you feel like you can't be a writer here, then pack it up and go be a writer somewhere else. Go to New York or California or something."

Sawyers' words suddenly played in my head. New York or California, maybe I could look into something like that.

I shook the thought out of my head, I didn't need to decide anything right now and I didn't want to make a rash decision. Turning off the water, I stepped out and wrapped a towel around my body. I walked out of the steaming bathroom and back into my room, shutting the door behind me.

Once I was back in the comfort of my bedroom, I changed into a pair of black leggings and a light blue tank top before squeezing the excess water out of my hair. I stood in front of my mirror and looked at the mess of hair in front of me. I didn't even know where to start, it was so tangled it almost hurt to look at.

After 5 minutes of aggressively yanking my hairbrush through my hair, I let out a frustrated groan and tossed the brush on the ground. "God damnit."

I placed my palms over my hand, sucking in a deep breath to try and calm myself down. There was literally no reason for me to get so upset about the tangles in my unbrushed hair, but at this very moment it was the most frustrating thing.

"Everything okay?" I heard Sawyer's voice so I dropped my hands and looked at him through the mirror. I hadn't even heard him come up the steps, but he must have heard me.

"I'm fine." I lied.

"You sure?" He asked with slight hesitation.

I threw my arms up in defeat. "I haven't brushed my hair in 3 days and it's been in a bun and now I can't fucking brush it. My arms are tired and I've been trying to brush this knot out for 5 minutes and I can't get it undone! I just keep brushing and brushing and brushing and it won't come out!" I exclaimed, tears pooling in my eyes.

Sawyer immediately rushed over to me, wrapping his arms around my waist and pulling me into him. "Hey, hey it's okay."

I buried my face into his chest, tears falling down my cheeks. I don't think I was crying about my hair, but at this point I didn't even know.

Sawyer held me against him for several minutes until my shoulders stopped shaking and I was just sniffling every couple of minutes. He pulled back slightly so he could look down at me before saying, "can I help you brush your hair? I can see if I can get the knot out."

I didn't know what else to do, so I nodded.

"Sit down on your bed. Let me see if I can help you." He said before he walked over to the hairbrush that was on the floor. I walked over and sat down on my bed, sitting with my legs crossed. Sawyer stood behind me and slowly started to run the brush through my hair. "Let me know if it hurts, yeah?"

I nodded, letting him know I would. He was a lot more gentle than I had been and my head was thankful for that. He took his time brushing through my hair in silence. My heart swelled at the kindness he was showing me right now. I was thankful that he wasn't giving me the cold shoulder still, but this felt like an entirely new Sawyer. He'd never offered to do anything like this before and I didn't know how to handle any of it.

He finished brushing through my hair about 10 minutes later. I turned around so I was facing him just as he set the brush down on the bed next to me. I looked up at him, meeting his softened gaze. "Thank you." I practically whispered.

Sawyer looked down at me, his eyes searching mine for something, but I didn't know what. "Anytime, Ave." He cleared his throat after a couple more seconds and motioned to the door. "Pizza should be here soon, wanna go downstairs?"

I stood up from the bed, standing directly in front of him. "Yeah, sure."

Sawyer nodded and gestured for me to go first. I walked out of my room and downstairs, finding a place on the sectional just in time for someone to knock at the door.

Sawyer and I both ate a couple slices of pizza. My stomach was incredibly thankful for finally giving it food, even if it wasn't the healthiest of choices. We were sitting on the sectional, Sawyer sitting next to me with his arms stretched over the back of the couch.

"I know that you're probably sick of people asking, so I'll only ask you one time and you can tell me to shut up if you want.. but seriously, how are you?" His voice was genuine and I knew that he was one of the people I could be honest with without him getting all weird or uncomfortable.

"Honest answer?" I asked.

Sawyer nodded.

"I'm sad and I'm confused and I'm exhausted and I'm starting to feel... numb. Numb to people asking me if I'm okay or telling me that they're sorry." I said honestly.

I'd run through almost every emotion possible since returning back home and it was one of the strangest things I'd ever experienced. I'd experienced so many moments of sadness and heartbreak thinking about all of the things I wouldn't get to do with my dad or all of the things that he would never get to see. I'd experienced moments of anger because I didn't understand why this had to happen to him. But I'd also experienced moments of joy, thinking and talking about the fun memories that I had with him.

I thought that I was going crazy. I even googled the grieving process just to confirm that I wasn't going crazy and that everything I was feeling was normal.

Sawyer looked at me and nodded. "You haven't been sleeping, have you?" He asked.

I shook my head. "Every time I fall asleep I replay the phone call with Callum. I wake up in a panic like it's happening all over again. It's just easier to stay awake, but I'm so fucking tired.." I sighed.

It was true, I was so afraid to go to sleep but my body was physically and mentally exhausted at this point. I wanted nothing more than to sleep for days on end, but I couldn't bring myself to do it.

"Would it help if you were sleeping with someone next to you?"
He asked.

His question confused me. "What do you mean?"

"You haven't really wanted to be around people, but sometimes
being alone intensifies feelings. Would it help if you tried to sleep
while someone was with you? That way if you start to have a bad
dream, either someone could wake you up or when you do wake up,
you're with someone and that might help calm you down."

I hadn't considered trying that, but it's not like I had anyone that
could just sit and watch me sleep. My brother had a million different
things that he had to take care of now and it's not like I had a
boyfriend I could cuddle up next to.

"Oh I mean, I.. I don't know. It might help, but I don't want someone to babysit me while I'm sleeping." I shrugged.

Sawyer chuckled. "Don't think of it like babysitting. If you want to
try and go to sleep, I'm not going anywhere."

"Oh, well thank you."

We talked for a little while longer, about the most random things.
We talked about my dad, we talked about school, we talked about
anything and everything before Sawyer turned on a movie. The
second the movie was turned on, my eyes got heavy. I was more than
sure that he did it on purpose, but I didn't mind.

My head bobbed, my eyes getting heavier by the second. It finally
fell to the side, meeting a warm, welcoming shoulder.

"She finally fell asleep and she's been asleep for a couple hours..
I know she hasn't been sleeping, I don't want to wake her." I faintly
heard a quiet voice.

"Are you sure? I don't want you to be stuck here all night." Callum?
Was that Callum's voice?

"Don't stress, I'm fine. Let her sleep. I'll stay."

"Thanks for keeping an eye on her today.." I definitely think that was Callum talking. He must be back home.

"You're welcome, man. Go get some rest."

The conversation faded out and I was brought back to a state of comfortable sleep.

"You need to come home.."

"You need to come home.."

"You need to.."

I gasped, my eyes shooting open again only this time I wasn't in bed. I was still on the couch, my head was on Sawyer's lap and there was a blanket over me.

I quickly sat up when I realized where I was laying, my heart beating so quickly I thought it was going to beat right out of my chest.

"Hey, hey you're okay! It's okay," Sawyer's voice rang in my ears. I looked over at him with wide eyes.

"I didn't mean to fall asleep on you, I'm so sorry." My voice was panicked, partially because of the dream and partially because I woke up with my head on his lap.

He shook his head, his tired eyes looking at me with sympathy. "It's okay, you fell asleep and I didn't want to wake you."

"I can go to my room, you can go home. I'm so sorry. I.. I'm sorry." I said again, feeling super awkward. The last thing I wanted was for him to feel uncomfortable and I was afraid that I'd done that by falling asleep on him.

Sawyer was quick to shut it down, pulling me into him again. "Hey, stop. It's okay, I don't mind. That's probably the first time you've really slept in days. If you're going to go to your room, I know you aren't going to go back to sleep. I'll stay the night, it's fine."

He was right, it was the first time I'd slept for more than probably an hour comfortably in days. I didn't want to go up to my room, but I didn't want him to feel like he absolutely had to stay with me.

"I don't want to make you stay.." I whispered.

"You're not making me do anything, Ave. I'm here for you, okay? I always have been and I always will be." His voice made my stomach do flips, pulling on my heartstrings more than he ever had before.

"Is it going to be totally weird if I lay on the couch with you though? I don't think I can sleep all night sitting up." He asked me.

Yes. It would be.

But please, god please do it anyway.

"Oh, uh no. I don't want you to be uncomfortable.." I said.

I sat up so Sawyer could lay down. Considering we were on a sectional, I was expecting him to lay on one part of it while I stretched out on another part. What I wasn't expecting was for him to lay on his side and hold out his arms for me.

Yes, definitely weird.

I hesitated before I shifted so I was laying on my side next to him, facing him. Sawyer's arms situated themselves around me, holding me against him.

"Is this okay?" He asked.

It was more than okay. I'd never in my life felt so comfortable before.

I glanced up at him as I nodded. "Yeah,"

"I promise I'm here if you have another dream. I'm not going anywhere." He whispered.

I closed my eyes, taking in both his words and his scent. We'd never been this close before, this intimate. It felt weird, but it felt so... right?

This should have been more uncomfortable than it actually was. I should have told him that he could lay down and that I would sit up or that I would lay on a different part of the couch. I should not have willingly crawled into his open arms to go back to sleep. But he held his arms out to me, so he wanted me here. Right? He wouldn't have done it if he didn't want me laying this close to him.

Our legs found themselves tangled together as I drifted back into a state of sleep, the feelings of sadness overcome by a feeling of relief being held by the one person that could make any pain go away.

Chapter 19

"Shit!" I heard Sawyer curse from downstairs just as I heard what sounded like a bunch of pans falling. I quickly finished applying mascara before rushing down the steps to the kitchen. I found him kneeling down, picking up a couple sheet pans.

"Are you okay?" I asked, quickly kneeling down next to him. He'd been stressed all day, but refused to tell me what was going on in his head. I had no idea if it was because of his parents or if it was because of me.

Sawyer stood up with the pans, placing them on the island with a small huff. "I'm fine."

I quickly grabbed his hands, forcing him to take a minute and look at me. "You're not fine. What's got you so stressed out? Do you not want me to have dinner with you? I can leave." I offered. If that's what was bugging him, then I'd rather him just have dinner with his parents and I could figure something else to do. If he let me borrow his car, I could go have dinner myself so that he could enjoy the night with his parents.

Sawyer quickly shook his head, taking in a deep breath. He held onto my hands, his grip a little tighter than normal. "No, don't leave. I want you here." He started. "I don't know, I always get anxious when I see them because it feels as though every time I see my mom she's worse than she was before. And what if she starts asking me questions about you? What am I supposed to tell her?"

I felt bad that he was anxious to see his own mom because she was sick. But I'm sure if I had to see either one of my parents like that, I would feel the same way.

However, another part of me was beginning to feel frustrated with his inability to just sit down and figure out whatever we were. I felt like we would both feel better about so many things if there was a label, at this point literally any sort of label would do. But he couldn't make up his mind or figure out what he wanted that to be, so we were both just walking around confused and a little frustrated by it.

"Hey, I know that it's hard to see your mom when she isn't doing well but it's important that you spend time with her. She loves you and she just wants to spend time with you. And if she asks you a question about this, we'll figure it out. Tell her we're taking it slow, laugh it off and remind her that I'm Callum's sister, I don't care. Whatever you need to tell her to help ease that anxiety off of you, I will go along with it." I was trying to help ease any of the anxiety that he was currently feeling.

As frustrating as this situation was becoming, I wasn't going to make things worse by telling him that he needed to figure everything out in the next 20 minutes before his parents showed up.

Sawyer pulled me into a hug, wrapping his arms tightly around me and holding me to his body. I could feel the anxiety radiating off of him and I wanted nothing more than to fix it in any way that I could.

"Why don't you go upstairs and get changed. I can finish dinner." I offered.

He pulled away just slightly so that he could look down on me. The look in his eyes filled me with something that I couldn't quite put my finger on. My heart swelled and I knew that I wanted him to look at me like that all of the time. He leaned down and pressed his lips gently against mine before muttering a thank you.

I smiled up at him when he pulled away from me. Sawyer pecked my lips again before walking out of the kitchen and upstairs to get himself changed. Once he was out of the kitchen, I reached into the freezer to pull out the garlic bread that we'd bought to go along with the pasta. I placed a couple pieces on the baking sheet before sliding it into the oven and setting a timer. I looked at the pasta that was sitting on the stove, it was almost done, everything just needed to mix together and warm back up. All of the food smelt delicious, it was making my already hungry stomach that much more hungry.

I stirred up the pasta before leaning back against the island and closing my eyes. I took in a deep breath trying to mentally prepare myself for the night ahead of me. It did feel a little weird, having dinner with Sawyer and his parents. This felt like something we would do if we were a couple, but I knew the only reason this was actually happening was because I was still staying at his house. I was more than positive that if Callum and Dani were in their own house and I was staying with them, I would not have been invited to eat with them.

I'd told Larissa about it this morning, because I was nervous myself but I was trying to hold it together. I couldn't decide if she'd made me feel better, because she just further watered the seed in my brain that Sawyer did want to be with me; he just didn't know how to do it. She kept telling me to just go for it and that Callum didn't seem like the type to be mad about something like that for very long. I knew deep down that she was right, but Sawyer wasn't ready to face that yet and I couldn't force him.

Dinner hadn't been going too bad, I'd stayed quiet most of the time just listening to Sawyer and his parents talk about different things. I'd seen his mom just a couple weeks ago at the wedding, but she somehow looked weaker than she did that day. I still wasn't sure exactly what was wrong with her, Sawyer didn't like to talk about her often or in many details. She was such a sweet woman, she always had been. His dad was pretty quiet, he seemed to just observe rather than engage in the conversation.

"Everything was really good, honey." Sawyer's mother spoke up again, looking over at him. His smile was gentle as he looked across the table at her.

"Thanks mom. Couldn't have done it without Ave though." He glanced over at me, keeping that gentle smile on his face. His hand that was under the table was resting on my leg, he gave me a small squeeze when he said my name.

I laughed and shook my head. "I didn't do much, Sawyer here did most of it." I said, glancing over at his mom. I really enjoyed watching the two of them talk. Even though he was incredibly anxious before she got here, he wasn't showing any of it now that she was in the room. His actions and words were so gentle when it came to her, partly because it was his mom and partly because it looked like he was afraid to be anything but gentle. Maybe he was afraid he would break her already fragile state.

Sawyer's mom smiled at the two of us. "You two are pretty cute."

"Mom," Sawyer muttered.

Here we go.

She shrugged, "Honey, I haven't seen you look this happy in so long. You look like you're at peace when you're sitting next to her. You danced at the wedding, when's the last time you danced with anyone?"

Whoa.

I could feel Sawyer's body tense next to me. He waited for a minute and I could tell he was trying to figure out what to say back to her. "Please don't make things weird." He laughed awkwardly. "We're taking things slow, figuring things out." He sounded a little unsure of himself and it made me a little uneasy.

"What's there to figure out? What's with you younger kids making everything so complicated." His dad joined in, forcing me to let out a breathy laugh.

"I think we're both trying to figure out what to tell Callum." I admitted, glancing up at Sawyer to make sure he was okay with me saying that. I wasn't trying to interfere or overstep, but I wanted to help him with the conversation if I could. I didn't want him to feel like he was alone in defending whatever it was that we were. He looked down at me with a soft smile before glancing back to his mom just as she started talking again.

"Are you afraid he'll be upset with you?" She asked, her eyes bouncing back and forth between Sawyer and I.

I let Sawyer answer the question, I wasn't sure what he wanted to say and what he didn't want to say. "Mom, Ave is his sister. What are we supposed to say to him? Welcome home from your honeymoon, by the way I started seeing your sister, don't be mad?"

I liked that Sawyer had such a good relationship with his mom that he was okay talking about this with her. It was almost like he wanted her advice and I really loved that.

She narrowed her eyes, giving him a look that even made me want to sink back into the chair. "You're thinking too hard about this. Callum is your best friend, is he not?"

"Uhh, yeah?"

"and he's your brother, who wants what is best for you. Is he not?" She said, shifting her focus to me.

I did sink back a little before I nodded. "He is, yes."

Sawyer's mom threw her arms in the air, "Then I don't see an issue. He wants what is best for both of you. I've gotten to know him pretty well over the years and I know that he loves both of you with his whole heart. If he's got a brain up there, even after all those years of football hits, then he'll say the exact same thing I did."

I had to look down at my lap to hide the smile that had formed on my face. She was sitting across from the two of us really just telling us both how it was and it was making me want to laugh. She was making things seem much less complicated than both of us were making it out to be.

"And what did you say, mom?" Sawyer asked. I could hear the humor in his voice.

"Finally!" She exclaimed.

This time, I really did laugh. Sawyer started laughing next to me and I could feel the tension freeing itself from him.

"Finally? Really?" He chuckled.

"Oh honey... A mother knows everything. My dear son, you've always looked after her and taken care of her. Sweet Avery, it's no secret that you had a little crush on him. It was just a matter of time until Sawyer realized the same thing." She said it like it was the most obvious thing in the entire world.

My face heated, embarrassment flooding into my cheeks.

"You got really grumpy after she moved away and since she's been home this summer, I can see the light coming back into your eyes." She smiled.

I couldn't help but notice that Sawyer's mom was the second person to say that his mood had changed since I'd returned back home. The morning of the wedding when I was doing Dani's makeup, she basically told me the same thing.

"Okay, I think we can change the subject now." Sawyer said, shaking his head and ignoring his moms comment.

The rest of the evening with his parents went well, I helped Sawyer clean up the table after we'd finished eating before we sat in the living room and continued talking for a little while longer. Sawyer's mom went on about how much she missed the house and how she loved that Sawyer had kept it basically the same.

It made a lot more sense that Sawyer had kept the place the same, he did for his mom. He didn't do it because he didn't care or because he was lazy and didn't feel like it. He kept the house the same because he knew how much this place meant to his mom and he wanted it to still feel like her house.

I was standing in the kitchen, washing some of the dishes when his mom walked into the room. Her movements were slow, she had a hand on her lower stomach like it was bothering her.

"I just came in to say goodbye." She said with a gentle voice.

I turned off the sink and quickly dried my hands with a towel. "It was so nice to see you again." I smiled at her.

"It's always a pleasure getting to see you." She leaned against the island, glancing over at me. "Do me a favor, will you?" She asked.

I nodded, "Of course."

I had no idea what she was about to say to me, but I was willing to do almost anything for this woman.

"Cut him some slack. Callum is important to him. They've been together for so much and I know he's afraid of upsetting him. But I can see how important you are to him too. I can see it in the way he looks at you and the way that he acts around you. Just be patient with him, please." She said softly.

I listened to Sawyer's mom speak, taking in her words. I was frustrated with Sawyer, but listening to his mom somehow lessened the frustrations. I already knew that Sawyer was afraid of talking to Callum, but her words helped to not second guess his actual feelings so much.

"Thank you. I know that Callum is important to him, he's important to me too. We're just trying to figure out what to say to him or how to tell him." I agreed.

"You're good for him, Avery. Please don't forget that." She said before taking a step closer and pulling me into a hug. "You two take care of each other." She whispered just before she pulled away.

I hated the way that she said take care of each other, but I had to force myself not to think too much of it. "Thank you. Hopefully I'll get to see you again before I go back." I smiled at her.

The way she looked at me left a heavy pit in my stomach, but she nodded and walked out of the kitchen. I followed her into the living room so that I could say goodbye to Sawyer's dad, but he wasn't in the room.

"Dad's outside, let me help you to the car." Sawyer said to his mom.

I watched the two of them for a moment before walking back into the kitchen so I could finish the dishes.

I had finished the dishes by the time Sawyer was walking back inside and into the kitchen. I turned around to dry my hands to find him standing in front of me. He immediately wrapped me into a hug.

"Sawyer, my hands are wet!" I laughed.

"I don't care." He mumbled, squeezing me tight against him. I wrapped my arms around him, resting my head against him.

"Thank you for today." He said, resting his cheek against my head.

"Why are you thanking me? I didn't do anything special."

Sawyer let out a small sigh. "You did though. Thank you for helping me make dinner and calming me down about everything. I know that my head has been all over the place, but I really do appreciate you helping me relax about everything. And even when my mom was nagging us both, you helped me get through it without getting upset." He spoke his thoughts to me.

I pulled away just slightly so that I could look at him. "Hey, you know I'm happy to help. I get it, this whole thing is a lot and it's just adding onto the stress you're feeling about your mom. I'm trying--" He quickly cut me off mid sentence.

"Hey no, wait. Before you keep going, it's not adding stress onto anything. You aren't doing anything that's stressing me out and if I'm making you feel like you are, I'm sorry. If anything, it's probably the other way around. I'm probably stressing you out."

I shook my head. "No it's okay. I get it, it's a lot and it's confusing and I know Callum is in the back of both of our heads. It's fine. I just want you to know that whatever I can do to make things easier for you, please let me know and I will. I know you were stressed out this morning and I hate seeing you like that, so let me help you where I can." I said.

"Come on." He said before taking my hand and pulling me into the living room. "Come lay with me." He let go of my hand and laid down on the sofa before holding out his arms as an invitation.

I giggled before climbing onto the couch and into his arms, snuggling into him. We'd been doing quite a bit of snuggling since this whole thing started, but this felt different. This was the silent comforting kind of snuggling. We laid like this after my dad died and I couldn't sleep. He held me, his embrace reminding me that he was there for me and that I was going to get through everything. Obviously, his mom was still here but this felt similar. Laying here with our arms wrapped around each other, but this time it was me reminding him that he was going to get through all of this with his mom and that I was right here for him.

"I like this." I said after a couple minutes of silent snuggles.

"You like snuggling on a tiny couch?" He asked with a light chuckle.

"I mean, yes actually. This is comfortable. It's like we can just lay here for hours and not say a word, but we're both comfortable and happy doing so." I admitted. "It's different than cuddling in bed."

Sawyer nodded, seeming to understand what I was trying to say. "It is different, but it is comfortable." He said.

I closed my eyes before I started to speak to him. "Remember when you held me after my dad died? It's like that. It was weird, because we'd never been that close before but it was the first time I felt like things would be okay after he died. You didn't have to say anything to me, you just let me know that you'd be there if I woke up again and you held me all night. It was the first time since he died that I didn't wake up in the morning because of that dream. Your arms were still around me and I just felt... safe." I voiced my thoughts for the first time to him. I'd never told anyone how that night made me feel, it was a thought that I didn't feel like needed to be shared with anyone until this moment.

Sawyer moved one of the arms that was around me, moving his hand to my face. He lifted my chin before saying, "open your eyes." When I did, he started to speak again. "You never told me that before."

I searched his eyes, trying to figure out what I wanted to say next. "I don't know.. Maybe I was afraid too. That day, I'd started thinking about moving away. I knew the house was going to sell and I couldn't just live with Callum. I went back to school, started looking into things a little more, and by the time we all came back into town again things were weird between us again. Time had passed and I was afraid to bring it up again because we barely spoke, so I left it alone and then I was gone."

Sawyer sighed, his face falling a bit. "I really am sorry. I'm sorry that I made you feel that way."

I shook my head, "Don't, it's okay." I didn't want the conversation to turn that way, so I quickly steered it back in its previous direction. "Regardless of what was said and what wasn't, my point is that it made me feel comforted and it made me feel safe. And I'm forever grateful for that, so yes this is different than cuddling in bed."

He moved a strand of hair from my face before putting his arms back around me. "It makes me feel safe too." He said quietly.

I didn't speak right away, wanting to give him time to elaborate if he wanted to. "My heads been spinning in a million different directions non-stop for a while now. You came home and it started spinning in a million and one directions. But I don't mean that in a bad way. I just feel like I don't know how to turn anything off, but this... this helps turn everything off. My head feels quiet for the first time in a long time."

I listened to his confession, my heart swelling three sizes. I wrapped my arms tighter around him, giving him a squeeze. I didn't know how to respond to him, but I knew that I didn't need to right away. I felt his arms tighten around me just slightly and I knew that right now all that was needed was that silent comfort.

I loved knowing that I could help his thoughts quiet down, even if it wasn't for long. I knew exactly how he was feeling, so I liked knowing we were both able to do that for each other.

The feelings that I had for him when I was younger were growing stronger by the day. Neither one of us knew what to do about the situation, but it was more than obvious that we both had feelings for each other. It was just a matter of properly navigating them. But that didn't matter right now, what mattered was lying here in Sawyer's arms, comforting him the same way that he's able to comfort me and silently reminding each other that we were both there for one another, no matter what.

Chapter 20

Sawyer

Dani and Callum were returning from their honeymoon tomorrow and I couldn't help but feel nervous about everything. I knew they'd be moving into their house in a couple days and a part of me didn't want Avery to go with them. I wasn't sure what things were going to look like with them being back, but I knew that if she stayed with me, at least we'd still be able to spend some time alone without looking suspicious. I knew she was going to hate the fact that I was basically asking to sneak around. I hated it too. We were far too old for things like that, but I couldn't help it.

My head was a mess, trying to figure everything out. The more time I spent with Avery, the more I found myself wanting her to stay in Maine. I didn't want her to go back to California, I wanted to keep her here and I wanted to figure things out with her.

I kept going through different scenarios in my head, trying to figure out how to navigate things and how to talk to Callum about this entire situation. Every time I got anywhere, I'd talk myself out of it. I couldn't even understand why, I had no idea what I was so afraid of. Was I that afraid of pissing off my best friend? Was I that afraid of trying things with Avery because I was afraid of what would happen if things didn't work out? Was I afraid of dragging her into my own personal issues? It's not even like I had that many things wrong with my life. It was just that the biggest thing wrong with my life was my mom and she was quite literally the most important person in my life. All of my focus had been on her for so long, that I was almost afraid if I stopped focusing on her that things would take a turn for the worst.

I knew she was frustrated. I was also frustrated. I was so in my head about everything that at this point, I had no idea how to even get out of it. My thoughts were spiraling and I'd never in my life felt this way about anyone. All of the girls that I'd ever dated or hooked up with in the past had been easy. They were easy relationships and maybe that's part of the reason they didn't work out, they were too easy.

With Avery, things aren't quite as simple. I've got more going on now that she's trying to come back into my life and her brother is an entirely new level of discomfort and complications. It's not that I didn't want to work on it, I just felt like I'd never had to put this much thought into things before and now that I did, I couldn't get a single thought in order.

I think that's why a part of me had been keeping things mostly physical, at least in conversation. That was the part that was easy for me. It was easy for me to talk to her about sex because it was easy to keep that surface level. But I knew that I couldn't keep doing that, I knew sooner or later she was going to want a deeper conversation.

I kept going back to the conversation I had with her on the couch after we had dinner with my parents. She voiced her thoughts to me and I voiced my own right back. I told her exactly what was going on in my head and I told her that she helped make all the noise in my head stop. That was probably the most I'd talked about my feelings in a while and it felt strange. I liked it, but it also made me uncomfortable. I liked being open with her, but I was also afraid to be that open again. I was afraid to let her in on everything because I'd never been that open with anyone and what if I said the wrong thing?

Things used to be so easy for Avery and I. When I saw her as a little sister, I never questioned anything that we ever spoke about. I always wanted to know everything that was going on in her life and she always wanted to know everything that was going on in mine. We talked to each other all the time, we joked about things, things were never complicated. Of course, the second I stopped knowing how to be around her I made things complicated between us. Now I never know what I'm even going to say to her. I still feel that pulling in both directions. The part of me that wants to joke around with her and have fun. The part of me that wants to listen to her talk for hours on end about anything and everything.

Then there was the part of me that felt like I needed to put a barrier between us. Things had picked up so quickly after Callum and Dani went on their honeymoon and there was that part of me that was nervous by it all. That little voice in my head was telling me that I needed to take a step away from her because this was wrong.

But then there was a new part of me... one that was surfacing more and fighting more with the part that wanted to distance myself from her. That part of me was stronger than the friendship part of me wanting to have fun and make her laugh. It was the one that had my heart beating faster each time I looked at her. It was the part of me that melted each time I held her hand or kissed her.

That third part was the part of me that I didn't understand.

I loved spending time with her. I loved having her stay with me. I loved listening to the sound of her voice and the sound of her laughter. I loved the way her body felt against mine, both in bed and out. I loved the way that she made me feel. She made me feel confident in myself, she made me feel like the old Sawyer. The Sawyer I was when my mom was healthy and I didn't worry so much about things. I loved that she could sense when I was stressed out or anxious and immediately stepped in to help calm me down.

So why was all of this so confusing? Why was I so conflicted? Shouldn't this be easy? My parents ended up together with no issues. When Callum meant Dani, there were no second thoughts in his mind and she was it for him almost immediately.

I hated that I couldn't figure out what to do about Callum. It's not like Callum was a bad or mean person. I couldn't even justify it myself as to why I was so afraid to talk to him about anything. I think a part of it was that I couldn't even get my own thoughts in order, so what was I supposed to tell him?

Hey Callum, I've been seeing your sister but I have no idea what to do about it because I can't decide if I love her or if I want to distance myself from her because things are just too complicated right now.

Love.

Whoa.

There was no way that the things I was starting to feel for Avery was love. There was no way that things would be this complicated if it was love. That's not what love is supposed to feel like, right?

How could I even love her and start something with her a month before she is due to go back to California? What the hell would that even look like for us? If we were going to figure something like that out, I would need to talk to Avery about more than just sex because our relationship clearly couldn't be physical if she was on the literal opposite end of the country.

Fuck me.

My mom was right the other day though. She mentioned that I looked happier and even at peace when I was next to Avery. I do feel happier being around her and she actually does bring a sense of peace that I haven't felt in a very long time.

So why was all of this so confusing for me?

Why couldn't I make sense of any of this?

Chapter 21

Dani and I were sitting on the couch, waiting for Sawyer and Callum to return back home from picking up pizza. Dani and Callum were back from their honeymoon and I know it was only a matter of time before Dani fired a bunch of questions my way. When they first got home, they were the ones getting questions fired at them. I'd been so excited to hear all about their trip and they were both excited to share their adventures with us. They'd brought us both home a little gift, even though there was no reason for them to do it but the gesture was incredibly sweet.

Dinner came around and Sawyer offered to go pick up a couple pizza's for us. Callum, having not seen his best friend in a couple of weeks, said he'd tag along. Sawyer looked slightly nervous to go, but he agreed and the two of them left about 15 minutes ago. I tried to continue asking Dani questions, trying to get her to show me more pictures to keep the focus on her rather than myself.

"So are you going to tell me why Sawyer looked like he was going to throw up when Callum said he'd go with him to get pizza?" Dani asked as she scrolled through the pictures on her phone.

"I have no idea what you're talking about." I lied.

Dani put her phone down, narrowing her eyes at me. "You're so lying. What is he hiding from your brother?"

I scooted away from her, resting back on the sofa. "Who said he's hiding anything?" I asked, not wanting to give into her even though I knew that she knew something was up.

"Callum may not have noticed it, but he's a boy. I'm not, he's been tense since we got back and the second he was able to get out of the house he was excited. Callum mentioned coming with him and he looked like a deer in the headlights." She said with a laugh. "So let me ask again, what is he hiding from your brother?"

I folded my arms, trying to decide the best way to go about telling her everything. "What isn't he hiding..." I started with a small laugh.

Dani waited for me to elaborate, but I didn't right away. "Did you have sex with him?"

I didn't answer.

"You did! How many times? When did it start?!" She exclaimed, firing off the questions exactly like I expected her to.

"Uhhh, I mean like.. we fooled around after you guys had your makeshift bachelor and bachelorette parties... but uhh, we had sex... the night of your wedding?" I confessed with less confidence than I had when I spoke to Larissa about everything.

Dani's eyes went wide. "First of all, you messed around with him before my wedding and you didn't tell me?!"

I shrugged. "You were occupied with the wedding, didn't think it was the right time."

She rolled her eyes. "Ugh. So you hooked up after the wedding. Was that it? Was it just that one time? Are you dating now?" She questioned.

I ran a hand through my hair, unsure of how to answer her question. "No, that was not it. We hooked up.... multiple times while you guys were gone." I said with a breathy laugh. That part was the easy part to talk about, it seemed to be the only thing that wasn't confusing. Sawyer was pretty vocal with me about his want to hook up, it was anything past that which left me in a puddle of confusion.

"But no, we aren't dating. I really don't know what we are." I revealed.

"What do you mean? Are you like friends with benefits or something?" She asked me.

I let out a small groan. I actually hated that term and I didn't want to be considered friends with benefits with Sawyer, but at this moment in time that was precisely what we were. We hadn't really spoken about what our relationship was past the physical part of it. I knew that he told me there was a possibility of us dating, but we really hadn't discussed anything further.

"Dani, I don't know. He basically said he didn't want to put pressure on anything and just wanted to figure it out slowly. Then he told me that dating was not out of the realm of possibilities. But we're both sort of afraid of talking to Callum, I think he is more so than me but it's been a thought in my head too. That's why he was weird about getting into the car with him, he's probably afraid he's going to slip up and accidentally tell him something." I blurted out all at once.

Dani sort of paused, seemingly taking in everything that I was saying to her. With her not adding anything in, I took the opportunity to continue my rant.

"I'll be honest, it's been frustrating. I thought that I was over Sawyer and that I wasn't crushing on him anymore, but spending so much time with him and doing all of the things that we've done... I know that I'm not. Snuggling with him at night and holding his hand? It's things like that, god it's been so amazing. Sometimes he gives me this look that screams to me that he feels the same way... But then when I finally feel like we're getting somewhere, he takes it back to focus on the physical side of things." I huffed.

"I can only imagine how frustrating that has to be for you. It's sort of like you're dating without him being fully able to commit to it." She responded, taking the words out of my mouth.

"Dani, that's not even all of it! He confessed that he started looking at me differently after I graduated from high school. That was what, 5 years ago? That's why he became so distant, he had no idea what to do with his thoughts so he just pushed me away. Then while you were gone, we had dinner with his parents. His mom went on and on about how happy he looked when he was with me and how she hadn't seen him so at peace in so long!" I was almost yelling at this point, just trying to release the pent up frustration I was having about all of this.

I had no idea how much of this I was truly supposed to be sharing with her, but I'd already told Larissa about it so I didn't think it mattered to tell Dani too. I needed her advice considering she actually knew Sawyer and Larissa didn't.

She didn't say anything for a minute, she looked like she was trying to figure out how to navigate the situation or figure out what to say. I was glad that it wasn't just me struggling with how to deal with the situation.

"So he definitely has feelings for you." She finally said after a couple of minutes of silence.

I lifted my gaze to meet hers, waiting for her to elaborate on her short but meaningful sentence.

"He definitely likes you, he just doesn't know what to do about it. That's probably why he's trying to keep things on the physical side and less on the emotional side. He's clearly enjoying the sex, I mean who doesn't enjoy that." She started with a light laugh.

"But he's letting you have dinner with his parents. He took you to one of his soccer games and he even admitted that he started looking at you different years ago, long before you came back this summer. It seems to me like he's getting too in his head about Callum and the idea of Callum being upset with him. He needs to get over that and admit his feelings to you. Once he does that, he needs to talk to your brother." She finished like the solution was simple.

I listened to my sister in law speak, taking in her words. They were essentially the same words that I'd been telling myself, only when it came from her it sounded so much easier. I was afraid to talk to Sawyer about any of this because I was afraid that doing so would cause him to push himself away from me again. I was almost okay with stringing myself along with him simply because I was afraid of what would happen if I said anything that might change it.

"I have no idea how to talk to him about this though. What if I piss him off and he just gives up? Dani, I'm terrified that if I say something, he's going to mention that I'm going back to California at the end of the summer anyway and that it would be better to just call everything off. He's going to realize it's not worth it putting this much energy into us because I'm just going to leave in a month." I voice my thoughts and my fears to her, realizing that I'd been holding them in.

I know it sounded bad, but I was afraid if I reminded Sawyer that I was leaving he was going to realize that whatever this was between us wasn't worth it to him. That it wasn't worth him being afraid to talk to my brother.

Dani sighed, reaching over and placing her hand on my leg. "Say he wants to call things off before you move, would you rather him do it now and get it out of the way or would you rather him wait until right before you go back and string you along for another month."

She brought up a good point. If he ended things now, things would feel a bit awkward for the rest of the time that I was home but at least I would be done with it and it would clear up the confusion. If I waited, I'd get more time with him and I'd get more time to possibly figure things out but it would hurt more if it came to an end anyway. Although, I knew that no matter what I was going to be heartbroken regardless if he decided to call it quits.

"I don't want him to call things off at all. It doesn't matter when he does it, I'm going to be heartbroken." I confessed my spiraling thoughts out loud.

"I came home thinking that my feelings for him were gone. When I got here and saw him, I thought that I probably just thought that he was still hot. It's not like that's such a bad thing... but the feelings are definitely still there and with every single little thing that he does, they come barreling out that much stronger. If he tells me that this isn't worth it then I'm going to be crushed."

"Avery, you need to talk to him. You need to figure out what exactly is going on inside his head. If all of this confusion is just because of Callum, I can try to help you figure out a way to talk to him about it. I really don't think that Callum is going to be mad at either one of you, but especially not you. He's going to be more upset that you both spent the last couple of weeks thinking that you couldn't talk to him than he would be upset that the two of you are together." Dani said as she gave my leg a comforting squeeze.

"Can you talk to him for me?" I half joked.

"If he doesn't get his shit together after you talk, then I will talk to him." She laughed.

I rolled my eyes but laughed. "Deal."

The four of us were seated in the living room, Dani and I were on the couch sitting behind Callum and Sawyer who were on the floor playing a video game. I didn't know why they were on the floor and I hadn't intended on sitting behind Sawyer, but Dani practically made me. She claimed she wanted to sit next to me so that she could show me pictures, even though she'd basically shown me everything earlier. Callum hadn't questioned it, but I could see how tense Sawyer's shoulders were. Every now and then I'd knock into him with my leg or nudge him with my arm, but he didn't really pay me much attention.

I tried not to think too much about it, I knew he was doing it because of Callum. It was just a little difficult going from snuggling and holding hands to Sawyer barely looking at me. It almost felt like the distant Sawyer from before I moved away, the one who barely spoke to me and the one I didn't know how to be around.

"Sooo, Ave what are we doing for your birthday?" Callum spoke up, glancing back at me quickly before looking back at the game he was playing on the tv.

"What?" I asked.

"Your birthday is next Friday! I haven't been able to celebrate a birthday with you in three years and it's on a Friday, we're absolutely doing something." He said it like it was obvious.

I'd honestly been so caught up in everything else that I'd forgotten about my own birthday. I was going to tell him that we didn't have to do anything, but I didn't feel like putting up an argument with him. "We can go out. I don't really care what we do." I said.

"Wanna go back to that club we went to after you first got home?" Callum asked.

I hesitated just slightly before saying, "Uhh yeah, sure we can do that. That sounds like fun."

I thought back to the night that the four of us went out to the club. That was the night that Sawyer pulled me off to the side to dance with me. It was the first time he kissed me. My breath caught in my throat just thinking about it.

I wondered what it would look like, going with them again. Would we tell Callum by then? Would Sawyer dance with me again or would we just awkwardly stand there all night, even though he made it a point to tell me we weren't doing that the first time we went. The last time it worked out because we were there to celebrate Callum and Dani. That made it easy for us to separate from them and find a spot alone amongst the crowd. If we were going for my birthday, I knew it wasn't going to be as easy.

"Don't sound too excited." He laughed. "Sawyer, you down to come? Shit, you guys have spent so much time together lately, feels like you have to come with."

Both Sawyer and I tensed this time, immediately overthinking his comment. What did the two of them talk about in the car? Did he tell him something that I didn't know about?

"What are you talking about?" I asked for Sawyer, wondering what he meant.

"What? I mean you've been staying with him since you got home. I know that we normally hang out all together but somehow you two managed to survive a couple of weeks without me and it wasn't totally weird or without killing each other. I don't know about you, but I think that deserves a celebration." He said with a laugh, completely oblivious.

Sawyer relaxed a little bit. He leaned back into the couch, discreetly leaning against my leg.

I sucked in a breath at his touch. It was the first time he'd initiated any sort of touch today and my body reacted to it right away.

"Yeah, sounds like fun." He said, his voice relaxed.

"Sweet."

The boys played games for a couple of hours while Dani and I sat behind them and watched. The four of us talked the entire time, catching up on random different things. Sawyer mentioned that we had seen Tyler on the Fourth of July, obviously leaving out all of the comments that he'd made and the fact that we'd been there on what felt like a date. Callum went on about how cool it was that he was a married man and joked that he couldn't wait to be in Sawyer's wedding.

"Who says that you're going to be in my wedding?" Sawyer joked.

"So you do actually plan on getting married one day?" Callum practically gasped.

"What the fuck does that mean? Why'd you say it like that?" Sawyer grumbled.

Callum glanced over at him, looking at him like he was dumb. "When's the last time you had a girlfriend? I haven't seen you with a girl in ages. Don't look at me like I'm crazy for being surprised that you want to get married."

I shifted uncomfortably in my seat behind Sawyer. I had no idea just where this conversation was going to go, but I was already slightly uncomfortable with where it was.

Sawyer spoke up again, "Just because I haven't dated a girl in a while doesn't automatically mean that I never want to get married."

"When's the last time you slept with a girl?" My brother asked with little to no remorse.

Now my face was bright red and I was actually uncomfortable. I had no idea if Sawyer was going to be honest with him and tell my brother that he'd slept with someone in the last couple of days or if he was going to lie.

Sawyer chuckled, a very breathy chuckle. "Honest answer?" He asked, glancing over at Callum.

Callum glanced over at him and nodded. "Honest answer, even if it's been a couple months dude. I won't judge."

They had this.. guy best friend look on both of their faces, it almost made me laugh.

"Two days ago." He said, completely honest and open.

My eyes went wide, practically bursting out of their sockets. I glanced over at Dani, whose facial expression basically matched mine.

Callum paused the game, throwing his controller on the ground. "You're fucking with me right now." He turned his body to face Sawyer, wanting all the details. Even though, he most definitely didn't want any of them.

"I'm not." He shrugged.

"Who the fuck with?!" Callum practically exclaimed.

Now it was Sawyer's turn to set his controller down and turn his body so that he was looking at my brother. His body was still leaning against my leg, his subtle touch being the only thing comforting me. He got himself into this conversation and I wondered how he was going to answer the string of questions coming from Callum.

"Just this girl." He answered briefly.

"Do I know her?" My brother questioned.

"Maybe." Sawyer replied.

If only you knew, Callum.

"Are you still seeing her?" Callum asked.

I glanced down at Sawyer, wondering what his answer to this question would be. Was he still seeing me now that Callum was back?

"Hoping so." He answered, leaning just slightly further into me.

I looked away from the two of them, trying to hide my smile from the boys.

"Why the fuck didn't you tell me about this before?! What the hell, dude."

Sawyer shrugged and chuckled a bit. "Just trying to see where things go." He, again, answered honestly. If only my brother knew the real meaning behind these statements that Sawyer was making.

"Well damn dude. I hope everything works out. You deserve it." He said before standing up and stretching his arms out. "But I'm exhausted, so I think I'm ready for bed." He yawned as he looked down at Dani.

"Me too. Night guys." She said as she stood up from the couch. She smiled at Sawyer and I before the married couple walked down to the basement. I saw her smile, but I also didn't miss the subtle look that she gave me before she walked away.

Sawyer waited until the basement door was shut before he stood out and reached out his hand to me. I took it and he pulled me off of the sofa. We shut off the lights and walked upstairs together. I wondered if we'd go back to sleeping in separate rooms or if we'd still share one, it's not like Callum or Dani came all the way upstairs for anything.

Sawyer didn't say anything as we walked upstairs, so I took it as a sign he was unsure of what to do and I walked towards the guest bedroom.

"If you're more comfortable sleeping in separate rooms now, we can." I offered, standing in front of the door.

He was still holding my hand and I could tell his mind was bouncing between thoughts. He reached behind me and twisted the doorknob before pushing the door open, still not saying anything. I was expecting him to tell my goodnight, but instead he took a step forward, forcing me to take a step back into the room. When I realized what he was doing, I backed up until I was standing fully in the room. Sawyer followed and gently shut the door behind me.

He wasn't saying anything at all, so I said the first thing that I could think of in an attempt to break the ice. "So that girl that you had sex with two days ago, you're hoping you can still see her?"

Sawyer's eyes darkened a bit before he nodded. "I am." He responded simply.

"For sex or are you looking to get married?" I asked with a smile, hoping he would get that I was just joking and wasn't trying to make this a serious conversation.

"Definitely for sex, but you know..We're still kind of seeing where things take us." He said. The way he said it was different than the other times he'd said it and it almost made my heart skip a beat.

"Are you trying to see her tonight?" I asked, my voice lowering just slightly.

Sawyer's lips turned into a smirk. "If she'll let me." His voice lowered into that sexy, slightly raspy voice he gets when he's horny.

I threw my arms around his neck. "Oh she'll let you." I leaned up and pressed my lips to his, wanting nothing more than to feel him against me.

Sawyer walked us backwards until we were both on the bed. He was hovered over top of me, his hands exploring every inch of my body like it had been too long since he'd last touched it. His lips moved from mine and down to my neck, trailing kisses along until he found my sweet spot.

I let out a small gasp, one of my hands finding the back of his head and holding it to my neck. I whimpered when I felt his teeth nip the spot. He'd barely touched me and my body felt like it was on fire. I wasn't sure if it was his comments or the fact that we were once again having to sneak around like teenagers afraid of getting caught by their parents.

Sawyer slipped his hand under the tee shirt I was wearing, moving his hand up and dragging the shirt along with him. He pulled away from my neck so he could pull the shirt over my head. The second it was off, his lips were against my skin again.

He pressed his sweat pant covered hips against mine, earning another gasp from me. My hips moved on their own, wanting to feel him against me in any possible way.

"Someone's eager tonight." He said with a raspy chuckle. "What if I want to take my time with you tonight?" He grinned.

"Please, Sawyer.." I whispered, not wanting him to take his time.

He shook his head and kissed all over my chest, lowering himself to kiss down my stomach. When he reached my hips, he pulled down the sleep shorts I had on, leaving me in my bra and underwear.

He lifted his hand, touching me over the fabric. I gasped, everything about his touch feeling so amplified for some reason.

He teased me for a couple minutes, just barely touching me over the fabric of my underwear. I moved my hips, trying to get more from him.

"Okay babe, okay. Relax." He whispered, hooking his fingers into my underwear and pulling them down. Before I had a chance to think about begging him for more, I felt the warmth of his tongue against me. Immediately I tossed my head back against the pillow, my lips parting in pleasure.

God I loved when he called me babe.

My hips had a mind of their own, bucking up to try and get closer to him. One of his hands pressed down on it, holding it to the mattress. The other one snuck down, two of his fingers sliding in with ease.

I squeezed my eyes shut, one of my hands settling in his hair while the other covered my mouth. I bit down on the back of my hand, whining into it. His tongue and fingers worked together, moving at the perfect speeds. He'd speed up every couple of minutes, earning muffled whines from me. Every time my breathing would pick up, he'd slow back down. It was driving me crazy.

I cried out into my hand, my back arching slightly off the bed. "Sawyer.. Sawyer.." I whimpered, feeling myself losing it. My grip on his hair tightened, my legs started to shake as they tried to close around his head.

I bit down on the back of my hand, not hard enough to hurt but hard enough that I knew it would leave a mark just as I felt myself fall off that cliff and letting the pleasure fill my body.

My shaky legs relaxed after a couple seconds, my chest rising and falling as I tried to catch my breath. I loosened the grip I had on his hair as I felt him pull away from me. He pulled his shirt over his head before climbing up so he was hovering directly over me again.

"You're beautiful." He mumbled before lowering himself down and pressing his lips against mine.

I loved the feel of him pressed against me, I loved the way it felt when he touched me. This time around was different than the others. Not only because I was forced to be quiet, but he took his time with all of his movements. Everything was slow and intentional, it made everything feel a million times better.

I loved everything about it.

I think I loved him.

Chapter 22

My eyes fluttered open at the sound of a knock on the bedroom door. I was dead asleep and didn't realize what was going on until I heard a voice from the other side of the door.

"Sis! I'm back with the moving van, we're going to start bringing boxes out so we can get this done as quickly as we can!" I heard my brother's voice.

What?

I rubbed my eyes and shifted to sit up when I felt a pair of arms around my waist.

Fuck.

"Aves? You awake?" He called out, knocking again.

Fuck. Fuck. Fuck.

"Sawyer, Sawyer wake up." I whispered in a slight panic, shoving his arms off of me. Sawyer shifted on the bed, groaning. "Shut up!" I whispered.

Sawyer rubbed his tired eyes, looking at me with confusion.

"Aves! Come on sis, I promise I'll buy you food later!" Callum groaned.

Sawyer's eyes immediately widened after hearing my brother's voice on the other side of the door. We both knew we'd be helping them move today, we'd spent the last couple of days since they'd been back helping them pack up their things. Sawyer and I had agreed we'd either not share a room last night or we'd get up early enough to not have something like this happen, but here we were.

"You have to move." I whispered to Sawyer. "Go... in the closet or something!" I shoved him again, his tired body not catching itself which landed him on the floor with a thud.

"Avery, you okay?!" Callum questioned, his voice going from annoyed to concerned.

My eyes immediately moved to the door when the knob started twisting. My eyes widened in panic, throwing my legs over the bed. I stood up just as the door opened up, revealing my concerned brother.

I stood by the bed, looking over at him as he stood in the open doorway.

Fuck me. This is not how I wanted this day to start.

"Did you just fall?" he asked.

My eyebrows scrunched in confusion. Sawyer was lying on the ground by the bed and he was asking me about falling?

"Did you hit your head or something? Seriously, are you good?" He asked again, staring directly at me.

"I'm good?" I said, confused.

"Uhh, okay. Well anyway, I just got back with the moving van. We're going to start loading stuff into it. We shouldn't have to make too many trips, so I'm hoping it won't take all day. Hurry up and get dressed, I'm going to go make sure Sawyer is awake." His voice still held confusion and concern. But the second he mentioned getting Sawyer, I panicked.

"No!" I called out a little too quickly. "No, I just mean I can go get him. Go start carrying some of the heavier boxes upstairs so Dani and I don't have to." I tried to defuse my panicked state with the first excuse that I could think of to get Callum to walk downstairs.

"Yeah sure, I'll do all the hard work by myself." He rolled his eyes.

I folded my arms. "Do you want my help or not?" I asked, bringing out my annoying sister card because I knew he wouldn't question it.

"Jesus, okay. Just hurry up." He said before turning around and walking out of the bedroom, closing the door behind him. When I heard his footsteps run down the steps, I climbed on the bed so I could peak on the other side.

"Sawyer?" I asked, confused when I didn't see him. Sawyer poked his head out from under the bed, earning a small shriek from me. "Fuck!" I groaned.

"Think he saw me?" He asked with a light chuckle.

"No I don't." I replied with a roll of my eyes as I got off of the bed.

I shuffled over to the desk, sorting through some clothes that I had folded and placed on top of it. I grabbed a pair of leggings and a cropped tee shirt so that I could wear something comfortable to help my brother move into his new home.

"Damn, hottie." Sawyer said with a grin as I changed out of my pajamas and into the chosen outfit.

"Shut up and go change." I shoved him to the door after I was changed. Before he opened the door, he leaned down and pressed a light kiss to my lips.

"Not going to do that all day, so a quick one before we go downstairs." He grinned, filling my belly with butterflies. He pecked my lips again before pulling the door open. He peaked out before quickly going into his room.

I waited a minute before I shuffled downstairs. I didn't see Callum right away, but I saw the front door open and Dani walking inside.

She glanced at me and immediately grinned. "Sawyer was in your room, wasn't he?" She asked immediately.

My jaw dropped and I looked behind me to see is Sawyer was behind me. "What the fuck?" I asked with a laugh.

"Callum said he couldn't get you up and you were being weird when he walked in. Sawyer was hiding wasn't he?" She asked with a smirk.

I started to respond to her but Callum walked through the open front door seconds later, not giving me a chance to. My face must have given it away because she mumbled a quiet knew it right before walking back downstairs to the basement.

Callum saw the quick interaction which caused him to give me yet another confused look before he shook his head and motioned for me to follow him to the basement. I walked downstairs after him, letting him know that Sawyer was awake and would be down after he changed.

When I reached the basement, I saw all the boxes that we'd packed up over the last couple of days. There were some furniture pieces that the boys had taken apart and needed to be moved. I had no idea what the actual plan was today, but it looked like they'd started moving the boxes first so that's where I started as well.

I reached the top of the steps with a box in my hand when I saw Sawyer in a pair of sweatpants and a tee shirt. It was amazing that he made the most simple outfits look good. He looked behind me for a second before looking back at me and winking as I walked past him to go outside. I bit down on my bottom lip, trying to hide a smile as I made my way to the moving van.

We'd spent the entire morning and part of the afternoon moving Dani and Callum into their new house. The house was really cute and I couldn't wait to see what it looked like once they were completely moved in and everything was decorated.

Callum and Sawyer were in the master bedroom putting together the bed frame so the married couple didn't have to spend another night on a mattress on the floor. Dani and I were in the kitchen, unpacking a couple boxes of kitchen things.

"Do you know if you're going to come stay with us here?" She questioned.

I glanced over at her as I unwrapped a couple of plates. I hadn't thought about it much because I hadn't actually spoken to anyone about it. I was positive that Callum would bring it up and I'd end up bringing all of my belongings over here. It didn't make much sense for me to stay with Sawyer without my brother. I was honestly surprised that no one had brought it up until now.

"To be honest, I have no idea. Callum hasn't said anything to me, but he might assume that I'm going to come over here. I mean, if I do, at least I can help you unpack while I'm still in town." I voiced my thoughts to her.

"Do you want to stay with Sawyer?" She asked, lowering her voice just slightly. Even though the boys were in another room, it was a one story house and we weren't trying to be loud.

I shrugged as I thought about my answer. "I wouldn't be mad about it, obviously. If I stayed with him then we wouldn't have to sneak around so much. But I have no idea how that would go over.

Would Callum think it was weird if I wanted to stay with Sawyer without him?"

I almost wondered if Callum was at all suspicious of anything between the two of us. It's not like we were actively doing anything in front of him, but we'd had a couple small moments in the last couple of days that made him look at one of us weird. I was sure this would be another one of those moments.

"I'm sure you could come up with an excuse that he wouldn't question. If anything, just tell him that our house is a mess and we don't have a guest bed yet, so you would have to sleep on an air mattress or the couch." She suggested a couple of excuses that I could use to help fool my brother into letting me stay with his best friend.

"I mean it also depends on what Sawyer wants, if he doesn't want me to stay over there anymore then I'm not going to." I muttered.

Dani laughed, rolling her eyes as she unwrapped a glass cup. "He definitely is not going to say that. You guys have been sharing a room still, so I'd say he will be happy to do that without having to worry about it."

I paused mid unwrap of another plate. "What are you talking about?" I asked, trying to act like I didn't know what she was going on about.

"Oh please. I told you this morning I knew he was in your room, which just means that you've still been sharing a room." She stated as a matter of fact.

I was about to try and give her any sort of excuse that I could when I heard the boys making their way into the kitchen. I was almost thankful for their interruption because I couldn't think of anything to say back to Dani. She knew that Sawyer was in the room with me and I couldn't think of an excuse to try and deny it. Instead, I stopped walking and unwrapped a couple of bowls, putting them into their assigned cabinets.

"Hey sis, were you planning on staying with us for the rest of your trip?" My brother asked, directing his attention to me when he walked into the kitchen. It was almost like he knew we were just talking about it.

My eyes bounced between the two boys who were leaning against opposite walls. I wanted to see the look on Sawyer's face. I wanted to know what he was thinking but I couldn't read his expression as quickly as I wanted to, which left me very little to work with.

"I actually hadn't thought much about it." I said honestly. It was also my way of giving myself a tiny bit more time to think of an actual answer. I knew he was going to want one before the end of the night.

"I actually forgot to buy an air mattress. Things have been so busy getting things ready to move, it slipped my mind. But I can go out and buy one tomorrow, you can sleep on the couch tonight. I know it's not really the most comfortable, but we can make it work." He offered.

I was about to speak up again when Sawyer started talking, drawing my attention back to him.

"You can stay at my place if you want to." He said, focusing his attention on me. I could tell there was an underlying meaning there. He couldn't just come out and announce that he wanted me to stay with him instead of my brother, so instead he was voicing it in a way that was more of a polite offer.

"Oh, I don't want to be a bother." I shook my head, trying to make it seem like I actually didn't want to be a bother to him. Both Sawyer and I knew that was a lie though. It was only so that my brother didn't question anything.

"Yeah dude, I know that we've been a lot and you haven't had the place to yourself in a while. I don't want to ask you to house any of us any longer." Callum's older brother voice came out, speaking for me like I was a kid that needed to be babysat.

Sawyer folded his arms over his chest as he shook his head. "At this point, I'm pretty used to all of you being in my house. It's probably going to feel weird when everyone's gone. It's really not a bother."

He shifted his attention from my brother back over to me. "Seriously, all of your stuff is already unpacked and at my house. Seems a bit pointless for you to pack it all up to come here, unpack it, just to pack it right back in a couple of weeks when you go back to California."

I hated the fact that he'd brought up the fact that I was leaving in just a couple of weeks, but I knew he didn't mean anything bad by it.

"Plus, our house is a total mess with unpacking and having an actual mattress is way more comfortable than an air mattress." Dani added, trying to help me out.

I glanced over at Callum and shrugged. "I mean, they both have a point. I'm fine with staying over there if that's okay."

Callum's eyes bounced between Sawyer and I for a minute before he spoke up again. "Are you sure? I seriously don't want to be a bother and I don't want either one of you to feel weird staying together even though I'm back."

"We managed just fine while you were on your honeymoon. I think we can manage for a little while longer." Sawyer chuckled. He sent a quick glance my way with the tiniest smirk on his face, if you weren't paying attention you would have missed it.

"Plus, it's not like we won't hang out. Let's be honest, we'll probably still end up spending more time together than apart." I laughed. "I already told Dani that I would help you guys unpack and we've got my birthday in a couple of days. But Sawyer is right, we managed just fine while you were away. I think we'll be fine now." I finished with a smile.

Callum ran a hand through his hair but nodded. "Okay, okay. If both of you are sure that you're okay with it. But you know if you want to come over here, you absolutely can at any time."

"I'm not a kid, Callum. I think I'll be okay." I laughed.

Callum rolled his eyes. "I know you're not a kid, Ave. I just want to make sure that you're comfortable and okay."

Sawyer pushed his body off of the wall and walked up to me, slinging his arm around my shoulders. My eyes widened for a split second before he rubbed the top of my head with his knuckles. The second I felt his knuckles touch my head my eyes narrowed as I went to shove him off of me. He tightened his grip on my shoulders so that I couldn't push him away.

"You know she'll be fine with me, Callum. I'll take good care of her." His voice was full of humor, but both of us knew that statement was another double meaning one.

Callum immediately started to laugh, easing my nerves almost instantly. "I'm so happy that you two are getting along with out me. This is literally my dream, my best friend and my little sister." He said with a laugh.

My shoulders tensed at his comment and Sawyer stopped rubbing my head, taking his arm from around my shoulders.

"We have always gotten along. What are you even talking about?" I asked, even though I knew there was a period of time where we actually didn't get along at all.

"You know what I mean! You always wanted to hang out with us when we were younger. I had a feeling that you had a crush on Sawyer and that's why you always wanted to tag along." He started.

"Then you went off to college and got all cool. You stopped wanting to hang out with us. Then you moved across the country. Sawyer was going through some shit and I really didn't know what to expect this summer. But my point is, I'm glad that you two are getting along okay and things feel normal again." He voiced all of his thoughts at once.

I'd say I was surprised that Callum mentioned me having a crush on Sawyer, but at this point it's been brought up so many times that I couldn't be surprised. I really did not hide it as well as I thought I did, even Callum had picked up on it.

I was also, in a way, glad that none of us knew what to expect going into this summer. I thought I was the only one coming into things a little lost, but it turns out all three of us were feeling the exact same way.

"Oh my god, Jones. You had a crush on me?" Sawyer gasped, once again acting like he had no idea.

"Ahh come on, don't act like we didn't talk about it." Callum grinned.

This surprised me.

"Excuse me?" I narrowed my eyes at both of them, hating the fact that the two of them had talked about me crushing on Sawyer.

"Ahh, okay Callum is right. We did talk about it a couple times. No need to be embarrassed though, we're all adults. It's okay that you had a crush on me when we were younger." Sawyer joked.

"Yeah sis. We're just giving you shit. It was a long time ago, I think enough time has passed that we can make jokes about it now." My brother chuckled.

"Exactly. It was a long time ago. Why are we still talking about it?" I folded my arms and groaned. Even though I had to pretend like it was indeed a long time ago and not going on right now, I was annoyed that we were talking about it. The idea of Sawyer and Callum talking about me having a crush on him was so embarrassing for my younger self.

"I think it's sweet that you had a crush on Sawyer." Dani added in, immediately causing me to shoot her daggers. "Come on, you can't tell me you two wouldn't have made a cute couple." She said with zero remorse.

Oh. My. God.

I stiffened again and this time, I felt Sawyer stiffen next to me.

"Sawyer and Avery, a couple?" Callum asked.

When I glanced in his direction, he was looking between Sawyer and I like he was trying to imagine it. I absolutely hated the anxiety I felt waiting on him to vocalize his thoughts about it.

"Weird," was all he said.

Weird.

"Weird?" I asked, wanting clarification.

He shrugged his shoulders, his eyes still bouncing between the two of us as he said, "My best friend and my little sister. Yes, a bit weird."

I had no clue if he meant weird in a bad way or just... weird. I was afraid to ask him for any more clarification though because I honestly wanted the conversation to be done with.

I felt the immediate tension between Sawyer and I. I was already afraid to have to deal with that later today. I decided not to ask any other questions or further the conversation and instead, turned around to continue unpacking the box that I'd been working on before the boys walked into the room.

The rest of the evening was spent unpacking boxes until all four of us were exhausted. Sawyer and I asked the two of them where they wanted certain things, but that was really the most I spoke. I was lost in my own thoughts after the conversation in the kitchen. I had so many questions and so many things I wanted to say, but I had no idea how to go about anything and I knew that I needed to talk to Sawyer privately before I did anything else.

Before Sawyer and I said our goodbyes to Dani and Callum, I let them know that I would come back and help them unpack whenever they wanted me to. We also finalized our plans for my birthday.

The ride back to Sawyer's house was quiet, almost too quiet for comfort. I think we were both in our own heads about the conversation, trying to dissect it and figure out what Callum meant when he said weird. It went from joking around to uncomfortable with one, tiny word.

I had no idea what was going to happen between Sawyer and I now. We were both a little on edge with Callum back home anyway. But now that we both knew that he thought the idea of us being together was weird...

Now things were weird.

Chapter 23

Happy birthday to me.

Nothing about this night was going according to plan. The look in Sawyer's eyes and his actions towards me were two completely different things. The look in his eyes told me that he liked the way I looked, that he thought I looked good. He liked the black skirt that I had on and he liked the lacy top that gave him a view of what I knew he was enjoying looking at. However, his actions weren't at all matching that.

He'd been much less vocal today. When he told me that I looked good, it was barely above a whisper before he walked past me and downstairs to meet my brother so we could head out. I was feeling much less confident in myself. On my birthday of all days. I was feeling like the two of us were backtracking to the Sawyer that didn't want to talk to me, the distant Sawyer that made me walk around on eggshells.

It all started when we got back from Dani and Callum's house, the night that the two of us helped them move in. Ever since Callum made that comment about us being weird, he'd been incredibly distant from me. We were still sharing a room and he'd even still kiss me, but things felt uncomfortable and I felt incredibly uneasy about everything.

Things felt weird.

I let it go at first. I was more than sure that he was just trying to figure things out in his own head. I know that after Callum made his comment, I got in my own head about it so I was more than positive Sawyer was doing the exact same thing. I had expected to talk about it with him, but he wouldn't bring it up and I was honestly afraid to.

We were slowly going back to not knowing how to be around each other. The only difference now was that it hurt a lot more than it did before. When he did it after I graduated, it hurt but more than anything I was just confused. I chalked it up to him getting older and being busy. Now, after everything that had happened between us I was just hurt.

I just hated how quickly everything took a turn. It happened because of one little comment and now there was so much distance between the two of us that it was actually a little scary.

I thought that today would be different, it was my birthday after all. I thought that maybe he would get out of his head and just enjoy the day with me. We weren't supposed to be hanging out with anyone until the evening, so I thought that the morning would be better at least. I was wrong in every sense of the word.

He was acting the same, if not worse today. He wasn't just distant today, he was cold. He didn't even actually tell me happy birthday. He'd spent the entire day busying himself and basically ignoring me so I really shouldn't have been so surprised when he'd brushed past me with a whisper of a compliment before we left the house.

I put a lot of effort into the way I looked tonight and I shouldn't have. I thought that maybe it would grab his attention, but half way through doing my makeup I was mad at myself for even thinking like that. I shouldn't have spent my birthday getting ready so that I had a chance of him telling me I looked good. I should have done it so that I could feel good on my special day. I should have done it for myself, but instead I was spending the entire day getting ready in hopes that it would give him something to talk to me about for more than five seconds.

There was not a single ounce of me that wanted to be out with everyone at a club. I wanted to be curled up in bed by myself. Dani had tried to talk to me about everything before we left Sawyer's house, but I brushed it off. I didn't want to go into details about anything, especially not as we were trying to leave his house.

We were standing by the car, waiting on the shots that Callum had ordered for everyone. The vibes were definitely off tonight and I was more than positive everyone noticed. Sawyer was leaning against the bar with his back to me, my brother leaning back next to him. Dani nudged my arm, grabbing my attention.

"You sure you're okay?" She asked, loud enough so that I could hear her over the music but quiet enough that it was just for me.

"I have no idea. It's my birthday and you'd think we were at someone's funeral." I groaned. My eyes glanced over at Sawyer briefly before they bounced back over to her.

"Want me to talk to him?" She offered.

I had no idea what good that would do. If anything, it would probably just upset him. I assumed that if Dani talked to Sawyer, he would be mad at me for talking to her about whatever it was that we were. But at this point, I was willing to do anything to get him to talk to me.

"And tell him what? To stop being a dick?" I asked with a light laugh.

Dani shook her head. "I don't have to tell him I know anything if you don't want me to. I can just pull him to the side and ask him if he's okay because he's acting weird. That's not a lie, he is being extra quiet tonight."

I contemplated for a minute if I really wanted her to try and talk to him. "If you really want to try and talk to him then go for it. Maybe you'll be able to get something out of him. He's pretty much been like this all week, I haven't been able to get him to talk to me about anything."

The boys turned around moments later, shots in their hands. Dani and I stopped our conversation as Callum handed me one of the shots. The three of us raised the shots up, Dani raising her plastic cup full of soda.

My fingers grazed Sawyer's, forcing my eyes to look in his direction.

"To the birthday girl! Cheers to 24!" Callum said.

"To me," I smiled.

"Cheers to 24!" Dani said with excitement.

"Cheers." Sawyer grumbled, barely loud enough to hear over the music. His eyes met mine for a split second before he looked away and downed his shot.

I quickly tossed mine back and reached between the boys to set my empty cup down on the bar just as Dani spoke up.

"Birthday girl needs about three more of those!" She grinned. "She's not drunk yet and she needs to be. Baby, order her a couple more please."

Callum laughed at his wife before he looked over at me for confirmation. I quickly nodded, almost wanting to beg him for more alcohol just so that I could get drunk and forget about everything that was going on.

"You got it." He chuckled before turning around to face the bar.

"Sawyer, can I talk to you?" Dani asked, turning her attention to him.

He shot her a confused look, but shrugged and nodded silently letting her know that they could talk somewhere. She motioned for him to follow him before the two of them walked away from the bar, leaving me alone with my brother. I quickly scooted into Sawyer's previous spot and leaned against the bar, facing Callum who was talking to the bartender.

"You okay? You don't look happy." He asked after he turned his attention to me.

"I'm okay." I lied with a smile.

"Are you and Sawyer okay? Not trying to sound mean or anything but you both look... miserable." He said cautiously, letting me know that he had actually caught onto the weird vibes.

"I mean yeah. I know you said he had a lot going on right now. I think I'm just trying to stay out of his way." I said, half lying this time. I did feel like I was resorting back to staying out of Sawyer's way and he did have a lot going on at the moment, but it wasn't what Callum thought.

"Did anything change with his mom that you know about?" He questioned, assuming that was the reason for him being unusually quiet.

I shrugged. "I'm not sure. He hasn't really said a lot the last couple of days." I said honestly.

I wanted to tell him that Sawyer was being distant because he mentioned that things would be weird if the two of us were a couple. I wanted to ask him what that meant so that I could tell Sawyer, but once again I was so afraid of making things worse than they already were.

"Did something change... between the two of you?" He asked cautiously.

My eyes widened slightly at his question and I decided it was best to play dumb. "What are you talking about?"

"I don't know!" He was quick to get defensive. "I just feel like things are weird between you two specifically. It seems like it's more than just him having an attitude because he's got shit going on... It was just a question."

I wanted to push back a little bit without outright admitting anything to him.

"Nothing has changed between the two of us. It's not like anything would, you said it yourself it would be weird." I made a roundabout attempt to get him to further tell me what that statement meant.

"I mean it would be weird! We've had this dynamic for so long and so yes, it would be weird for that to change. It would be weird for me to watch my best friend, who I know can be a total dumbass and dickhead sometimes with my little sister. My little sister that I already worry about every single day." He spoke, not giving me a lot to really work with.

"And is that such a bad thing for the dynamic that we have to change a little bit?" I asked, pushing further than I probably should have just as the bartender came back over to us with six shots. He placed them in front of us before turning to serve the other people at the bar.

Callum split the shots in half, giving me three and keeping three for himself. Before he had a chance to respond to my question about our dynamic changing, I picked up one of the cups. I didn't say anything, I just gave him a look that silently told him to pick one of his up. Once he did, we tapped the plastic cups and tossed the shots back together.

We both took a couple of seconds to regain composure before either one of us started to talk again.

"I never said it would be a bad thing. I get it, change can be good. But why does it even matter? Do you still have a crush on him or something?" He asked with a tone that I couldn't properly read.

I hated the fact that he'd asked me that question, so instead of answering it right away I picked up another shot and waited for him to pick one of his up. Again, we tossed them back together. My head was already starting to feel lighter.

"And what if I did?" I asked without even really thinking about it.

This time, Callum picked up the shot. I picked mine up and we swallowed the third shot. He stacked all the cups together and pushed them out of the way before he turned his body so he was fully facing mine.

"Do you?"

"I don't know!" I groaned. "Maybe! But it doesn't even matter because it's never going to happen!" I exclaimed, tossing my arms up in defeat.

"The dynamic would change. I'm going back to California. I'm your little sister and that would make things weird. There's way too many factors that would make it impossible so even if I did still like him, it doesn't matter." I listed off the reasons why there was no way that Sawyer and I would end up working out. The second I said everything out loud to my brother, I immediately made myself upset.

"Aves.." He started but was cut off by Dani and an even more upset looking Sawyer walking over to the bar. He immediately stopped talking when they walked back up to us, a confused look spreading across his face. I knew that the conversation was over and for the time being, I wasn't going to get to hear whatever Callum was going to say or possibly how he felt about everything. He didn't look angry at all, but I wanted to know what he was going to say.

"I need a shot." Sawyer spoke up.

"Me too," Callum said, his tone changing.

"Me three." I muttered.

Sawyer ordered himself a couple shots. Callum only ordered one for himself and me considering we'd just downed a couple back to back. As soon as they were in front of us, we tossed them back without a word to each other.

I grabbed Dani's hand, wanting to just take a step away from the boys. "Dance with me?"

The two of us walked over to the dance floor and started to dance together. I wanted to ask her about the conversation with Sawyer, I wanted to know what they talked about and why he looked so upset or angry when they walked back over. But on the other hand, I didn't want to talk about it anymore. I didn't want to ask her about it because it was my birthday and I just wanted to have a good time.

My body was warm and my head felt lighter, all the effects of multiple back to back shots.

Dani quickly caught onto the idea that I didn't want to talk about Sawyer and instead of telling me anything, she just danced with me and enjoyed the music. I would ask her about it in the morning, but for now I just wanted to celebrate and stop thinking about everything for a couple of hours.

The rest of the night was a lot more fun, I'd lost count of how much alcohol I had consumed and I steered clear of making any sort of attempts to talk to Sawyer. Whenever Dani and Callum wanted to dance together, I would dance by myself. I'd actually ended up talking to another group of girls that were there, so if I wasn't dancing by myself I was dancing with them.

Sawyer kept mostly to himself, a drink in his hand the entire time. He didn't make any sort of attempt to dance with me and I didn't ask.

By the time we'd loaded ourselves into the car, I couldn't even think straight. Sawyer and I sat in the back, Callum in the passenger seat and a sober Dani in the driver's seat. My head rested against the window. My eyes were open for a couple of minutes but everything was passing by so quickly that it made me dizzier than before, forcing them to close.

I wanted to feel the warmth of Sawyer's hand on my thigh. I loved when he put it there without asking. It always let me know that he was there. But tonight, it wasn't there. I didn't feel the warmth of his hand against my thigh. I didn't feel the tingles that erupted from under his thumb as he moved it against my skin in the most comforting way.

I got nothing.

When we arrived back at his place, I stumbled out of the car. Callum's window was down so after I shut the back door, I leaned into his window. "Text me when you get home, yeah?" I asked, my words slurring just slightly.

"You going to be okay?" Dani asked, leaning against the steering wheel. I knew her question held a much deeper meaning, but I shrugged in response.

"Who knows." I answered.

"You sure you don't want to come home with us?" Callum asked.

"Yep." I shifted on my feet. "Brother, I'll be good. Promise. Go home and hang out with your beautiful wife. Be nice to her, okay? She's a good one." I grinned, pointing my finger at Dani.

"Get some sleep. Text me if you need anything." My brother said in a serious tone.

"Got it, dude." I gave him a lopsided thumbs up before I practically dragged myself to the front door. I was surprised to find Sawyer waiting for me, I thought he'd be inside with the door closed in my face.

We walked inside and I leaned against the wall, raising one of my legs up to pull my heel off. "Fucking hell." I mumbled. I had to lift my foot up a couple times, losing balance each time I lifted it.

"You're going to fall." Sawyer said from in front of me.

I looked up at him, narrowing my eyes. "Well at least my shoes will be off."

Sawyer rolled his eyes but bent down, unclasping the strap on each of the heels I had on. He grabbed my arms and helped me step out of them, leaving them by the door.

"Oh so now you want to be nice to me. That's cool." I mumbled without even thinking about it as I walked past him to go to the stairs. All I wanted to do was go to bed.

"What the hell is that supposed to mean?" He asked in a confused and annoyed tone.

I spun around so that I could look at him, immediately losing my balance when I did. My head was spinning like crazy.

Fuck me.

I sat down on one of the bottom steps, needing to take a minute to get myself together. All of my emotions were starting to come to the front in one big, confusing mess. My drunken brain couldn't make sense of any of them.

"You've been mean to me all week!" I blurted out after a couple of minutes.

Sawyer leaned against the back of the couch, running a hand through his hair. "I haven't been mean to you." He said, brushing me off like I was being dramatic.

"You've barely spoken to me since we moved Dani and Callum into their house. I feel like I'm walking on eggs.. eggs--" I paused, my brain feeling like it wasn't keeping up with what I wanted to say to him. "Fucking eggshells around you for the past week! That's not fair to me."

"I'm not making you walk around on eggshells." He defended himself, again brushing me off.

The fact that he was dismissing my comments so easily was making me angry. I just wanted to talk to him about everything and he wasn't letting me.

But I also hated that we were having this conversation when a ridiculous amount of alcohol had been consumed by the both of us. There was no way this was going to end well.

"You're making me feel like you did before I moved!" I cried. "I told you that before I moved away, I thought every little thing I did pissed you off. I thought... I thought I was doing everything wrong and you're making me feel like that again!" My voice immediately got louder because I hated that he was pushing me away again.

"I told you, I've got shit going on." He shrugged, making it seem like it wasn't a big deal.

I pushed myself off the steps, stumbling over to him. "Sawyer, you're pushing me away!"

"What do you want me to do then, Avery? Because I don't know what the fuck I'm doing anymore." He said, his voice cold and sharp.

"Talk to me!" I cried out. "You can't just push me away when things get complicated!"

Tears were starting to form in my tired, drunk eyes. My heart was hurting right now and I didn't know what to do to fix it. I was willing to do anything for him. I wanted to do anything I could to make things easier for him, but he wouldn't talk to me to figure things out together.

"Things have always been complicated!" He raised his voice. "Things were complicated the minute I decided to look at you differently! Then you waltz in three years later and things just got messy!"

"So it's my fault? I came back and fucked everything up?" I asked, lowering my voice a bit.

"I didn't say that!" He defended.

"You just said things got messy when I came back!" I yelled. "What do you want me to do? Would you like me to leave? Do you want to just distance yourself completely from me so that you don't have to deal with the complications that come along with me anymore?" I practically spit at him.

"I didn't fucking say I wanted you to leave! Why do you think I asked you to stay with me and not your brother?!" He exclaimed, pushing his body off of the couch.

I watched as he paced around the living room, running his hands through his hair in a stressful manner. His shoulders were tense and his steps were hard. He was just as upset as I was.

"Exactly! You tell me that you don't want me to leave but then you walk around acting like you hate me! Sawyer, I'm exhausted." I said with a sigh, lowering my voice again.

Sawyer stopped walking and looked over at me before he started speaking again. "I'm exhausted too, Avery. I have no idea what the fuck to do about any of this. Then you go off and tell Dani everything and she comes asking me about it like it's any of her god damn business."

He brought up Dani talking to him tonight out of nowhere, I still didn't even know what the two of them had said to each other. My head was spinning impossibly fast at this point, I was drunk and so exhausted from everything about the day.

"Dani was just trying to help." I whispered.

"Why does it matter to her?! It's not her business!" He said, his voice getting louder again.

"Because she cares, Sawyer! And I needed someone to talk to because you keep stringing me along and I don't know what to do about it!" I yelled. "You're making things so difficult because of one person!"

"That one person is your fucking brother!" He yelled right back at me.

"I know! I fucking know that he's my brother! Everyone reminds me every goddamn day of my life that the amazing Callum Jones is my older brother!" I cried, a couple stray tears falling down my cheeks. I had to grab the back of the couch, partially out of anger and partially for balance.

"And so he makes one comment about us being weird and then you get all weird!!" I shouted at him, all of my anger just releasing at him all at once.

"Would you like me to call him and tell him to come back over so I can tell him I've been fucking his little sister?!" He asked. I couldn't help but flinch at his choice of words.

That's not at all what I wanted. In fact, I wanted him to call my brother and tell him that he had feelings for me so that he could just admit it to himself. I knew there was no way that we'd be fighting like this if he didn't.

"Would you like me to tell him that the reason I asked you to stay at my house even though he's back is so that we could continue hooking up without having to worry about being suspicious? Or that the first person I've has sex with in so long, I can't even be happy with because there's too many fucking complications that come with it? Or that---"

"Was this all I ever was to you!?" I cut him off. Everything that he was saying felt like a punch to the gut and I was tired of it.

"Was I just a complicated hookup?"

"That's not--"

"I'm sorry that I'm so fucking complicated to you that you can't just enjoy hooking up. I'm sorry that being with me is so much of an inconvenience that you just have to push me away to make yourself feel better! I'm so fucking sorry Sawyer that I ruined everything by coming home." I cried.

"Ave, stop." His voice was quieter now.

"No it's true! I came home and I fucked everything up for you. Your life was clearly easier when I was on the other side of the country." I sniffed, wiping my eyes with one of my hands.

"I was one less complication.." I whispered.

Sawyer walked up to me, grabbing my shoulders and forcing me to look up at him. "I never said you were a complication."

I shoved his hands away from me. I didn't want him to touch me. I didn't want any sort of comfort from him right now.

"No, I was just making your life complicated." I mumbled. "Listen, you said you didn't want to put pressure on this, right? You said you just wanted to see where things go, right? Maybe it's just a little too complicated for that." I whispered through a shaky voice.

"Ave, come on. Don't say that." Sawyer sighed.

"Then tell me that we're okay! Tell me that we can make this work. Tell me that you can tell my brother about us and that things won't be weird." I cried, begging him to tell me that we could work through the complications.

All I needed him to do was tell me he would try. That was it. If he told me he would try, then all of this could be okay.

"I just..Everything is just..." He started.

"You know what? It's fine." I cut him off, not wanting to hear whatever he was going to say because I knew it wasn't going to be what I needed.

"We're both drunk. I think it's better if we just sleep it off." I mumbled before turning around and walking away from him before he had the chance to say anything else to me.

I stumbled a bit as I walked up the steps and made my way into the guest bedroom. I didn't know if he'd come into the room or not, but at this point I wasn't going to be surprised if he decided against it.

I didn't even change clothes when I walked into the bedroom. I shut the door behind me and went straight to the bed. The second I was lying down, I curled up and started to cry again. This wasn't at all how I'd envisioned talking to Sawyer about everything. I thought we'd be able to sit down and have a real conversation about everything. I had no intention of talking to him about it when there was alcohol involved.

I was confused about where we stood at the beginning of the day, when he wasn't talking to me at all. But now after that, I didn't even know where to start with whatever it was that we were. I had no idea what any of this meant for us but the pit in my stomach told me that it wasn't headed anywhere good.

Happy fucking birthday to me.

Chapter 24

Thump. Thump. Thump.

There was an uncomfortable pounding in my head before my eyes even forced themselves open. A sea of nerves and nausea swam in my stomach and the room spun as I slowly rolled onto my back. My arm stretched out to the side of the bed next to me, unintentionally feeling for another body.

Instead of feeling a body next to me, all I felt was the cold, empty side of the mattress. I slowly turned my head so that I could confirm with my eyes that I was indeed alone in the bed. The second I saw the empty side of the bed, thoughts of the previous night came flooding back. I replayed bits of the conversation between the two of us, the words coming back before I could stop them.

Oh so now you want to be nice to me. That's cool.

You've been mean to me all week!

I don't know what the fuck to do anymore.

Would you like me to call him and tell him to come back over so I can tell him I'm fucking his little sister?

The second the words from last night entered my brain and started to replay, I knew I was going to be sick. I forced myself out of bed, stumbling as I exited the bedroom. My body felt like it had been hit by a truck, the pounding in my head immediately getting ten times worse.

I started to head towards the upstairs bathroom but I heard the shower running which let me know that Sawyer was awake and in the shower. I covered my mouth with my hand and started down the steps as quickly as I could. I needed to make it to the bathroom before I got sick all over the floor.

I almost stumbled over the last couple of steps due to how quickly I was rushing down them. Luckily though I caught myself before accidentally giving myself any sort of injuries.

As soon as I was on the main level, I rushed into the half bath. I knew it was only a matter of seconds before I was throwing up all over the floor. The second I was in the bathroom, I was on my knees in front of the toilet throwing up all of the contents in my stomach. My entire body shook, tears falling down my cheeks as I emptied my stomach into the toilet.

Tears from throwing up. Tears from exhaustion. Tears from fighting with Sawyer.

I felt so sick and so overwhelmed.

24 is off to a great start.

I sat in front of the toilet for a while. Each time I thought I was done, I'd start coughing up more. I knew that my stomach was empty but my body was trying to get rid of more. It was starting to hurt, my brain was not working well enough to be able to tell my stomach that it was indeed empty and that it could relax.

My arms rested on the rim of the toilet, my head resting on top of my arms. I knew it was disgusting but I didn't have time to think about it and I could barely keep my head up.

I heard the sound of a knock on the open bathroom door. I lifted my gaze to see who was standing there even though I already knew who it was because there was no one else here. My tired, tear filled eyes immediately met Sawyer's.

What a sight to see for him.

I hated the fact that he was seeing me like this. If things hadn't ended the way they did last night, I wouldn't care as much that he was seeing me hunched over the toilet. I wouldn't have cared because it simply would have been me getting sick because I had too much fun on my birthday, as one should.

Instead, I was laying against the toilet in tears partially due to the alcohol and partially due to the anxiety I was feeling from the fight that we'd gotten into.

His hair was still wet from the shower, little droplets falling down his forehead. He had on a pair of sweatpants and nothing on top.

"I heard you when I got out of the shower." His voice was soft, softer than normal.

"Sorry," I muttered, closing my eyes again.

"I brought you some water."

I didn't want it. I didn't want anything from him right now.

Even though I knew I needed it, I could get it myself when I finally got up and out of the bathroom.

"Can I help you up?" He asked.

I shook my head against my arm. As much as I wanted to leave the bathroom and go lay back down, I knew I needed to wait a couple more minutes. As empty as my stomach felt, I was afraid that I would get sick again if I left the bathroom. "Then can I sit with you?"

My eyes fluttered open again so that I could look up at him. He was still standing in the doorway, leaning just slightly against the door frame with a water bottle in his hand.

Why did he want to sit here with me?

"Sure," I mumbled.

As soon as I gave him the okay, Sawyer took a seat on the floor of the small bathroom. He placed the water bottle next to me before crossing his legs. He looked like he was sitting as far away from me as he could while still sitting in the actual bathroom. He didn't make any sort of effort to try and soothe me or comfort me, I'm sure he could tell that I didn't want it.

"You didn't come into my room last night." I whispered, closing my eyes once again so I didn't have to look at him.

"I didn't think you wanted me to." He confessed.

We both went to bed with the same thought. I didn't think he wanted to come to bed with me and he didn't think I wanted him to come to bed with me.

Miscommunication at its finest.

"I'm so sorry for ruining your birthday." His voice sounded genuine, but I didn't respond to him. I didn't really know how. Nothing was going to make last night better. I knew we needed to talk about what was said yesterday, but there wasn't a single ounce of me that wanted to do that when I was laying against a toilet.

"You didn't even tell me happy birthday yesterday." I whispered.

Sawyer cleared his throat. He didn't respond right away, he may have an excuse for everything else that happened but he didn't have an excuse for not telling me happy birthday.

"I was a dick yesterday, I know. I ruined your day and I really am sorry. Things are just..." He trailed off.

"Complicated and weird?" I finished his sentence using the two words that were most used for whatever it was that we were.

"Yeah..." He said with a sigh.

I opened my eyes and slowly lifted my head so that I could look over at him. Sawyer was now sitting with his legs bent and his arms crossed over his knees. At this moment, I don't think either one of us knew where we stood in our whateveritscalledship. I knew that I was mentally and physically exhausted and I was sure that he was too. I hated that I was so afraid to ask him where we stood and what was going to happen next.

"We don't have to talk about it right now, but I am sorry if I made you feel like you were the complication and I'm sorry if I made you feel like you were doing something wrong." He stated, his voice was still just as soft as it was when he'd first entered the bathroom.

I didn't want to tell him that it was okay because I didn't want this to happen again if I did tell him that everything was okay. I didn't want him to apologize now if he was just going to continue to distance himself from me and push me away from him. All I really wanted was for him to either figure things out with me or tell me that things were over. I couldn't keep doing the back and forth with him, it was starting to hurt way too much.

"I think we both have some things that we need to think about." I said quietly.

Sawyer nodded in agreement. "Right."

We didn't know what any of this meant for the two of us, but we both knew that we each had a lot to think about. Sawyer and I both needed to think about what we wanted. Sawyer needed to figure out if this was worth the stress and I needed to figure out just how much more of my heart I was willing to give him.

"I think that I'm going to shower and lay back down.." I said before I reached up and flushed the toilet one last time. When I was standing fully off of the ground I leaned against the wall, my body feeling incredibly weak.

Sawyer reached over and grabbed the bottle of water off of the ground before he stood up and handed it over to me.

"If you need anything at all, please let me know. I can run out and grab you anything you need too." He offered before he walked out of the half bath.

After I showered, I took a short nap to try and sleep away the aches I was feeling in every single part of my body. I'd ended up talking to Larissa for a little while, although I didn't feel like talking on the phone for long so I ended up telling her I'd call her back later. She knew something was wrong but trusted that I'd call her to talk to her about everything when I was ready. I appreciated her not digging for details.

I was sitting on the bed, trying to figure out if I wanted to finally eat something. I knew that I needed to and every once in a while, my stomach would growl to let me know that it wanted something to eat but there wasn't a single ounce of me that wanted to walk downstairs and get food. I could have texted Sawyer, but I still didn't want his help with anything.

I was still trying to make sense of everything that had happened between Sawyer and I. I couldn't get over how quickly things had taken a turn. One minute things were fine and the next they weren't. All it took was my brother saying one word and everything that happened between Sawyer and I was being thrown out the window like it didn't matter anymore.

The bedroom door opened, causing me to look over at the door. I assumed it was Sawyer walking into the room but my body immediately relaxed when I saw Dani walking in with a fast food bag in her hand. I didn't even know she was coming over, she hadn't texted me to tell me.

She obviously saw the confused look on my face so she said, "Sawyer texted me."

After she walked into the room, she closed the door behind her and walked over to the bed where she took a seat next to me. She handed me the bag of food and I opened it to find a large fry and some chicken nuggets.

"Thought you could use something simple and greasy to eat. He said that you hadn't eaten anything today." She said, her voice soft.

I pulled the fries out of the bag and popped one into my mouth. My stomach was in knots still, but it was thanking me for finally giving it something. I knew I needed to force myself to eat or I would just feel even worse.

"Thank you." I sighed.

"Wanna tell me what happened after you got back yesterday?" Dani questioned, cutting straight to the point.

"Wanna tell me what you two talked about?" I countered.

Dani nodded her head before saying, "Fair enough."

She kicked her shoes off and lifted her legs onto the bed to cross them so she could sit more comfortably. I pulled the chicken nuggets out of the bag as she situated herself, picking one up and taking a bite of it.

"Truthfully, we didn't talk about much. I asked him if he was okay because it looked like something was bothering him. When he tried to brush me off and tell me that he was okay, I asked him if it was because of whatever was going on between the two of you.." She admitted.

I listened to her tell me what they talked about, not wanting to interrupt.

"He was really upset that I knew about it. He tried to tell me that it was between the two of you and that it wasn't anyone else's business. So of course, I pissed him off when I told him that it was actually between you two and Callum. I also told him that he was letting things affect him more than he needed to, which really made him mad. After that, he basically told me to fuck off and then he walked away." She finished.

Jesus.

"Dani you didn't have to do that..." I sighed.

I wasn't upset with her that she'd tried to talk to him, I was the one that told her she could. I felt bad that he was being rude to her though, she didn't do anything but try to help us. A part of me thought that maybe if someone else tried to talk to him about Callum that it would help, but it obviously did the exact opposite.

"I didn't say anything that wasn't true. I told you, he's getting too in his head about things." She stated with a shrug.

"I don't get it though. If he was that mad at you yesterday and didn't want you involved with any of this then why did he even text you today?" I questioned. I was surprised that he'd asked her to come over.

"He said you guys got into it last night and you needed someone to talk to. He also apologized to me for our conversation." She said.

I nodded. I remembered yelling at Sawyer about how the only reason I'd talked to Dani about us was because I needed to talk to someone about it and Dani cared enough to listen. I guess that made sense that he'd asked her to come talk to me, he was smart enough to know that I needed to talk about everything and that after ignoring him all morning, I wasn't ready to talk to him yet.

"So what happened after we dropped you off?"

I sucked in a breath before recalling all of the details back to her. I told her every little detail from last night, from the yelling to the tears to the thoughts of walking away from him. I told her about how Sawyer still didn't know what he wanted and how he just kept telling me that everything was complicated. I told her how lost I was feeling and how heartbroken I was.

Talking about everything made the nausea I'd been feeling this morning surface again, but I knew I needed to get everything out. I knew I needed to vocalize my thoughts to someone else before I could think about talking to Sawyer about everything.

"Wanna know what's funny though? When you pulled Sawyer off to the side last night, I actually started to talk to Callum." I admitted with a small laugh.

Dani's eyes widened.

"Did you tell him?" She asked.

I shook my head to her question as I gathered my thoughts about the conversation Callum and I had when we were at the club last night.

"No. I mean, not really no. He asked me if Sawyer and I were okay, he said we both looked miserable." I started. "He asked me if anything had changed between the two of us and that kind of led into him asking if I was still crushing on Sawyer." I confessed.

"And did you tell him you did?"

"I basically told him that I had no idea but that even if I did, it didn't matter because there were way too many complications, one of them being that I was his little sister and that would make things weird." I said with a shrug.

"What did he say about that?" Dani asked as she sat up a little bit straighter, clearly wanting to know what her husband said in response to all of this. This was one of the biggest question marks for us right now and I knew she wanted to hear what he had to say. The issue was that I didn't even get to hear all of what he had to say, I was cut off before he could voice all of his thoughts.

"Well before that, he was saying that it would be weird if the dynamic changed between the three of us... but then he went on to say that change can be good. It was a little confusing." I groaned. "After I told him that nothing would happen between the two of us because of a long list of reasons, he started to say something to me but you and Sawyer walked back over and he never actually finished what he was going to say."

While I waited for Dani to say something, I picked up the water bottle that had been sitting next to me since this morning. I finally unscrewed the cap and took a small drink from it.

"Talk about bad timing." She said with a shake of her head. "However, I do think it's a good thing that you talked to him! It seems to me like he's not really mad at the idea of you two being a thing. Did you talk to Sawyer about it?"

I shook my head again.

"No, I didn't really get the chance to. Everything sort of blew up last night really quickly. I think I was a little afraid to tell him that I talked to him because Callum made one little joke about it at your house, saying things would be weird, and everything went downhill from there." I sighed.

"Do you think it would make it better to talk to him about it though and tell him what happened? Even though you didn't get his full answer, Callum doesn't seem super upset about it. I'm sure that he didn't mean weird in a bad way." She started.

"I think he's right in saying that the dynamic would change if his best friend and little sister started dating. I also think he just might not know how to act around you two for a little while because it would be weird for him to see you two together like that. He'll probably be worried about what would happen if the two of you ever broke up. But I genuinely don't think he's coming from a bad place when he says any of this. I think if he was upset about it or angry about it, he would have shot you down last night when you tried to talk to him." She voiced her thoughts.

I listened to my sister in law speak, taking in the idea that maybe my brother wasn't actually upset about the idea of Sawyer and I being together but more so worried about what the changes would bring for all of us. We'd all known each other for so long at this point that his concerns were valid. Things would change and if Sawyer and I ever did break up, things would be even weirder between the three of us.

How could I even be thinking about breaking up when we weren't even technically together?

After a couple minutes I spoke up again. "I honestly have no idea if that would make it better or not."

It was the truth, I was at a loss right now. I had no idea what was going to help the situation and what was going to hurt it. I didn't know if Sawyer would be mad at me for even bringing it up to Callum without him, even though we really didn't talk about everything in much detail. He still had no idea what was really going on between the two of us.

"It can't make it worse, right? Maybe it's what he needs to hear." She said, just trying to help in any way that she could.

"I just don't know at this point. I don't know what is going to make the situation better. I have no idea what to do anymore. What if he gets mad at me for talking to Callum without him?" I voiced another concern to her.

"Callum is your brother and he brought it up first, if Sawyer gets mad at you for that, then he's got some bigger issues." She said as a matter of fact.

She did have a point. I was allowed to talk to my own brother and he was the one that brought it up to me. He asked me if everything was okay between Sawyer and I and I was just answering his questions. There was no reason why I wasn't allowed to speak to my own brother. On top of that, I really didn't tell him anything.

Dani and I sat in silence for a couple of minutes, both of us seemingly in our own thoughts. There were so many thoughts running through my own head right now, it was hard to keep them all straight.

"Can I ask you a question? You don't have to answer if you don't want to." Dani finally spoke up again.

"I mean yeah? You're already asking me questions." I said with a laugh. She'd been sitting here asking me questions since she walked into the bedroom with a bag of greasy food, I had no idea why she felt the need to ask me if she could ask me another one.

Dani looked at me for a minute, her eyes searching mine as she contemplated her next words.

"Do you love him?" She finally questioned.

Oh.

Well that was not what I was expecting.

I'd spend weeks just trying to figure out how I felt because I came into this summer convinced that I was completely over the little school girl crush that I had on him. I quickly learned that I still found him insanely attractive, but that turned into realizing I still had a crush on him, which turned into feelings much deeper than that.

"Like I said, you don't have to answer me right now if you don't want to... But I do think if you love him, if you really think that you do... then you should talk to him." She spoke.

"I think you need to tell him how you feel and you need to make sure that he really hears everything that you're saying to him. Tell him that you talked to Callum and tell him that Callum will get over everything. If you don't talk to him, openly and honestly, he's never going to get out of his own head and you'll never move on from where you guys are right now." She finished.

I knew that she was right. I knew everything that she was saying was exactly what I needed to do. I knew that if I felt the way that I thought I felt, I needed to talk to him about it and I needed to tell him everything. I needed to lay it all out on the table and hope that everything goes the way I want it to go.

The problem with all of that was that it was going to be one of the scariest things I've ever done. I was going to have to sit down and tell Sawyer that I loved him. I was going to have to tell him that I talked to Callum and that I wanted to talk to Calum with him. It was the only way that I was going to figure out what was going to happen between the two of us.

I was going to finally have to hear if Sawyer thought all of this was worth it or if he was ready to give everything up and that thought alone made me sicker than I'd felt this morning.

Chapter 25

----

3 years ago

"What time does your flight get in tomorrow?" Larissa asked me from the other side of the phone.

"I should get there around 2." I smiled brightly at her through the screen.

"Ahh! I'm so excited to finally meet you in person!" She squealed.

I couldn't help but giggle at my future roommate. I was beyond excited to take the step and move away from Maine. California was on the literal opposite side of the country and I couldn't wait to be there. It had been pretty nerve wracking searching for places to live, especially when I'd never been there before and had no idea what I was really looking for. I got lucky when I found Larissa, we hit it off immediately so I knew it was the right choice and I couldn't wait to officially move in with her tomorrow.

"I'm excited to finally meet you too." I said with a laugh.

To say I was nervous was an understatement. I'd never really been out of my small hometown so this was a huge deal to me. I was just tired of being in a place that no longer brought me joy. I had no idea what California was going to hold for me, but I was feeling more hopeful than I'd felt in a long time and that was enough to bring me excitement.

"Should I make a huge, embarrassing sign for you?" She joked.

At least I think she was joking.

I rolled my eyes. "Please, do not. Or I'll have to find a new roommate."

Larissa gasped. "You haven't even seen the apartment and you're already talking about getting a new roommate?!"

"If you bring an embarrassing sign with you to pick me up from the airport and that is how I meet you in person, yes I will be finding a new place to live and a new roommate." I laughed.

Larissa rolled her eyes but nodded. "Okay, fine. I won't bring an embarrassing sign with me." She agreed.

"But! you better make sure that you get a ton of sleep tonight because I have so much to show you when you get here! I'm so excited to show you around! You're going to love it so much I just know it!" She said, her voice full of excitement.

I loved how excited she was about everything, it was already making me feel more comfortable and even more excited to go. I'd never really had girlfriends before so this was a new thing for me. I liked how easily the two of us got along and I hoped that it stayed that way even after I was there.

"Aves! Come here, I need to show you something!" I heard my brother call me from down the hall.

"Uhh, let me call you back. My brother needs me." I said before sitting up on my bed.

"Ooooh, tell hottie brother I said hi!" She giggled.

I fake gagged at her comment before saying, "gross. I think his girlfriend is here too, so sorry about that one."

She rolled her eyes but nodded. "Whatever, text me later!"

We said our goodbyes and I threw my phone on the bed before walking down the hallway of my brother's apartment.

"What do you need to show me?" I asked as I got closer to the living room. I didn't see him when I walked into the room so I called out his name.

"Kitchen!" He called.

I couldn't help but roll my eyes. I figured he wanted to show me something stupid and he couldn't even meet me halfway. I turned to the left so that I could walk into the kitchen. As soon as I walked into the kitchen I saw my brother standing there with two other bodies next to him.

"Surprise!" Callum said with a huge smile on his face.

"I know you're leaving tomorrow, but we wanted to do something for you before you left us." His voice was full of excitement and happiness.

Sawyer was leaning against the counter to the right of my brother, Dani was on the left of him holding out a cake.

"You did not have to do that." I let out a breathy laugh.

"Well duh, I know we didn't have to. But it's your last night here and we just wanted to have a little send off party I guess." He said as he walked up to me, wrapping me in a tight hug.

"Callum, you act like I'm never going to come back." I laughed, but hugged him back.

"I know that you're going to come back and I know that I'm going to come visit you... but California is literally on the opposite side of the country, like you couldn't have picked anywhere closer?" He joked.

"Kidding. But seriously, I'm allowed to be upset that my baby sister is ditching me to go live the coolest life ever." He said as he pulled away from me.

"You have to send us all the pictures, Avery! I've never been to California before but I've heard it's beautiful." Dani said from behind Callum. She put the cake down on the counter and smiled at me.

"I will, I will." I agreed.

I was thankful that my brother had done this for me, it was really sweet. It had been a really good day overall. I'd finished packing up all of my things this morning and had spent a majority of the day hanging out with Callum. He'd taken me out to an early dinner and then mentioned something about having to run into work. I didn't even question it and used the time to triple check my bags and call Larissa. I had no idea that he'd been planning a surprise for me, I was surprised that he'd hid it so well.

I almost felt surprised that Sawyer was here. A part of me thought that he would have made up some excuse about being busy, but I also knew that because he'd known me for so long that my brother probably talked him out of any excuse he'd tried to give him.

"I got you a little something. It's nothing crazy because I know you weren't trying to pack a lot." Callum said to me. He turned around and grabbed a small box off of the kitchen counter and handed it to me.

"Don't let him take all the credit, I helped him pick it out." Dani said with a laugh as she pulled a couple of plates out of the cabinet.

I laughed at her comment before I opened the small box. Inside of it was a green mug with an etched out image of a lobster on it. I'm sure to anyone else, this probably would have been a really stupid gift but I knew exactly why he gave it to me.

"To remind me of home?" I asked with a smile.

Callum grinned proudly and nodded. "I knew you'd get it."

It was simple but I loved it. I knew that even though I was excited to get out of our small town, I was going to miss it and I was going to get homesick. This was a nice gesture to help when I was feeling homesick.

"I love it, seriously. Thank you both." I said with a smile.

I put the box down on the small kitchen table behind me before I gave my brother another hug. I pulled away from my brother before walking around him so that I could hug Dani as well.

After I released Dani, she cut into the cake. She cut four pieces and handed a piece to each of us.

I'd almost forgotten Sawyer was standing in the kitchen with us, he hadn't spoken at all since I'd walked in. It wasn't surprising, again I was more surprised he was even there. But I did hate the fact that I was about to move so far away and he was barely speaking to me. I was convinced he was only here because my brother had told him to come so that he could say goodbye to me.

Sawyer had gotten a little better after my dad passed, especially after the night we fell asleep on the couch together. It wasn't long after that though that he resorted back to barely speaking to me. I really hated that I was leaving on these terms, but I was glad that I was going to get to say goodbye to him at least. I was also hoping that being so far away from him would help me get over the annoying crush that I'd had on him for so many years.

"Are you nervous?" Callum asked before taking a bite of his slice of cake.

I poked the cake with my fork and sighed. "I wish I could say that I wasn't, but I am. But I'm also excited to see a new place and experience new things." I said honestly.

"You can always come back if you hate it." My brother said with a soft tone.

I laughed at his comment and shook my head. I didn't even want to think about the possibility of hating it. I was fully planning on living this experience to the fullest. There was no part of me that could stay in Maine anymore, trapped in this tiny hometown with the same people. I needed to move on and meet new people, try new things.I needed to figure out who I was as a person. I needed a new space to write and a new place to write about.

"We'll see where it takes me." I smiled.

We spent a good amount of the evening on the couch just talking. We relived memories and looked up things to do in Santa Monica. Callum made me promise that if I finished a book and it got published, that I'd come home to tell him in person. I couldn't help but laugh at my big brother, but I appreciated that he had faith in me and my writing skills.

Sawyer had been a bit tense all night, but he did talk to me. It wasn't much, but it was hard to stay silent when we were reliving so many fun memories between the three of us. I made Callum tell Dani a couple of stories that he didn't want to, but I thought she needed to know if she was going to continue to date my brother.

After a while of laughter and sharing stories, Sawyer finally pushed himself off of the couch. He stretched his arms over his head before saying, "I think I'm going to head out. I don't want to be the reason you guys are up late."

"I'll walk you out." I said without thinking about it.

Sawyer turned his head to look down at me from my spot on the couch, a confused look on his face. I had no idea if I was about to make things even weirder than they already were, but this was my last chance to really say goodbye to him before I left.

"Come on, we've known each other for how many years? I'm about to move across the country, I think I'm allowed to walk you outside so that I can say goodbye to you." I quickly defended myself.

"Uh yeah, sure that's fine." He seemed unsure, but agreed to let me walk him out to his car.

My brother stood up, giving Sawyer one of those bro hugs just as I was standing up from my spot.

"We still on for next weekend?" Callum asked as he pulled away.

Sawyer nodded before he started to head to the door. "Yeah, just text me."

I slipped on a pair of shoes and followed him to the door. "Be right back!" I said to my brother and Dani before I followed Sawyer out of the apartment.

I truly had no idea what to expect out of this, but all I wanted was a proper goodbye from Sawyer. The last couple of years had been weird between the two of us but Sawyer was someone that I cared deeply about and I couldn't forget that just because he was acting a little funny. We'd shared a lot of good moments together and he was someone that had been there for me when it felt like I didn't have anyone else. Those moments weren't going to disappear just because we'd had some distance put between us.

I quietly followed him down to his car where he stopped in front of it. He hesitated for a minute, his hands fiddling with his car keys. He looked nervous, like he wasn't sure what to say. It immediately made nerves bubble inside of me. He hesitated for another moment before his eyes finally met mine.

"So, you're really doing this?" He finally asked. I couldn't quite read his tone, it made me feel that much more nervous. "I am." I responded simply.

"Good for you, Jones. Get out of this small town, go do some cool shit."

I laughed at his response, it was something that I wasn't expecting. "I will try my best to do all of the cool shit."

Sawyer scratched the back of his neck for a minute before he said, "I uh, actually have something for you too."

My eyes widened a little bit. I wasn't expecting him to get me anything. Things had definitely changed between the two of us, so him giving me something before I left was surprising. I wondered why he didn't give it to me while we were inside when Callum had given me his present. Had I not walked outside with him, would he have not given it to me? I watched him as he took out a small velvet bag from his pocket before he reached his arm out to hand it to me.

"I guess your brother and I are pretty alike. We had similar ideas." He chuckled.

I glanced up at him before looking down at the little bag in my hand. Slowly, I pulled the strings on it apart to open it up before pulling out what looked to be a golden necklace. On the chain, there was a round pendant with a lighthouse etched into it.

My heart swarmed with something I'd never felt before.

"To remind me of home..." I whispered, this time not as a question but as a fact.

I ran my thumb over the lighthouse, admiring it for a minute. I don't know what I expected, but I was definitely not expecting this. My heart was pounding, butterflies were swarming through my belly uncontrollably.

"Sawyer, I love it. Thank you so much." I whispered before finally looking up at him, meeting his eyes again.

"Uh, want me to put it on you?" He asked.

"Please." I said before nodding.

I handed him the necklace and turned around, moving my hair out of the way for him. I immediately felt goosebumps appear under the sweater that I had on as I felt him putting the necklace around my neck. His fingers grazed the back of my neck as he clasped it, almost making me suck in a breath of air. Once he was finished, I moved my hair back and turned around so I could face him once more.

I didn't say anything at first, I wasn't sure what to say. But I knew that I needed to say something before he left without another word.

"Listen, I know things have been a little... I don't know, strange. But I really am going to miss you.." I admitted to him. It was true, I was unsure what the future held for the two of us. I had no idea if I was going to talk to him after I moved, but I did know that at the end of the day, I was going to miss him like crazy.

Sawyer grinned, a grin that he hadn't given me in quite a while. He pulled me into an unexpected hug, his body immediately warming mine up by at least 10 degrees. I wrapped my arms around him without hesitation, inhaling his scent that brought nothing but comfort as I hugged him back."I'm gonna miss you too, Jones."

He didn't let go of me right away and I didn't let go of him. I didn't want to, I knew as soon as I let go it meant that he was going to leave my brother's apartment and I wasn't sure when I would see him next.

Unfortunately, he did pull away from me before he cleared his throat. "I should get going.."

"Oh right, yeah." I stepped away from him. "See you around?"

Sawyer opened his car door and nodded. "See you around, Jones."

I watched him as he got into the driver's side of his car and started it up. He didn't close the door right away, glancing at me through the windshield. I gave him a small wave before I forced myself to turn around, a small ache in my heart immediately making itself known when I heard the car door shut.

I wanted to turn around and tell him so many things, but with the way things had been going between us I knew that I couldn't. I wanted to tell him to come back inside with me so that I could hang out with him for a little while longer. I wanted to promise him that I would call him as soon as I got to California so that I could tell him about it. I wanted him to promise me that we'd still talk even though I was gone. But I didn't do any of that, I couldn't.

I needed to escape this town and escape him. I needed to do something for myself, for once in my life even if that meant walking away from him. Even if that meant walking away from the one person who sometimes felt like my best friend, who sometimes felt like my older brother's best friend who treated me like his own little sister, who sometimes felt like a person that I couldn't please no matter how hard I tried.

I needed to walk away from the back and forth, no matter how badly it hurt to do it.

I had to wipe a couple of tears from my eyes before I walked back inside of my brother's apartment. I also tucked the necklace into my sweater. I didn't think he'd notice, but just in case he did I didn't feel like answering questions about it or even talking about it.

"Hey guys, I think I'm actually going to go lay down. I know that I'm not going to get much sleep tonight, so I'm just going to try to get whatever I can." I said to my brother and his girlfriend after I shut the front door behind me.

"Alright. I've got my alarm set, but if I'm not awake just come get me." Callum gave me another hug before I walked into my bedroom.

I set my alarm and plugged my phone in before shutting off the light and laying down. My fingers held the lighthouse pendent around my neck as I closed my eyes.

Here's to the adventure of a lifetime.

Chapter 26

B ut I do think if you love him, if you really think you do... then you should talk to him.

Dani's words kept repeating over and over again in my head. They had been since she left the house two days ago. I knew that she was right and I knew I needed to talk to Sawyer, but I was struggling with figuring out how to do it.

Sawyer and I still hadn't talked about anything, but he had been less cold than he'd been to me on my birthday. Things were still very awkward between us, but I think he was starting to realize how much he was hurting me and maybe even himself by the way he was acting.

At least that's what I hoped he was realizing. I still couldn't wrap my brain around how quickly things had changed between the two of us. One minute, he was telling me that a relationship between us was possible, the next minute he was telling me he wanted nothing to do with me, the next minute he was still distant but starting to talk to me again. My brain was an absolute wreck trying to make sense of everything.

Things had taken a turn so quickly that it almost felt like someone had slapped me in the face. Even though I still hadn't really talked to him about my birthday, other than the little that was said in the bathroom, I couldn't stop thinking about it. I couldn't stop thinking about just how cold he'd treated me. I hoped that things would change after I talked to him.

I also felt like I was running out of time and I was tired of walking around unsure of what was going on between the two of us. I needed some sort of an answer before I went back to California, even if those answers broke my heart.

Sawyer was on his way home from work and I was standing in the kitchen, waiting on the lasagna I'd made to finish cooking. My heart felt like it was beating a million beats a minute and my palms were sweating with nerves. I'd gone back and forth literally all day, trying to decide what I wanted to say to Sawyer, trying to decide if I even really wanted to talk to him. But I knew that if I pushed it back any longer, I wasn't going to do it at all and I was going to leave without knowing what was going on between us.

I'd spent the last couple of days doing a lot of reflecting. Going back and forth with Sawyer was killing me, but I couldn't deny the way I felt about him if I tried. I knew I was far beyond the point of crushing on him. I also knew this was more than someone that I simply wanted to hook up with. My feelings were undeniable at this point.

I was in love with Sawyer Evans.

The timer that I'd set on my phone went off, breaking me from my nervous thoughts. I quickly turned it off and opened the over, checking to make sure that the food was actually finished cooking. When I saw that it was, I slipped on some oven mitts and pulled it out of the oven before placing it on the stove to cool off. While I waited for that to cool off, I grabbed a couple of plates out of the cabinet to place on the dining room table. Just as I placed the second plate down, I heard the front door open letting me know that Sawyer was home from work.

Almost instantly, I sucked in a nervous breath. I tried to shake my hands off on my jeans before I walked into the living room, just as Sawyer was closing the front door. He had his binder and water bottle in his hand like always.

Sawyer glanced in my direction when he heard me walking into the living room. "Hey." He started. "It smells really good in here."

He kicked his shoes off by the front door and set his binder and water bottle down on the coffee table before making his way over to me.

"Hey. I uh, made dinner. Are you hungry?" I asked. I hated how anxious I felt about all of this. I hated that I had no idea how the conversation was going to go and I just hated all of the uncertainty.

"Actually, yeah I am."

We walked into the kitchen together and I grabbed the two plates that I'd just put on the dining table. I placed them on the counter next to the stove before grabbing a spatula so that I could put some lasagna on each of the plates. I walked the two plates back over to the table and set them down as Sawyer shut the fridge, a bottle of wine in his hand.

"Want a glass?" He questioned.

I was silently thanking him for pulling out the bottle of wine. I hoped that it would help ease some of the nerves I was feeling, even though I doubted that it actually would.

"Please." I nodded.

I don't think anything was going to help calm my nerves at this point, but I was willing to try. I was sure that if it got too quiet between us, Sawyer would actually be able to hear just how loud my heart was beating.

Sawyer grabbed two wine glasses and poured wine into both of them before he brought them over to the table, setting each of them down next to the plates. We both took a seat at the table, both quiet and trying to figure out what to say. The tension between us was thick, it almost made it hard to breathe.

"How was practice?" I finally spoke up after a couple minutes of silently eating.

Sawyer took a sip from his wine glass before glancing over at me. My shoulders unintentionally tensed just slightly when our eyes made contact.

"It was good. We've got a game on Thursday." He said before taking another bite.

I nodded, hating that we were having such an awkward conversation.

"I'm glad practice went well. I hope the game goes well too." I glanced down at my plate, my hands shaking with nerves as I pushed the food around on my plate.

"Michael asked me if you were coming to the game."

I lifted my gaze again to meet his. There was an ounce of hope in his eyes that gave me the smallest amount of hope that maybe things would be okay.

"Oh, I mean... would you want me to go?" I asked, unsure if he actually wanted me to tag along.

Sawyer shrugged a bit. "You can come with me if you want to."

I wasn't sure what to make of his comment, the hope in his eyes didn't match his words. I just nodded and lowered my gaze back to the pasta on my plate.

"I don't think I have anything else going on." My voice was quiet, I didn't want to show too much enthusiasm, but I also didn't want it to seem like I didn't want to go.

"Cool."

"Cool." I repeated.

The next couple of minutes were spent without words, the only thing you could hear was forks against plates. The tension had not yet been released and I was almost positive you could cut it with a knife if you really wanted to. I went to take another bite, but my shaky hands dropped the fork on my plate causing a loud clatter to echo in the silent air.

"Fuck," I mumbled and quickly picked it back up.

"You okay?" He asked.

I sucked in a breath before looking over at him, meeting his eyes again.

"Can I talk to you about something?" I said, a little too quick. I had to talk fast or I would convince myself not to say anything.

Sawyer set his fork down, his eyes remaining on mine. He nodded, "What's up?"

I hated how relaxed he seemed, because it was the exact opposite of how I was feeling. He seemed like nothing was bothering him and that he didn't care about the tension between us, meanwhile my hands were shaking so bad that I couldn't even hold my fork.

"I... I need to talk to you about us." I stuttered.

He visibly tensed in his seat but nodded his head, giving me the go ahead to say whatever I wanted to say.

"Okay, sure."

It was almost like he knew I was going to be the one to bring everything up, he was just waiting on me to actually do it.

"I don't really know where to start... I know that things have been weird and everything's been so hard..." I started, trying to figure out how I was going to say what I needed to say.

I'd tried so many times over the last few days to rehearse what I wanted to say to him, but every time I tried I hated the way it would come out and I'd have to start again. The difference was that whatever was going to come out, I couldn't take it back and start again. He was going to hear it.

"I know that my brother has played a pretty big role in all of this, because we've both been a little afraid to talk to him about this, about us. But I think maybe we should try to talk to him. I know that it's not going to be easy, but I realized that I—"

I was cut off by Sawyer's phone ringing in his pocket.

"Shit, sorry." He mumbled, pulling his phone out of his pocket. I thought that he'd silence it and call the person back, but his face fell a bit when he pulled it out and saw who was calling him.

"Ave, it's my dad. Can you give me just one minute?" He asked, looking at me with eyes that were apologetic.

I nodded quickly. "No, it's okay. Go ahead."

I knew that he was probably afraid that his dad was calling him to tell him something about his mom, so I didn't want to make him ignore the call.

"Just one minute. We can keep talking, I promise." He said. His tone of voice told me that he was serious, he wanted to continue the conversation after he got off the phone.

That made me feel better because it made me feel as though he was actually listening to me and hearing me out, that he really did want to know what I wanted to say to him.

"Seriously, it's okay." I repeated, wanting him to know that I didn't mind.

He answered his phone, putting it to his ear. "Hey dad."

I watched him as he answered the phone. I couldn't hear the other end of the phone, but within 20 seconds of listening to his dad his face paled.

"Jesus Christ, is she okay? What did she hit?" He stood up from the table, his voice sounding panicked.

He listened to his dad talk for about a minute before he said, "I'm on the way. What room is she in?" His hand was running through his hair, his face full of worry. "Okay, I'll be there soon." He said before hanging up the phone.

The second he hung up, I stood up from my chair to meet him. "Is your mom okay?"

"She fell, hit her head." He said quickly.

I gasped, not expecting him to say that. I had no idea what to say because I had no idea if she was okay or not. I followed Sawyer into the living room, watching him put on his shoes.

"I'm so sorry, I have to go see her. We can finish talking later, I promise. But I have to go." His hands were shaking as he slid his shoes onto his feet.

I quickly shook my head, not even caring about anything that I was going to say to him. Everything between us could wait, right now I needed to make sure that he was with his mom.

"Please don't apologize, you need to go see your mom and make sure she's okay. This can wait. Do you want me to come with you?"

I wasn't so much asking to go with him, but more so just wanting to be there for him if he needed support.

He stood up from the couch a couple minutes later, looking around for his keys. "Where the fuck did I put my keys?" He groaned. "You don't have to come with me, I don't want to make you go."

I saw his keys inside of his soccer binder, so I pulled them out to hand to him. "Keys." I said quietly. "I don't mind going if you need some extra support."

It wasn't until he reached his hand out to take the keys that I saw just how badly they were actually shaking. I wasn't about to let him get behind the wheel in this state. I'd done this before and I knew how dangerous it was. I knew his head was all over the place and the last thing I wanted was for him to get into an accident himself.

"I'll come with you, but I'm driving." I said, not handing him the keys. He didn't question it, so I slipped on a pair of sandals and grabbed my wallet before walking to the front door.

"Let's go." I said.

The two of us walked out of the house, I locked the door behind us before going down to his Jeep. I unlocked it and hopped into the drivers seat. It took me a minute to adjust to the drivers seat of his car, not only had I not driven a car since being in Maine, but I hadn't driven Sawyer's Jeep before. I had a second of nervousness before I remembered that it didn't matter, that I just needed to get him to the hospital.

"She's at MDI." He said as I backed out of his driveway.

"Got it." I said before starting down the road to get him to the hospital. The drive was pretty quiet, I didn't know what to say to him and he was pretty nervous. His legs were bouncing with nerves, his breathing was a bit heavy. I took my right hand off of the steering wheel and reached over to him, holding my hand out for him to take.

He hesitated just for a moment before placing his hand in mine. I interlocked our fingers and gave his hand a comforting squeeze, silently letting him know that I was here for him.

My hand never left his until I needed to park and turn off the car. We both got out of the car and I quickly locked it and went to Sawyer's side. Without question, I took his hand in mine again and looked up at him with reassuring eyes. I had no idea what we were walking into, but I wanted him to know that I was here for him. He held my hand as the two of us walked inside the hospital.

We made our way inside and to the Emergency Department where Sawyer chatted with the lady at the desk, letting her know that he was here to see his mom. She mentioned that it was family only, but I obviously didn't mind. After a couple minutes of talking to her, Sawyer was handed a badge and directed where to go.

When we walked away from the counter, he hesitated on going to the door. "I'm sorry you came with me and can't even come back."

I shook my head and squeezed his hand again. "Don't apologize. I'll wait out here for you. I'm not going anywhere, okay?"

He hesitated for a moment before pulling me closer to him and wrapping his arms around me, giving me a tight squeeze. I squeezed him before he pulled away from me.

"I'll be right out here." I reminded him.

"Thank you, Jones." He said with a weak smile before he turned to walk back through the doors.

Once he was gone, I found a seat in the waiting area and pulled out my phone. I dialed Callum's number and put the phone to my ear. It wasn't late, but I had no idea what he and Dani were doing tonight.

"Hey sis." He said when he picked up.

"Hey,"

"You okay?" He asked, picking up on my concerned voice from just that one word.

I sighed, shaking my head. "I'm at MDI with Sawyer. His mom fell and hit her head."

Callum let out a breath, "Jesus Christ. Do you know if she's okay?"

"I have no idea, we just got here. His dad called him while we were eating dinner. He was all sorts of worried, so I told him I'd drive him here. He just went back to see her. I just felt like I needed to call you and tell you." I told him.

I had no idea if Callum needed to know this, but something in me just needed to call him and let him know. Sawyer and Callum knew almost everything about each other and I knew that he'd tell Callum about it eventually, so I knew it wouldn't hurt to call him.

"Do you need me to come down there?" He asked.

"No I don't think so. I'm just waiting in the lobby until he comes back out. I'll let him know I told you and one of us will keep you updated." I told him.

"Okay, well if you need me to come just text me. I'll keep my phone on me."

"Alright, love you." I said.

"Love you, sis."

We hung up the phone and I put it back in my pocket. I sat back in the chair and looked around the waiting room, just looking at all of the people in the room.

This night had not turned out the way that I had expected at all. I was so close to confessing to Sawyer that I was in love with him when we got interrupted. I wasn't at all upset about it, I knew this was way more important right now and I was going to do anything Sawyer needed me to do. I didn't care if we were here all night, I fully intended on staying in this lobby until Sawyer was ready to go back home.

I just hoped that his mom was okay. The nerves that were in my belly were still there, but now they were there because I had no idea what was going on behind the double doors that Sawyer had walked behind. I had no clue if she was okay or what was going on and I could only hope that everything was okay.

Chapter 27

Sawyer

I sat next to the hospital bed, my moms hand in mine. She had a pretty nasty cut on her head that had been stitched up. My dad told me that she'd been standing on a stool to reach something in their laundry room when she slipped and fell. When I asked her why she didn't just ask my dad, she said that he'd been on the phone and she didn't want to wait for him. I couldn't help but shake my head at my mother's excuse, but I wasn't surprised. Even with her growing weaker, she'd always been a stubborn one and didn't like asking my dad for help when she thought she could do it herself.

Doctors had been in and out of her room, asking all three of us questions and writing down things that we'd tell them. My mom had been in and out of hospitals for the last year or so, but this was the first time we'd started getting any sort of answer as to what was actually going on with her.

Any other time she was at the hospital, for various reasons, or even just at the doctors office, no one could figure out what was going on. I don't know if they really didn't know or if they just didn't care to figure out the answers. I'd spend so much time researching things and asking questions, but I was always told that I had no idea what I was talking about. It was beyond frustrating and it was part of the reason my mom's health stressed me out so badly. It would be one thing if I had some sort of an answer, because I could look into things that would help her. But right now, it seemed like we were running in circles with no end in sight.

The doctor had said he wanted to run a couple tests on my mom. I didn't know what they were for, but I was glad that he wanted to run some extra tests on her. She'd gotten her blood drawn and they said it would take a couple of days for it to get back to us. My mom was told to stay in the hospital until the results came back.

"Did you come by yourself?" My mother asked me, breaking me from the storm of thoughts swarming in my head.

I looked over at her on the bed and shook my head. "No, Avery is in the waiting room. She was with me when dad called and she drove me here." I told her.

My mom gave me a weak smile. "Such a sweet girl."

I nodded in agreement. I was really thankful that Avery had driven with me and even told me she'd stay in the waiting room until I was ready to leave. She didn't have to, especially since she couldn't even come back into the room with me, but I didn't want to tell her to leave so I was grateful when she told me she'd wait without me having to ask. Especially after all of the shit that I'd put her through, she didn't owe me anything and the fact that she was here without question really made me think about how I felt about her.

"Are you two dating yet?" She asked me for what felt like the hundredth time.

Since my parents came over for dinner, my mom hadn't stopped bugging me about making things official with Avery. I didn't have the heart to tell her to drop it because I couldn't figure out what was going on in my head, so I let her say whatever she needed to say about it.

"I know, but you know I just want what is best for you. You're my baby boy." She started. "Mothers always know best and I can see that she is good for you."

She gave my hand a weak squeeze.

Even though she was sitting in the hospital with a bandaged forehead, she was sitting there asking me about my love life. It almost made me want to laugh.

"Shouldn't we be focusing on you? Not me?" I joked.

"I might be here for a while, there's plenty of time to focus on me. But right now, I want to talk about you two." She smiled, her gentle mom smile over at me.

So that's exactly what we did. I let her ask me questions and I did my best to answer those questions. My mom was someone that I'd always gone to for advice and she even offered it when I didn't want it. I wanted to tell her everything about what had been going on between Avery, but I stuck to answering the questions she'd asked. I didn't think now was the right time to go full in with the details.

I talked to her about Avery until she looked like she was ready to fall asleep. She tried to get me to open up more about what exactly was going on in my head, but I kept the answers brief. When her eyes started to flutter, I could tell she was fighting it so I gave her a hug and told her I was going to let her get some rest. I knew if I stayed, she'd stay up to keep talking to me so I needed to let her get whatever rest she could.

Avery and I walked back into my house. I kicked my shoes off and threw the keys down on the coffee table. It was incredibly late and I was exhausted. I knew that Avery was too so I figured we'd both go to bed soon.

"I'm going to clean up dinner." She spoke up, her voice confirming just how tired she actually was.

I knew she wasn't going to go to bed until I did though, that's just the kind of person she was. She cared so deeply about everyone in her life, even me, the one treating her like garbage.

When I'd walked into the hospital lobby to get her, she was half asleep in a chair. Immediately, I felt guilty for making her wait out there for me but when I tried to apologize to her, she basically told me to be quiet and that it didn't matter, that she didn't mind. I knew she was being honest. I knew she really didn't mind, but I still felt guilty for making her wait out there for me for hours.

I walked into the kitchen behind her. She was walking our half eaten plates to the trash can. I grabbed the wine glasses and dumped them out in the sink before rinsing them out. I grabbed a lid for the pan she'd used to cook the lasagna and put it on the pan. It had been left out for a while, but I didn't care to fully clean it up right now. It could go in the fridge for the time being, I'd clean it up in the morning.

We finished moments later. Avery stood by the sink, her body language also showing me how tired she was. I walked up to her and wrapped my arms around her, pulling her into me for a hug. I didn't say anything right away, I just held her close to me. Even with all of the stress and distance between us, at this moment I was thankful that she was here with me.

"Thank you." I whispered after a couple minutes of just silently holding each other.

Right now, I didn't care about anything that had happened between us or even anything that was going to happen. I didn't want to think about it. I was standing there so incredibly thankful for Avery just being there with me tonight while I went to check on my mom. There was no real reason that she needed to go with me or take care of me, especially after pulling her back and forth and for refusing to get my thoughts in order. But she did anyway and I don't even think I could thank her enough for that.

"Let's go lay down." She whispered. "You have to be exhausted."

We pulled away from each other, but I grabbed her hand and led her upstairs. I walked into my bedroom and the two of us laid down on the bed. Neither one of us changed, we just laid down. I immediately wrapped my arms around her again and pulled her close to me, just holding her.

Something about lying here just holding her made my heart beat faster. Having her in my arms almost felt like it would make all of my problems go away. With her, everything felt like it was going to be okay. As cliche as it sounds, she was the light that I needed to guide me out of the darkness that I was feeling.

"You were trying to tell me something earlier." I whispered, referring to the conversation that we had started right before my dad had called me. I knew that it was about us, she had been saying that she wanted to talk to Callum, but I didn't really get much more than that.

"It's not important right now." She said, her voice quiet.

I knew she was lying. I knew it was important, especially if it was about the two of us and her trying to say she wanted to talk to her brother. But I also knew that right now, she was trying to keep the focus away from us and instead keep it on my mom and making sure that I was okay.

But I wanted her to know that I thought it was important. I wanted her to know that I wanted to hear what she had to say. If she wanted to talk to Callum, then I wanted to hear what sort of plan she had about that and how she really felt about everything.

"It is important." I responded.

She shook her head. "I didn't say it wasn't important, I said it's not important right now." She clarified, even though I already knew that.

"Is your mom okay?" She asked, changing the subject back to my mom before I had the opportunity to get her to say anything else about us.

I really hadn't said much since the two of us left the hospital, I didn't really give her any sort of updates either. I think my brain was just too all over the place to really try and talk about anything.

"Honest answer? I have no idea. I mean, her head yeah her head will be okay. But they are running some tests on her to hopefully find some answers." I said.

I realized then that I hadn't actually told Avery anything about my mom. I told her that she was sick, which was true. But I hadn't actually given her any real details about what was actually going on or the real reason everything about the situation was stressing me out so bad.

Avery tilted her head up a bit to look at me, the look on her face told me she was confused. "Answers?" She asked.

I nodded. "I told you she's been sick for a while. She hasn't been doing well, but we have no idea what's going on. It's part of the reason why I don't like talking about it. Every time I ask anyone anything or try to tell anyone about it, they tell me it's not that or that I don't know what I'm talking about." I admitted to her.

It's not that I was trying to withhold information from her, I just hated talking about it with anyone because I didn't know what was actually wrong with her. It's hard to explain the situation to someone when I don't even know what's going on.

"I don't know if they finally saw something, but they wanted to run a couple more tests on her tonight and I'm hoping that after this, we'll have some sort of answer." I said to her.

If I was being honest, I was almost afraid for them to find an answer, even though I'd been asking for one for months. I was afraid of what the answer would actually be. I was afraid that it would be something that couldn't be fixed and I had no idea what I would do if that was the case.

"Sawyer, I'm so sorry I can only imagine how frustrating that must be for everyone. For your mom for having to deal with all of this and for you and your dad, trying to get answers for her and being shut down. I hope that you are able to get an answer soon."

I shut my eyes for a moment and nodded. "Me too."

I felt Avery's hand move from around me to my cheek, her palm resting against the side of my face in the most comforting way. "Whatever happens, I'm here for you. I mean it, okay? I'm not going anywhere."

I opened my eyes again so I could look at her. Our eyes locked and immediately, I felt that tug in my heart that I'd been feeling for a little while now, but was slightly afraid to admit that I had been feeling. The look in her eyes held nothing but the truth. Avery wasn't going anywhere, at least not emotionally. I couldn't help but remember that physically, she was leaving me in the next couple of weeks.

"Thank you."

Things had taken quite a quick turn between Avery and I. We both got a bit uncomfortable after Callum got home, but it definitely came from me more than it did her. The idea of him being home and finding out about us before I was ready for him too just set me back further than I expected. I wasn't trying to distance myself from her as much as I did, but something about him vocalizing the idea of us being weird... that sent me over the edge.

I still felt horribly guilty over how I treated Avery in the days leading up to her birthday and then especially on her actual birthday. It really drove a wedge between us and I hated that. I didn't mean to treat her as cold as I was treating her, but I couldn't stop it after it started and I didn't understand why. I think I just got so in my own head that everything I did came out so wrong and I didn't know how to fix it.

I knew that we had so much to talk about and figure out, but right now that could wait until later. Right now, all I wanted was to listen to Avery's soft breathing as she slept in my arms. Her hand had fallen down to my neck as she succumbed to sleep, her head nuzzled into my chest. I felt comfortable. The thoughts swarming my head were slowing down and my focus was on her and the feeling of her sleeping in my arms.

"We're going to figure this out.." I whispered.

Chapter 28

It had been about a week since Sawyer's mom fell and ended up in the hospital. It had been about a week since I almost told Sawyer that I was in love with him. It had been a week of emotional confusion on both of our parts. I think we were both putting our whateveritscalledship to the side while Sawyer focused on his mom. It was what he needed and I wasn't trying to get in the way of that.

Even though we were putting things to the side, we'd been less distant in the last week or so. Sawyer had been much less cold to me. Things were still tense, but I think both of us were just trying to make the best of the weird situation. As bad as the night was, I think that being able to remind Sawyer that I was there for him and that I wasn't going anywhere almost helped the two of us. I think it helped him to know that I was okay with holding off on figuring out things between us while he figured out what was going on with his mom. I was doing everything I could to not complicate anything and just let him know what I was fully supporting him and anything that he needed.

My heart was aching for him because I knew he was frustrated that they weren't getting answers from anyone. I had no idea what was going on, but now that I knew I felt like everything else was starting to make more sense. It made sense that he didn't want to talk about the situation with anyone, because anytime he did his ideas and thoughts just got shot down. He probably didn't want people asking him a bunch of questions that he didn't have answers to either.

I was young when my mother died, so I don't remember it happening at all. My dads death was also pretty quick and unexpected, so it's not like I had to deal with any of the premature death feelings of knowing something was wrong and having to plan and deal with any of it. I really had no idea how he was actually feeling, but I was doing everything I could to support him in any way that he would let me.

He'd been at the hospital for several hours now, much like he'd been every evening for the last week. Whenever he had free time, he was spending it at the hospital trying to get things figured out and check on his mom. Each night that he'd come home, I could sense his frustration and I knew it meant things hadn't really changed or that they still didn't give him an answer.

Tonight felt different though and he wasn't even home yet. I hadn't heard from him in a while, so I wasn't sure how long he was planning on being there. He'd been texting me to let me know when he was coming back, but tonight I'd heard nothing since he arrived at the hospital.

I was curled up on the couch, the tv on in the background but not really paying much attention to it. My mind was anywhere and everywhere, my thoughts like a tornado just spinning around. There was a notebook next to me, I'd been writing in it here and there.

There was nothing to be proud of written down, just a bunch of jumbled notes and thoughts that I was trying to put on paper and make sense of. It was hard to make sense of things when everything around me just kept getting more and more confusing.

I heard Sawyer's car pull into the driveway moments later. My eyebrows drew together in confusion, I wondered why he hadn't texted me to tell me he was on the way. I assumed that he'd just gotten distracted or that he was just tired. He had been at the hospital longer today than he had been the last couple of days. However, when he walked through the front door I could tell almost immediately that something was wrong.

His body was stiff and his face was red. I stood up from the couch to face him, but I didn't say anything. I think there was a part of me that was afraid to even say hello to him. The atmosphere changed the second he opened the door and I had no idea what was about to take place. There was a small part of me that even wanted to run away and hide.

Sawyer kicked his shoes off and tossed his keys down, looking over at me with an expression that I couldn't decipher if my life depended on it.

"What happened?" I asked, my voice barely above a whisper.

His face was red like he'd been crying, but he looked like a mixture of all of the bad emotions a person could have. I hated the look on his face, I hated the stiffness in his body and the way he was looking at me. Something bad happened.

He choked out a laugh that split my heart in half. I hated the sound of it.

"Sawyer, talk to me." I slowly walked up to him. He hadn't even moved away from the door, so I wanted to move closer to him. I needed to figure out what was going on.

When I tried to reach for his hands, he moved away from me like he didn't want me to touch him. He finally walked away from the front door so that he was standing away from me again. My heart ached when he walked away because I didn't understand what was going on.

I turned to face him, but I didn't say anything else. I waited until he was ready to talk to me and tell me what was going on in his head.

"She's got cancer." He finally choked out. "She's got fucking Ovarian Cancer and I tried to tell someone, anyone, to see if she had cancer and no one would fucking listen to me."

I unintentionally let out a shaky breath as I listened to him. I didn't want to interrupt him before he was done. I wanted him to be able to say what he needed to say and get out whatever he was feeling.

"I couldn't even listen to them when they were telling me about what they could do to help or how long she has, I just started seeing red. How can they just let that go on for so long and continuously tell her that she's fine when she obviously isn't fine? Fucking idiots." He spat out.

He was so angry and now I understood why. I can't imagine what was going through his head right now. He told me that he'd been trying to figure out what was wrong with his mom for months and everyone told him that he had no idea what he was talking about, so I can only imagine how frustrating it must be for him to get news like this after being told everything was fine.

I slowly walked up to him again, but this time I didn't touch him. I slowly walked up to him again, but this time I didn't touch him.

I didn't want to anger him even more than he already was, but I wanted to comfort him.

"Sawyer, I'm so sorry." I know it was the one thing that everyone says when things like this happen. When someone gets sick or someone dies, it's a human instinct to say that you're sorry. Even when it's not your fault and you have no reason to apologize, it's the only thing anyone can think to say.

I remember after my dad died, I became almost numb to the phrase because I was so sick of hearing it.

Sawyer shook his head, he refused to look down at me and I hated that. "It's just one more fucking thing." He mumbled.

"How can I help? What can I do to help you?" I asked him. I didn't know what to do or say, but I just wanted to help him.

He let out another choked laugh.

"There's nothing that you can do, Avery." His tone was cold. Colder than anything he'd ever said to me.

Panic was starting to rise in my chest.

"No, Sawyer... I'm here for you. Remember?" I tried to remind him. "I can't fix this, but I'm here for you."

Sawyer turned to walk away from me again, he didn't want to be anywhere near me right now and it was causing a storm to form in my stomach.

"No! You're getting ready to leave again! You aren't here for me. You're leaving in less than a month. Don't you get it?" He spit out in anger.

I almost flinched at his words, taken back by everything that he was saying. Of course I knew that I was leaving soon, but that didn't change the fact that I cared so deeply about him. Physically, I was leaving but that didn't mean I wasn't going to be there for him emotionally. I didn't want him to go through any of this alone and I was almost willing to do whatever he needed, even if that meant figuring out how to stay here a little longer.

"Sawyer, where is this coming from?" I asked, my voice shaking.

"Don't act like you haven't thought about it!" He started. "I know we've both been thinking about it but neither one of us will bring it up! We've been ignoring it like it's going to go away, but it's not going away! It's never going away! So now we just need to deal with it like adults and deal with whatever comes with it!"

I could tell he wasn't just talking about the two of us. He was talking about his mom and how everyone had been ignoring whatever symptoms that she had and now they were having to deal with it. But all of his anger about his mother's situation was being directed towards me.

"We can deal with it together. I meant it when I said I was here for you." I practically begged him to listen to me try to tell him that I was there for him.

I walked up to him and placed my hand on his arm to try and get his attention again. He didn't want it though, he pulled himself away from me, not letting me comfort him in any way.

"We're not dealing with anything together. I have to deal with this shit by myself." He shrugged me off.

"You can't help me from the other side of the country. We both knew this was coming, it was just a matter of time until one of us decided to finally suck it up and deal with it." He started. "Well, this is me dealing with it."

"What are you saying?" I asked as tears started to pool in my eyes. I felt a lump forming in my throat, nausea taking over my entire body. "I think you know what I'm saying."

I despised the fact that he wouldn't actually say it out loud. Out of pure anger, I wasn't going to let him not say it to my face so I forced myself in front of him so he couldn't walk away from me again.

"Say it out loud. I want to hear you say it. If you want to give up on us, then I want you to say it to my face." I said with all the strength that I had.

Deep down, I knew this wasn't the time for any of this. He wasn't in the right mindset and he was upset about everything with his mom so he was taking it out on me. But now my heart was starting to hurt too and at this point, everything was being laid out on the table.

Sawyer finally looked down at me after a minute and the second we locked eyes, I felt my heart break in two. He was looking at me with nothing but anger and even hate. All the strength that I had to ask him to say the words out loud was gone. I felt myself wanting to shrink back. I wanted to take it back, I didn't want to hear him say it loud anymore. The second he said it to me, I knew it would be done with and there was nothing I could do to take it back.

"I'm done with whatever the fuck this is, Avery. I can't do it anymore. You're getting ready to go back to California, we might as well just get this over with. There's no point in continuing to fuck around when you're leaving and I have bigger things I need to deal with now. Things have gotten too fucking complicated for both of us and I can't deal with it anymore." He said.

He spoke the words like they were easy for him to say, like none of this mattered to him anymore.

"So that's it?" My voice cracked, but I tried to hold it together.

"What do you want me to say, Avery? We're not dating. We fucked around for the summer and now it's time for me to deal with some real fucking issues in my life. If that's not okay with you then you need to grow up."

Every single thing he said was another punch to the gut. Sawyer had never spoken to me this way before, even in his moments of distance or feeling like he was angry with me, he'd never been this mean to me.

I was practically speechless at this point. I didn't even understand how we'd gotten to this point. A part of me thought that he was just angry right now and he needed to let it out but that we'd be okay in the morning, that we could talk about everything and figure things out together. But he was letting me know that he didn't want any of that. He was done with this, with us and I didn't think there was anything I could do or say to fix it.

"It's probably best that you stay the rest of this trip with Callum. You probably should have gone with him when he moved out. Things would have been easier for both of us if you had." He said, like he'd forgotten that he was the one who had asked me to stay with him.

"Fuck you, Sawyer." I said, my voice barely above a whisper.

"Don't act like you're surprised that this is coming to an end." He said harshly.

"If you wanted to call things off, then fine! But there's no reason why you need to be a fucking asshole about it like I'm just some random girl you decided to have a summer fling with! Don't fucking act like you don't care about me because I know you do! You can tell yourself whatever you need to make yourself feel better, but I know there is more to this than just me moving back to California! I'm sorry that you're dealing with all of this with your mom, I genuinely am and I hope that she's okay but this isn't an excuse to take your anger out on me." I started.

"I've been nothing but patient with you all fucking summer while you complicated things! I've been doing every single thing I can to make sure that you aren't getting in over your head and that we're moving at your pace because I know how much Callum means to you. I waited 10 years for you to kiss me, I thought what's another month or so while you try and figure out whatever it is that you need to figure out. And now you have the audacity to sit there and blame me for this ending? Get over yourself."

Every ounce of anger and heartbreak was spilling out of me as I yelled at him. I wanted him to know exactly how I was feeling. I wanted him to know that I did everything I could for him this summer and that the way he was treating me hurt.

"This is why they tell you not to get with your best friends little sister." He mumbled.

I almost wanted to laugh, because I couldn't believe that he had just said that to my face.

"Go to fucking hell." I spat at him before turning and booking it up the staircase. I slammed the guest bedroom door shut and the second I was alone my knees gave out. I sat on the floor with my palms covering my face and sobbed.

Dani was on her way to pick me up from Sawyer's house. I ended up texting her, telling her that I needed to stay with her but I didn't tell her anything that happened. I'd spent about 30 minutes throwing my stuff into my luggage, not caring about organizing it. I didn't even care to check if I had everything that I needed, I knew I could deal with that later. I just needed to get out of this house as quickly as possible.

Once I had everything, I pulled all of my stuff downstairs. I let my suitcase thump against the staircase with each step that I took, hoping that Sawyer would hear me leaving. I'd heard him shut the door to his bedroom at one point, so I knew he was upstairs and I wouldn't see him on the way out. I had the smallest amount of hope that if he heard me leaving, he'd walk out of his room and tell me to wait. I thought that maybe he'd take back everything he said and he'd talk it out with me.

He didn't.

When he didn't come out of his room, I knew that I couldn't be in the house for a second longer so instead of waiting in the living room I dragged all of my stuff outside and into the driveway where I stood and waited for Dani.

It didn't take long for her to arrive and as soon as she saw me with all of my stuff outside, she was out of the car helping me load my stuff in it. We both settled into the car when we were finished and she quickly pulled away from the house and down the road.

"Want to tell me what happened?" She asked after a couple minutes of silence.

The second she asked the question, I started to cry again.

"Oh honey, I'm so sorry." She said without even knowing what happened. All she knew was that something happened between Sawyer and I.

I folded my arms over my chest and looked out the window as tears streamed freely down my cheeks. My heart was completely shattered into pieces. I don't know how I expected Sawyer and I to actually end the summer, but regardless of if we were going to be together or not, this was not at all how I expected things to end.

I thought we could try and make things work when I left and even if we couldn't, I figured that we would at least end it mutually and on good terms. I never in a million years expected him to look at me with such hatred and to end things on such a sour note. I know things were hard for him right now, especially after getting the news that his mom had cancer. I knew he was just angry about all of that but I never expected anything that happened tonight and now I had no idea what to do.

I hated that he'd just single handedly tore my heart out and stomped on it like it didn't matter.

I hated that after so many years of being friends with him, this was how it ended.

I hated that he really didn't believe that I was going to be there for him through this.

I hated how much I cared about him and how much I wanted to help him through this pain

I hated that after everything he'd just said to me, I didn't hate him at all.

Right now, I hated the fact that I loved him.

Chapter 29

I faced the wall of my brothers bedroom, a blanket pulled almost all the way over my head. I had no idea what time it was and my stomach was trying to nudge me and tell me I was hungry, but I didn't care. I had no desire to eat at all, I was so nauseous that I was sure I would throw up if I tried. My face was puffy and my eyes were burning from the amount of tears that I had shed over the last however many hours.

After Dani helped me carry my stuff inside last night, she'd walked into her bedroom to talk to Callum. I assumed she was telling Callum that I was staying with them, but when they walked out of the room together a couple minutes later, Dani told me that my brother was going to sleep on the couch and that I was going to sleep in their room with her.

The look on Callum's face told me that he had a million questions he wanted to ask me, but he didn't say anything to me. I knew that it pained him not to say anything because I knew he wanted to know the exact reason why his little sister was showing up to his house in tears. But he either knew that he needed to wait until morning or Dani had asked him not to ask me about anything.

When we walked into their room, she didn't ask me questions or make me talk about anything. She just laid down on the bed with me and wrapped her arms around me like she was hugging her sister or her best friend. Of all of the things that had occurred over the summer, the one thing I was most thankful for right now was how close Dani and I had become. She'd just picked me up and let me stay with her without question and I was incredibly thankful for that.

I'd heard her leave the room earlier, but I didn't move or make an attempt to get up. I hadn't slept much, I'd spent most of the night crying and replaying Sawyer's words in my head over and over again. There was a tiny part of me that wanted to go back over there, after he had some time to decompress and hopefully think about everything. But the bigger part of me knew that it wouldn't be a good idea for either one of us and that I needed to stay exactly where I was.

The bedroom door opened and I heard two sets of footsteps entering the room. I wanted to pretend like I was asleep because I knew they were going to make me talk to them about everything that happened and that meant I had to finally tell my brother the full truth about Sawyer and I.

I thought that I was going to have to do this with Sawyer, but now I had to have the conversation by myself and I knew his reaction was going to change simply based on everything else that I had to tell him now. If we'd been able to work things out together, I think the conversation would have been okay but now I knew that Callum was going to be angry because of how last night went.

"Hey sis." Callum's voice was soft, like he was afraid of sending me over the edge.

I felt the bed dip from behind me, so I knew that they sat down. I took in a breath before slowly rolling over so that I could face them.

The second I saw the expression on both of their faces, I wanted to turn back around. Both of their faces were filled with pity and that was the last thing I wanted at this moment in time.

"Hi." My voice was hoarse.

"How are you doing?" Dani asked me, her voice equally as soft as Callum's.

I tilted my head and looked at her, smiling weakly. "Peachy."

Callum huffed, clearly not finding amusement in my answer. "Seriously, Aves. What's going on?"

I slowly sat up on the bed, resting my back against the headboard and pulling my knees to my chest. I wrapped my arms around my legs and let out a sigh.

"Honest answer?" I asked, directing my attention to my brother.

I don't know when that became our thing, but whenever we weren't sure how much detail to give to one another or how truthful to be, we'd answer with honest answer? Sawyer, Callum, and I had been doing it to each other for years now.

"Yes, honest answer. I want you to tell me the exact reason why you showed up to my house last night as an absolute sobbing mess." He was no longer his usual joking self. He was beyond serious, wanting to know exactly what happened that made me react the way I was currently reacting.

I looked over at Dani, silently asking for her support and confirmation that I needed to talk to my brother. She gave me the slightest of nods which made me shift my focus back to Callum who was patiently waiting for me to start speaking.

"Remember when you asked me if something had changed between me and Sawyer?" I asked.

Callum's eyes narrowed, but he nodded.

"I wasn't completely honest with you.. things have changed between the two of us." I started, unsure of where to go from there.

"What did you guys like hook up or something?" He asked.

I don't think he was actually expecting me to say yes because when I didn't answer his eyes went a little wide.

"Oh fucks sake. You did, didn't you? When? How many times? Jesus, are you guys dating now?" He started firing off questions at me.

"Callum, relax with the questions. Let her talk." Dani said, her voice remaining calm.

"We did... uh, I mean throughout the summer." I confessed. "But then you made a joke about it and made that comment about it being weird and Sawyer started to get distant. He spent the entire summer thinking about you and about how pissed off you were going to be at him for hooking up with me. But that's the thing, Callum... it wasn't just a hookup." I sighed.

"I mean, at least I didn't think it was... It's no surprise that I had a crush on him forever, so this was like... a dream come true to put it that way. We connected in a way that was way more than hooking up, but I think he was just in his own head about everything because he couldn't stop freaking out about you finding out." I finished.

Callum listened to me explain to him what had gone on between Sawyer and I since I had been home. I was completely honest with him about how things started to heat up before him and Dani had even gotten married and that they'd escalated right after the wedding. He listened to me explain to him that I'd always had a crush on Sawyer, even though I knew he already knew that part. But I also told him that Sawyer admitted to thinking about me differently before I left for California three years ago.

"So it's more than sex. You two obviously like each other--" He started, but I cut him off.

"Callum if you want me to be 100 percent with you... I um.." I hesitated for a minute. "I know it's probably weird for you, this is all probably weird for you, but I think I'm in love with him." I admitted.

Callum let out a breath of air and ran his hand through his hair.

"Holy shit." He mumbled.

I had no idea what was going through his head. I knew this was a lot for him to take in. His little sister showed up to his house in tears the previous night with no explanation and then admitted that she'd been hooking up with his best friend and then admitted that she was actually in love with his best friend. I was really throwing everything at him at one time and I'm sure he had a thousand and one questions.

"Right. So you love Sawyer. Did he say that he loved you back? I'm confused as to how we got to this very point in time." He wasn't really letting me into his thoughts, but I wanted to finish my side of things before he let me into his side.

"Well, I never told him. I was going to tell him the other day, but he got the call about his mom and that's the night I called you at the hospital. I never got around to telling him because it didn't feel right to unpack these feelings when he was dealing with his mom in the hospital." I told my brother about how I wanted to talk to him about everything, but the timing just didn't feel right because of everything going on with his mom.

"Anyway, last night he got home from the hospital and well, they got some answers to what's going on with his mom..." I had no idea if I was supposed to tell Callum or not. It didn't feel like my place to say anything, so I decided to leave that part out for now so that Sawyer could talk to Callum about it when he was ready.

"I could tell something was wrong as soon as he walked inside. He was mad, really mad. I tried to get him to talk to me but he really didn't want any part of it..." My voice started to waiver so I took a minute to collect my thoughts. Dani and Callum waited patiently as I got myself together.

I closed my eyes, hugging my knees closer to me as I replayed the conversation from yesterday and the harsh words that Sawyer had spit at me. I recalled the details to Callum and Dani, telling them that he said he had other things he needed to deal with and that I shouldn't have been surprised that our summer hookup was coming to an end. I really wasn't trying to paint Sawyer in a bad light to my brother but there was no way to sugar coat the conversation that had taken place the previous night.

"He told me that I should leave and come to your house. So I called Dani, packed my stuff and here we are." I finished. My eyes were still closed, but I could feel the tears forming again. I was honestly impressed that I still had some left.

Neither of them said anything for a couple minutes, I think they were both just soaking in all of the information that I'd told them. I finally opened my eyes, uncomfortable with the silence, and looked over at Callum. Immediately, I could see the anger starting to bubble up inside of him.

"Callum, please don't go do anything stupid." I begged. "He's upset about his mom and I think that's why everything happened the way that it did yesterday. I mean I guess it's like he said, I'm leaving soon anyway so it doesn't even matter anymore." I was honestly defeated, but I still found myself wanting to defend him.

"Avery, you're my little sister. I have every right to be pissed at him for treating you this way!" Callum said, his voice raising just slightly out of anger.

"I'm not saying that you can't be mad, I'm just saying please don't do anything stupid. I'm not trying to get in between your friendship with him, that's one of the reasons we were afraid to tell you anything. I didn't want you to be mad at either of us." I begged him.

The last thing I wanted was for him to hate his best friend. I never wanted to get in between their friendship and I hated that even now, that's exactly what I was doing.

Callum's gaze softened a bit before he started talking again."Ave s, I'm mad because of how he treated you last night and I'm mad at him for thinking that he can treat you like you're just some random hookup."

"If you're sitting in front of me telling me that you are in love with him and there's a chance, even after all of the dumb shit he pulled last night, that he is in love with you... how am I going to be mad at you for that? I'm upset that you didn't think you could talk to me about all of this, but of course I'm not mad at you for feeling the way that you feel." He spoke his thoughts.

I listened to everything that my brother was saying to me. I should have been relieved, but it only made me feel worse. We could have told him about everything before but both of us were too afraid to.

"You said it yourself, it would have changed the dynamic and things would have been weird." I said, trying to defend why I was afraid to talk to him about everything.

"And what else did I say to you? Change doesn't always mean bad. Avery, I was trying to talk to you about this on your birthday. I always knew that you had a crush on Sawyer and yeah, we did joke about it together when we were younger. I didn't know how serious it was though and if I ever made you think that you had to hide that, then I am sorry. I always thought Sawyer looked at you like a little sister, I never considered the fact that he could have feelings for you but I guess he was just hiding that from me too." He started.

"The dynamic would change between us, because I'd definitely have to kill his ass if he ever broke your heart. Much like I want to do right now...." He groaned. "It would be weird to watch you kiss him and do couple-like things together but I would get over it and get used to it because it would make you happy. Aves, all I have ever wanted was for the two of you to be happy, no matter what that looks like. You both are so important to me. You know that."

His words struck me right in the heart and I couldn't help the sob that choked out before I could try to stop it. Another strong wave of sadness crashed through me as I listened to him speak. It hurt so much more knowing that we'd gone the entire summer afraid to tell my brother anything, when we should have just been honest in the beginning. It would have changed things between the three of us, but at least we could have figured it out together and we wouldn't have reached the point that we'd reached last night.

"It doesn't really matter now. He said he's done with everything, I was just another complication to his life." I said quietly. "There's no point in fighting for it when he clearly only wanted to hook up."

"Do you really, truly deep down think that this was just a hook up to him?" Dani's soft voice spoke up to ask. She had been pretty quiet, letting Callum and I talk about things. She'd been the one trying to tell me that Callum wouldn't be mad, so she was just letting us finally talk about the things we should have discussed before now.

I glanced over at her, thinking over her question. Deep down, I did believe that it was more than a hookup. Sawyer told me that he cared about me, but he was just afraid of what things would look like if we decided to become a couple. The entire situation was just confusing to him. But he even told me there was a possibility of us becoming a couple.

However, I couldn't help but believe him when he said that this was all just a hookup to him. He'd talked about the physical aspect of things a lot more than the emotional, so it was really hard to believe that this was anything more to him.

"I really want to believe that this was more to him... but after last night it's just hard." I closed my eyes again and sighed. "I believed him for a minute after we had dinner with his parents, but things got messed up so quickly..."

I thought back to the dinner that we had with his parents, after dinner his mom walked into the kitchen and asked me to be patient with Sawyer. I really did try. I tried so hard to give him what he needed and to be patient with him, but there was only so much I could do when he stopped giving anything back to me.

Callum reached out, placing a hand on my knee. He gave my knee a quick squeeze.

"Sis, I know that I can't say much to fix this for you but I am sorry about all of this. I'm not going to make excuses for him this time, because how he handled the situation was not okay." He sighed. "But I need you to know that whatever you're feeling about him right now is okay. If you're upset with him, I'm here to do what I can to make you feel better. If you're angry at him, I'm angry too. If you're in love with him and want to try to make things work, then I really need you to know that I just want you to be happy."

I shifted and scooted closer to my brother so that I could hug him. I leaned into him as he wrapped his arms around me, tears falling down my cheeks again.

"I just want what's best for you and if that means working things out with him, we'll handle the changes together. Okay?" He rubbed my back as I cried into him.

"Thank you," I whispered.

I had a lot to think about.

It was really nice to hear that Callum was going to support whatever decision I made, but I didn't even know if I had a decision to make. Sawyer had made it pretty clear that he didn't want anything to do with me. There was just something inside of me that was quietly begging me not to give up on him yet.

"Promise me that you won't say anything to him about this, at least not right now? I just need some time to think about things and I don't want to make things worse." I asked him.

I just needed to make sure the situation didn't get any worse than it already was. I was positive that Sawyer knew I was going to end up talking to Callum and telling him about us, but I didn't want Callum to say anything stupid. I especially didn't want him doing anything if I was considering making an attempt to talk to Sawyer before I left. I knew I needed to give Sawyer space and time to focus on his family and not me, which meant I needed to give him time away from the situation as a whole. If Callum came barging into the house upset that he'd made me cry, it wasn't going to help the situation at all.

"I won't say anything." He promised.

Now I just needed to sort out what my next steps were. I'd fully planned on giving Sawyer time away from me, but I needed to sit down and figure out if I was going to try and see him before I left. I still had about a month left in Maine... a month that I didn't even want to spend here anymore. After all of the emotions that I'd run through in the last 14 hours, I was beyond ready to go back to California and get away from all of it.

I was ready to be back with Larissa and get back into my normal routine of things. I was ready to get away from the emotions that were circulating in every ounce of me. I was ready to do the exact same thing that I did after my dad passed away, escape all of the pain and deal with it another time.

Chapter 30

"**Y**ou sure that you're wanting to come back early?" Larissa said to me. Her phone was propped up on something as she made herself lunch in our little apartment that I missed so much.

I was laying on Callum's couch, waiting for him to get home from work while I FaceTimed my best friend.

"Yes. I can not stay here any longer." I groaned. "Plus, it's only like 2 weeks early so it's not like it's anything crazy. I still have some time to finish packing and hang out with Callum. I just don't want to be here anymore." I confessed to her.

"Still no word from Sawyer?"

I shook my head, even though she had her back to the phone. "Nothing. I've gone back and forth, trying to decide if I should say anything to him... but I am afraid that he'll just tell me to fuck off." I admitted with a light laugh.

"Babes, he probably wouldn't tell you to fuck off... You're actually the one that told him to fuck off, remember?" She laughed.

"I had a good reason to say that!" I defended.

Larissa turned around to look at me through the phone screen again. "You're not wrong, I'm just saying. What if he is sorry and wants to talk to you, but he doesn't think you want to talk to him?"

I hadn't actually thought about that. I did tell Sawyer to go to hell, so there was maybe there was a chance that he actually did want to apologize and talk to me, but was under the impression that I didn't want that. It was a valid point, but I really didn't think that he wanted anything to do with me.

"When Dani went to get the couple of things I forgot, he didn't even say anything to her. He didn't ask about me or anything." I groaned. "So he doesn't want anything to do with me, trust me."

I'd secretly hoped that when Dani went over to his house, he'd ask her how I was doing. When she came back and I tried to ask her about it, she just shook her head and changed the subject.

"Well, regardless. I'll be happy to have you back. I've missed you this summer, so I'll happily welcome you with open arms. I just wish you were coming back under better circumstances, you know?" She said with a sad smile.

I nodded, agreeing with her. I was excited to be back with her, but I also wished it was under better circumstances.

"Trust me, I wish I was coming back happier too. But what can you do, right? I'm just excited to be back with you. I've missed you so much. I wish you were here with me right now." I said with a sigh.

"You'll be back soon enough and we'll get drunk and have a chick flick night so that you can get all of your tears out and then be done with him." She laughed.

"Thanks, Larissa." I smiled at her through the phone.

"Hey, I'm gonna go eat lunch. But call me later if you need anything, okay? You'll be back here really soon and I've got the biggest hug waiting for you here in California."

I smiled at her again. We said our I love you's before hanging up the phone. I set my phone down and leaned my head back, closing my eyes. This summer had not gone the way I expected, even though I went into it with little expectations. I went into this summer thinking that Sawyer wouldn't even pay me any mind.

I didn't expect him to kiss me, to hook up with me, and for myself to realize that I was in love with him. I didn't expect anything with his mom, I didn't expect him to end the summer the way that he did.

When I first came home, the only real expectation that I had for myself was dealing with the feelings of sadness about my dad. However, since being home I hadn't actually had many thoughts about him, or at least as many sad thoughts as I thought I would.

I remembered that when I first got home, I'd told myself that I wanted to go see my dad's old house. I wanted to go visit him at the cemetery and I hadn't done either of those things. I had barely even acknowledged my dad and I was a little mad at myself for that. I had little time left in Maine, especially if I was leaving early, and I knew I needed to find time to go visit him.

When Callum got home from work, he sat down on the couch next to me. "How are you doing?" He asked with caution like he'd done the last couple of days. He'd been walking tip toeing around me, like anything he did or said would set me off into a fit of tears.

"I told Larissa I was coming back early." I said to him, not really answering his question.

Callum sighed, showing me how sad he was about it. I'd talked to him about the idea last night and even though he was upset, he didn't fight me on it. He knew why I was going back and he respected the decision.

"And you're sure that you want to go back?"

I nodded. "It's only a couple weeks early, I need to leave so that I can just clear my thoughts. I need to feel like I can breathe again."

Callum nodded. "Whatever is best for you. I support it." He said sadly.

"Can you do me a favor?" I asked him.

"Anything."

"I uh, told myself when I first got home that I wanted to drive by dads old house... and I want to go visit him. I kind of forgot about it and I really want to do it before I leave. If you don't want to come with me, can I at least borrow your car?" I asked him.

Callum looked at me for a minute before he nodded. "Wanna go now?"

I wasn't expecting him to do it right now, but I nodded. "Uh yeah, sure we can go now."

He stood up from the couch and said, "let me go change. We can leave in like 5 to 10 minutes."

I stood up after him and nodded, letting him know that I was going to change as well. Callum walked into his bedroom and I walked into the guest bedroom, shutting the door behind me. I quickly changed out of the pajamas that I still had on and into a pair of shorts and a tee shirt. I slipped into a pair of shoes and combed my fingers through my hair before I walked back out of the bedroom so that I could wait on Callum.

He walked back out a couple minutes later and asked me if I was ready to go. When I told him I was, the two of us walked out of the house and to his car. As soon as I was in the SUV and buckled, a wave of nerves crashed through me. I hadn't seen my dads house since I left, I had no idea if it looked the same or if anyone occupied it any longer. After our dad died and we couldn't live in the house any longer, Callum ended up getting an apartment. I lived with him for a bit, but it wasn't long before I moved away.

"Do you know if anyone lives there?" I asked him as he took off down the road.

"I'm honestly not sure. I haven't been by it in a while." I wasn't sure if he'd know, but it was one of those things that most people would know about in a small town.

I just nodded and turned to look out the window. My legs bounced with nerves. I was afraid those feelings of grief would come back when I saw the house.

When we pulled down the street that the house was on, I felt the anxiety building up inside me ready to burst out. There was a lump in my throat the size of a golf ball. I couldn't stop my legs from bouncing, I was picking at my fingernails trying to calm down. It didn't take long for Callum to pull up near the house. He parked along the street a couple houses down, but you could see it clear as day.

The moment my eyes laid on the house, I felt like the air had been sucked out of my lungs. It seemed as though every possible emotion a person could go through was flooding through my veins in a matter of seconds.

For the first time in three years, I was staring at the house that I'd grown up in. Quickly, all kinds of memories started flooding back into my brain.

Memories of Callum and I running around in the backyard, riding our bikes around in the front. Our dad yelling at us to watch for cars whenever he'd catch us in the street. Memories of sitting on the front porch, watching Callum and Sawyer play basketball out front because I always wanted to hang out with them when they'd let me. Memories of coming back to our house after football games and going on about how good the two of them played because I was always so proud of them.

Memories of picking the boys up from parties and having to sneak them inside to try and hide them from our dad, even though we all knew he would never be mad at them for drinking. Memories of my dad taking me shopping for prom and helping me pick out the perfect dress. We spent hours looking at dresses together, I know he didn't want to be out that long but I never forgot how much it meant to me.

I remembered saying goodbye to the boys each year they'd go off to college and greeting them both whenever they'd come back home. I remembered prom night, getting dropped off by Jake and surprised by the boys. I remembered each time I had to say goodbye to my dad for his work trips and planning dinner dates with him whenever he would return.

So many things played out in my mind, so many memories that I'd forgotten about until this very moment. My bottom lip quivered as tears started to pool in my eyes.

The last memories I had in this house weren't great. After my dad died, I hid in my childhood bedroom, not wanting to face anyone or talk to anyone about anything. I remember Sawyer brushing my hair for me and then lying on the couch with me while he comforted me. After that, we were being told we needed to get out of the house. I don't even remember packing up my things, it all happened so quickly. It was like I was forced out with very little time to even process the events that were taking place.

"Wow," I whispered.

Callum glanced over at me and smiled a soft, sad smile. "You okay?"

I shrugged, my eyes staying focused on our old house. "It's... strange. Looking at this house that we both know and loved and seeing that it's someone else's now. It's like our memories of it were wiped away and now someone else is making new memories there." I voiced my thoughts to my older brother.

"We had some good times in that house." He chuckled.

"Yeah, remember that time you and Sawyer got so drunk your senior year and lost your ride home. You had to call me to come pick you up, I didn't even have my official license yet... But you made me come pick you up and then you threw up in the front yard." I said as I finally tore my eyes away from the house to look at him.

I couldn't help but laugh as I recalled the memory. I was so afraid to drive to pick him up because I wasn't allowed to drive by myself, but I did anyway because I wanted to make sure they got home safe.

Callum rolled his eyes but laughed. "I'd rather forget about that, but yes I do remember that."

"Or the time that dad was teaching you how to drive and you backed over my favorite toy at the time and broke it into like 20 pieces." I giggled.

"You didn't talk to me for a whole week."

"Remember when we threw our first party when dad was away and you were so afraid he was going to be mad that you cried and yelled at me and Sawyer?" He laughed.

This time I rolled my eyes. "Listen, I didn't break rules like you two did. I was genuinely afraid he was going to be upset." I defended.

"Dad didn't care about shit like that. We weren't stupid. He told us not to break anything and not to cause trouble, we didn't do either of those things." He shrugged.

"Did you ever hate that he was gone so much?" I asked, changing the subject just slightly. I used to get so irritated that he would leave on trips so often. I always hated having to say goodbye to him and I would always try so hard to plan something for the two of us when he'd get back in hopes that he'd understand that I just wanted him home with me. I never understood why he was always gone.

"I mean sure it got annoying that he missed out on things, but he was always there for the important shit. I don't think I hated it because I was normally with Sawyer or you when he was gone." Callum shrugged.

It didn't bother me quite as much when Callum lived at home, because he was right. Whenever dad was gone, Callum was there to keep me company and hang out with me. Sawyer would join in a lot of the time too, that's why he spent more time at our house than Callum did as his. When dad was gone, Sawyer was hanging out with us so that I wasn't alone.

But after the two of them had gone off to college, I ended up alone most of the time anyway. Dad trusted that I would be fine by myself, so he didn't really slow down his trips. The only difference was that I no longer had my brother to spend time with.

"Yeah, you got lucky being the older one. You had to take care of me when he was gone. Then you left and I had no one else to hang out with." I shrugged. It's not that I didn't have any friends when I was in school, but I didn't really hang out with people outside of school like my brother had so of course it was easier for him.

"You were always reading or writing, I always thought you enjoyed the alone time." He admitted.

He wasn't wrong, but it did get lonely. "I don't know, sometimes I hated it. It got boring."

We were quiet for a couple minutes, both of us just taking things in.

"Can I ask you a question?" I asked.

Callum turned to face me and nodded.

"How'd you find out? You were still in school, so who called you to tell you?" I asked him a question that I'd wondered about for a while. We didn't really have any other family, so I was always curious about who called Callum and how he found out about it.

Callum shifted in his seat, not expecting my question. "I was at school, yeah. I was walking to one of my classes when I got a phone call. When I answered, it was an officer asking me if I was Callum Jones. I had no idea what it was about, but he'd basically told me he needed me to come down and speak with him. I'd told him I was at school, but he told me it was important." He started.

"I had this gut feeling, so I ran to my car and started driving. I went straight to the station, told them who I was and who had called me. When he sat me down, he had this look in his eyes... I'd never had anyone look at me the way that he was looking at me. And then he told me what happened. I don't even remember what happened next, it's kind of blurry. We talked, but I don't remember what was said... I just remember repeating that I had to call you."

My heart ached as I listened to Callum recall what had happened the day he found out about our dad. I had no idea that was how he'd found out, I'd always been afraid to ask him. Now that I knew, it made me sad. I was thankful that I found out through Callum, but I had no idea he had to find out by someone who wasn't even related to us.

"I had no idea.."

Callum shook his head. "No it's okay. It wasn't something that I felt like you needed to know at the time and I just never brought it up."

Thinking back on it, I genuinely don't remember Callum showing his emotions to me during that time. We didn't really talk about it, because I didn't want to talk to anyone about it. I wanted to be left alone and then I left for California.

"How did you handle everything so well?" I asked.

Callum laughed at my question. "I wouldn't say I handled it well."

My eyebrows scrunched together in confusion. "What do you mean?"

"I was pissed, for a long time. But I wanted to make sure that you were okay more than anything, so I didn't want you to know that I was mad. I tried to do what I could to take care of you, make sure you finished out the school year okay and then get you moved into my apartment. Sawyer and Dani helped, I think they saw more of the anger than you did." He shrugged like it wasn't a big deal.

"Callum, you didn't have to hide your emotions from me. We were dealing with the same pain, you didn't have to hide that." I said.

He shrugged again. "Yeah, but you're my little sister. I needed to make sure that you were okay."

"I'm sorry that I didn't notice that you were angry. I was so confused and dealing with it myself, that I didn't even question how you were feeling. When it looked like you were doing okay, I didn't think about it I just thought that was your way of dealing with it." I felt guilty that I truly didn't notice my brother's anger about the situation.

"Don't feel bad, it's okay. Everyone deals with things differently. You were more upset and I was just... mad. I was mad at him even though it wasn't really his fault, because I was pissed at him for leaving us." He shrugged.

"And then I left you right after." I said sadly. If I had known how angry Callum was with my dad for leaving us, I'm not sure I would have left. It made me wonder if he'd been mad at me as well.

"You sure did." He said, but his voice held humor. "I was surprised when you told me that you were moving to California, I almost didn't believe you. I figured this was your way of dealing with the situation and I'd never in my life seen you that excited to go on an adventure like that. I was upset that you were leaving, maybe even a little angry. But, it was kind of cool for me to get to see you become your own person and go on this journey by yourself."

I looked over at my older brother as he spoke. He confirmed that he had been upset that I left, which made me feel bad. But even though I felt a tinge of guilt, I liked hearing the actual thoughts he had about me moving away. He'd always just told me he was excited and happy for me, but I knew deep down there was more to that.

"You know a part of me was thinking that someone would talk me out of it. When I made the decision, I was terrified to go and I kept telling myself someone will convince you not to go. Someone will tell you that it's a bad idea and you can stay home... and then no one did." I said with a laugh.

"We were all shocked, but you seemed pretty set on it. You had a plan before you told any of us. I talked to Dani and Sawyer about it after you announced it, we all thought you were going to take it back. But then you didn't and then you were taking off on this adventure all alone." He started. "I was terrified for you. My baby sister, in a state on the literal opposite side of the country where you don't know anyone... yeah it was terrifying. But I trusted you. I knew you were doing what was best for you and like I said, that's all I've ever wanted for you."

I smiled at my brother and his loving heart. I was incredibly thankful for our relationship, it almost made me not want to go back to California. I was going to miss him, I did every single time he left to come back home after a visit.

I never hated my dad for leaving on trips and I never hated him for leaving me three years ago, but I was, in a weird way, grateful that he'd left so many times because it helped bring Callum and I closer together. We were always there for one another when we needed it and I knew that was something that would never change.

"Ready to go visit him?" He asked, referring to our dad.

This was the part that I was dreading more than anything. I hadn't been to the cemetery since the funeral, so I hadn't even actually seen his headstone in person. I wanted to go before I moved, but I couldn't bring myself to do it.

I sucked in a nervous breath but nodded. "Yeah, let's go." I turned to look out the window again as Callum drove us away from our childhood home, away from the memories that the house would forever hold.

I hoped the new family would make memories that were as fun as the ones that we made.

Chapter 31

Dani was sitting on the floor next to me helping me fold my clothes. We'd been fairly quiet as she helped me pack up my suitcase. I was leaving tomorrow and both of us were a bit sad about it. I was excited to go back, excited to get back into my routine and try to get over everything that happened between Sawyer and I. But I was also sad about leaving.

At the beginning of the summer, I was ready to go back to California the second I landed in Maine. But as the summer went on, things changed and I started to become a little more sad about the idea of going back. Right now, I was excited to put some space between me and all of the pain that I was feeling, but I was more sad than I expected to be about going back.

"I'm really glad that we were able to spend so much time together this summer." She said as she folded a shirt.

I glanced over at her and nodded. "Me too. It's been really nice." I smiled.

It's not that Dani and I didn't talk before I came home, but we had definitely become a lot closer in these few short months. We'd texted on and off before, but I was confident that I would be talking to her a lot more often after this trip. Dani had been the one next to me this entire summer as things heated up and then exploded right in my face. I was beyond thankful for all of the listening she'd done and for all of the advice that she'd given me.

"Thank you for everything this summer. For letting me talk about Sawyer all of the time, making sure I didn't do anything stupid while I was drunk, picking me up when I called you crying, all of the above." I said to her.

"You don't need to thank me, that's what I'm here for." She said with a light smile.

I placed some folded clothes in my suitcase, trying to make sure I was folding everything nicely so that it would fit properly. I'd bought a couple things since being home so I knew it was going to be an even tighter squeeze this time around trying to get these bags closed.

"I'm sorry that the summer didn't end the way you thought it would."

I shook my head. "You don't need to apologize about it, you didn't do anything. It happens." I shrugged.

"Well I know I didn't do anything, you know what I mean. It was a pretty shitty way for things to end and that sucks." She said.

I laughed. "It does suck, but what can you do?"

It was true. Everything about the situation sucked and I hated the way things had ended, but at this point in time I really had no idea what else I could do about it.

"Have you talked to him at all?" Dani asked.

I shook my head.

"Does he know you're leaving early?"

"I have no idea. I don't know if Callum talked to him and told him, but I haven't seen him or talked to him since I left his house to come here. I thought about reaching out, to check in on him or to see how his mom is doing but I think I've been a little afraid too." I admitted.

I wanted so badly to text him and ask him how he was doing. I wanted to ask him how his mom was feeling and if there was anything I could do for him. But I knew I couldn't do that, I knew he didn't want that.

Dani didn't say anything, she just nodded.

"Do you know how he's doing? Or how his mom is doing?" I asked, wanting to check just to see if she knew anything that I didn't. I had no idea if she or Callum had talked to Sawyer at all, but I needed to ask.

She glanced over at me with a sad smile. "I know Callum talked to him. He called him to check in on his mom, Sawyer told him what the doctors said. As far as I know, she's doing okay. Sawyer is... a little beside himself."

My eyebrows scrunched, my heart immediately aching when she mentioned how Sawyer was feeling. "Did Callum um, tell him... about.." I trailed off.

"About you two? No. He told me that it wasn't his position to bring it up to Sawyer and that if Sawyer wanted to talk to him about it, he was going to let him bring it up. He tried to keep the focus on his mom. But he did say that he could tell Sawyer was, I don't know... I don't want to say hiding something from him, but being a little distant I guess." She tried to explain to me.

I was a little surprised that Callum hadn't told Sawyer about our conversation, but at the same time I was happy that he was waiting until Sawyer came to him about it. I knew that Sawyer was aware

Callum knew something, there was no way he didn't know I talked to him about everything. I was more than positive that's why he was being distant when talking to my brother.

Was he waiting for my brother to try and talk to him about it? If that was the case, things were going to get really complicated between the two of them. Eventually, one of them is going to have to sit down and talk about it and I really hoped it was Sawyer who would initiate the conversation with my brother. However, at this point in time I wasn't sure he ever would.

"I hate that I still want to comfort him... I feel like I shouldn't want to, but knowing that he's beside himself is breaking my heart." I said with a deep sigh.

Dani gave me a reassuring smile. "Don't feel bad about wanting to comfort him, especially with the way that you feel about him. You know that he's going through this tough time with his mom and you want to be there to make sure that he's okay. Don't beat yourself up about it, it's okay."

It made me feel a little better but I still felt dumb for wanting to go and comfort Sawyer. He was there for me during one of the lowest points in my life and I wanted absolutely nothing more than to be there for him right now, despite everything that had happened between us.

"Do you think you're going to try to reach out before you leave? I mean I know you're leaving tomorrow." She asked.

I shrugged as I thought about my answer.

"I don't really know. It's not like I have much time if I'm going to. I want to, because there was so much left unsaid and I want to see how he's doing. But I also feel like I need to leave it alone. I want to give him the space that I know he needs and I'm afraid if I try to say anything to him, it's going to make it worse and there is literally no time to fix any of it anymore."

Dani nodded, understanding my dilemma.

"Don't feel like you have to go and talk to him, especially if you think it will make things worse. But I will say if you think there's a change it will help or make things easier for you before you leave, then don't feel like you can't talk to him. The two of you have so much history that isn't going to be erased just because things got complicated."

"I know things were a little weird before you left to move to California and now things are just straight up... twisted and complicated. I just want to make sure that you are doing whatever you need to do to leave with as much peace as you can. I know there are things being left unsaid and if you think saying them to him will help the situation, then you need to tell him before you go." She voiced her opinion.

I took in her words, unpacking everything. I knew she was right. When I left three years ago, things were weird. Now they were just complicated and super messed up. I was once again leaving on a note that I wasn't the most happy with, but at least this time around I could talk to the person and at least attempt to say my peace.

At this point, it was just a matter of finding the actual time to do it and working up the courage to do it. I had so much that I wanted to tell Sawyer. There were so many things left in the air and unspoken. The door between us wasn't fully closed and if I was going to leave, I knew I needed to fully close and lock the door so I could leave it here.

I truly hated that I never got to tell him how I felt about him. I hated that we'd left things off saying this entire summer was nothing more than a hookup. I wanted to scream at him and tell him that he was lying and that it was all so much more than that. I wanted to look him in the eye and tell him that I was ridiculously in love with him and that I'd never loved anyone the way that I loved him. I knew if I left without telling him, I was probably never going to get the chance to say it again.

I had no idea what things were going to look like after I left. At this point, I had no idea if Sawyer and I were ever going to talk again after this trip. The idea of never speaking to him again was gut wrenching. I couldn't imagine coming home and not speaking to him, not seeing him. The thought was physically painful. Dani was right, we had too much history for that to happen.

I knew if there was any hope in keeping some sort of relationship with Sawyer, even if it was a weird one, I had to do something before I left. I couldn't leave things the way they were.

"Hey Dani, do you have any paper lying around?" I spoke up after a couple minutes of us folding in silence.

She glanced over in my direction, shooting me a confused look. "Yeah, I'm sure I can find you some after we're done. Why?"

"Just something I need to do before I leave for the airport tomorrow." I said before looking back down at the shirt in my hand.

I had so much that I wanted to say to Sawyer. I knew I wasn't going to do it over the phone and I wasn't sure if I'd be able to actually get everything out if I was standing in front of him. I wasn't even sure he'd let me see him in person. Writing out my thoughts was the next best idea. I knew I'd be able to vocalize the things I wanted to say to him if I was writing it out on paper. I just had to figure out how to get it to him. I wasn't sure if I wanted to give it to him before I left, if I could find the time, or if I wanted to have someone else give it to him to make sure that I was already gone by the time he looked at it. Regardless of how the letter arrived in his hand, I knew this was the only way I was going to express everything that I needed to say to him.

Chapter 32

Dear Sawyer,

I know that you may not want to hear from me, but I'm taking a chance and writing you this letter because there's some things I need to tell you before I go back to California. I wanted to start by saying that I am sorry if I messed up this summer for you or made it more complicated than it needed to be. I know that you're dealing with a lot with your family and if I added any more stress, then I am sorry. It was never my intention.

I know that neither one of us knew what to expect going into this summer, so I think we were both taken for a little bit of a wild ride with all of the events that took place. When I came home, I didn't even know if you were going to speak to me. I had no idea that I would be kissing you, that I'd be hooking up with you, and that with all of that, I'd be falling in love with you.

Yes, I said it and I mean it with my whole heart.

Sawyer Evans, I am so in love with you that it hurts.

Everyone knew that I had a crush on you when we were growing up, it wasn't as big of a secret as I thought it was. You were my brother's cute best friend that was so nice to me every single time you saw me. If you didn't expect me to have a crush on you, then you're insane. But it was always just that; a crush. I knew in my heart that I never had a chance with The Sawyer Evans. I was the crazy one for thinking I ever did. I knew the type of girls that you liked, I listened to you talk about them all the time. I also knew that I'd never measure up to them. But to me, that was okay because even though you were my brother's best friend... you were my friend too.

When we were younger, you never made me feel like I wasn't allowed to hang out with you. If you were getting food, you'd get something for me too. When I hugged Callum after football games, you would hug me too. When you two were playing games, you would try to include me wherever you could. Even as we got a little older and you went off to college, you'd come home and pick things back up with me like we were never even apart.

I think maybe there's a part of me that has always loved you, but I thought I was too young for any of that. It didn't make sense for me to feel like I loved you, so I told myself that I was just confused or that I was just being dramatic.

Then something changed and you started growing a little distance from me. There was a pain in my heart that I'd never experienced before. I thought I was losing you. But the weird thing was... it never made sense to feel like I was losing you because you were never mine to begin with. How could I lose something that I never actually had? You were there, but you weren't. You pulled me back and forth and I went along with it because I wanted to do anything that would make you happy.

I still do.

So that's why, even after everything this summer I am still in love with you. I still want you to be happy, even if that means you crumble this up and pretend like you never read it. I promise I won't be mad at you if you do.

Whatever happens from here, I just need to get my truth out. I need to know that you know how I feel about you.

The night that your mom fell, I was actually going to tell you that I loved you. Things were getting really complicated and I couldn't hold it back any longer. I thought maybe if I tell you how I feel, if I can convince you to talk to my brother with me, that things would be okay. That we would be okay...

Then you got the call about your mom and I knew immediately that wasn't important anymore. The only thing that was important to me in that moment was making sure you were where you needed to be. You looked nervous, so I drove you to make sure you got to the hospital okay. I sat in the waiting room because I knew that you might need a hug when you came back out. I wanted to be there for you, because I love you and I hate seeing you in pain.

You tried to ask me what I was going to say later when we got back to your house, but I knew that it still wasn't the most important thing. I didn't want you to focus on the stress that was the two of us when you were already stressed about your mom.

Sawyer, I was trying to make things easier for you... I wanted to do what I could to make this less complicated, but you didn't let me try.

I gave you space, because I knew it was what you needed.

But the night you came home after you found out your moms diagnosis... You've never looked at me the way you looked at me that night. I can still feel my heart breaking with that look that you had in your eyes. Every time I think about you, I see that look. You wanted nothing to do with me anymore and I knew in that moment, no matter what I did, no matter what I said... it didn't matter. You had your mind already made up.

I could have told you then. I could have told you how I felt, but I didn't want to do it out of anger. I didn't want to do it when I knew that it didn't matter anymore. I didn't want you to feel like I was trying to trap you into staying with me by finally telling you how I felt about you.

So instead of telling you anything, I let you talk. I let you tell me that this was all just a hookup. I let you tell me that you had bigger things to deal with and that I just needed to grow up. I listened as you reminded me that I was just your best friend's little sister and that you never should have started anything with me in the first place.

Listening to everything that you were saying, I knew that you weren't just talking about us. You were talking about your mom too, I was just the punching bag taking all of the hits.

I let it happen, because I know how it feels. I know the feeling of needing to let everything out even if it's being directed at the wrong person. I know the pain of something going wrong with your parents and it isn't something I would wish on anyone.

I'm should also say that I'm sorry that I told you to fuck yourself and go to hell... I never meant it, I was just mad.

I was so mad at you for telling me that this summer was just a hookup, because it wasn't to me and deep down I know it wasn't to you either. If that's what you need to tell yourself, then that's okay but I know that it was more than that...

But I guess it doesn't matter now. I'm going back to California, just like you want. One less complication in your life. But I couldn't leave without saying all of this to you.. so here we are.

If you've made it this far into the letter, then I do want to say one last thing... I want to say thank you.

I know, it sounds crazy saying thank you after all of this.

But truly, thank you Sawyer.

Let's be honest, if it weren't for you there's no way I would have moved to California three years ago and found myself as a person. I would never have even considered moving out of the state if you hadn't put the idea in my head.

If it weren't for you, I would have told myself I could never become an author. Even though I haven't yet, I would have given the dream up completely years ago.

I probably wouldn't have made it through my dad's death if it weren't for you. Even after the distance that was put between us, you showed up for me when I felt like the entire world was crashing down around me.

If it weren't for you, I wouldn't have started writing again this summer. I never told you this, I was afraid if I brought it up there would be all of these expectations that I would actually stick with it this time. But being back around you, it made the wheels in my head start turning again.

If it weren't for you, I wouldn't know what true love looks like.

And not the true love that you see in movies or books that's all mushy and doesn't have any problems. But the real love. The love that's good, bad, ugly, and so beautiful all at the same time.

I know that things didn't go the way we expected, but I guess that's a part of life. Things happen that you don't expect. Sometimes that's good and sometimes that's bad.

So thank you. Thank you for being there for me, in my best times and also my worst times.

I'm so sorry that I can't be there for you like you were for me. I'm sorry that I'm going back to California while you're here in Maine dealing with all of these burdens. I'm so truly sorry that you feel as though I'm leaving and that you can't talk to me...

But here's the thing, Sawyer. I've always been there for you... and I never planned on leaving. I've always been cheering you on. Through every football game, through every girlfriend, through each graduation and celebration... I've been cheering you on whether you see it or not.

All I have ever wanted is for you to be happy, no matter what that looks like for you.

So this is me telling you that I am still here for you. I may be going back to California, but I'm always here for you if you ever need me. I'm still cheering you on and rooting for you. I'm still supporting you in any way that I can.

I'm still loving you.

I think I always have.

And I think I always will.

Love, Jones

Chapter 34

I felt so sick to my stomach as my brother pulled up to the airport. When I told him that I needed to stop at Sawyer's place on the way there, he looked at me like I was crazy. I told him that it was something I needed to do before I left and that it would take less than five minutes. I had no intention of talking to him, I simply wanted to drop off the letter that I'd written to him.

Whether or not he was going to take the time to read it, I had no idea. I couldn't control what he did with it, all I could do was drop it off to him and hope for the best.

When we arrived at his house, the Jeep wasn't in the driveway which let me know that he wasn't home. I breathed a sigh of relief knowing that I wasn't actually going to run into him. Callum tried to apologize, he thought I needed to talk to Sawyer. I told him I didn't need to talk to him, that I just needed to drop something off.

He pulled into the driveway and I quickly got out of the car. I pulled the letter out of my purse and walked to the front door. I looked around for a minute, wondering where to put it to make sure that he'd see it. I bent down, lifting up the corner of the welcome mat and sticking the envelope partially under it. When I took a step back, you could clearly see the envelope so I was hoping that he would notice it.

I got back into the car and Callum drove away, questioning what I'd left for him. I just told him that I had a couple things that I wanted to tell him before I left and that I'd left it there for him to read himself if he wanted to. He didn't question me further, I think he understood that I didn't want to explain anything else to him and that it was simply something that I felt I needed to do before I left for California.

He pulled the car up to the curb and put it in park. Dani, Callum and I all excited the car. Callum opened up the trunk and started to pull my bags out while Dani wrapped me in a hug.

"I hope your flights go well, please text us when you land. I'm going to miss you so much, thank you for everything this summer." She said. When she pulled back she had tears in her eyes, which immediately made tears form in my own eyes.

I was not expecting her to cry.

"Oh god, please don't make me cry." I laughed. "I promise I will text you when I land. Thank you for everything this summer, seriously. You've done so much for me and I couldn't be more grateful. You're a wonderful sister and I'm super thankful that you're here to keep an eye on Callum while I'm away. I'm going to miss you a lot." I choked up at the end, shaking my head to try and keep the tears from falling.

"Oh screw you, don't make me cry!" She laughed.

Once Callum got all my bags out of the car and on the sidewalk, he closed the trunk and then pulled me into a tight hug. He didn't say anything at first, he just hugged me tightly. I fake coughed, he was hugging me almost as tight as he had when I first arrived home at the beginning of the summer.

I almost made a joke about it, but instead I hugged him back just as tightly. He was about to pull away from me, but I held onto him as I actually started to cry.

"Oh sis," he said as he held me for a couple extra minutes. "I'm going to miss you."

I finally pulled back from him and wiped my eyes. "I'm going to miss you too." I sighed. "Thank you for convincing me to stay the entire summer. Even though I'm leaving a little early, I'm really glad that I stayed the entire time. It was really nice getting to spend so much time with you guys."

Callum wiped a tear from his eyes and laughed. "I'm glad I was able to convince you. I'm sorry the summer didn't end the way you'd hoped, but I'm glad that you got to stay and hang out with us for as long as you did. I'm already looking at the calendar to see when we can make it over to see you." He smiled.

"Just let me know, I already can't wait." I smiled.

I pulled him into another hug and rested my head on him for a minute. "Please make sure that he's okay. He's going to think that you hate him, I'm sure that he knows that you know... Make sure he knows that you don't hate him." I whispered.

Callum squeezed me again, nodding. "I'll take care of him, I promise."

"I love you." I whispered through my tears.

"I love you too, sis."

We pulled away from each other and I once again wiped my eyes. I grabbed all of my bags after saying my final goodbyes to my brother and his wife. We waved to each other before they got back into the SUV and I headed into the airport.

I almost wanted one of those movie scenes to happen. The one where the girl is getting ready to take off on her adventure but the guy realizes he made a mistake and comes running to stop her.

But this wasn't one of those movies.

Sawyer wasn't coming to the airport to stop me.

I was leaving, hoping with everything that I had in me that he'd read the letter.

The California air hit differently as Larissa and I drove back to our little apartment with the windows down. It was almost 5, but my body was still back on Maine time so it was around 8 and I was already tired. I hated the fact that I was going to have to adjust to this again. It was difficult having to adjust when I got to Maine and now having to flip it back the other way, I was annoyed.

Larissa and I didn't talk a lot on the drive back, I think she knew that I was in my head about a lot of things and she was waiting on me to be the first one to talk. I just had no idea what to say. It's not that she didn't know what had happened between Sawyer and I, so I just felt like I was repeating myself over and over again. There was nothing else I could do at this point to change what happened, so it almost felt pointless to talk about it.

We finally arrived back at our apartment after getting stuck in traffic for a while. Larissa helped me pull my stuff upstairs and into my room. I practically threw all the stuff down, deciding I'd deal with it another day. I didn't care about unpacking, I just wanted to sit in my own bed and try not to feel too sorry for myself.

I laid down on the bed, Larissa lying next to me. "I missed you." She said with a light laugh, trying to lighten up the mood.

"Ugh, I missed you too. So much."

"It's good to have you home!" She smiled.

I rolled onto my side and nodded. "It's good to be back."

"I know that you probably don't want to talk about it, so we totally don't have to talk about it for long but I have to ask. Did you talk to him before you left?" She asked quickly.

I laughed at the way that she'd asked, trying to speed up the question to get it out as soon as possible. "I didn't."

"Oh..."

"I wrote him a letter though and I left it on his front porch." I said.

"A letter? What did it say?" She asked.

I rolled onto my back again and looked up at the ceiling. "I told him everything. I told him how I felt."

Larissa gasped. "You told him that you loved him?"

I nodded. "Sure did. I didn't think I could come back without telling him, but I didn't really know how else to do it... it felt like the only way I knew how to tell him. So I wrote everything out and I had Callum stop at his house on the way to the airport. He wasn't there, so I left it on the porch. I don't even know if he's going to read it, but at least I got everything out and the only thing I can do now is wait to see if it changes anything."

"Wow that's some pretty heavy shit."

I laughed. "Yep."

"I can't believe Callum wasn't upset when you told him too, that's pretty crazy. It's like he knew deep down that there was something between the two of you." She voiced her thoughts.

I shrugged. "Callum isn't a mean guy, so I don't feel totally surprised. If anything, it's kind of annoying knowing that he wasn't actually mad about anything. It made me feel like I should have just told him myself earlier and dealt with Sawyer being a little mad. At least everything would have been out in the open and we could have dealt with it together."

"Yeah I guess that's a good point." She said.

"Nothing to do now but get back into my routine, get some clients back on the books, and wait to see if Sawyer says anything. If not, try to move on and get over it." I said with a sigh.

"Well, I heard that Jamie is still into you.. so if things don't work out with Sawyer, you can always give him another chance!" She giggled.

"Larissa! What the hell. That is so not happening no matter what. How do you even know that?" I asked with a roll of my eyes.

"What? It could! He's still hot, don't deny it. We're friends, he told me." She said like it was obvious.

"Whatever, it's never happening again so you can tell him I said that." I laughed.

"Ugh, fine." She groaned.

"Anyway, I need to take a shower and I think I might have an early night tonight. We can catch up on everything tomorrow, I want to go get coffee and go down to the beach. It's been too long." I said as I sat up on the bed.

"Coffee and the beach, sounds perfect. I'll just be in my room, let me know if you need anything." She said and rolled off my bed before she exited my bedroom.

I pulled my phone out of my pocket, immediately annoyed with myself for hoping there would be a message from Sawyer. I was going to need to hide my phone if I was going to be acting like that. I did have a text from my brother though.

Callum- Text me when you get back to your apartment please. Me- I made it back, sorry I got distracted talking to Larissa.

He texted me back a couple minutes later.

Callum- No worries, thanks for letting me know. Try to get some rest tonight, you need it. Me- That's the plan. Miss you guys already. Callum- We miss you!!

I threw my phone down on my bed and stood up before walking out of my bedroom and into the bathroom I shared with my best friend. I grabbed a towel out of the tiny closet in the bathroom before I turned on the water.

I stayed in the shower for longer than I needed to, getting lost in my own thoughts after I scrubbed down my body and my hair. My brain was all over the place and I just wanted it to shut off for 10 minutes.

Once I decided it was long enough, I turned off the water and pulled the curtain back. I wrapped the towel around my body and stepped out of the shower. I gathered up my clothes from the floor and opened the door to go back to my room.

The second I opened the door, I was pulled back into the moment at Sawyer's house when he caught me getting out of the shower. When he asked me if I always walked around other people's houses in little to no clothes. When he told me not to keep track of his schedule because he liked our little run-ins.

I quickly shook the thought out of my head and went back into my bedroom, closing the door behind me. I opened up my suitcase and pulled out Jamie's tee shirt. I hadn't worn it in a while and a part of me was doing it out of spite because Sawyer had told me if he saw me wearing it he'd rip it off me.

I put on a pair of underwear and the tee shirt, my mind taking me back to the first night I got home. When Sawyer had found me in a tee shirt and then the day after when he told me I looked good in nothing but a tee shirt.

I let out a small groan, I was not about to relieve moments with him with every single thing that I did. I was going to drive myself crazy if I did that.

I pulled my brush out and stood in front of the mirror in my room, running the brush through my wet hair. The second the brush got caught on a tangle, I was taken years back to after my dad died. The night Sawyer brushed my hair for me because I couldn't do it myself. The night he stayed on the couch with me because I hadn't gotten proper sleep in days.

"Fuck me." I groaned.

Once I was finished brushing my hair, I looked around at the stuff on my floor. I was exhausted, but I felt like I needed to start putting things away. Maybe if I put everything away, it would help take Maine off of my mind. So that's exactly what I did, I started unpacking my suitcase. I hung up a bunch of different clothes in my closet and put away a bunch of things in my dressers.

Different articles of clothes made different memories pop up in my head. The dress that I wore the first night we went out, the first night Sawyer kissed me. The dress I wore to the wedding, the first night Sawyer and I had sex. The bathing suit I wore on the Fourth of July. The shirt I wore for my birthday. The pajama's I had on the night he told me to leave. Everything brought back memories and I ended up finding myself on the floor in tears again.

I hated the pain that I was feeling in my heart. The pain that wasn't just emotional, but physical too. It was making me sick to my stomach.

This was heartache at its finest and I had no idea how to handle it. I'd never experienced a pain quite like this before, because it was so much different than the pain I felt when my dad died.

When my dad died, I was grieving him because he wasn't here anymore.

With Sawyer, I was grieving him and he was still here.

It was completely different and I had no idea how to handle it.

"Stupid fucking shoe, stupid fucking memories." I said as I threw a heel that was in my hand at the shelf in my closet.

The second I threw it, I heard it hit something and a box fell off the shelf and onto the floor in front of me.

I looked down at the contents of the box that had spilled out as I picked it up so I could put it back. It was just an old box of random things; letters, cards, pictures, movie tickets, things like that. I started picking everything up so I could put it all back, but when I went to put them back in the box something caught my eye.

Immediately, the string that was holding my heart together pulled a little tighter. I picked it up with my other hand before I put everything else back in the box.

The necklace.

I turned over the little gold pendent to reveal a little etched lighthouse.

The lighthouse that Sawyer had given me before I left for California the first time. The one he'd given me to help me remember my home.

I held the necklace to my chest as quiet sobs started to spill out of me.

Even 3,272 miles away from him, he was everywhere.

I had no idea how I was supposed to recover from this.

Not when there were so many reminders of him, in everything I did and everything I had.

Chapter 34

S awyer

When I came home, I didn't even know if you were going to speak to me. I had no idea that I would be kissing you, that I'd be hooking up with you, and that I'd be falling in love with you.

Yes, I said it and I mean it with my whole heart.

Sawyer Evans, I am so in love with you that it hurts.

I reread the words that Avery had written to me for what felt like the hundredth time.

I had no idea what day she was leaving, I hadn't talked to her since she'd left my house the night I found out my mom had cancer. I couldn't stop thinking about the way that we'd ended things, the way that I had ended things. I was really pissed off about my mom and I took every single ounce of my anger out on her. I knew it wasn't fair, but once the words had escaped my mouth there was nothing I could do to try and take them back.

I knew that I had hurt her, but I had no idea how to fix any of it. Truthfully, a part of me didn't feel like it mattered. She was leaving soon and I thought that the damage had already been done and that there wasn't anything I could do to change what happened.

When I came home from practice a couple days ago, I didn't expect to find a letter under the mat at my front door. I picked it up, thinking that it was junk that someone had left. I saw my name written on the outside and I immediately recognized Avery's handwriting. My heart dropped the second I saw it and I'd never rushed inside of my house faster than I did that day.

I sat down on the couch and tore the envelope open. I wasn't sure what I was expecting from her. I figured that maybe she was going to tell me how angry she was at me or how upset she was with me about how things ended.

What I wasn't expecting was for her to tell me that she was in love with me. The second I read the words on the paper, all of the air in my lungs disappeared. I read and reread the words a couple of times to make sure that I was reading them correctly.

I read the entire letter, over and over again. She poured her heart out to me in this one letter, even after I'd practically torn her heart out and stomped on it like it didn't matter.

I felt like a dick before, but I was confident now that I was the biggest asshole on the planet. I'd spent the entire summer so in my own head about how I felt about her, that I'd been pushing away my own feelings and being completely oblivious to hers. Even after I started feeling like maybe I did love her, I doubted it. I told myself that things were way too complicated for it to be love, it just didn't make sense to me.

But here she was, telling me that she was in love with me and that love was messy sometimes. She even thanked me.

I didn't deserve a thank you. I didn't deserve anything from her. She deserved so much better than anything that I could ever give her.

After I read the letter a couple times, I drove to see my mom. It felt stupid, asking my mom for advice on this because I felt like I already knew what she was going to say.

When I sat down and told her what had happened, she looked at me with such disappointment.

"Sawyer, why did you push her away?" My mom asked me with a sad look in her eyes.

I sighed. "Mom I didn't know what to do. I've never felt the way I feel about her with anyone else and I didn't know how to handle it. My mind has been so focused on making sure that you're okay that it was becoming too complicated. I still don't know what to tell Callum, so I just told her I needed to end it." I didn't exactly tell her how I ended things, because I didn't want her to know all of the things that I'd said to Avery.

"Do you love her?" She asked.

I ran a hand through my hair. "I do, but I fucked up."

"Watch your mouth." She rolled her eyes. "If you love her, then you need to tell her."

"She's already gone. What am I supposed to do?" I asked.

My mom laughed. "Call her? Text her? Go to California." She said like I was an idiot.

"Go to California?" I asked like she was crazy.

"What? You want to express your love for her? You want to fight for her? Then go to her and fight for her. Show her that you're serious and that you want to make up for what you did."

I'd been back and forth on what to do since I talked to my mom. She made it seem so easy. Just go to California and fight to get her back. It was so much easier said than done. I had no idea what I would say to her if I saw her. I had no idea if she'd want to talk to me still, let alone forgive me.

The one thing I did know was that I needed to talk to Callum before I did anything. I knew that he knew about the two of us, there was no way that he didn't at this point. But he hadn't mentioned anything to me about it and he'd been checking in on me with my mom, so I had a feeling he was waiting on me to talk to him about it.

I knocked on the door of Callum and Dani's house, hoping that Dani wasn't home so that I could talk to Callum by himself. I waited a couple minutes for him to answer. His car was in the driveway, so I assumed that he was home.

I was about to knock again when the door opened, revealing my best friend on the other side.

"Hey man," I said, sort of awkwardly.

"Hey." I couldn't quite read his tone, but it didn't seem to hold a lot of anger so I was taking that as a good time.

"Mind if I come in? I think we need to talk." I scratched the back of my neck.

Callum stepped aside to let me inside. "I think we do too."

He absolutely knew.

I walked inside of his house and he shut the door behind me. The two of us walked into the living room and took a seat on the sofa. I had no idea where to start with him, there was so much that I wanted to say to him. I had no idea what he knew and what he didn't, but I was assuming that she'd pretty much told him everything.

"I'm assuming that you know about Avery and I." I started after a couple of minutes, wanting to start with the most obvious thing.

Callum looked over at me, one of his legs loosely crossed over the other. "She told me."

"Everything?" I asked.

He nodded. "I think so."

I closed my eyes for a minute and took in a breath. "So you know what I said to her then."

"I do."

Fuck me.

"Callum, first of all.. I'm sorry that I didn't say anything to you. I should have talked to you about everything long before now. I should have told you how I was feeling about her and I shouldn't have gone behind your back about anything. I'm really, really sorry about that." I started.

I knew that I fucked up. I should have talked to Callum the second that I started looking at his sister differently, but instead I decided to be afraid and hide it.

"You started looking at her differently years ago but you never told me." He said, his voice remaining calm. There was the smallest hint of sadness in his voice, I could just barely hear it but I knew it was there.

I opened my eyes and looked over at him. She really did tell him everything.

"I didn't want you to be pissed at me, man. Avery is your little sister and I'm your best friend. I really didn't think it would be a good look if I told you that I was starting to look at her as more than a friend." I admitted.

I hated the fact that I kept that from him. I felt like an idiot.

"Regardless, I know that I should have said something to you a long time ago and I never did. I didn't even know what to do with my feelings, so I tried to ignore them and it just made everything ten times worse. I thought if I just pushed her away, that it would make it better but I only ended up hurting her." I sighed.

"Then everything happened this summer and it just became so complicated. I made everything complicated because I couldn't understand my own feelings and I was afraid of hurting you. But once again, instead I hurt Avery and I feel terrible about it. I fucked everything up and I know there's no words that I can say to make it better right now and I know you probably want to punch me in the face, but I'm fucking sorry dude." I spit out, spilling my heart out to my best friend.

"Listen, I'll tell you the same thing I told her. I'm sorry if I made you feel like you couldn't talk to me about this. I know that I made a bunch of stupid comments about things being weird, but I was never going to be mad at either of you. It would take some time to get used to and you know I'd have to kill you if you hurt her, but I would have gotten used to it." He said, which felt like a total punch in the gut.

As much as it felt good to know that Callum would have been okay with Avery and I being together, at this point I hated hearing it. I would have rather him told me there was no chance of him being okay with it because him being okay with it was making everything worse. I was more than sure Avery felt the same way when he said it to her.

"But you really fucked this up and you're right, I do want to punch you in the face for hurting her the way that you did. You treated my sister like the random girls you used to hook up with and that doesn't sit right with me." He said, his voice finally showing a hint of anger.

"I know I fucked it up. There's no excuse for the way I talked to her. I'd just found out about my mom and she was just there, I took everything out on her and I said a bunch of shit that I didn't mean. I let her walk away from me and the second I did, I knew I fucked up but I didn't know how to fix it." My voice was starting to become shaky and I hated the way that I was feeling.

"Do you love her? And don't lie to me anymore. Don't fucking think about me right now, think about my sister. Do you love her?" He asked.

I looked over at him, studying his face for a second before I nodded.

"Look at me and tell me that she was more of a hookup. Tell me that you love her." He said, wanting me to say it out loud.

"She was always more than a hookup, Callum. I love her, I do. I think I have for a while, I just didn't know what to do about it." I finally admitted my feelings to my best friend.

It was true. Avery had always been more than a hookup, I just didn't know how to deal with the emotions I was feeling so I used it as an excuse. I kept telling myself that it was physical, I tried to keep the conversations on the physical side in hopes that it would push the feelings away.

It never did.

"If you love her, then I need you to go tell her that you love her. You need to find a way to go tell her. Because as much as I know she doesn't want to admit it, she loves you so fucking much. Even after all the shit that you did to her this summer, she loves you and frankly I don't know why right now. But what I do know is that you need to fix this." He started.

"You need to find a way to fix her heart, because right now it's in pieces because of you. And I swear to god Sawyer, if you ever hurt her the way you did before she left... I'm not holding back next time. I don't care what you've got going on, she just wants to fucking help you because that's who she is as a person. She's not a punching bag that you get to take your anger out on." He finally finished.

I took in his words, listening to him tell me that I needed to fix things with his sister and that he'd kill me if I ever did this to her again.

"I'm going to fix this, I'm going to do whatever I can to fix this with her." I said to him. If she was going to give me a second chance, I was never going to hurt her again. I planned on doing whatever I can to make things right with her, I was just silently praying that she'd give me the chance to do this.

I was thankful for Callum and the person that he was. He was definitely a much better friend than I was, but it was something I'd known long before this. Callum's heart was unlike anyone else that I'd ever known. I shouldn't have been surprised that he just wanted us to be happy, it was in his nature.

I was the one that was too afraid to do anything because I couldn't even make up my own mind. I think I used him as an excuse while I tried to figure things out and that simply wasn't fair to anyone involved.

But now that I had a little bit more of a clear head, I planned on doing everything I could to make things right.

I knew that I needed to go to California. I knew I needed to talk to Avery and tell her how I felt.

I needed to tell her that I was in love with her too.

Chapter 35

One month later

I followed Larissa through the busy building, people shouting around us directing others where to go and calling out names to get people's attention. Larissa was doing a shoot today and had managed to get me a makeup gig. Things had been a little slow since getting back to California, I wasn't trying to book as many clients as I had before. My mind was still a little all over the place, so it took me a while to get back into things.

When I wasn't working or being forced out in public by Larissa, I'd spent most of the last month isolated in my room behind my laptop. Surprisingly, I'd done a lot of writing. I'd practically forced myself to get all of my thoughts out in hopes that it would help keep them out of my head. It didn't work most of the time, the thoughts were still racing around my head. But at least throughout all of this, a spark of creativity had been lit inside of me.

"Larissa, you're getting ready with the rest of the girls over in Room B." Some lady that was walking by said to my best friend before pointing to the left.

"Got it!" She cheered. We made a left and walked towards a door that said B in big red paint.

When we walked inside the room, a couple other girls were inside getting their hair done. Larissa said hi to the girls and walked over to a chair that had her name on the back of it. I had no idea what this was even for, she hadn't told me anything about it. She just said that I was doing her makeup and maybe a couple other girls and that I would get more direction once I was there.

I watched my best friend sit in the chair and look at me like she was hiding something.

"What?" I asked.

"So there's a couple things I didn't tell you about this gig." She said and smiled innocently at me.

I rolled my eyes as I set my bag down. "What."

"I'm sort of just in the background of this one, with the girls.." She started.

"Okay?" I said, confused as to why that mattered. I didn't really care where she was going to be standing for this, that part didn't matter to me as I wasn't involved in any of the actual photographs.

"Well, I sort of forgot to mention that Jamie is going to be here?"

"Jesus Christ, Larissa. You're joking, right?" I huffed.

"It's fine! I was talking to a friend of ours and she mentioned it to me, said that he was looking for a couple extra girls and since we already knew each other it was pretty easy to get me in on it." She said, telling me how she got the gig.

I truly didn't care how she got it, I was just annoyed that she didn't tell me that my ex boyfriend would be here. I wasn't in the mood to deal with any of that, I didn't want to run into him and I definitely didn't want to hold any sort of conversation with him.

"I'm hiding in here literally the whole time, I don't want to talk to him." I said with a sigh.

Larissa looked up at me, I couldn't tell if she looked apologetic or not. "You're not hiding in here! I want you to watch it, you've never come to anything with me before and it's really fun! He'll be so busy with the shoot that he won't even see you and if he tries to talk to you after, then I'll tell him to go away. I promise."

I rolled my eyes again, still irritated. "I'll think about it. Anything else you decided not to tell me today?" I asked, hoping that she had no more surprises for me.

She opened her mouth to speak when a lady with a clipboard walked up to us and said her name, grabbing her attention.

"Is this Avery?" She said and looked at me.

I nodded, "That's me."

The lady nodded and started to explain to me what I needed to do with Larissa and then asked me to work on one of the other girls in the room. I was excited that I was getting to work on Larissa and another girl, even though I knew there was a chance that I'd get to work on other people I wasn't sure if I would really get the opportunity to, so I was excited.

Once she was finished explaining everything to me, I opened my bag and pulled out all of my supplies. Someone else came over to start on Larissa's hair as I started on her makeup. While I was working, I'd asked her what the shoot was even for, especially with Jamie being the lead person in it.

The woman that was working on her hair asked me if I knew Jamie, so of course I told her that I used to date him.

"You're joking? You dated him? He's so hot!" She said with a laugh.

"He's a real piece of work." I half joked.

Jamie wasn't a bad person, but he and I had a lot of issues and there was a reason why we weren't dating anymore. He wasn't an unattractive person, so anytime anyone said that he was hot it just made me laugh because even though we weren't together anymore, I couldn't lie about his looks. He was attractive and everyone knew it.

"Are you seeing anyone now?" The woman asked.

I internally flinched at her question but shook my head as I tried to remain composure. "Not currently, no." I said with a light smile.

"Good for you, you're young. Have fun while you can." She offered her advice and I smiled politely and thanked her. She didn't need to know about anything that I was feeling or going through, she was simply making conversation and being polite.

It felt like we were in Room B for ages getting everyone ready, I'd ended up helping with an extra girl as they were running a bit behind schedule. Even though it felt like we'd been in the room for a while, everything was happening and moving so quickly that I almost couldn't keep up. I wasn't used to the fast pace, it was overwhelming.

I looked at Larissa in the mirror after she got dressed, smiling at my best friend. She was absolutely stunning and there was no denying that.

"You look so hot." I laughed.

Larissa turned around to face me and smiled. "Wouldn't look this hot without you, so thank you! I wish you could do this with me every time!" She giggled.

"Girls! We need you out here in 2!" Someone called from the doorway.

"You'd better get out there, don't want you to get into any trouble." I laughed.

"You're coming out, right? You'll watch?" She asked with hope in her eyes.

I glanced at all of my stuff spread out on the countertop. "Let me put this away and then I'll come out. I'll be quick, I promise."

Larissa didn't have much time to argue, so she nodded and then walked out of the room with the rest of the girls. Once they were gone and there were only a couple people left in the room, I started to gather up my things again. I just wanted to get everything packed so that it wasn't out in the open. I hated leaving my things out and I knew I was just going to be thinking about it if I walked out of the room before cleaning it up.

Once I was finished, I glanced at myself in the mirror. I'd ended up pulling my hair back into a messy bun halfway through getting the girls ready as I was tired of it being in my face. My eyes looked tired, they didn't look as lively as they normally did and I hated that. But even after staring at my reflection for a couple minutes, I wasn't even staring at the tired expression on my face. My eyes were focused on the little gold necklace that hung around my neck.

After I'd found the pendant in my closet, I cried about it for a while but I put it back on and I hadn't been able to take it back off. I still hadn't heard anything from Sawyer, I hadn't really gotten any updates from my brother or Dani either. A part of me knew that I was only hurting myself by wearing the necklace, because it was the thing I stared at each time I looked at myself in a mirror. But I couldn't bring myself to take it back off, it was the one thing that kept me feeling like things would be okay even if they never would be.

I found myself slowly going back into the anxious state I'd been in almost every day since returning back to California, so I forced myself out of Room B so I could go watch Larissa. I made sure to stay out of everyone's way, standing in the back but in a place where I could see what was going on.

I watched as the girls posed around and behind Jamie, keeping him the center of attention. It was so loud, so many directions were being given, flashes were going off, camera's were shuttering. I had no idea how she did this, I would definitely crack under pressure if I had to be the one on the other side of the camera. I'd be so self conscious of the way that I looked that I would never photograph properly.

It was fun to watch though, I liked being able to see her in action. She'd talked to me about this countless times, but it was an entirely different experience getting to see it myself. I'd never understood what she meant when she'd talk to me about certain things, but this was really cool to get to see.

I stood and watched for a while, I had no idea how much time had passed but I knew that we were going to be here for a while.

"Avery Jones?"

I heard my name so I turned around to follow the voice. "That's me," I said, trying to find the person that had said my name.

A man in a security outfit walked up to me and said, "There's someone here to see you, Ms. Jones."

I shot him a confused look. There shouldn't have been anyone here to see me, this wasn't even my shoot. I was here with Larissa and no one else that I knew in California even knew that I was here with her today.

"You can follow me." He said and turned around before I even had a chance to ask him who was here. I looked around for a second before I quickly followed behind him. It felt stupid, following someone that you didn't know to go meet a mysterious person, but here I was.

"We aren't allowed to bring him back unless he walks back with you. If you would like to talk to him out here, you can. If you'd like to bring him back, he'll just have to walk back with you." He informed me.

He?

I was about to ask him who was here, but he stopped walking which caused me to abruptly stop walking. I lifted my gaze and the second our eyes locked my breath caught in my throat. The world around me stopped momentarily, I thought that maybe my mind was playing tricks on me.

There was no way that he was here.

There was no way he was in California.

How did he know where I was?

"Larissa told me to come..." Was the first thing he said to me.

"Would you like to stay out here or would you like him to walk back with you?" The security officer said to me.

It took me a couple seconds to process what was just said to me.

He talked to Larissa and she told him where to go.

She knew he would be here and she didn't tell me.

"Ms. Jones?" The officer said, grabbing my attention again.

"Sorry, he can um... he can come back with me." I said, my mind not even thinking straight. It was running a mile a minute and I couldn't keep up.

I had no idea if I wanted him to come back with me or not, but I wasn't sure what to expect and so I felt like it would be better if we were inside because at least I could find a distraction if I needed one.

The security guard let Sawyer through and immediately I started walking back to Room B. I didn't look to see if Sawyer was following me because I knew that he was. When we got back to the room, my chest was so tight that I felt like I was going to pass out. A couple of the other people that helped get the girls ready were still sitting in the room.

I cleared my throat to grab their attention, "I'm so sorry... would you mind if we had a couple minutes to talk?" I asked, my voice coming out a lot more shaky than I meant for it to.

They all quickly nodded and walked out of the room without question, leaving me alone with Sawyer. Neither one of us said anything for a couple minutes, we just stood there waiting for the other person to say something.

"You're in California.." I finally said, breaking the silence.

"I know that you weren't expecting me and I'm sorry to barge in so unannounced... I got a hold of Larissa and when I told her that I was coming, she told me where you'd be today. I contemplated waiting, but I needed to see you as soon as I could." He started. "I don't even know where to start, there's so many things that I want to say to you.. I read your letter. I read it and then I reread it so many times I've lost count."

I let out a shaky breath when he confirmed that he'd read the letter I'd written him before I left. It confirmed that he knew that I had fallen in love with him.

"Avery, I fucked up. No amount of words will ever make up for what I said to you. But I am so, so sorry. I'm sorry for making you feel like you didn't mean anything to me or that you were only ever someone I was hooking up with. I'm sorry for making you feel like you were the reason things were complicated, because you were the exact opposite. You tried to make things easier and I was the one complicating them." His voice was shaky, he was nervous.

I felt the tears starting to pool as I listened to him talk.

"I'm so fucking sorry for pulling you back and forth all summer. For making you think that things were going on the right track and then pulling away from you the second things were getting good for us. I'm sorry for taking out all of my anger on you. I was so mad about my mom and you were the first person I saw and I took it out on you. I'm sorry that I spent the entire summer blaming the fact that you were Callum's little sister as the reason I couldn't figure things out."He was spilling his heart out to me.

"Callum being your brother was a huge factor in my confusion but the truth is... I was confused about my own feelings. I told you that I started looking at you differently years ago and it was true. But this summer, everything became even more different and I didn't know how to handle the feelings I was having about you. Avery Jones, I fell in love with you this summer and as much as I told myself that it wasn't true, I was just afraid of the feelings and because of that, you had to suffer the consequences and no amount of apologies will ever make up for that."

My lips parted just slightly as I listened to his confession.

"I don't know if you'll ever forgive me for what I did to you and I understand if you don't. I don't know if I would forgive me either.. but if you think that there's even a chance that you still love me the way that you said you did... know that I will spend every single day making it up to you because I am so in love with you that it hurts." He repeated the words that I'd used in the letter I wrote him which immediately made my broken heart swell.

His words were a lot to take in. After everything that he said to me in Maine, I had no idea what would happen if I ever spoke with him again. I thought that if we were going to talk, it would be quick apologies and then we'd move on. I was not expecting him to admit all of these feelings to me.

"You were right in saying that this summer was more than just a hookup. I know it was for you and I'm sorry for not realizing that it was more than that for me until it was too late. It may be too late now, but I needed to tell you how I felt and I needed you to know how sorry I am about how I ended things with you. I never meant for things to end the way that they did." He said after a couple minutes of me still not saying anything.

I was honestly in shock and didn't know how to respond. Every time I started to think of something to say, he'd start talking again and I would lose it all over again.

I couldn't believe that he'd come all the way to California to tell me this. He traveled across the country to come and find me to tell me that he'd messed things up and to tell me that he loved me.

Maybe forgiving him was stupid, maybe it was a mistake... but it was a stupid possible mistake that I was willing to take one more chance on.

"So you love me, huh?" I finally spoke up.

Sawyer looked at me dumbfounded, but the stupidly beautiful grin started to spread on his face as he said, "You have no idea how much I love you, Jones.."

He took a step closer to me, his hand going to my neck where the gold necklace hung. He picked up the pendant in his hand and said, "And I'm hoping that you still love me too..." He dropped the necklace and moved his hand to cup my cheek.

"Sawyer Evans, even after all the stupid shit you put me through.. I am still so in love with you that it hurts.." I whispered.

That was all he needed. He closed the distance between us and pressed his lips to mine. The worn down string that was holding my heart together tightened, pulling it together tightly as I kissed him back.

We kissed for a minute, a desperate kiss from both of us as we held each other close. I'd known that I had missed him, but I hadn't realized just how badly I had missed him until this very moment.

This kiss was soon interrupted when the door flew open and a bunch of girls started to walk into the room. We quickly pulled apart and my eyes immediately found Larissa, who was practically smiling from ear to ear.

"I see you were able to find the place okay." She joked to Sawyer.

"Let me ask you again, any other surprises for the day?" I asked my best friend.

She shook her head and laughed. "This time, there are no more. Now, you two get out of here. I'm going to hang out with a couple of the girls, I'll leave you the apartment for a couple hours." She giggled.

I quickly picked up my bag and hugged her, whispering a quick thank you to her before Sawyer and I walked out of the room. We walked through the busy building together, at one point Sawyer had laced his fingers through mine.

We were walking together when I heard the unmistakable British accent talking behind us.

Sawyer leaned down so he was closer to my ear and said, "Jamie?"

I laughed and nodded, "Jamie."

We walked out of the building and to a car that I assumed Sawyer was renting. He unlocked it and helped me put my things in the backseat. He leaned down and pressed his lips to mine again.

When he pulled away I looked up at him for a minute before asking him the question that I was almost afraid to ask. "Does Callum know you're here?"

Sawyer cupped my cheek again with my hand and nodded. "He actually told me that if I didn't come, he was going to kick my ass for being stupid. He knows I'm here and he's expecting a phone call tonight... I told him I wasn't sure if it would be a phone call with just me or one with the two of us, but that I was hoping it was the two of us..."

My heart swelled again as I listened to him tell me that he'd talked to my brother. I had no idea what the conversation actually held between the two of them, but it made me feel a million times better knowing that they finally talked.

"I'd love to call him with you."

We called my brother that night. He had a million questions for both of us, but the biggest one was him asking us what the next steps were. It left us both in silence for a minute because we hadn't talked about it before we'd gotten on the call with him.

But Sawyer quickly caught his guard and said to me, "Callum I know it's probably still weird for you to hear but I love your sister and I'd love to be able to call her my girlfriend."

And that is how I ended up finally being the girlfriend of the boy I'd had a crush on for 10 years, the boy that I'd fallen in love with years ago but didn't even realize until he was slowly breaking my heart.

Love is funny like that. It sneaks up on you when you aren't expecting it. Sometimes you think you're in love, but it's really just lust. Sometimes you think there's no way I could love that person, but then it hits you like a train all at once.

I didn't know what the future was going to look like for Sawyer and I. I didn't know if he was going to stay in California with me. I didn't know if I was going to go back to Maine with him. I didn't know what things were going to look like for his mom. I had no idea how the dynamic between the three of us; Sawyer, Callum, and myself would look like. I didn't have the answers to any of these things.

But at this very moment, I was okay with that.

Because the one thing that I was sure of was that I was in love with Sawyer Evans and Sawyer Evans was in love with me.

Epilogue

T hree years later

I practically sprinted to the front door of my brother's house, eager to finally be home to meet the new baby. I tried not to slip in the snow that covered the ground, but even if I had it was truly the least of my worries. Sawyer and I had gotten into town late last night and both of us knew that it was too late to come visit. We were staying at Sawyer's dad's place as I didn't want to overcrowd Callum and Dani. I could hardly sleep, I was too excited to wake up and visit the new family. I'd been getting constant updates from Callum and Dani throughout her pregnancy and even after the little one was here, but it killed me that I couldn't actually be home for the birth. I'd been counting down the days until we arrived back in Maine so we could finally meet the little one.

"Babe, hurry up oh my god!" I groaned, waiting for Sawyer to meet me at the door.

"Go in without me, weirdo. You don't need to wait, this is your brother's house, not mine." He said with a laugh as he closed the car door and started up the steps to the front door.

Fair point.

I knocked on the door and walked in quietly, unsure if the baby was sleeping or not. "Hello?" I said quietly when I walked in, not seeing anyone in the living room.

Callum walked into the living room seconds later, a smile on his face. "Aves!" He quickly walked over to me and wrapped me in a hug. "Hi sis."

I hugged him and smiled, "Hello!" I was still talking quietly, still unsure if the baby was asleep or not.

"You don't need to be quiet, she's awake. Dani's just in the nursery feeding her, she'll be out in a couple minutes." He said with a laugh.

I heard Sawyer shut the front door behind me a couple seconds later. Callum grinned and gave his best friend a welcome home hug.

"How's California life treating you, man?" He asked, even though they talk to each other literally all the time.

After almost two years of doing long distance, Sawyer made the move to California. Both of us had gone back and forth for quite some time, trying to decide if he wanted to move to California with me or if I wanted to move back home to Maine with him. We both traveled back and forth as often as we could, for a while I did more than he did because of everything going on with his mom. I never minded though, I wanted to be there for him however I could.

His mom passed away and while I was home for the funeral, he told me that he wanted to move in with me. I made him wait. I knew the reason he wanted to make the sudden move and I knew that it didn't actually help the grieving process. He helped his dad get a couple of things in order and a few short months after that, he said he was actually ready to make the move.

I had to sit down and talk to Larissa to tell her that Sawyer wanted to move in with me. Our apartment wasn't big and I had no idea how we were going to make that work. Funny enough, she told me that after our lease was up, she was looking to move in with her girlfriend and needed to talk to me about that anyway.

It worked out, she moved out and into her girlfriend's place and I officially took over the apartment with Sawyer. Things had been going really well between us. I think we were both a little nervous to see what life would look like officially living together, but everything had been working out really well.

"It's definitely different from being home, but it's nice. I like being out there." He said with a smile. He wrapped his arm around my shoulder and pulled me into him. "It's nice not having to jump back and forth anymore too, just being able to be with Ave all the time."

Callum fake gagged. "Gross." He said but then laughed. "Just kidding, I'm glad that things are going well."

I was about to respond when I heard a door open. My eyes immediately shot down the hall where Dani was walking out holding their daughter.

My eyes immediately started to water as she walked into the living room.

"Hi Avery." Dani said with a smile.

I met her by the couch with a smile. "Hi Dani." I said before looking down at the little girl in her arms. She was so beautiful, it was actually insane. She looked like the perfect mixture of Callum and Dani.

"Wanna hold her?" She asked.

I sat down on the couch and held out my arms. "Please." I'd been waiting for this moment for so long, I didn't think I could wait another second.

Dani gently handed me the little girl and I situated her in my arms, making sure to be careful of her neck. A couple tears slipped down my cheeks as I stared at my beautiful niece. I couldn't even believe she was real. My brother had a baby and she was so beautiful.

"Ugh, she's perfect." I said with a light laugh.

After a couple minutes of just staring at her, I gasped. "I'm home, tell me her name. I've been waiting so patiently!"

I had no idea how I'd forgotten that they refused to tell me her name. They said they wanted it to be a surprise and that they wanted me to learn the full name after I met her. It just made waiting to come home and see her that much harder.

Callum and Sawyer sat down in the living room with Dani and I. Dani looked over at Callum and nodded with a smile on her face.

My brother looked over at me and grinned. "Scarlett, meet your Aunt Avery." He said, his eyes focused on his daughter for a minute.

I smiled when he said her first name, it was such a pretty name.

"Avery, meet your niece. Scarlett Avery Jones."

It took me a minute to register what he'd said to me, I was focused on repeating her first name in my head as I stared down at her. When it hit me that they'd used my name as her middle name, I gasped.

"You're joking." I said, looking over at my brother.

He shook his head, "Wanna see her birth certificate? As soon as we found out we were having a girl, I knew I wanted to try to put your name somewhere with hers. I talked with Dani about it and she agreed almost immediately."

I let out a laugh as more tears fell down my cheeks. "Oh my god." I didn't even know what to say. I wasn't expecting it and it warmed my heart so much.

My brother and I really didn't have any family left, so when he told me that he was having a baby I couldn't help but be excited that our family was growing a little bit more. It was really just him and I left and the fact that he'd done something so special was something I would never get over.

"Scarlett Avery." I repeated with a smile, looking down at the little girl. "I love her so much."

"We love you, Avery." Dani grinned.

"I love you guys."

I handed her off to Sawyer so that he could hold her too. I want to say that he was awkward holding her, but he did it so naturally it was impressive.

"I can't believe you have a baby, dude." Sawyer said to Callum, in awe that his best friend was a dad.

Callum laughed and nodded. "Me either."

"But I'm really happy for you. This is great, she's beautiful." He said with a smile.

I loved everything about this moment, the four of us just sitting around admiring the new little addition to the friend group. She was the most perfect addition and I couldn't wait to spoil her every second that I could.

I watched my boyfriend hold my niece, my heart filled with so much joy. He glanced over at me and gave me the smallest of nods before his eyes danced between Callum and myself. I shot him a confused look, not understanding what his look was about.

"Ave has something she needs to tell you too." He said.

My eyes widened. I was so not expecting him to say anything, I was not planning on mentioning anything to my brother right now. I was fully planning on keeping the attention on them and Scarlett.

"What? Aves, are you pregnant?" Callum gasped.

"Jesus! No." I groaned.

"Damn, that would be so cute if you were." Dani giggled.

I rolled my eyes at her comment but laughed. "Definitely not pregnant."

"Well what's going on? What do you need to tell me?" He asked.

My eyes met Sawyer's again and he nodded at me, a gentle smile on his face almost as if he was encouraging me.

"Remember how you made me promise that if I ever published a book I'd come home and tell you in person?" I started.

Callum's eyes widened and he started to speak, but I quickly shut him down.

"I didn't publish anything! Don't get too excited. But I finished my first book and I submitted it to a couple different publishers." I said shyly.

"She's got a meeting set up in a couple weeks." Sawyer added on.

"Aves! That's incredible!" Callum gushed.

I shifted in my seat and shrugged. "It's just a meeting, I don't know what's going to happen. There's a chance that nothing will come of it."

I was afraid of getting my hopes up if I got too excited about it.

"But there's a chance it will become published! You've dreamed of this for so long, sis this is amazing. I'm so proud of you." Callum said with a huge smile.

I relaxed my shoulders, my heart swelling hearing my brother tell me he was proud of me. I was proud of myself too. As terrified as I was about it not working out, I was excited with the small chance of my dream finally coming to life.

"So his dad is back in the old house?" Dani asked as she parked the car in front of Sawyer's dads place.

"Yeah. When Sawyer told him that he was moving to California, his dad told him he would move back into the place. I guess he didn't want it to sell because of how much his mom loved it." I answered.

"That's sort of sweet. I never realized how much of an attachment you can have to houses." She said.

I shrugged. "There's just so many memories that are a part of them. I think he did it to feel closer to her because of how much she loved the house. I get it, whenever I'm home if I have time to drive by our old house I will. I like to see what it looks like and if anything's changed, mostly just because of the memories that Callum and I made growing up."

"Okay, that's sweet." She laughed.

Dani and I hopped out of the car and started making our way towards the front door. We'd been home for a couple of days now and I wanted to give Dani a little mom break. We'd gone out for coffee and to get some lunch while Sawyer and Callum hung out at Sawyer's dads place. Callum said he wanted to check in on Sawyer's dad, so they spent a couple hours there.

When we walked inside, Callum was sitting on the couch holding Scarlett giving her a bottle. He looked over at us when we walked in and smiled, nodding a little hello.

"Where's Sawyer?" I asked when I didn't see him.

"He's out back on the deck." Callum said in response.

"Why the hell is he outside? It's cold and it's snowy." I laughed. I was about to take off my jacket, but stopped after his comment.

My brother shrugged. "I don't know, he said he'd be back. He's been out there for a couple minutes though, want me to go check on him?" He said and stood up, keeping the bottle in Scarlett's mouth.

I shook my head. "No it's fine, I'll go check on him."

I walked through the living room and dining room to get to the back door, confused as to what Sawyer was doing outside. The only thought that I had was maybe his dad asked him to fix something, but it was pretty cold out so I can't imagine what would be so important that he absolutely had to fix right now.

The second I glanced out the back door, my eyes immediately widened. I slowly slid the back door open so that I could step outside. Sawyer was standing out back, rose petals were spread amongst the snow covered deck. The little outdoor table that still sat off to the side had a couple of lit candles on it.

"What is happening right now?" I said before I could think to stop it.

Once I was outside, I stepped through the snow to walk up to Sawyer whose hands were in his jacket pockets. He looked like he'd been standing outside for a little while now, his face was a little red.

Before I could ask him what was happening again, Sawyer dropped down to one knee.

"Oh my god." I gasped.

He pulled his hands out of his pockets, one of them holding a small box.

"Shut up," I whispered.

Sawyer grinned and opened the box. "Avery Alexandra Jones, we've been through it all together. We've known each other for ages, we've seen the ups and the downs, we've seen each other at our very best and we've seen each other at our lowest of lows. You've continuously celebrated every single win that I've ever had and you've helped me through some of the darkest times I've ever had."

His hands were shaking, I couldn't tell if it was from the cold or nerves.

"I know that I've taken you on a little bit of a rollercoaster, but thank you for sticking with me and showing me true patience. I love you with every single fiber of my being and I want nothing more than to continue waking up next to you for the rest of my life. Avery Jones, will you marry me?" He finally asked.

I didn't hesitate for a second.

"Yes, oh my god! Sawyer, yes!" I cried. I extended my left hand that was also shaking, partially from the cold and partially from nerves and excitement. Sawyer took the ring out of the box and slid it onto my shaky finger. He stood up and wrapped his arms around me, pulling me in for a kiss.

"I love you so much." I laughed in between kisses.

"He finally did it!!" I heard my brother from behind us. I turned around and Callum, Dani, and Scarlett in the doorway.

"You knew why he was out here didn't you?" I asked with a laugh.

"Duh." Callum said like it was obvious. "Now come inside so we can celebrate! It's freezing!" He laughed.

Sawyer blew out the candles that were sitting on the table before the two of us walked inside. We both took off our jackets and I glanced down at the ring on my finger, smiling brightly.

"Let me see!" Dani squealed, holding out her hand. I placed my hand in hers and let her take a look at it.

"Ahh it's so beautiful! Congratulations!" She said and pulled me in for a hug.

Callum hugged Sawyer. "Congrats man, I'm really happy for you." He said as he gave him a quick pat on the back.

He then turned to me and hugged me. "My baby sister is getting married, holy shit." He laughed. "To my best friend!"

"Guess that means we'll officially be brothers." Sawyer said with a laugh.

Callum grinned as he pulled away from me. "Man, all those years of calling you bro. Now you'll actually be my brother. Crazy."

I couldn't help but be happy about how excited Callum was for the two of us. When Sawyer and I first started talking about our relationship years ago, we were both concerned about what Callum's reaction would be to it. Neither one of us wanted to make him upset or hurt him. Things were a little weird in the beginning, I don't think any of us knew how to act but we quickly got over it and Callum has been super supportive the entire time.

If you would have told my 16 year old self that we were going to be marrying Sawyer Evans, I probably would have thought you were playing a joke on me. I would have said there was no way that Sawyer Evans was into me like that, he looked at me like a little sister and nothing more than that.

If you would have told my 23 year old self that we'd managed to sort out our whateveritscalledship, I also probably would have thought you were playing a joke on me. Even three years ago, this seemed like something that never would have happened because there were too many details that we couldn't figure out.

But here I was, standing in Sawyer Evans' childhood home with the most important people in my life. My brother and his wife had their first baby and I was engaged to the man that I'd been in love with for so many years now.

"Are you going to call Larissa and tell her?" Callum asked me.

I nodded, "I will in a little bit. I'm just enjoying the moment right now." I smiled.

Sawyer wrapped his arms around me and pulled me in for another kiss. "Avery Jones, I'm so in love with you that it hurts." He said with a grin.

We still said that to each other, but it held a different meaning now. Back then, it did hurt how much I loved Sawyer. But now, it's more of a reminder that love isn't always easy and sometimes it does hurt. But there's not a single thing that I would change about us.

"Sawyer Evans, I am so ridiculously in love with you that it hurts in the best way."